Aching Prosperity
(Rathúnas Tnúthánach)

Tyrone Alexander

To order additional copies of this book, contact:
Xlibris
1-888-795-4274
www.Xlibris.com
Orders@Xlibris.com
736179

Acknowledgments

I want to thank my family and friends who gave their support for the dream of this book and its story in the years it took to complete.

I would also like to thank Dáithí Sproule and the Center for Irish Music in Saint Paul, Minnesota for invaluable help and inspiration with Irish language and music.

Much thanks also goes to Ireland, its people and culture for inspiring me with their beauty and melodies. I hope that everyone of Irish heritage will appreciate this book and what it reminds of their ancient culture.

- Tyrone Alexander

Contents

Chapter One

*A*lastar ["Ah-lah-stahr"][1] felt the wind's downy goodbye as it rushed through the trees around him. He lay against the foot of a great, white oak at dusk trying to sleep. He never went so far up the mountains before. The day's leisurely march up the mountainside held no effort at all. *It'll be an easy journey*, he thought. *Four or five days at most.*

He never made the trip to the Canal Valley before, but the distant mountain range was always in view from the green fields of his home in Netleaf. They constantly called him to go, but something or another held off the urge and everyone said there was nothing but dry rock and sand there, so he never went. But now he needed to gather choice wood for carving and making tools. He had exhausted the supply of rare wood in his home range, and his father's stock from the valley was gone long ago. He had to gather a new selection of valuable and pre-dried wood. Dry wood was more stable to carve, and it would save him much time and expense if he didn't need to kiln the stock. The desert valley already prepared things the way he needed.

Alastar drifted to sleep. The chill air bit through his senses as he rushed through a dark void. Layers of misty clouds ran past and left cool dew on his skin. He began to shiver when suddenly, a loud *SNAP!* broke the silence. He startled awake and quickly opened his eyes, but everything was a gray blur. Afraid to move, he quickly blinked his eyes to clear his vision. Slowly, the pale white branches of the oak tree above him solidified and sharpened in his view. The branches glowed eerily around the edges with the full moon shining behind them.

[1] There are many Irish dialects that sound very different. This book prefers a North Irish "Ulster/Donegal" accent for pronunciations. See the dictionary at the end of the book for a complete pronunciation guide.

Chapter One

Alastar thought the moon's stare was chilly; a cold dew he had just visited and fell headlong from. The full moon was always a reminder of frigid yearning after he was spurned by Nuala ["New-ah-lah"], his first love - an unexpected rush of adolescent love for a friend he had through childhood. He recalled the poem he wrote for her and how he snuck it through her bedroom window on a first full moon of spring.

His attempts to win Nuala's love ended with long shards of broken glass remaining in his heart. She chose to only remain friends, and then left the isle soon after to travel with her parents. He thought her leaving Eritirim ["Air-rih-cheer-rim"] was a convenient excuse to avoid the awkward closeness they shared after he revealed his feelings. That was just a few years ago, but the sting of rejection lingered and sapped his strength as if he had just fallen into a frosted mountain lake. Alastar's heart had remained frozen and brittle. He never wanted to take interest in another girl since then.

After some moments of silence, Alastar began to calm as he remembered where he was. Then suddenly again, another loud *POP!* pounced through the air, and he sat up. He felt the sharp tingle of fear all around him. He scanned his surroundings quickly. His horse, Éimhín ["Ay-veen"], was nearby, tied to a thick bush. Éimhín's familiar ruddy, chestnut silhouette gave Alastar comfort. His sturdy frame was motionless and showed no concern at all.

Alastar continued to look around. The small fire he made near his feet was now just a mass of red glowing coals but still very hot. *There couldn't be any wolves or mountain lions around here,* he thought. The herds and predators kept to the lowlands where the grazing was lush and plentiful. It was cool and dry here; nothing to support large beasts. He recalled mountain rams weren't seen here for generations. Ever since the highlands became so dry, large animals were a rare sight in the mountains.

His thoughts kept churning through scenarios as he counseled himself of potential threats. *What about bears?* He remembered recent sightings reported by friends, but they weren't this high in the mountains. The image of a large menacing bear rushed into his mind and Alastar moved to clutch his ironwood staff that lay by his side. He had meticulously carved it with relief sculptures of a grape vine and scattered clusters of grapes. The vine wound up the staff and ended underneath a large ball wrapped in a nest of leaves at the top - the image of a pearl treasure he had in his mind when he carved it.

The ironwood had a dark, rich grain with veins that made the staff appear like it was made of golden brown marble. The long staff was as beautiful as it was sturdy. It elegantly showed Alastar's master craftsmanship. Few people could carve such hard wood as he did, especially at his age - not even twenty years old.

Alastar felt strengthened as he held his staff ready. Nothing moved in the dark air. Still silence for another minute. Then another loud *POP!* shot out. This time a small object jumped out of the hot coals onto his chest. Alastar jumped up with a yelp, dropped his staff, and flailed at his chest trying to brush off whatever touched him.

"What was that?!" Alastar exclaimed. He didn't see anything around him as he stood looking about. Éimhín was looking at him now. "Did you see that, Éimhín?" he questioned. Éimhín gazed at him unconcerned and looked away. "Ahh, what da ya know? It was somethin'."

Alastar knelt down and looked into the glowing coals closely. There were a few round objects with stemmed caps nestled among the hot coals. Then just as the word, *acorn*, came to him, one of them popped loudly like the others and sent Alastar jumping again.

"Acorns! Éimhín. Just acorns. You can relax now," he said with a sheepish grin. Alastar picked up a twig and knocked out the rest of the acorns from the coals. *They must've fallen there from the branches above,* he thought. The tree looked very dry, so the acorns were ripe to fall and pop quickly in the heat of the coals.

The moon was still high and shining bright as Alastar gazed upwards through the branches again. *Still hours from dawn,* he thought. *Surveying the landscape at night might be interesting.* He climbed the great oak as far as he could.

The air was cold far up in the tree and a slight breeze made the dry leaves rustle softly. He could see up towards the summit clearly now. The firs and other evergreens replaced the oaks and maples where he had stopped to camp. He was about halfway up the mountainside. The trees became much sparser toward the summit, and the terrain became rough with rocks. *It will be slower traveling tomorrow,* he thought.

Alastar turned around as he perched on the branch and looked southeast toward his home. The air was very clear and he could barely see the twinkling of the sea far off on the horizon where his village was. The mountain forest extended for a long ways until it broke into the plains beyond. The loosely packed treetops looked like a patchy carpet of dark blue speckled cotton balls in the moonlight. As the wind blew through the forest, the leaves shifted and shimmered dimly for brief moments in spots here and there. Seeing his home was a soothing sight that washed peace over him, like a warm blanket in a cold room.

Alastar never imagined living anywhere else. Riding Éimhín in the open grassland, fishing in the sea, all his friends and family, and the satisfaction of woodworking – his life in Netleaf filled him with joy. Only one thing was missing. Alastar wondered if Nuala would return. He felt a family of his own would complete his life.

He remembered her long, dark hair and how it fell about her

fair shoulders, like a streaming waterfall that billowed on smooth, white boulders. Netleaf didn't have a lovelier girl. Alastar felt a warm chuckle as he remembered what his mother said after he was spurned by Nuala - *Don't feel bad about Nuala. You don't want ta be with a girl, hair dark as a raven when yours is light as a walnut. Did ya ever see a raven in a walnut tree? And did ya notice how thin she is? You'd think her well-moneyed parents would feed her a chicken now and then.*

Alastar smiled. His mother was always good at making him laugh. Then a long sigh filled him as his heart wished to see Nuala again. Alastar's yearning made him tired; he felt the frozen lake waters surround him again. He climbed down the tree and lay back down to sleep.

The sound of birds singing woke Alastar as the sky shifted from midnight into bright blue. *This is what father must've felt like on his trips to the Canal Valley,* he thought. It was a rare trip for anyone, because the dry valley had few resources to offer. For a woodcarver, though, it was a treasure trove. His father, who taught Alastar the craft of woodcarving, made the journey just a handful of times. Alastar never went with his father before he died, though. He was 14 when he passed and remembered his father's stories of the valley very well. He couldn't wait to see the bare, rocky landscape filled with hills and cliffs of red and tan layers. He thought it'd be like exploring the surface of a huge, bumpy agate shining in the sun; so foreign to the lush, green fields and forests of home.

Generations ago, the Canal Valley was green and fertile. It left behind abundant remnants of trees and bushes along the many dug out water channels. No one knew who made the canals. The valley was desolate and abandoned since the time of Netleaf's settlement, but the old stories told of the central canal running down the valley a full 16 miles from somewhere in the mountains. It continued northeast toward the sea and became dammed up just a walk from shore. Many smaller channels branched out of the main canal, like the roots of a great tree that sent life into the land instead of the other way around. The whole valley must've been green from the great amount of dead trees and bushes his father told him about.

Alastar walked and led Éimhín through the large rocks and pine needle debris on the mountainside. The summit was just a short reach now. "We're almost at the top," he noted to Éimhín, "It wasn't so difficult after all. Was it?"

At the crest of the mountaintop, Alastar paused. He labored to breathe in the thin, cool air. They had not stopped to rest at all since moving out at dawn. Now he felt the quick and steady push up the mountain was worth it. *Hardly midmorning,* he noted to himself. *We'll be heading back home tomorrow.*

He gazed downward at the valley, awestruck at the wide expanse of dry, red and brown land that stretched from horizon to horizon everywhere. Amazed at the contrast from the land behind him, he said, "Wow, Éimhín, look! The other side is red like you. It does look like a grand agate stone. No polished sheen or dark ridges like your mane and tail, so I'd say you're still a sight prettier." Éimhín gave an acknowledging nicker.

Alastar looked down and back and forth through the valley below looking for a good destination. Whatever was alive and green was hidden from sight. The rocky desert filled the canyon with bare crags and sandy soil everywhere. "Good thing we brought enough ta eat. Doesn't look like there's anythin' ta chew on down there. No water either. But there's a lot of dead trees, just like father said."

Off to his right, on the far side of the valley, a brief, sparkling glint caught Alastar's eye. There was a large cluster of dead trees in the area that were arranged in neat rows. *An old orchard,* he thought. It looked like a good place to find a variety of wood. The water would've been plentiful there. It was reachable in a couple hours.

"I have our target, Éimhín. But first, time for a midday chewin'." Alastar went to Éimhín's side and took out some apples and bread from a saddlebag for their early lunch. "We need a rest before we go huntin'."

After resting, they made their way down into the valley. It was a slow and careful meander through the boulders and brush. Alastar had never seen such a dry, rocky place. All the foliage was dead brown and withered, save for very small patches of long, wispy grass and clusters of round plants covered in long, thin thorns. *Pincushion plants,* Alastar recalled from his father's stories, *except all the packed needles point outward.*

The only trees on the mountainside were a few lonely desert mesquites, which were all dead as well. Alastar broke off a branch from a mesquite tree and smelled it. It still had a faint sweet, fruity fragrance. *Grand wood for cooking and smoking food,* he thought. Alastar collected a bundle of mesquite branches to take home. His mother would love to roast meat with it.

As Alastar continued into the valley, he wondered how it could be so dry when the other side of the mountains was so green and lush. He'd seen rain clouds travel over the mountains all the time, but anything needing a fair drink here was long dead. The valley walls were even more barren than the floor. There weren't any dead remains of trees or anything else there. *The water must not have reached beyond the valley floor,* he thought. The Canal Valley's history was puzzling. Who would carve out so much land to bring life to a place that appeared to be cursed with thirst?

"Good thing we don't need ta stay long," Alastar told Éimhín,

"After two days, we'd be on the ground tryin' ta lick the dew off the rocks in the mornin'... well, if there is any dew to suck up, anyway."

On the valley floor, Alastar looked up at the high mountain walls. The mountainsides didn't roll and rise smoothly like the other side. It was cut steep in the valley. Alastar felt like he had descended into a deep trough made of red clay. He imagined water filling the trough again and sprouting all the valley with emerald leaves and flowering blossoms.

The valley bottom was fairly flat and a couple miles wide throughout. It was covered with dead bushes and trees all along the trench. It was clearly a thriving, if sparse, forest long ago. Judging from the size of the trees, the valley must have been watered from the canals for centuries. Some large areas had no trees or bushes and were blocked off in neat segments; the remains of crops. *What did they grow here?* Alastar wondered.

As they made their way northeast toward the orchard, Alastar collected various wood from trees and bushes along the way. Some had familiar shapes and composition but were slightly different from the foliage back home. Maple, walnut and yew were easy to identify. He only collected a few branches of these since they could be found near home. Other plants were not recognizable at all, and he wondered if they were from the green days of the valley or did they come when the desert claimed the land?

Some hours passed before Alastar grew tired. They were at the bank of the main canal. Alastar had strapped many large bundles of wood to Éimhín's back. He didn't realize how much wood he picked up until he paused to look for a moment.

It was pitiful. Éimhín looked like a tired, long-legged turtle who huddled inside a huge, bumpy, brown shell. Alastar felt bad and said, "Sorry, Éimhín. I'm a bit of a packrat. . . Tell ya what. I won't pick up any more until we get ta the orchard."

Éimhín made a loud snort and moved his head toward the other side of the canal. Alastar looked past him and saw the first straight rows of the orchard, just a minute off in the distance.

"Oh, right then. No rest for the weary." Alastar was embarrassed and felt worse for Éimhín, so he got out a few apples and fed him. "Here's some good snackin' for ya. I packed extra. I sorta knew you were goin' ta carry a bit." Alastar gave a little uncomfortable smile and scratched his head. "That's why I didn't ride ya the whole time."

They walked slowly toward the orchard and Alastar realized Éimhín couldn't cross the canal with so much tied to his back. The banks were too steep, as tall as Alastar – almost six feet high. *That's all right,* he thought. *I'll just run to the orchard myself and come back.*

"Rest here," he told Éimhín. "This is the farthest we'll go. I'll be right back." Alastar jumped down into the canal as Éimhín watched him with a plaintive expression. Alastar looked back at him and noticed his sad face. "Don't look so worried. I'm not gonna bring back too much wood. We'll be headin' home before ya know."

Alastar started walking to the other side of the canal on the hard packed ground. The floor was a lattice of cracks littered with drab, smooth rocks and driftwood. *Just a lot of muddy clay,* he thought.

The actual trough of the valley was not as breathtaking as the agate-like canyon it was in. When he looked up again, a bright glimmer shining above the tops of the dry, spindly orchard trees caught his attention. He stopped. *Was that the same bright flash I saw from the summit this morning?* It disappeared just as quickly as it did in the morning.

Alastar moved forward again still looking up at the valley wall, and again a bright flash shot into his eyes, then nothing more.

He froze, perplexed, and squinted to focus at the spot. He could see nothing odd there; just the bare red-brown cliff face. However, below the spot, almost hidden from view behind the tops of the trees were scattered clusters of short, light green bushes. They seemed to be full of thriving leaves. *Interesting,* he thought. They were the most vibrant living plants he'd seen in the valley.

Alastar moved forward again expecting to see the bright flash. It didn't come, but he was surprised again when a short row of sparkling white symbols slowly appeared on the rock wall above the bushes. Shocked, Alastar stopped again and stared. He felt his heart start to race. The Canal Valley had unexpected surprises, but rocks glowing like lanterns, brighter than day, was a sight he never encountered or even heard of before.

The glowing symbols continued to sparkle and shifted their radiance as if shimmering opal flowed through them. They were too far away to see clearly or read, but they weren't disappearing. Alastar looked back at Éimhín and yelled, "Do ya see that?! Somethin's odd here." Éimhín stood motionless and gave a subdued whinny. "Does nothin' excite ya?" Alastar asked annoyed. "This is the most amazin' thing we've ever seen!" Then the thought of the symbols disappearing went through his mind and he ran toward them.

His body forgot the fatigue it felt and after sprinting across the orchard, he found himself looking up the valley wall. The glowing symbols were just above the full bushes. *Can't be more than 50 feet up,* he thought. *It won't be hard to get there.* Alastar could now see the row of symbols was actually five separate, brightly shining pictures, like the relief carvings he did in wood, except the symbols weren't cut into the rock. They seemed to glow on the surface of the rock wall.

Alastar started to walk quickly up the mountainside when he noticed something else strange. It made him stop with surprised confusion. Not far to the right of the symbols, a large stone archway popped into view; literally popped. It was just around a slight bend in the valley wall and nearly invisible against the mountainside behind it. But when Alastar started to walk upwards, his perspective shifted and the archway could be seen moving differently against the background.

What is this place? Alastar wondered. He moved his head back and forth while looking at the perfectly proportioned stone arch. It wasn't a natural formation. Its round beams were completely symmetrical and gracefully became thinner toward the top. The arch was almost invisible if Alastar didn't move, but it popped out of the background when his viewpoint changed. The effect mesmerized him for some moments as he swayed back and forth with giddy amazement before he remembered the glowing symbols.

Alastar continued up to them. They still glowed bright. The first showed two swans that faced each other. They stood atop a flat board with their wings held up and heads craned downward towards their bodies. He lightly brushed across the image with his fingertips and could only feel the rock wall. But as he moved his fingers across it, the opalescent image shifted its light more rapidly. Strange, he thought.

Alastar continued to swipe his fingertips across the next symbols: a horse leaping right with a long, flowing mane and tail, a thick cross with arms of equal length, a smooth, polished round gemstone mottled with dark and light areas, and a thick arch made of many arcs of equal width, like a rainbow. The light in all the symbols flowed more rapidly as he touched them and then slowed down again when his hand went away from them. It was the most amazing thing to Alastar. *Was this magic like the legends told of? Should I be afraid?*

Unsure what to do next, Alastar looked at the bushes below the symbols. They were interesting as well. He broke off a pale green leaf and smelled it – a strong, earthy sweet aroma. *Sage,* he recognized. But it didn't look like the sage back home. These had flattened, light green, leafy stalks with small leaves, like evergreen plants with a tinge of frosty covering. The sage bushes he knew had much larger leaves and normal, thin round stems. Sage was a rare herb that was useful for different things, so he broke off bundles to keep. *Perhaps this desert sage would be useful.*

Alastar began to feel calm now. The symbols kept glowing without change as the minutes passed. *There must be a reason for these symbols and the arch,* he thought. *They must go together somehow.*

Alastar looked at the stone arch and saw how it framed the center of the valley beautifully. The agate layered walls of the valley funneled into a dot on the horizon inside the stone arch's graceful curves. He'd never seen the world displayed with such beauty. Only a master artist could create such things. Alastar knew it required careful planning and patient skill to create works like the stone arch. His experience carving wood, where mistakes were permanently etched, made that obvious to him. Stone was no different. *But who would create this? And who would, with the skill enough to make it camouflaged until you were close enough to see it?*

Astounded, Alastar looked back at the glowing symbols. The flowing opal light kept moving through them, silently pacing and waiting. "What am I supposed ta do?" he muttered softly.

Swans - a horse - Alastar looked back across the canal at Éimhín. Then at the horse image again. The image did appear to show Éimhín's familiar sturdy silhouette - a strong work horse but also nimble and fast. Alastar scratched his head in bewilderment. *It couldn't refer to Éimhín, could it?*

A thick cross - a polished gem - and a rainbow. . . or an

arch? Alastar looked at the stone arch again. *Could it be?* But the rainbow image was consistently thick all around, while the stone arch was tapered thinner at the top. He looked back at the symbols and something about the gemstone image jumped out at him. *The setting around the gem is also tapered thinner at the top and bottom like the arch!* Intrigued by this detail, Alastar pressed his forefinger down on the image of the gem to trace the setting around the gemstone. When he touched it, the image suddenly changed its color to a brilliant gold light, like warm, rich sunlight. Startled, he took his finger off the image and it slowly changed back to the flowing, white opalescence.

Why didn't it do that before? Alastar wondered. *Did pressing it do anything?* He looked back at the stone arch and everything appeared the same. Alastar turned to the symbols again and swiped his hand across the images, left to right. They reacted the same way as before and flowed quicker with the white light inside. Then he pressed down on the swans with the tips of his fingers, and sure as he thought it would, the image changed to glow bright gold.

This must be some sort of puzzle, Alastar pondered. *It's giving clues about how it works, but how is it solved?* He took his hand off the swans and the gold light faded back to the white flow.

What happens if I make them all gold? Alastar quickly pressed down on all the symbols before they would fade back to white. The gold radiance held constant, and once more, his curious persistence was rewarded. Bright flashes of gold light and loud crackling noises came from the stone archway. He turned to look and saw it covered in sparkling gold points of light that obscured the view of the valley through it.

Alastar stared in awe. The glittering gold curtain of light faded and gave way to a view of the Canal Valley again. . . except there was a problem. The view of the valley through the archway was now thriving with green forest everywhere on the valley walls and a river flowed down its center.

"What is this?" Alastar said in confused wonder. He walked toward the archway to get a better look. Halfway there, he leaned far right to peer around the arch so he could see the valley without looking through the archway. Behind the arch, the valley appeared normal – a desert dry, giant agate. Then he looked through the arch again and the valley was a lush, emerald green canyon as far as he could see. *Was this an illusion?*

Alastar went straight up to the archway. *A caravan could go through here,* he thought. The arch was big enough to move a herd of cattle through, three or four cows wide. The whole world seemed to be changed on the other side of the arch. He could see farther to the right into the green valley from his close viewpoint at the arch, like he was looking through a huge window. The green valley through the arch wasn't simply an image painted there in the air. It appeared the stone arch was a doorway into a thriving version of the valley.

Alastar wanted to stick his head through the arch doorway and look around one of the stone beams to see if the world was also changed behind him, but he was afraid to enter. He sensed there was a tangible barrier at the doorway, as if the air was thick with energy. He stepped backwards some feet and found a rock. He threw it into the arch doorway and the stone went through with a metallic *ZING!* sound as it pierced the portal barrier. The rock landed in the green side of the valley without event. *I should be able to go through without harm,* he thought, but as the thought came to him, the view of the green valley began to fade in and out with a rhythmic pulsing. *What's happening?*

Alastar looked back at the glowing symbols and saw they were also fading in and out, synchronized with the view in the archway. Something else was happening to the symbols too. He ran back to them for a closer look.

The last symbol of the rainbow was slowly disappearing from the right. Alastar put his hand on the image, but nothing changed. All of them continued to flash gold, bright and dim, matching the archway's rhythm. And the symbols were disappearing, being wiped away, right to left.

Alastar became alarmed as he saw the rainbow symbol vanish and the next one start to disappear. *My chance to go through the portal might be gone with the symbols.* He frantically pressed and swiped at the symbols again to try and stop them from changing, but nothing he did helped. The doorway into a new world was counting down.

Maybe I can reactivate the doorway once the symbols are gone, he wondered. *But what if they're gone forever?* Alastar started to panic. He sensed he needed to explore the other side of the portal. The symbols spoke to him in a silent language. Somehow he knew they spoke a message to him… about him, and the stone doorway was an important piece of the puzzle.

What do I do? Go through the archway now?

Alastar looked back at Éimhín. He couldn't leave him. Besides, the symbols appeared to be about Éimhín too.

What do I do? Wait for the symbols to disappear and try again, or go through now? I'm at a crossroads without a di. . . rection - "A crossroads!" Alastar burst out. *Is that what the thick cross means?*

Minutes had passed as he pondered things and the flashing gem symbol was now almost gone. He had to decide quickly. The symbols were large, but they would be gone in less than ten minutes.

He was at a crossroads – go through the doorway now and experience something truly amazing or remain here and risk losing the opportunity… but he could continue life here. He was happy with it. However, he wanted to know what was on the other side.

Then Alastar wondered if he would be able to return from the other side. Fear and panic gripped him. He closed his eyes for calm and in a flash he decided.

This is something important, and I can't let it pass by. I will go on faith, he said. Alastar took off sprinting as fast as he could to Éimhín. He ran out of breath at the edge of the canal, so he stopped briefly and looked back at the symbols. They were half gone. The sight gave him a resurgence of strength, and he ran back to Éimhín's side.

"Éimhín! We have ta go!" Alastar panted as he cut off the many bundles of wood from him. "We'll only keep the most interestin' wood. Just two bundles. Good thing I'm an organized packrat. Already have the good stuff bundled together." Alastar looked at the symbols again. Only two were left.

"We'll use the other bundles… never mind. Can't talk now!" Alastar muttered quickly. *Éimhín is ready to ride,* he thought, *but he won't be able to climb out of the canal.* Alastar grabbed the extra bundles of wood, fast as he could, and threw them into the canal. He chased after them quick as a cat after a mouse. Éimhín stared at his odd behavior and gave a confused neigh.

When Alastar reached the wood, he franticly threw the bundles against the opposite wall of the canal and ran to them again. Then he piled them into steps that Éimhín could use to get over the canal wall. Finished, Alastar looked at the symbols again. Only one was left.

Alastar blew a loud whistle and yelled to Éimhín, "Here, boy!"

Éimhín immediately circled back some steps and made a running jump into the canal. He rushed toward Alastar and stopped by his side. Alastar was so tired he could barely mount Éimhín, but once he got on, Éimhín knew exactly where to go. He quickly turned around and went to the middle of the canal.

Éimhín reared up on his hind legs and whinnied fiercely. "Go!

Go like ya never did before!" Alastar told him. Éimhín galloped hard toward the canal wall and leapt clear out of the canal without even touching the crude steps Alastar had made.

"I didn't know you could do that!" Alastar said with surprised exuberance. "Why'd you let me tire myself out with all that wood?" Éimhín replied with a satisfied whinny, but Alastar couldn't tell if his horse was satisfied about making the jump or seeing him haul all the wood across the canal.

Alastar kept his eyes on the remaining symbol – the swans. It was half gone as they entered the orchard. The ride to the base of the valley wall was swift, but the remaining symbol was disappearing quickly.

"Careful here, Éimhín, the climb is rocky."

Surefooted, Éimhín barely slowed as they went up the mountainside and passed the flashing symbol. It was just a small, vertical bar now, and Alastar slapped Éimhín's rear to push him faster. They charged toward the stone arch as the image of the green valley faded in and out. The desert valley could be seen stronger through the arch now when the image faded. The door was closing.

"*QUICK!*" Alastar urged. Almost there, Alastar looked behind them and saw the symbol make its last blink. Then he felt the push into the portal. It was like moving through a misty waterfall, and the rushing *ZING!* sounded around them to accompany the cool, tingling sensation. They were through.

*É*imhín continued to gallop fiercely as Alastar saw the stone arch pass by. The red-brown valley behind them faded out and the stone arch turned green. It became completely covered by vines and fruit. He looked ahead and gave Éimhín a tug on his reins. "Whoa!" he said to stop him.

He fell onto Éimhín's neck and patted him on the shoulder. "Your heart must be beatin' faster than mine. Well done, boy." He straightened up again and looked all around. They stood perched atop a high ledge that overlooked the valley. In the quiet of their rest, Alastar could hear the world was now bursting with the sounds of life – birds, insects, and a rushing river below them.

"Would ya look at the valley now. Greener than the deepest emerald everywhere! So many trees." Alastar was amazed at the sight. He'd never seen a forest so thick and alive. The valley was covered in dense forest with huge oaks that reached into the sky. The only places not covered by the forest were the long, winding river and a few vertical cliff faces too steep to hold soil. Alastar could see the familiar agate layers of the desert valley in the exposed cliffs, but this place was perplexing.

Why was there no evidence of such a thick forest in the Canal Valley? Was this the same place? It must be, he thought. The valley walls and flow of the canyon here matched exactly what he saw in the desert valley. *But what happened to all the soil and forest? Millions of trees and the river.*

The river was a pure blue reflection of the sky and wound about the floor of the canyon, like a loosely coiled string as if a thread of the sky had fallen lightly to earth. The central canal had looked nothing like the river. It was dug straight as can be down the center of the valley, and he didn't recall seeing any evidence of this winding river in the Canal Valley. More mysteries were presenting themselves, but Alastar felt at ease. The changed valley made his heart feel the peace of home – green and welcoming.

"Does this place confuse you?" he said as he got off Éimhín and led him back toward the stone arch. As they walked, Alastar noticed most of the mountainside there was covered in bushes and small trees that were draped with grape vines and fruit just as the arch was. Alastar took out his staff and looked at its intricate carvings of vines and grapes. He carved it using the small wall of vines his mother cultivated in her garden as reference. He never had seen them in the wild before; certainly never in so much abundance.

Do grapes always grow so well here? Alastar mused. He remembered what a difficult time his mother had growing the vines. They needed constant care, it seemed. The valley here, though, appeared to be naturally covered in fruitful vines.

Standing at the archway, Alastar noticed how much its thick, round beams now reminded him of his carved staff. The grape vines wound around it in a similar way as he had carved into the wood, complete with scattered clusters of perfect, round fruit. *A strange coincidence,* he thought, especially since the vines at home didn't spiral and wind but simply crawled loosely about the small fence lattice in the garden. In his heart he felt the forces of destiny were lining up to show him he was in the right place.

Grapes weren't native to the isle, at least the Eritirim he knew. His mother's grape vines were imported by a traveling merchant from the sea. No one else in Netleaf could keep the vines alive either. Somehow his mother kept them growing. All a part of destiny's intricately, precise weaving of thread upon thread to fix the eyes on the tapestry of one's true destiny.

I'm meant to be here, he thought. Alastar corrected himself, "*We're* meant ta be here, Éimhín. The shinin' rocks had ya in it too. I'm sure of it." Éimhín was eating the deep purple grapes that hung on the arch. "Enjoy this treat. I never could sneak ya many grapes before. Mother always caught me sneakin' 'em. She knew every little cluster that popped out of her garden." Alastar smiled as he remembered home. *Home... was Netleaf still here in this changed world?*

"We have ta go home now, Éimhín. I hope everyone is still in Netleaf over the mountains." Alastar looked through the archway and pulled Éimhín away from eating. "Sorry, boy, we can't bring grapes. I don't have a good carrier for 'em. They'll squash on the way."

Alastar lead Éimhín through the archway. It was now still and graceful. It showed no signs of the once tangible portal that was inside it. They walked back to where the glowing symbols were. It was completely different there too. The cliff wall was covered in vines and leaves, and the sage bushes were gone. They were replaced by a different sort of bush; full of green leaves and branches that held bunches of small, white flowers that encircled clusters of green buds that hadn't bloomed yet. The bushes looked like someone had stuck bouquets of baby's breath buds into them, each with its own white halo of flowers.

Guelder Rose, Alastar recalled. They were just starting to bloom. When all the flowers are full, they crowd each other and make the clusters look like lumpy snowballs. They were always a nice sight in the spring, and the red berries coming from the blossoms in late summer made a great jam. His mother always had a good recipe for the few fruits of the isle.

Thoughts of continuing home replaced his reminiscing. Was he ever going to see the isle he knew before? Alastar brushed aside the greenery on the wall to look for signs of the symbols. He moved vines and leaves and felt the rock face all over the wall, but nothing indicated the symbols were there or could be brought back. Alastar looked over to the archway and wondered if they would be able to return. It was nearly invisible, just as it was in the dry canyon, except here the vines covering everything gave the stone arch its camouflage.

"Looks we'll be here awhile. Let's go see if Netleaf is where she's supposed ta be." Alastar started to lead Éimhín away when he saw the guelder rose flowers reacted strangely to Éimhín eating them. "What have ya found, Éimhín?" he said with surprise. They were giving off the same opalescent glow the symbols had flowing in them.

"Stop eatin' them, will ya?!" Alastar said alarmed as he tugged on Éimhín's reins. "I don't think ya should be eatin' glowin' flowers!" Éimhín gave a soft whinny, tugged back on the reins and started to eat the flowers again. "Tasty, eh? . . . Fine then. Don't complain ta me if ya start belly achin'."

Alastar touched the white flowers and their round petals glowed bright on contact. Touching the leaves and buds had no effect, though. Then a thought came to him. *What if the flowers are like the symbols and triggered the arch?*

"STOP eatin' the flowers! You could be eatin' the keys ta get outta here!" Alastar tugged hard on Éimhín again. Then he started to swipe and punch at the clusters of flowers trying to make something happen. Éimhín watched him curiously as he hopped around from bush to bush and attacked the flowers like a musician trying to play an oversized instrument.

After some futile minutes, there were broken white petals scattered on the ground. Alastar stopped trying. He stood confused. "I guess the flowers just do that. Nothin's happenin'." Alastar broke off a bundle of flowers to take. They continued to glow when he touched them. "I wonder if these glowin' ones are common here. I bet if I gave a bunch of these ta Nuala, she'd swoon over me for sure." Éimhín gave a humored nicker.

"Well, the next girl then... Ah, never mind." Alastar sighed and tucked the bundle of flowers partway into a saddlebag pocket. "Let's see if we can get ta the summit before nightfall. We should have a few hours daylight yet."

They started to walk down towards the valley floor. Alastar led with his staff tapping the ground rhythmically. It was a much different sound than in the Canal Valley. The ground here was soft and covered with short grass, dirt and leaves, while the dry valley was bare and rocky. His staff made a ticking sound as they went along in the desert valley, but he could barely hear the soft thud of his staff among the vibrant sounds of the forest here. The green valley seemed to change the cadence of his steps too. Alastar felt it was just the beginning of something that would wash over his entire being.

As they descended to the valley floor, Alastar noticed it was over a hundred meters deeper than before. The orchard under the cliff ledge was gone too. When they settled on the floor, Alastar could see how different the forest was compared to home. The forests along Eritirim's green coast and mountain range only held a few kinds of trees and almost no underbrush. They were sparse and colored only in various shades of green, but here it was packed with vegetation of all kinds that showed many colors in their leaves and blossoms.

However, the lush color wasn't the only thing that startled him. The forest canopy was dominated by huge oaks much larger than he'd seen before. Their trunks were as wide as the bellies of sailing ships 15 to 20 feet wide and their branches sprawled far above his head for hundreds of feet; more than twice the height of the largest oak trees he'd ever seen.

Underneath the canopy, there were many types of smaller trees and underbrush. Alastar had never seen such a forest. Variety exploded everywhere and it looked to be the peak of spring. Many trees and bushes were in bloom to complement the colorful leaves of silver, copper, burgundy and green. The view was like a kaleidoscope of sprouting gems in a vibrant haze of patina hues. It reminded Alastar of a forest painted in the colors of deep autumn, except the leaves were not dried and shriveled but bright and full of life.

"The view down here is just as breathtakin' as on the cliff top. I can't believe where we are. This forest must be ancient." Alastar looked about. Despite the dense canopy of leaves overhead, the forest below was very bright. Streams of light flooded down between the branches and the undersides of the leaves glowed golden light as well. In fact, everything in the forest had a warm glow about it, like it was literally lit with life.

The forest moved too. Alastar watched all the flitting insects flying about the flowers. The other flowers didn't appear to glow when they were touched, though. Alastar felt confident he found something special in the glowing guelder rose bushes. He made careful notes in his mind to keep track of where he was going. He thought finding the stone arch again would be important, but the thick forest looked the same everywhere, so they took a straight line towards the river. *I'll have to mark a tree once we get to the river,* he thought.

As they got close to the river, its sound of rushing water began to dominate the atmosphere. The forest started to change too. Smaller alder trees became more common. Their long, red fuzzy catkins hung from the branches like little foxtails strewn all about. Paired with the thick moss that grew on the alders, the catkins gave the forest a feeling of syrupy dew that made Alastar want to nap.

"Can ya smell the river? Fresh and crisp; it'll be a good drink," he said. The trees grew right up to the river bank. The valley didn't seem to have any ground that wasn't covered by foliage. The sight of the river flowing by gave Alastar a sense of orientation and familiarity, like the sparkling sea did back in Netleaf. At the river's edge, though, he realized a problem.

They couldn't cross here. The river was huge, at least three times wider than the canal, and the water was a rush and streamed around large boulders. It would be too dangerous to cross here.

First things first, he thought. Alastar got water sacs out and bent down into the river. The cool, rushing water quickly filled the sacs. They spent a minute resting by the river as Alastar thought about how to cross. Then the loud screech of a hawk rung into his ears, and he looked about. To the right just upstream on the same side of the river, he saw something that brought wonder and shock to his eyes.

A large white hawk with gold fringed feathers and a shiny blue beak perched in a small tree that was completely covered with vivid pink blossoms. It spread out its wings and tail feathers for a moment and Alastar saw a vibrant, blue V-pattern on the underside of its tail. The point of the V was at the tail's tip and its beak matched the V's color - a vibrant, deep and transparent blue, like a polished sapphire.

"What is that?" Alastar muffled. He tried not to alarm the hawk. It wasn't like any bird he'd seen before. It looked straight at Alastar with a piercing, authoritative stare and rang out another loud cry. Its low brow and serious face told him to take heed. Alastar stared at it nervously. Then it took off flying and cried out again.

Alastar watched as it circled over the river three times and then flew upstream slowly, screeching many times. Alastar kept watch of it as it came back and circled near them again. It still cried out loudly. After a few circles it started to fly upstream again.

Hawks don't often make so much noise, he thought, *or act that way.* Everything about this told him to follow. Alastar was quickly learning to pay attention to unusual signs. Things in this place appeared to be guiding and reassuring him of where he needed to go. He quickly mounted Éimhín and they started to ride upriver trying to keep the hawk in sight.

The bright hawk kept a close line above the river and flew slow enough for them to keep pace. They galloped a good half hour weaving through the trees along the river when Alastar noticed the river became narrow and shallow. Suddenly the hawk changed course and turned left. It flew straight up the valley mountainside, right as they broke through the edge of the forest.

Alastar stopped Éimhín and watched the bird fly over the mountain ridge, but instead of disappearing over the summit, it kept ascending, higher and higher, until it disappeared into the light, wispy clouds far overhead. *Strange,* Alastar thought, *I've never seen a bird fly so high.*

"Looks like this is where we cross." he told Éimhín. They stood on a pebbled beach where the river was much wider. It bowed outwards into a calm lagoon surrounded by the canyon walls. A high, thin waterfall flowed peacefully through a narrow opening where the cliff walls met in the middle. The rocky walls were covered by moist, green moss and tufts of grass here and there. The sun had already dipped below the summit of the valley on the right, so the lagoon was in shadows. The bright sunlight was found again on the other side of the valley. *That's where the hawk went; where we need to go,* he thought.

Alastar turned Éimhín left to cross the river, and they started to splash through the water. The river was only knee deep there. Alastar gazed to the right as they crossed and peered into the narrow gap where the waterfall fed the river. He could see the tips of green mountains beyond, far in the distance. *How far does the valley go?* he wondered.

As they neared the river's edge, the scratchy sloshing sounds of Éimhín's hoofs scuffing the wet pebbles met with the whirring buzz of something that flew past them. Alastar tracked the blur and saw it hover near some low lying flowers at the edge of the forest in front of them. It glowed dim blue as it hovered near the dangling red flowers. *Looks like a hummingbird,* he pondered, *but it's twice as big and glows like a blue ember.*

The flowers it touched lit up red as it struck them with its long needle-like beak. *More glowing flowers,* Alastar thought. But the bird didn't look like it was feeding on nectar. It jumped from flower to flower and hit them with its beak as if they were bells.

Alastar kept his eyes on the bird as they made it to shore. He slowly got off Éimhín, so he wouldn't scare it away. He walked cautiously toward it, and when he got closer, he noticed it wasn't a bird at all, but a tiny flying person with a long, thin horn on top of its head. Its glow was coming from the shimmering blue dress it wore. The fabric hung about its legs and made the dress look like a bird's drooping tail.

Astonishing! Alastar thought very amused. He looked back at Éimhín and whispered, "Are ya seein' this?" Éimhín appeared agitated and stomped a forefoot. "What'sa matter? Are ya blind? This is amazin'!" he retorted in a hushed voice. Éimhín gave out a loud whinny. The horned fairy was startled and zipped off. It disappeared with a trail of sparkling dust that fell shimmering to the ground. "Why'd ya do that, Éimhín?"

Alastar continued walking to the red flowers. They glowed constantly now and slowly dripped a red luminescent liquid. "Bleeding hearts," he said as he recognized the flattened, round blossoms that hung from the plant's stems. *Except they're really bleeding. . . and. . .*

Alastar's eyes widened as the glowing, heart-shaped flowers broke off, one by one, and floated into the forest. They left behind a trail of glowing red droplets on the ground, and Éimhín started to snort and neigh at Alastar.

"What'sa matter now?" he asked irritated and looked back at him. Éimhín gestured up the mountainside. "Right. Back ta Netleaf. . . We have time. There's still a couple hours daylight, and we have a curious hunt here." Alastar whistled for Éimhín and he reluctantly went over to him.

Alastar grabbed his reins and led Éimhín along the trail of glowing red drops. They went straight upwards and right onto a path through the wooded mountainside. The floating bleeding hearts were nowhere in sight, but their glowing trail was easy to see. It took them up and around to the other side of the cliff wall that the waterfall flowed through.

"We would've never found this trail by ourselves, Éimhín. Wouldn't ya say this is good fortune?" Éimhín answered with silence. Alastar felt his concern. "Are ya that homesick, boy? We're just gonna have some explorin' before we continue on," he reassured.

The glowing trail led them to the dark entrance of a narrow crevice that went through the cliffs. Its top loomed far overhead. *Must be over 30 feet,* Alastar thought. "The drops stop here, but it looks like we go in. It's gonna get dark and cramped. Don'tcha be worried. Looks room 'nough."

They started into the damp corridor. The light was dim, and it was barely wide enough to let Éimhín squeeze through. Alastar looked up at the sky, still bright blue, but now enclosed by dark, jagged rocks. "It's gettin' tight in here," he said as he heard the sound of scraping wood. The wood bundles on Éimhín were catching on the cliff walls.

Alastar stopped and looked back at Éimhín. He shifted about and tried to see if his staff was safe from damage. It was held jutting upwards in a leather clip that hung from Éimhín's left shoulder. *Too close to the rock wall,* he thought. *I'd best grab it.* Then he saw the guelder rose flowers were also very close to getting smashed and decided to get them too.

"I don't know, Éimhín. You got a bit chubby in this place," he joked while he squeezed past Éimhín's neck to take his staff. Éimhín sounded an annoyed nicker and leaned against the wall. Alastar was smothered. "Ugh! Éimhín!" he screamed, and Éimhín quickly released him. "Grand thing ya did! Now my clothes are wet and dirty. Aren't ya happy?!" he said with no amusement. Éimhín gave an acknowledging neigh in response. The humor left Alastar, but Éimhín's playfulness put a smile on his face. What a character, he thought. "A fine boy ya are," he said and pat Éimhín's neck.

Alastar lifted his staff out of the clip and held it up in the air as he moved farther back to grab the flowers. It was a struggle to get to the rear saddle bag. Alastar dirtied himself more against the cliff wall. "Grand, just *grand!*" he exclaimed. He thought he would make fun of Éimhín filling up all the space again, but then remembered getting pressed solid against the wall. "Er... Ugh, this place is bit of a bottleneck," he said and grabbed the flowers. Now both his arms were up in the air with the staff in one hand and the flowers in the other as he squirmed his way back to the front.

They continued through the craggy narrow a long ways. The ground was hard and rocky. Alastar's staff made the ticking sound he became accustomed to hearing in the Canal Valley, except here it echoed in the corridor like a hollow whisper that was smothered by the walls. As they went along, he noticed the echo become less prominent. The exit was near.

Soon the green light of the forest was seen reflected on the rock walls and the sound of a large waterfall drifted through the air. *That sounds a lot bigger than the waterfall we saw before,* Alastar thought.

The end of the corridor was covered in hanging vines that filtered the sunlight like mottled, green stained glass. Anxious to go through, Alastar went forward and pierced the loose vines with his staff first. Outside, he was suddenly engulfed in bright light. The sun's bright glare shone directly into his eyes. Everything was awash in bright white. Alastar looked away and raised his hand over his eyes to act as a visor.

He heard Éimhín come through the vines as he stood blinking and squinting. After a minute, the bright blur of white and green all around him sharpened into a view he could barely contain. They stood on another high ledge. This one looked out to a vast green landscape of high hills and cliffs. They had reached the end of the valley and found themselves at the edge of hill country, covered in green grass and sparse forests. The land was an assortment of countless peaked hills and plateaus that jut upwards from the rolling landscape. Vibrant green fields and forests stretched over the hills and valleys alike; green everywhere just as in the River Valley.

Alastar couldn't believe how alive the land was. The shores of the isle he knew where rich and green, but never so full and lush with life. The isle had become so thick with life that it condensed on his eyes. He could feel it all around him and penetrate him as if a vibrant energy connected him to the land.

"Can ya take that sight in? Mountain peaks everywhere. Not as high as the valley summits, but boy, doesn't it look rich? That's some grand grazin' land in the hills out there, Éimhín."

Alastar looked down and to the left slightly where a large rushing waterfall flowed. It was so high, he couldn't see its bottom.

This must be the river beyond the cliff walls, he thought as he scanned toward down the river where the mountains closed in to encapsulate the valley beyond. He could see downstream for some miles to where the calm lagoon was nestled just over the high cliffs they had just circumnavigated.

He turned his head back toward the waterfall and looked far to the left. Alastar was surprised to see the river meet the edge of a huge field of deep blue water there. It reflected the mountains and sky all around it, like a perfect mirror. *The lake in the mountains,* he recalled. *That must be the source of the river. . . and the main canal that the old stories told about.*

"We've found the mountain lake, Éimhín. The flowin' Mirror of the Mountains; never seen for generations since it dried up." Alastar felt the energy about him intensify as he realized he was in the presence of things only recorded in stories of ages long gone. The words and images of the mind had kept the stories at a distance, like fairytales and dreams too fantastic to be true, yet they were true. How fleeting and dim do memories become when they are removed from tactile sensation.

"Now we're right in the middle of what…" Alastar said with a spark of comprehension, "…once was." *Are we now in the past?*

Coursing Change

"*We* might've gone *A LOT* farther than we planned," Alastar said. He noticed a tiny plume of white smoke in the distance. It was just in view at the edge of sight, blocked from further view by the cliffs. He stepped out as far as he could on the ledge and leaned forward to get a better look. He saw the gently curving column of smoke came from a small house nestled at the edge of the lake. It was the last house in a loose group.

"Éimhín, there's a village not far off." Alastar tried to remember the stories about the valley and mountain lake, but couldn't recall anything about a town next to the Mirror of the Mountains. *It can't be an accident we were brought here,* he thought. "I do think I know where we'll go next. We'll get better oriented talkin' ta people there."

Éimhín shook his head and backed up a step with a neigh to show disapproval.

"What's with ya, Éimhín? We're not so far from Netleaf. I wanna see what we found here. Isn't your heart poundin' with adventure?" Alastar took Éimhín's reins and led him down toward the base of the cliffs. They had gone halfway when he faintly heard women singing inside the waterfall's loud rumble. He looked down at the base of the waterfall and saw three women there. They were washing clothes among the wet boulders and mist.

Right quick to get some answers, he thought. "I hope these gals are friendly, Éimhín. Let's just. . ." Before Alastar could finish his sentence Éimhín bellowed a loud neigh. It caught the women's attention, and they all looked up at them. Alastar kept walking down the mountainside as if nothing happened, though he began to blush.

He became suddenly aware the flowers he held were in plain view. "Why'd ya do that, boy? You've been actin' up a bit. Stop it!" Alastar muttered in frustration under his breath and tugged on the reins.

The women stopped washing and held relaxed smiles the whole time they approached. *Why wouldn't they smile?* Alastar thought. He was walking around the mountains holding flowers like a silly girl. Now he was keenly aware his face was flushed red. His cheeks felt so hot he thought they were glowing like embers. *Maybe the flowers weren't such a good token to carry around,* he thought. *Why did I even take them?*

Alastar tried to walk calmly in his embarrassment. As the distance narrowed, one of the women struck him with familiarity. She had shining dark hair and fair skin; it was as if he'd found Nuala in a waking dream. Her hair fell by her smooth shoulders just as he had remembered, just as beautiful as the waterfall that streamed among the boulders where she stood.

Alastar began to calm after seeing her familiar face. *But is it her?* he wondered. He didn't recognize the other women. They all wore simple, light tan blouses and long skirts of different shades each – gray blue, faded burgundy, and washed green, like the desert sage he collected. He thought their flax clothing was very plain and ragged.

The sage colored skirt reminded Alastar of the sage bushes and glowing symbols. The woman wearing it was an unfamiliar blonde, so his attention quickly went back to the Nuala look-alike who wore the drab blue dress. The last woman was an attractive, red-haired lady who was much older than the others. Alastar looked over 'Nuala.' He knew Nuala wouldn't wear such plain, worn clothing. *But maybe people are changed in this place too,* he thought, *like the land was transformed.*

Alastar stood by the river's edge and greeted the women. They all stood ankle deep in the riverbank just where they were when he first saw them. Their hair and clothes were wet and their skin was covered in droplets from the waterfall. Alastar couldn't help thinking how beautiful 'Nuala' looked despite her unadorned dress. She appeared like the light of spring to him; a lush, green leaf glistening with the first raindrops of the season. He kept wondering how she could be here. *Was this really happening?*

Alastar looked at 'Nuala' and asked, "Nuala, is it?"

The red-haired woman answered in a pleasant tone, "Where'd ya learn your manners, lad? You should be addressin' the eldest first."

Alastar felt the blushing heat come to his cheeks again. He made a curt bow and said, "Forgive me, ladies. I thought 'Nuala' would know me. I am Alastar Duer from Netleaf on the east shore of the isle." He looked at 'Nuala' and hoped she would say something.

"Right then. I'm Flann ["Flahhn"]," the red-haired woman acknowledged. "This is Ula ["Oo-lah"]," she said and gestured towards the blonde girl. "And I don't know who Nuala is, but you were addressin' Nola ["Noh-lah"]. We're from Loch an Scátháin ["Lahkh-in Sky-hine"][2]."

Loch an Scátháin, Alastar pondered. *That's Mirror Lake in the older tongue.* It was uncommon to hear it used outside of old stories and the elders' speech. More evidence they ran into the past. "Loch an Scátháin," he repeated. "You must mean the lake upstream."

"Sure. That it is. . . and the village as well," Flann said. "I've not heard of Netleaf, but by the looks of ya and your fine horse we could tell you were from the plains; one of the Eachraighe ["Ahkh-ree"]."

"Sir, is Netleaf near Lacharan ["Lah-kahr-run"]?" Nola asked Alastar with a spark of interest in her eyes.

---

[2] 'kh' in pronunciations is a hard, long 'k' + 'h' sound

The women saw him as someone of stature and wealth because of his well-crafted clothing, ornate staff and Éimhín's well groomed and fine build. The craftsmanship of his saddle, bags and bridle told them he was not a peasant or from anywhere they were familiar. The materials and workmanship looked entirely foreign to them. No one but nobles owned such valuable and well-made things. However, they did think the bundles of wood on Éimhín were an odd thing for him to haul if he was a rich man.

Alastar never heard of Lacharan and had no idea who were the Eachraighe (the Horse Riders). Eritirim had only a handful of towns on the green shores of the south and east. Beyond the mountain range was nothing but the vast desert agate where he had just come from. No reports of life from there at all. It was just the part of the isle that was dead and barren, even if it made up most of the isle.

Alastar tried to keep his confusion to himself. "I haven't ever run ta Lacharan. Don't know anythin' about it really," he said.

Flann grew suspicious. Lacharan was the largest seaport on the isle and the clan seat of the Eachraighe. Everyone knew it. *How can this Horse Rider not know anything about Lacharan?* she wondered. Flann queried Alastar, "What *are* ya doin' here then? The horsemen don't venture ta our side of the mountains. Not since the Áiteoir ["Æ-chor"][3] claimed rule. Have ya gotten word the isle is free ta roam again?"

Free to roam? The Áiteoir? How do I deal with all these odd questions? Alastar wondered. He told them, "I'm afraid I'm out of sorts here, ladies. We were out gatherin' wood for my stock and traveled a long ways. Wandered off much farther than we intended, really. We're a bit lost in this place and tryin' ta gather our bearin's.

[3] 'æ' in pronunciations is an 'a' sound as in ash, cat and hat, not 'ah' or 'ay' as in ago, pa, or hay

Then we stumbled upon you all. A good thing too, because we'd be needin' ta find a decent place ta rest the night."

"Sure enough," Flann acknowledged with hesitation in her voice. Alastar certainly seemed out of place, but he looked harmless enough. *Tall and fit, but certainly no burster,* she thought, *Hardly anything intimidating about him. No scamp looks the way he does and wanders about with guelder rose in his hand,* she mused.

"We have room for ya," Flann said. "Let us finish the wash first. We've nearly done." The women started to wash clothes again. They scrubbed them on the boulders under the flowing waters of the falls.

Nola couldn't help noticing Alastar watched her closely. She wondered about the flowers he had. He kept holding them like he was carefully protecting them from harm. He held them far from his body so they'd be cushioned by air on all sides. *A curious, funny boy,* she thought.

"Tell us, sir. Are those guelder rose for your Nuala?" Nola asked. Ula and Flann looked up from their work curiously.

Alastar felt he should give the flowers to Nola. *Can't be a coincidence I was led here and found her like this,* he thought. *She's so much like Nuala.*

"Oh…" he said bewildered. He was unsure what to do. He felt odd to give the flowers to Nola and nothing to the others, so he split the bundle into three equal parts. "I… I do believe these *are* for you." He stepped into the river and handed flowers to each of the women. The guelder rose still looked fresh after the long ride and trek through the cliffs. Alastar felt satisfied they held up well. Then he remembered their glow and said, "Go on, touch the white petals."

They lightly tapped the flowers with their fingers, but nothing happened. Alastar was confused. He remembered they glowed after he plucked them from the bush. "Try it again. They'll do somethin' amazin'!" he said with enthusiasm.

"How long ago did ya pick these?" Nola asked.

"Some hours ago, I'd say," he answered, "Why?"

Nola and Ula giggled softly. They all wondered how Alastar didn't know the flowers would stop glowing after the life's flow drained out of them. They thought he was acting strangely.

Flann replied with a look of concern, "Lad, you're not from Rathúnas ["Ræ-hoon-us"], are ya? Your head's empty of thin's of the isle. Wobbly as a newborn foal ya are. The flowers stop glowin' once the flow of life's gone out of 'em. All the radiants are like that – guelder rose, mouse ears, white beam…"

"Sure, sure," Alastar interrupted. He scratched his head in confusion. He thought his face glowed bright red for certain. *And what's this Rathúnas now?* he wondered. It sounded like she was referring to the isle. "Emm…" Alastar stammered. He wasn't sure what to say. "You could say we're not from this isle. Éimhín and I traveled a long ways. So far, in fact, I couldn't even say the distance we've gone. I do find myself a newborn here. I would appreciate your help ta get back in sorts."

Alastar sounded so sincere and appeared so helpless that the women felt they needed to help him. Flann also noted how cordial his speech was. Alastar's unusual qualities and simple honesty made her feel he was trustworthy. *The air about him is full of respect and knowledge, though not of common things,* she thought. *He seems to be an educated and well mannered young man; a rare combination even among the wealthiest of the isle, but he needs a good looking into.*

"We'll be certain ta help ya with what we can, lad," Flann replied. "We can't have ya wanderin' wobbly as ya are. Who knows what wild thin's would try ta claim ya. Rathúnas is not safe as it once was. The Áiteoir made the isle their personal haunt for all dark thin's of the world. The mountains around Loch an Scátháin are one of the last sanctuaries from Áiteoir control. Lacharan is the other. We're under truce ta keep ta our diminished borders these past years."

"You were a grand sight," Ula said. "We thought the Áiteoir released the travelin' restrictions, or better, they were beaten back."

Alastar felt relieved he would get help, but the Áiteoir troubled him. All his life he lived in a free and untroubled island. Reports of war only came from across the sea where the rest of the world seemed to ebb and flow in tumbling prosperity and suffering. It was not a world he cared to take part in.

"I'm sorry I can't be of much help," he replied. "The troubles of your isle are unknown ta me. But I am very grateful for your help. Please accept the guelder rose as a token of my friendship."

Flann and Ula nodded and smiled, while Nola said with eyes gleaming, "Gladly, sir." She brushed back her long hair with her left hand and tucked the guelder rose behind her ear. The gesture showed her pretty face fully, like the full moon had popped into view after the curtains were opened. She smiled at Alastar with a warm trust that melted away the shards of glass that remained in his heart.

Alastar felt his chest pound hard, and he started to feel warm. He felt the dry void in his chest start to glisten with life again when he saw Nola showing the affection he yearned for. *She must be the reason I was brought here,* he thought. *How could it not be destiny?*

Flann saw how quick Alastar and Nola became comfortable with each other and broke their moment of silent admiration. "Finished now!" she said quickly. "We're ready ta go." The women gathered the clothing and placed them in two large, round wicker baskets.

Alastar saw how heavy the wet clothes were and suggested, "Let's have Éimhín carry those baskets. He don't mind." Éimhín gave a soft whinny of a sigh, and Alastar patted his neck in reassurance.

"Nonsense!" Flann retorted. The baskets are drippin' wet, and how can you load such a beautiful horse? We'll be fine ta carry 'em."

"Sure… then let me carry the baskets," he said. He felt he was fit enough to carry them both the whole way to town. He placed his staff back into the saddle clip and took the baskets from them. "They're not so heavy for me," he said as he stacked one on top of the other. Then he lifted them up and straddled them with his arms in front of him. Flann took Éimhín's reins and led them along a trail that followed the river. Alastar and the girls followed close behind. The path soon turned uphill and Alastar began to strain from the load. He also noticed the baskets were leaking all over him.

Wonderful, he thought. The last time his pants felt like this was when he couldn't hold his bladder in the middle of the night. He ran to the outhouse leaking a stream when he was six or seven years old. Alastar started to smile as he remembered his father teasing him about it. "Ya should've listened ta me, boy, when I told ya to go before bed," he recalled him saying.

Ula broke his thoughts and asked him, "Sir, where did ya get that staff? I've never seen such beautiful carvin', and the wood glows gold, like polished hawk's eye gemstones. I've never seen wood flash so brilliant!"

Hawk's eye, Alastar thought. It reminded him of the bright hawk they followed up the river. He forgot it was leading them toward home. Alastar went back to Ula's question and answered, "I made it. About a year ago."

"You carved it yourself?" she asked. She was surprised he could sculpt the staff so expertly.

"Surely, I did," he said with a slight grunt. His brow showed beads of sweat from carrying the heavy baskets.

"That's amazin'!" she exclaimed. "You don't look old enough ta be a master carver."

"My father started me early. Just as soon as I could safely handle a knife and gouge." Alastar went back through his memory and recalled he started apprenticing soon after he had that outhouse accident. "Been carvin' over ten years, closer ta twelve."

"Then you're not an Eachraighe?" Nola asked.

"Right. But I'm a fair rider. I'm just handier with wood than most," he answered. His arms were starting to ache. "How far ta Loch an Scátháin is it now?" he asked.

"Only half hour," Nola said. "Are ya all right carryin'? Ya look peaked."

"I'm fine. Grand altogether!" Alastar reassured quickly. He tried to appear strong and capable. He thought about how he buried Éimhín under loads of wood in the Canal Valley. He never saw him so poor and tired. *I must be looking about like that now,* he thought, *and it's hardly been ten minutes.* "I'll never load ya up like that again," he whispered to Éimhín.

Nola couldn't hear what Alastar said. "What was that?" Nola asked him.

"Ah, nothin'. Just mumblin' from my mind."

The shadows grew long as they continued toward the village, but somehow the land still appeared bright and vibrant after the sun dipped below the horizon. Alastar knew something was odd when he saw the sky dimming but the land did not. He could tell things were brighter in this land when they were in the forest, and how the smaller trees and underbrush were unusually thick and alive under the shade of the huge trees. *I knew the forest was glowing with light,* he exclaimed to himself.

It was subtle before, but now he could see clearly that every plant kept glowing with sunlight after the sun went away. Alastar wanted to ask about the glowing landscape, but he didn't want to give them any further suspicions about where he came from. He looked over at the guelder rose in Nola's hair and saw that it wasn't glowing as all the rest of the foliage around them. It still looked alive and fresh, but its flame of life was gone.

They arrived at the edge of town faster than he thought they would. His arms and shoulders were sore and cramping, but he could have managed a farther distance.

"Here we are," Flann said. She noted the first house along the trail. It was a large double roundhouse, laid out like a figure eight, made with stone walls and a roof of thatch. There was a timber barn about half the size of the house on its left. The lake wasn't visible behind the trees that surrounded them, but the sound of water sloshing among the shore was near. It was a wonderfully familiar sound Alastar thought as he recalled all his time along the beaches of the sea.

Flann stopped them at the fence gate in front of the house. "We'd be stayin' here, Alastar." She looked at Nola and said, "Slán ["slahn"; bye/safe journey], Nola. We'll see ya tomorra'."

"Slán agaibh ["slahn ah-guv"; bye everyone][4]," Nola replied softly. She turned to Alastar and said, "I'll take these from ya." She took the baskets, set them down, and separated them. Then she looked at Alastar. "Thank you, sir, for carryin' 'em." She picked up one of the baskets and smiled at Alastar as she rose up. "Slán," she said to him and continued to walk down the trail.

Alastar's gaze kept on her as she walked the path. The glow from the plants and trees all around them made him feel like he was viewing a dream vision of Nuala walking away from him again; a

[4] 'g' in pronunciations is always a hard 'g' "guh" sound, not a 'j' as in jay or gee-whiz

gently swaying figure lit by a glowing corridor that disappeared around a corner. He wanted to follow her down the trail, but before he could do anything Flann broke his trance. "Ula, take Alastar and his horse ta the barn. Show 'em their quarters."

"Aye, Mam ["Mahm"; Mom]," Ula said.

Flann took the remaining basket and went into the house. Ula took Éimhín's reins and gestured Alastar to follow. She led them to the left and into the barn. Alastar looked about and figured the barn to be about the same size as his – about right to fit a dozen cows. The barn here was relatively empty, though; just a small cow, a horse, and a handful of sheep and goats were inside.

Ula led them to an empty stall. "This is for Éimhín. He'll be cozy here." She looked at Alastar with a cute smile and asked, "You have a fair glint for Nola, don'tcha? You seem very comfortable with her."

Alastar responded, "She reminds me of a close friend I lost some time ago. I thought I had run into her again when I saw Nola. Couldn't tell ya what a surprise it was, but I suppose they're not the same person."

"Right, it was Nuala wasn't it? I hope ya find your friend. Losin' people round ya isn't a fond thin'. I'd much rather roll in a bed 'a thistles than lose anyone else."

"Who've ya lost?"

"Near half the village since the warrin' with the Áiteoir began. Good we have a truce now, but we're cut off from the rest of the isle. Only travelers sanctioned by the Áiteoir can roam Rathúnas. That'd be most everyone on the isle since everyone surrendered; all but us in the Torthúil ["Tahr-hool"] Mountains and Lacharan. The Áiteoir separated our kingdom so we couldn't regroup together."

"Why did the Áiteoir make truces instead of continue their

take-over?"

"They didn't have the power ta hold the rest of the isle *and* finish the take-over. Torthúil is blessed. Our numbers were less, yet the Áiteoir were kept from advancin'. After two years of siegin', the Áiteoir struck the truce. So many died. The truce was welcome. It was quiet these past years, but we fear the Áiteoir plan ta finish their war for the isle."

Ula started to gaze into memories for a moment as she recalled the terrible years of war. Then she looked to the back of the barn and said, "You can stay in the loft. There's a decent bed and space for ya. Our farm hand used ta stay there, but he didn't live through the warrin'."

"Thank ya," he said. "I'll keep everythin' in order for ya."

"Don't worry about it, sir. I'll leave ya ta settle in. Join us in the house after."

"Sure, I will. And please, just call me Alastar. We're friends now."

Ula made a quick bow and nod and left the barn. Alastar turned to Éimhín and said, "Don'tcha think this is a might bit cozier than campin' on the mountain? Sounds like a safer place too, considerin' all that talk of the Áiteoir." Éimhín let out a snorting raspberry sound and shook his head.

"Still think we should've headed for home?. . . Soon enough. Ya have ta admit. We've learned a lot about this place from our side adventure. I think we're right where we need ta be. You did notice Nola, didn'tcha?" Éimhín stood silent as Alastar untied everything from him.

"Not so fond of her either? Sure then. You can be the one ta feel left out when we have our weddin' and all." Éimhín gave a nicker. Alastar patted him on his neck and shoulders and joked, "Ahhhh... I'd still let ya watch the ceremony… maybe from the barn window, is all."

Alastar picked up his staff and bags. He looked up towards the loft. It was fairly lit from the light that came through windows high in the barn walls. The light was softer than daylight, though, and the sky was dark. The glow came from the trees.

He carried his things up to the loft where he found a small table with an oil lantern and a small box bed with straw-stuffed linen for a mattress. Less comfortable than he was used to, but it would be a better night than camping on the cold summit.

Alastar left his things on the loft and went back down toward the barn doors. "Rest well now," he said to Éimhín. "I'll be back soon. Don't let the goats and sheep pick on ya."

He left the barn and turned toward the house. It was clearly dusk outside, but the glowing landscape provided enough light to see a long ways. However, he noticed the plants were not glowing as brightly as they were before. The energy from the sunlight was slowly leaking away. *The dead of night may still hold its darkness here,* he thought.

Alastar heard the sounds of the lake close by; gentle waves among rocks and reeds. He followed the sounds and walked to the back of the house. Between the many tree trunks in front of him, he saw the dim flickers of light dance off small waves on the water. He went straight up to the shore and scanned the view.

At dusk the lake was a dark, gorgeous, shimmering mirror that was bordered by glowing trees and plants all along its rim. He could see the far shore ahead and to the right where the river started, but towards the left, the lake reached farther than he could see. Only the faint glow that rose from the forest on its unseen shore was seen on the horizon.

It's not cold here, he thought. He always imagined the Mirror of the Mountains to be a frigid place, but the air felt as warm as the rich light that came from the forest glow. The rushing breeze along the lake hardly rustled the water at all, but it could be heard running swiftly through the leaves, like a tinkling chime muffled under pillows of wool. Alastar never imagined a place so peaceful and full of harmony. Eritirim had changed so much, even its sounds made a song when there was hardly a melody before.

Alastar turned back to the house. The windows were brightly lit by flickering firelight. *Time to meet the neighbors,* he thought.

"Alastar," Conall ["Kon-nul"] said as Alastar walked into the house.

"Sir," Alastar nodded. Flann and Ula were dressing the table for dinner. A large fire burned just behind them inside a stone fireplace. Conall evaluated Alastar keenly. Up and down he looked, trying to find any signs that he was an enemy. Then he moved to Alastar's side and stared at his face. Alastar turned his head to look at Conall.

"Do not turn your head, boy," Conall said firmly. Alastar looked straight ahead again with bewilderment while Conall continued to stare at the side of his face.

"Sure," Conall muttered. "Not Áiteoir. Their trackers have a piercin' spark in their eyes when you look at 'em from the sides. I would've gutted ya right here if you were Lorgaire ["Lore-geh-reh"]." A chill went through Alastar's spine. Conall was a large, strong blonde man and wore a long, blue gray léine ["lay-nyah"] tunic that hung just below his knees. His powerful legs stood like sturdy pillars over his leather sandals. Just one of his calf muscles appeared to be larger than both of Alastar's combined. The threat of being gutted quickly by him didn't seem so farfetched. Alastar wondered what would have happened if they met Conall instead of the women first.

"Never a Lorgaire had a demeanor like Alastar; no other

Áiteoir either," Flann said. "I told ya he was a fine boy. We could see that far off. When would ya trust your wife's intuition, dear?"

"When there's risk 'a war, I'll be proddin' the matters as need be," Conall replied. He moved in front of Alastar and patted his shoulders firmly with his hands. "Welcome, Alastar. Have a seat at the table." The two men sat down facing each other on opposite sides of the table. Flann and Ula continued to serve.

"I started the stew before we went ta the falls," Flann said. "Dinner's right quick for ya t'day, Alastar." She filled bowls with stew while Ula brought them to their seats. Then Flann sat down next to Conall while Ula gave everyone a piece of bread.

"It smells lovely," Alastar said. "I thank ya for your hospitality."

"It's our pleasure," Flann said. "Go on, get ta eatin'."

Everyone started eating. Alastar felt strange to sit down with Conall's family. It had been only him and his mother for the longest time. They rarely went to gatherings outside home, and most of his family had either died or left the isle to find their fortunes, much like Nuala's family had left. Life on the isle was often too quiet for some people, but Alastar's life in Netleaf was comfortable and well respected. His trade of woodcarving supplied them with decent things and all they needed.

Alastar wondered about Netleaf again. Does he still have a home here? What would he do if he didn't? Then thoughts of seeing Nola plunged his mind into daydreams of settling into Loch an Scátháin. *Surely, I could win her hand,* he thought. He only needed to secure a decent plot of land if his home in Netleaf was gone. . . Alastar hesitated. Suddenly he realized that if his home was gone, his mother, family and friends would be gone too; his whole life wiped away like the disappearing symbols on the cliff wall.

What am I thinking about? Alastar said to himself. *Shouldn't I be thinking about returning to my true home on the other side of the archway?*

Conall grew restless. "Alastar, lad. How did a pleasant young man like yourself venture inta the mountains? The Greerian ["Greer-ree-in"] sentries at our borders don't miss a thin'."

Alastar wondered if he should be completely honest about where he came from. But who would understand that? He could hardly understand it himself. And the arch was well hidden; perhaps it was meant to be kept a secret… Just then a loud knock came from the front door.

Ula got up and answered the door. "Braede ["Bray-dah"], won't ya come in?" she said.

Braede walked inside and met them at the table. "Conall, I heard we have a visitor ta Loch an Scátháin. Would ya mind another head at the table?" He was a thin, older man with rough, weathered skin and spindly, dry hair. He looked as if he spent his entire life walking under a desert sun or drying on the salty seas. Alastar had only seen traveling merchants appear the way he did; worn souls after many years of constant traveling. Everyone else appeared well rested, fair skinned, and plump by comparison.

"You're welcome at our table, Braede," Conall said. "Ula, set some stew for Braede."

"Certainly, Dadaí ["Dah-dee"; Daddy]," she responded.

Braede held up his hand to signal, no, and sat down at the end of the table. "I'll not be eatin'. I had my dinner. You all continue as ya were. I'll just be conversin' with the boy, if you're not mindin'."

"Sure then," Conall said.

Alastar started to feel fidgety having another inquisitor eye him closely. He looked at Braede and smiled. "Pleased ta meet ya, sir," he said with a polite nod of his head.

"Grand. What would your name be, lad?"

"Alastar, sir."

"Swan-bearer, is it? Interestin'," Braede said. "You're a curious fellow with such a fine steed and fitments."

Swan-bearer? Alastar wondered. He never knew his name meant swan-bearer. The term made him remember the symbol with the swans that faced each other. Now he knew the symbols were speaking of him and Éimhín. *What else did they say?*

Braede continued. "Nola said she'd never seen a horse and rider appear as fine and stately as you. Ya do look an exceptional lad and your horse as well. I had a quick look at him in the barn."

Alastar felt the heat of blushing come after hearing of Nola. "Thank ya, sir. I'm only as I am. Éimhín and I are as common as all else."

"Éimhín?" Braede asked.

"My horse, sir. His name is Éimhín."

"Right then. And ya deny bein' an Eachraighe?"

Braede was asking for a lot of details. *Did Nola tell this man everything?* Alastar wondered. "True. I am not an Eachraighe. I'm simply a woodcarver."

"A *woodcarver?!*" Conall burst out. "Ya have many a fine thin' for a woodcarver, lad. Are ya certain that's *all* ya are?" Braede looked at Alastar with suspicion. Alastar could feel him working out another question to pin him down with.

"Why are ya givin' the boy such a heavy questionin'?" Flann retorted. "He's a trustworthy lad. Won't ya let him eat in peace?"

"We're just makin' sure of things, Flann," Braede said. "Odd thin'. This boy walks inta the mountains without alertin' the sentries. Our Greerian patrols have eyes ya can't hide from, and certainly no horse rider can outrun their flyin' wings. We can't have anyone travelin' unknown ta us and breakin' the Áiteoir truce lightly. All in Rathúnas know this." Braede turned his head to face Alastar. "Everyone save this boy, anyhow. Nola said you were quite lost. Where did ya come from, lad?"

"I'm from Netleaf, sir, a small sea town."

"I've not heard of such a place on the isle or elsewhere," Braede said. "I've had much travelin' and a keen memory ta know."

"I'd say my home is much farther than you've ever traveled," Alastar said. "We wandered ta your isle quite unexpectedly."

"How can ya simply wander onta our isle, lad? Are ya from Rathúnas or not?" Braede asked with an intense interest.

"We're not of your isle, sir," Alastar answered. The plain truth was always best. His parents had taught him early that a man is only as good as his word. A good name is worth more than the riches of the world, his father always told him. "We simply arrived from the mountain valley. We were followin' the canal, emm… I mean, we were seekin' wood where the river was. Never went past your borders at all."

Braede gave an expression of shock. "Arrived from the valley… I see." He gave Alastar a smile and stood up. "It was a pleasure ta speak with ya, lad. Conall, see that the boy is cared for and that he stays in town for the time bein'. I must speak with the king of matters."

"Certainly," Conall replied. He looked at Alastar. "Ya heard him, lad. You'll be stayin' with us till we have further word. Braede doesn't think you're a threat, so I'm fine with ya here."

"Surely," Braede said. "I could've had ya put in the stocks, Swan-bearer. But there's other thin's you'd be meant for." He bowed to everyone. "I'll take my leave. Thank you all."

After Braede left, everyone continued to eat. Alastar began to relax slightly, though he didn't like the idea that his traveling was restricted. He had to know if Netleaf, or at least a town, was where his home should be. The hawk appeared to be leading them there, but what would have happened if they crossed the border? The talk of flying sentries and oppressive Áiteoir made him feel ever more a babe in the woods.

Alastar wondered who Braede was. He seemed to be an important person. "Conall, sir. Who is Braede?"

"Round Loch an Scátháin, he's the mill owner," Conall said.

"Hadn't always been, though," Flann added. "He owned stone mines in the north kingdom till round 'bout ten years ago. He fled here when the Áiteoir took the north. He used ta travel everywhere tradin' his stone. Now he's settled by our loch and is one of King Fuar's ["Foor"] envoys."

"I see," Alastar said.

"Braede's a bit of a rough talker," Conall said, "but ya needn't worry about him. He's a good man. Found a wife in Loch an Scátháin and has a quiet life. Built the mill too. Before him, we had ta grind grain ourselves."

"That we did," Flann said. "Just handfuls at a time. Fair bit a' effort ta make some bread. It was that or travel ta Cnoc na Rí ["Kruk nah Ree"] ta buy flour. That's where the king sits. I'm sure Braede will be leavin' for there in the mornin'."

Cnoc na Rí. . . Alastar recognized those words. It meant Hill of the King. "Where is Cnoc na Rí?"

"How could ya not have seen it, lad, wanderin' the valley?!" Conall said with further suspicion. "It's at the mouth of the River Bradán ["Brah-don"] where the sea meets our mountain waters. Did ya not say ya came here by the River Valley? Ya must've came ta our isle through there… on a boat. No other way inta the mountains without crossin' the borders."

Alastar hesitated to speak of the archway, but his choices were diminishing if he wanted the trust of these friends. "We didn't come by boat or pass near Cnoc na Rí."

"Then *how* did ya get here, lad?" Conall asked firmly.

"We came through a shimmerin' gateway from our isle," Alastar said with some trepidation.

"AMAIDEACH! ["ahma-jawkh"; absurd]" Conall exhorted. "Ya must think my head full 'a pebbles ta believe that! Or you're demented as a mainidh ["mah-nee"; lunatic]! I can tell you're no conjurer."

Flann and Ula were stunned. "You've seen a geata ["gæt-tah"]?" Flann asked.

"Don't tell me ya believe those old tales," Conall said. "Conjurin' is one thin', but the roamin' gateways are thin's 'a story."

"Bah!" Flann said. "You know as well as I. The thin's of this world are unexplainable."

"It's true, sir," Alastar said. "We came by an extraordinary gateway and ended up on your isle. It was all by inexplicable fortune. Now that we're here, I haven't a clue how ta get back."

"That explains your unfortunate lack of knowledge," Flann said. "I knew ya were a good lad, but your manner was puzzlin'."

"Simply a lost traveler," Ula said with sorrow. "You could be very, *very* far from home. The gateways have unimaginable power."

"What do ya know of the gateways?" Alastar asked.

"They're thin's 'a grand stories," Conall said. "Told ta folks ta amaze and dazzle."

"I'm afraid we only know what's told in folklore," Flann said. "They whisk travelers ta far realms as easy as it is ta step through a curtain."

"Right then," Conall said sarcastically. "The lad stepped through a grand doorway and now he's trapped here. That makes no sense at all, girls. Don'tcha recall the stories say no one goes through the gateways unless they're meant ta pass? The boy said it was blind fortune he got here. Ya can't just wander through! Never mind that no one ever told of findin' a gateway on Rathúnas or anywhere else."

"Blind or no," Flann said. "Alastar's meant to be here. That I'm sure of."

"Fine, there's logic in that. We'll get ta the meanin' of this however it goes. The king has people who understand thin's of this nature better than most. I'll speak with Braede in the mornin' about it. Anyhow, it don't change what's happenin'. You remain with us, lad, until we hear from the king."

Alastar acknowledged with a nod, "I'm grateful ta be with you folk. I truly feel lost on your isle and do want to find my home again."

"Don'tcha have a worry, lad," Flann reassured. "I promised we'd do whatever we can for ya."

*T*he landscape was dark having lost all its sunlight glow in
the middle of the night. Though the sun was still hidden, the dawn sent
its warm light across the lake. Alastar woke in the barn upon hearing a
loud, repeated WHOOPING! sound, like a large flute played with two
notes that oscillated swiftly, up and down, up and down... *Is that a
bird?* he wondered.

The barn was very dark. Alastar got up and stumbled about
to walk outside. "Do ya hear that thing, Éimhín? Not quite a rooster.
Pleasant melody; only loud, *very* loud. Puts me in bits."

Alastar walked to the lakeshore where the sound was coming
from. He noticed how 'normal' everything appeared. Nothing was
glowing as the night before. The land was just beginning to soak in the
sun's energy. All around was peaceful and slumbering... except for
that loud WHOOPING! call.

He looked around at the lake's edge. Most everything was
dim shadow reflected on a dark silver platter. No wind or movement.
Then off to the left, a large satin bird emerged from a patch of reeds
near shore. It floated into the open as it made its loud flute call. Alastar
strained to see what it was. He recognized its silhouette with a long,
arching neck and pointed, dagger beak to be a grebe. The tufts of
feathers that crested its head gave it a regal appearance. Alastar tried to
examine the bird, but at a distance it was dim and blurry.

Then the sun's brow appeared over the horizon and made all
before it shine brighter. Now Alastar saw the grebe had a mostly white
body and neck that shimmered as pearl with gray flecks on its back
and topsides. The sides of its head were patched with ruby feathers
that shimmered as well, like glowing cheeks. *A blushing bird,* Alastar

thought. "Did ya catch a glimpse 'a Nola this mornin'?" he joked softly.

An idea came to Alastar, and he went back to the barn. "It was a grand large bird, Éimhín," he said as he looked through his bundles of wood in the dim light.

"Here's a good piece." He lifted up a small branch of hawthorn with patches of darker wood mixed among the light. "It will come out nicely."

Then he went up the loft and grabbed his leather tool pouch. It was filled with his favorite wood crafting tools – a selection of smaller chisels, knives, gouges, files, rasps, punches and drills. He always carried his kit in his bag thinking he might need it wherever and whenever inspiration came to him. Inspiration is like a spark that leaps from windblown sails struck on the flint of mood – unpredictable as the wind blows, but a good artist learns to always be ready to catch the spark.

Alastar went back out to the lake. He sat down with his tools and the piece of wood he chose. He made very quick work of it with his skilled hands. The bark came off first. Then he cut off areas with knots and isolated a good section with the color transition we wanted - mostly light with a darker topside.

He whittled away the wood to make the rough shape of the grebe that still floated nearby. It only took him minutes to sculpt it out of the dead, dry wood. Alastar likened the carving process to making a new, beautiful creation from something once dead and unattractive, like a jeweler would cut and polish a brilliant gem from a bland piece of stone. The most common things could be transformed from a mute existence to one of radiant beauty that sung its own symphony simply by being.

Alastar held the rough sculpture up and examined its

proportions in the quickly brightening dawn. Its rough, faceted shape looked about right. He even took care to use the darker grain in the wood to fashion the grebe's rosy cheeks. Then he used files and rasps to smooth out the shape. Many minutes passed, and the landscape made a swift transition to the bright, glowing luster that Alastar noticed when he first came to Rathúnas. *The light of life is speedy to flare up but slow to go out here,* he thought.

Soon Alastar got out a small gouge and cut lines in the wood figurine to make the eyes, wings and general features. He held it up again, and looked at it from all sides. "Dandy grand!" he exclaimed. "Almost done." He looked about for the grebe on the lake. It was much farther away now feeding on a fish that was halfway down its gullet.

Alastar took out a rubbing stone for the final step and brought the wood surface to a satin-like luster that mimicked the grebe's shiny feathers. The polishing took as much time as the sculpting, but the results were brilliant. He had a keen grebe that sat nicely in the palm of his hand. He hoped Nola would like this gift. It only needed a nice wood stain to bring out its colors better, but he didn't have any with him. A simple water wash in the lake would have to do this time. Perhaps he could make an oil stain later if he could find the materials.

Alastar walked back towards the barn and saw Conall enter through the front gate. "A grand mornin', sir!" Alastar greeted.

"Mornin' ta ya, lad," Conall said. "I was gone ta catch Braede before he set out, but he'd already gone. Left right early, his wife said, so I sent a seabhac ["shawwk"] messenger ta Cnoc na Rí."

"Shawk?" Alastar asked.

"A hawk, lad," Conall answered. "Quickest way ta send word unless ya have means of enchanted kind."

A hawk? Alastar wondered if it was like the one they followed up the River Valley. "What does your hawk messenger look like?"

Conall thought his question was odd. "Have ya never seen a hawk, lad? An eagle, falcon? Have ya not any of 'em where ya came from?"

"Surely, I know what hawks look like, sir, "Alastar said. "I meant ta know if yours was white with a blue beak and V on its tail."

A shocked look sprung onto Conall's face. "You've seen the Seabhac Azure?"

"It led us up the valley along the river soon after we arrived on your isle."

"Now I know you're not a daft mainidh," Conall said. "Flann was right. Ya *are* meant ta be here. The Seabhac Azure is a trusted guide for very few. *Very few...* ya seem ta be someone of a special path, lad."

"*Special?*" Alastar said with denial. "I'm not sure of that, but I do feel Éimhín and I are meant ta be here as well. Your isle has a certain melody callin' out ta me."

"Trust me, lad. You're meant for something else altogether unlike what most of us are meant for. Flann could see it right off and promised ya our help. Took me some turns, but now I'm givin' ya my promise ta protect ya. Ya have my shield and sword at your side." Conall placed his right hand on Alastar's shoulder. "Don'tcha wander off."

Alastar nodded. "I welcome your safeguard, sir."

"We've had enough pleasantries, lad. Address me by name." Conall removed his hand from Alastar.

"Right. Conall it is. I was just goin' ta walk 'round the village. Get sorted out a bit."

"Good then. Stay in sight of town and you'll be fine. There's many miles ta the east border, but we're very close ta the new west border the Áiteoir have us pinned ta. We don't want ya alertin' the sentries or watchmen on either side."

"Certainly, sir, emm… uh, Conall. I'll not be lookin' for trouble."

Conall smiled and looked at the grebe in Alastar's hand. "Right. What's that ya have in your hand?"

Alastar lifted it up to show Conall. "It's a lake grebe I just carved."

"Mainidh me, lad. Ya *are* a woodcarver. That's amazin' workmanship. Just the image of that flutey bird hollerin' every morn come spring. He'll not hush till he finds his mate." Conall smiled again. He knew Alastar was fond of Nola. "When she comes they'll do a dance on the water, and there'll be chicks aplenty." Conall started walking towards the house. "May luck rise ta ya, lad… with your grebe."

Alastar put on a shy smile and felt blushing warmth come to his cheeks. He looked at the grebe in his hands and wondered how Conall knew it was for Nola. How did everyone know everything about him here?

He went into the barn and stored his tools away. "I'll be wanderin' about town," he said to Éimhín. "I'd take ya with, but I think this time you can rest at the Conalls'." Alastar was concerned Éimhín would behave shamelessly again, especially around Nola. Éimhín gave a quiet raspberry whinny. "But I'll tie ya up outside so ya have some fresh surroundin's." Alastar gave him some apples to eat and led him outside where he tied him to a tree near the lakeshore.

Alastar headed down the trail where he saw Nola walk the evening before. He carried the wooden grebe and swung his arms freely as he walked. He felt light with life, and his steps went swiftly as he scanned the area. House after house, he looked diligently for Nola, but there was no one in sight. *I can't be so early,* he thought.

Where is everyone?

He walked by a dozen homes along the trail. They were widely spaced, a couple minutes apart at his quick pace. After some time, he came to a much larger house made of stone blocks and a wood plank roof; a much sturdier construction than the other houses. It had a wooden round tower attached to it that was snug against a cliff. A trail led up the cliff and went towards the top of the round tower. It was the grain tower for the mill; Braede's mill.

The mill was quiet and still except for a few donkeys and other animals in the yard. Loch an Scátháin was a very small and motionless town from what he could see. The houses were modest stone and thatch structures and small. Besides the mill, Conall's home was the largest. Alastar wondered if he passed Nola's home yet. Braede had talked to her, so they either met on the trail or spoke at home. Possibly she lived at the mill.

Alastar went up to the door and knocked. "A good mornin'," he said loudly.

"Who is it?" a woman answered.

"Alastar. Friend of Conall and Flann, Ma'am."

The door opened. An older, chestnut haired lady stood at the door. "Alastar… Braede spoke of ya. I'm Brónach ["Broh-nahkh"], his wife. Ya can't be lookin' for flour. What could I do ya for, lad?"

"I was seeking Nola, Ma'am. Would ya know her house?"

"Sure I would…" Brónach hesitated as she looked Alastar over to gauge whether he could be trusted. She gave him a critical look. "Isn't it early ta be lookin' for her, lad?"

Alastar felt uncomfortable. *Of course it was early,* he thought. *I must look like a wide-eyed pup fresh out of bed.* "I have somethin' ta give her, Ma'am."

Brónach looked at the grebe in his hand. "Not a dradairín

["drah-dah-reen"], I hope."

"A dradairín, Ma'am?" Alastar asked. He fidgeted about under Brónach's sharp eyes.

"A small, useless potato… Ahh, pay no mind ta that," Brónach snapped. "I'm sure my niece is where she always is. Either with Ula or home, up the way near the south tip of the loch."

Niece… Nola was related to Braede. Alastar wondered if he would have to spend a lot of time with him. He didn't seem pleasant to be around.

"Up the way… grand, Ma'am. I thank ya for your help." Alastar bowed.

"A grand welcome ta ya, lad," she said.

Alastar walked away and continued along the trail. The forest became sparser along the left side opposite the lake. There were no homes for some minutes, but he saw small herds of sheep and goats with their shepherds in the pastures. The sight of activity gave him some comfort that he wasn't so odd to be walking about town in the morning.

The path started to curve right at the far southern edge of the lake. He found the next house set on the curving arc of land that bent around the lake there. It was another humble roundhouse nestled among trees by the lake. It didn't have a fence, but across the path was a large barn and crop fields. This was Nola's home.

Alastar walked farther up the path and saw the tract of land there was filled with crops. Small homes and barns dotted the flat fields right up to the patchy hills in the distance. People and animals were in the fields working, but the season was early and no sprouting was seen in the many rows of plowed channels.

He turned right and went to the door of Nola's home. He knocked. "A good mornin'!"

Alastar heard movement and footsteps inside. The door opened and a dark haired lady stood there with a smile. "A bright mornin' ta ya as well," she said.

He recognized the familiar features of Nola in her. "You must be Nola's mam, ma'am."

"That I am. You must be Alastar. Call me Mab ["Mahhb"], dear."

"Surely, Mab, ma'am. I'm lookin' ta speak with Nola."

"Simply Mab, please." She could see Alastar was a decent young fellow by his stand and demeanor. "Ya missed Nola. She went straight off ta the Conalls' ten minutes past."

Alastar was puzzled. He didn't meet Nola along the way. "That's odd. I didn't run inta her."

"'Course not, dear. She took the boat. Right fair quicker than foot. I imagine she'll be there if ya be headin' back."

"Right," he said. Alastar pondered if he should explore the rest of the town or go back.

Mab sensed his contemplation. "No need ta be in bits, dear. She spends most days with Ula and the Conalls'. She'd be there by now. Was off quick this morn' after chores. Your arrival seems ta have given toss ta her feet."

Alastar felt his cheeks heat up again. Mab was giving him the look of a mother ready to announce her daughter's wedding day.

"Grand," he said. "I was wonderin' how much farther the town is. Conall told me ta stay in sight of town."

"There's hardly anythin' else ta see. After the farmhouses, there are more homes along the lake for some miles. Same as you've seen. No one else worth visitin' that way," Mab suggested. "Dún ["Doon"; Fort] Tearmann is many miles on the road southwest, but I imagine they wouldn't know how ta treat ya there. They don't oft open the gate for strangers." She suddenly remembered to be a gracious hostess, "Ah!

Where are my manners?" She stepped aside and opened the door wider to welcome him in. "Cupán tae ["kupahn tay"], dear?"

"Tea? Thank ya, Mab," he said. "But I'd be runnin' back ta…" He was about to say, to see Nola, but he hesitated to show too much interest in her. He already appeared eager enough. He completed, "… ta the Conalls'."

"Certain ya would, but what sort 'a fella refuses a kind welcome? Come in!" Mab urged. She led him to sit at a table near the fireplace. An empty cup, spoon, and small, round pot with a wood ladle in it sat on the table. "Grand thin' I already started tae for myself." Alastar sat down and hid the wood grebe on his lap underneath the table.

Mab brought him a clay cup and small spoon to accompany her own. She poured milk into their cups and went to the fireplace to get a bronze pot from the fire. She came back and filled their cups with tea from the pot. "Pine needle and cherry blossom tae."

Mab sat down at the table and lifted the ladle from the small, round pot on the table. She dripped honey from the ladle into her cup. "Honey?" she offered.

"Certainly, thank ya," Alastar answered.

"We'd like ta stop by the Conalls' later, my husband and I. Learn more 'bout ya and what have ya. Nola said you were a very interestin' lad." Mab gave him a kind smile as she dripped honey into his cup.

Alastar hoped Nola didn't say anything about his apparent naiveté to her parents. No one wanted their girl to marry a simpleton. "It'd be a grand thing ta speak with ya and your husband later," he said. "I'd be lookin' forward ta it." He mixed the honey in the cup with his spoon and took a sip. The tea had a slight, warm citrus flavor that was accompanied by a fragrant pine and sweet floral scent. "Wonderful tea," he commented.

"It's Fionn's ["Fin's"] favorite - my husband," Mab said. "But he likes it without honey." She remembered Alastar was holding something before but chose to keep it hidden. "Was there somethin' ya wanted ta give Nola?"

"Sure," he answered. "I made her somethin'."

Mab smiled seeing that Alastar showed affection for Nola. "She'll find it a grand gesture, I'm sure."

"It's nothin' really," Alastar noted uncomfortably. "Just a small carvin' I did this mornin'." He was embarrassed to speak to Nola's mother about his fondness for her. He hurried and took large gulps of tea from his cup.

"Would ya like some bread, dear," Mab asked.

"Thank you, but no. I really should be goin'," Alastar said. He took a final gulp of his tea and got up.

"Sure then. We'll chat more later." Mab got up and escorted Alastar to the door. "May the road rise ta meet ya."

He gave her a curt bow. "Thank you, Mab. And for the tea. Good day ta ya."

"Slán, dear," she replied. She stood at the door and watched Alastar as he went back the way he came. She admired his pleasant forward nature. *A fine groom for Nola,* she thought. Loch an Scátháin lost all her young men in recent years, but now her hopes for Nola to have a family soon were rekindled.

On the way back, Alastar's steps sprung quickly with thoughts of Nola. He kept thinking she must've hurried to see him again. The thought made him feel snug as if she had already wrapped her arms around him. What would he say to her next? Thoughts of being with her turned in his mind the entire way back, and he arrived at the Conalls' gate before he could settle on anything to say.

He saw Nola and Ula feeding Éimhín behind the house. He walked to them and couldn't help smiling when he saw Nola hold the bucket to Éimhín's muzzle and lightly stroke the top of his head. *Éimhín is going to grow soft for her,* he thought.

"Grand mornin', girls," he said.

"Slán, Alastar," they replied.

Nola looked at him with a beaming smile. "We're givin' him a good helpin' of oats and clover. Ya left him starvin'!" She was anxious to see Alastar again too. After hearing about his unusual journey and that he was blessed with the Seabhac Azure, she felt sure they were meant to meet.

"Ya ran off early, Alastar," Ula said. "Where'd ya go?"

"I was lookin' through the village. . . and seekin' Nola." When she heard him say that, Nola's face lit aglow like the land did in the dawn. Her pale cheeks flushed with red and Alastar thought she was the most beautiful thing he'd seen on this isle or his own. He lifted up the grebe he made and held it out for her. "I carved it this mornin' for ya when the lake grebe woke me." He looked about the lake for the grebe but it was nowhere in sight.

Nola smiled and tucked her hair behind her left ear as she did at the falls. Alastar quickly remembered how she tucked the guelder rose in her hair before. "Sorry, this won't tuck in your hair so well as the flowers."

Nola took the grebe from him and looked at it.

"It's not a dradairín either," he said. The girls burst out in laughter.

"Who told ya about that?" Nola asked. She tried to keep composure while Ula giggled.

"Your aunt, Brónach." Alastar was very curious about the dradairín seeing how amused the girls were. "What is the dradairín about anyways?"

"Father had turned mam's shoulder many years back," Nola said. "Before I was born, she was heavy with me, and he tended the fields so long for days and days. Mornin' ta sundown, he'd be gone and left mam with Brónach and my brothers without ever comin' in ta say a word. They didn't have help back then, and my brothers were still too young, so father did all the work himself.

"When he came back in the evenin's, he'd be so ragged. It was during the harvest, and he went straight off ta bed without so much as a kiss for mam. After two weeks of bein' ignored, she asked him, 'My name may mean happy, but have ya noticed a smile on your pregnant wife's face lately?'

He could hardly say a word, much less think. 'What's this now?' he asked mam. She was furious he had no idea what she meant and ran out the room ta sleep with my brothers."

Alastar thought Nola was cute recounting her parents' story. She was full of expression. "Right. Your father made your mother angry, but how's that funny?"

"I'm not finished," she continued. "The next day he asked Brónach why mam was angry at him. He felt awful about it, so at lunchtime when he'd just have a quick bread in the fields, he came ta the house with somethin' hidden in his hand ta give ta mam.

"She still had fire in her eyes, but she held out her hand for the gift. He put a small potato in her hand. Fit right in her palm and shaped naturally like a heart." Nola drew a heart shape in the air with her fingers. "He found it during the harvest and thought it would show how much he loved her.

"Mam looked at it and saw it was blotched with many dark spots of rot. It couldn't be eaten, and she felt it was worthless for the weeks of agony without him. She scolded, 'Ya gave me a small, useless potato ta nuzzle me with?! A dradairín?!'" Nola laughed. "She was so *furious!* She threw it out the window and told him how a good husband would just give simple affection ta his wife every day, in the small moments, without ever thinkin' about it. That's all she wanted. Father never gave her useless gifts after that, but he made her more than happy from then on. He's always givin' her fondness and such."

Ula smiled and teased Alastar, "Are ya *sure* that grebe is not a dradairín?"

Nola smiled at him. Alastar tried to appear comfortable, though his slight swaying side-to-side gave away his nerves. Being around Nola made him feel like his heart would overflow with joy. "It could pass for a potato, I suppose," he said.

"It's beautiful," Nola said. "Thank you, Alastar. We have somethin' for ya too."

"Right," Ula said. "Father is havin' a céilí ["kay-lee"] for ya."

Alastar was surprised and apprehensive. He didn't want to have too much attention drawn to him. "A *céilí?* Why would he want to have a party for me? I'd much rather have small quiet meetin's."

"It's too late. Conall already has a runner spreadin' the word," Nola said. "It's good time for it. The town hasn't had a social for years; since the truce stopped the fightin'."

"Grand," Alastar said with sarcasm. "Your father didn't consider I've got no fancy dress or clean clothes even." Besides the leather long coat he packed, the only clothes he brought were on him – light leather pants and boots and a white linen shirt covered by a sleeveless leather vest. His clothes were still soiled from exploring and sweating in the valley.

"Sure, ya don't quite look fit for a gatherin'," Nola said. "But we won't let that banjax anythin'." She looked at Ula. "Get your mam ta find some clothes for Alastar and fix a bath for him. Then we can wash his clothes and have 'em ready and dry for the céilí tonight. It's still early and the sun's bright t'day."

"Right," Ula acknowledged. She left to go into the house.

"*Tonight?!*" Alastar exclaimed. "That soon?"

"Right. Conall doesn't want ta wait," she said. "He thinks the king will be callin' for ya, so he's fixin' it for t'night."

The thought of having to go before their king made him more nervous than having the céilí. His life was always quiet and left alone by the outside world. Eritirim didn't have a king. It hardly had a population at all. The few towns were scattered, peaceful and largely self-sufficient. His knowledge of kings came from stories and travelers. Kings always seemed to be fighting their neighbors and warring. Alastar was glad to live on a tranquil island, but now suddenly he found himself carried into churning waters that he had little control over.

"I haven't a clue what I'm supposed ta do for the king," Alastar said. Éimhín finished the bucket of feed and Nola set it down. "Thank ya for feedin' Éimhín. He can get hungry." Alastar patted and stroked Éimhín's neck. "I'd say he could eat more than a whole herd of goats."

Nola giggled and Éimhín gave a discontented neigh. "Nonsense," she said. "He's a fine horse with a healthy appetite. Let him eat all he wants. No one here's seen a finer horse than he. He's taller and stronger than ours. Even the Eachraighe don't have horses like him."

"Have ya seen their horses?" Alastar asked.

"I have. We used ta travel ta Lacharan ta buy and trade all the time; before the warrin'. We haven't gone for years now. Many of the Eachraighe live there. The lands outside the city are full of horse ranches. The horses of Rathúnas are prized all 'round, but Éimhín is an even grander sight. I'm sure they would pay mightily in Lacharan for

Éimhín. Put him right off ta breedin'.""

The thought of selling or losing Éimhín was disturbing to Alastar. He could never part from him. "I couldn't ever leave Éimhín ta someone else," he said. He looked at Éimhín in the eye and continued to stroke his neck. "My dad bought him when he was still a foal almost ten years ago. A merchant from the mainland had a mare that gave birth during the sea voyage. I could barely ride a horse then, but when I saw Éimhín I begged to have him. He wasn't yet weaned, so my dad bought the mare too. Dad said they were the best horses he'd ever seen too."

Alastar felt sad his father didn't live to see what a fine pair he and Éimhín had become. After his death, Alastar spent much more time with Éimhín. They developed a tight bond that replaced the one Alastar had with his father.

Nola saw the sadness in Alastar's eyes. It touched her to see his feelings. Most men around her were the rough and rugged kind; they rarely showed tender emotions. She looked into his eyes and asked softly, "Are ya alright, Alastar? You could bring tears ta a stone."

Alastar turned to face her. He was startled to see her staring intimately into his eyes. He stammered, "Sure. . . I'm just missin' my dad. He died a few years after we got Éimhín." Her steady eyes quickly washed his sadness away. He held his gaze on her as well. They were standing so close to each other that Alastar felt if he could just lean forward enough, she would lean into him too and they'd kiss.

He tried leaning forward and just when it appeared she was moving into him, Éimhín whinnied and shoved Alastar with a swift movement of his head. Alastar almost fell flat down on the ground but caught himself. Nola covered her mouth with her hand and giggled. "Emmm… I'll just check on your bath," she said and walked away smiling.

"Éimhín!" Alastar whispered. "I should've known. I should've *known!* Ya banjaxed my first kiss with a girl! Now I'm startin' ta think Nola had a good idea sellin' ya off ta some Lacharan horse breeder." Éimhín gave an amused neigh. "Right," he said irritated. "You have your fun. I'll be going in ta clean myself up."

Inside the house, Flann was boiling a cauldron of water to heat the bath with. "Alastar," she said, "the bath is nearly set." She led him into a small room where a large, round wood basin sat next to a small table. Ula poured water into it from a bucket and Nola stood beside her. Alastar looked and smiled at Nola. She smiled back reassuredly.

Flann looked inside the tub. "Just a few more buckets," she said. Ula and Nola left with buckets in hand. Flann looked at Alastar who stood waiting."Have ya not taken a bath before, lad? Start your undressin'."

Alastar hesitated. He didn't want to undress in front of her. "Sure... I, emm..."

"Ya needn't be shy. Ya appear mighty comfortable 'round Nola," she teased. Flann and Ula saw them from the window when Éimhín foiled the kiss. "Are ya certain you're followin' what's right? You've taken a quick likin' ta Nola, but there's many a pleasant girl here." Flann was thinking like Mab; Alastar would be a fine groom for her daughter.

"Certainly true," he said. Alastar sensed from her tone she was suggesting Ula was a good match for him. "Ula is a very fine woman as well. I only know what my heart feels. I feel I already know Nola."

"Our hearts are often deceived by passion and thin's that flicker 'a light. Just don't be too hasty ta grab after what you're not certain of."

"I will... But as far as undressin', my mam was the only woman ta see me bare. I'll just wait for the bath ta be ready and get in by myself."

"Modest through and through. No one's gonna stare under your breeches, lad." She left to get the hot water.

The girls came back with buckets of water and dumped them into the basin. "Right done," Ula said huffing. "Let's help mam get the hot water." They left the room.

The women came back with buckets full of steaming water and poured them in. Alastar sat down on a bench by the wall and took off his boots and socks. "Girls, don'tcha look at Alastar," Flann joked. "He's right sensitive about his knickers. Turn 'im scarlet just ta talk of 'em." Alastar started to blush and the girls laughed. "Your bath is set, lad. I'll bring ya some clean clothes in a jiffy. Soap is on the table."

The women left the room. Alastar undressed and got into the bath. He had barely sunk into the tub when Flann came back and set a light blue shirt, brown trousers, and a towel on the bench for him. She took his dirty clothes and left again.

Alastar heard the women talking in the next room. Nola went outside to wash his clothes while Flann and Ula started to fix lunch. The warm bath was soothing. He leaned back in the tub and tried to stretch, but the tub was only large enough for him to sit in a crouched position. He started to feel very tired and rested the back of his head on the thick rim of the tub. All the morning activity had drained him and he quickly fell asleep.

He woke an hour later. It was quiet in the house, but he could hear the birds sing outside. He finished washing in the cool water and got out. He dried himself and put on the clothes Flann left for him. It was quickly obvious the clothes belonged to Conall. They were many sizes too large. He saw Flann had left his belt with the clothes. At least the pants wouldn't be dropping to his knees.

He walked out the room. The clothes flapped about him as he

moved. He felt like he was draped with flags; a five year old wearing his father's clothes. The house was empty, but he noticed a sandwich on the table with a note next to it. It read: The sandwich is for you, Alastar. We didn't want to wake you.

Alastar looked out the windows to see if anyone was outside. No one was around. Éimhín was still by the lakeshore, and he could see his clothes hanging on a line in the sun. He went outside to see if they were dry yet. They still felt wet.

"Where did everyone go?" Alastar said to Éimhín. Éimhín gave a little nicker. "No idea, eh?"

Alastar went back inside and ate the sandwich. He thought a ride through town would be a good idea. Éimhín could use a stretch of his legs, and he might as well see the whole village. After eating, he got Éimhín saddled to go.

They took off at a fair trot down the trail. People were outside their homes now, working and visiting with neighbors. It was only a handful of minutes to reach Braede's mill on horseback. Alastar turned Éimhín left to go up the cliff trail at the mill. There was another path there that went farther up the mountain.

They went up the mountain for a minute, winding along on the trail with thick bushes on either side. Alastar could see Nola's house and the croplands as they wound upwards, back and forth on the zigzag trail. The farms formed a beautiful patchwork of parallel lines in rich, dark earth that covered the area a long ways to the south and west. Alastar thought there was a large excess of cropland to nourish the few inhabitants of Loch an Scátháin. *Perhaps they trade most of the crop with neighboring cities,* he thought.

Alastar stopped at the top of the trail where there was a shed and a large wooden cage with birds in it. A large perch stand with an attached flagpole stood near the cage. He looked up the flagpole and saw a long red, triangular banner at the top. The flag hung limp, but he could see parts of a crest in the folds of fabric - pieces of a horse, crown and wings.

He got off Éimhín and peered into the cage. It was large enough to walk in. There were three hawks inside, all very normal in appearance; light gray or brown with some black markings, nothing like the Seabhac Azure, which was also larger than these birds. Each hawk wore a collar with a leather tube on it. These were the seabhac messengers Conall talked about. Alastar had heard about birds being used to carry messages, but he couldn't fathom how to train them for that. Many miles from place to place, there and back without fail; simply amazing.

He walked to the edge of the plateau to survey the landscape. They were very high on the mountain and Alastar could see most of the lake below. Its reflective surface spanned all the way from the right and filled most of the land underneath. He continued looking toward the left and saw another town far off to the southwest, past the farms in the plains. *That must be Dún Tearmann,* he thought. It was a large square fort town enclosed by a wall of some kind.

Directly in front, the hill country stretched far out. *The hills must have belonged to the Torthúil Kingdom before the truce,* Alastar thought. *Conall said the new border stopped where the hills began.* He wondered what lay in the country around him. The scale of Rathúnas felt so large and foreign. He had explored the green side of his isle in a month of summer without much fanfare. There was hardly anything new to see, but now he felt it could take a lifetime to discover the isle. He couldn't help wonder what was in store for him here.

Then thoughts of settling into a quiet life with Nola came back to him. There was plenty of room in Loch an Scátháin to plant a new home. Alastar felt he belonged here. He was led to this place by very unusual means after all.

Alastar mounted Éimhín again and they went back down to the lake trail. They continued to Nola's house where he stopped to see if she was there. No one was home, though. Where were his friends? He scanned the fields. They didn't seem to be out there either.

They continued around the lake until the trail started to curve north again. There was a large longhouse in the corner where he saw people gathering and stacking wood outside. He saw Conall and the others preparing the grounds for the céilí in a large grass courtyard next to the lake. The area was bordered by blossoming trees full of bright pink flowers, just like the tree he saw in the River Valley. About a dozen people were busy stringing ribbon and decorations around the area and building large wood piles for bonfires.

Alastar rode up to Conall and jumped off.

"Alastar, lad!" Conall greeted. "Ya didn't drown in the wash. I have ta say, ya look mighty thin in my clothes."

Nola was hanging a lantern on a rope that was strung around the perimeter of the courtyard. She looked at Alastar, smiled and continued to work.

"I must've shrunk in the wash," Alastar replied.

"Right. Only the best garments shrink in the wash. Remember that, lad," Conall said smiling.

"Thank ya, sir. You didn't need ta go through all this trouble and finery for my sake. I'd prefer quiet meetings…"

Conall interrupted, "Amaideach! Don'tcha act the maggot now, lad. We're treatin' ya as a true son 'a Loch an Scátháin. You'll have our finest welcome."

Alastar felt bad to push off their friendly hands. "Forgive me. I grandly accept this honor."

"Right ya will. Don't let me hear ya talk like that again, or I'll have ta start calling ya a mainidh for certain."

"For certain. Keep me in check." Alastar smiled.

A man about the same age as Conall approached. He was strong and well built, though not so much a burster in appearance as Conall, more rugged than intimidating. He extended his hand to Alastar.

"Alastar, a fond welcome ta ya. I'm Teague ["Teeg"]." He had brown hair and was shorter than Alastar.

"Grand ta met ya, Teague," Alastar responded.

"Teague's our bird keeper and scribe," Conall said. "A fair poet as well, lad. Ya might hire him ta write somethin' nice for your grebe," he chuckled.

"Grebe?" Teague asked.

"Ahh, the boy's taken a likin' ta a fair Scátháin girl," Conall said.

Alastar felt flustered. Would he not have peace to admire Nola?

"Ula?" Teague pondered.

"It would be a fine match, for certain," Conall said. He put his palm on Alastar's shoulder. "But it isn't my lovely Ula." Conall could see Alastar wasn't comfortable speaking of personal matters. "Let's not gab like a brood 'a hens, fellas."

Alastar smiled. "Right. Teague, we were just up the mountain and saw the hawks."

"Ahhh," Teague said. "Did my fair Bress come back yet? We sent her off ta Cnoc na Rí at dawn."

"The perch was empty, sir. But there were three birds in the cage," Alastar said.

"Sure then," Teague noted. "They're takin' some time ta respond. Braede should've arrived there early in the mornin' judgin' from when he left."

"That *is* unusual," Conall said. "We should've gotten word by now." He looked at Alastar and felt concerned the king was deliberating too critically on the boy. King Fuar was often suspicious of things, especially now during the uneasy truce. "Well, we'll have word soon. Let us keep ta our work. We have a céilí t'night." He looked at Alastar and said, "Alastar, lad. I have ta send ya off. You can't see the preparations until we're ready. Go back ta my home and rest. We'll be comin' back there ta get ya soon 'nough."

"Certainly," Alastar acknowledged. He wanted to speak with Nola, but he knew the whole town would talk of it if he showed his affection now. "I'll see ya back at home," he continued and went back to Éimhín and rode away.

*T*he sun was getting low on the horizon. Its reflection blazed across the lake in fiery ripples. Alastar started to groom Éimhín by the lakeside at the Conalls'. "Best ta get ya fussed up for the céilí, boy. The afternoon ride has your hair in knots."

They had been out among the countryside for another hour after leaving the town longhouse. They explored the east side of the lake and river, up to the falls and the impassable point where the river poured into the valley through the rising cliffs. Alastar thought of crossing the river to explore the other side of the lake, but it was too deep to cross without swimming. After relaxing a while at the falls, they returned to the Conalls'.

Alastar had his own clothes on again. He looked as fresh and new as the day they rode out from Netleaf to complete their simple errand of wood gathering. It was only two days ago, but it felt like they were years to Alastar. The sudden changes of seeing the desert valley and then being immersed in the magic and beauty of Rathúnas made him feel disconnected from his old life. His mind and spirit felt transported just as far as his body had gone through the gateway.

The isle made him feel renewed, though he was the same person; he didn't feel the same. He felt like a completely different person in Rathúnas. Was it the new surroundings, the people?. . . Nola? Alastar felt those things were the reason for his new sense of being, but no, those were all possible where he came from.

He could have moved to a different town or country altogether and found new beginnings, even another 'Nuala.' The simple act of changing your surroundings doesn't change the person, not in the long term. His new sense of being was the realization that the world was not as he thought it was. Things that seemed impossible were in plain sight; a world that appeared small and comfortably known was now full of wonder and infinite possibilities.

Alastar felt it throughout his body since he arrived in Rathúnas - an invisible connection deep in his soul, but it wasn't the magic of Rathúnas he felt. He was feeling the re-coupling of a lost connection to everything. Many lose it after settling into a comfortable existence with what is known. But now, the sudden thrust of destiny's flow woke his instincts to see everything with the eyes of a child again. Anything was possible, and he thought of taking up a new life in Rathúnas.

"We may be buildin' for us a new life here, Éimhín," he said.

Éimhín gave a mindful whinny. "Sure, sure. I know. We need ta check if our home in Netleaf is here yet. Ya know we're under orders ta stay here."

The sound of horses galloping up to the house caught Alastar's attention. He went to the front of the house. Conall and Teague were on horses. "Come now, lad!" Conall shouted. "Ya look ready."

Alastar noticed they wore formal clothing with dull red mantles over their léine shirts. The capes covered their shoulders and appeared to have hoods. The fabric was buckled neatly at their right shoulders with large penannular ring clasps while small U-shaped fibulae clasps secured the left side to their shoulders. All the clasps were gold. The ring clasps pinned the mantles to their shoulders with a large needle, and each clasp was covered with a round shield engraved with the kingdom's seal; Teague's ring clasp had a silver shield while Conall's was gold.

The shapes on the shields caught Alastar's eye as they glinted in the sun. The kingdom seal was a leaping horse inside the shape of a kite shield with a crown on top, wings on the sides, and a crossed sword and spear in the background. The symbols seemed to match the crest he saw on the red banner at the hawk cage. He wanted to look closer but Conall reminded him, "It's time ta go! Get ta yer Éimhín!"

"Right!" Alastar acknowledged. He saddled Éimhín and they all left for the céilí at a moderate pace. Now that he saw some horses of Rathúnas beside Éimhín, Alastar could see what Nola meant. Éimhín was clearly stronger and larger framed than their horses. It wasn't that their horses appeared weak by any means. Éimhín simply stood a head higher and had a stately build to him, like he was bred for nobility.

"We heard back from the king," Conall said. "They haven't seen any sign of Braede. It was late afternoon when they sent Bress back with the reply. It seems Braede has gone missin'."

"Troublin' business," Teague said.

"Has this happened before?" Alastar asked.

"It hasn't. Braede has always been reliable," Conall said. "We don't know what ta make of it. The king has sent out a party towards Loch an Scátháin ta search for him. . . and King Fuar sends his welcome ta ya, lad. His royal chancellor travels here with the party to meet ya. He will decide if ya should go ta the king."

Alastar wondered if he would have to go to Cnoc na Rí. Seeing the royal city would be quite an event, but he had other things on his mind that he wanted to explore first. Netleaf was one. Seeing Nola again was the other. He couldn't wait to see her again.

They arrived at the longhouse and to Alastar's surprise, there were two short lines of men on horses that formed a corridor into the courtyard. The scene was vibrant with the courtyard bordered by the pink blossoming trees and shimmering lake. Many people waited inside the large courtyard. The whole town was there. They were dressed in finer clothes than he'd seen since arriving, though they were still simple designs compared to Alastar's intricately crafted clothing.

The styling was attractive in a naturally flowing way, and the colors were vibrant compared to Alastar's plain white and brown clothing. Their clothes appeared to mirror the simple, colorful glow of the land around them.

Many of the women's dresses matched the bright pink blossoms of the trees and Alastar wondered what kind of trees they were. "What sort of trees line the courtyard?" he asked.

"Cherry," Conall answered. "Sweetest fruit of Torthúil."

"I've not heard of cherry."

"They're large red berries. Good for all sorts 'a jams 'n sweet thin's."

"Like guelder rose berries?"

"AMAIDEACH! Not even. You can eat cherries right off the stem and they won't give ya the runabout if ya eat too many." Conall turned to face Alastar and Teague. "Fellas, ride in behind me." He raised his hand and two flag bearers at the end of the corridor swung their long flagpoles back and forth a few times. Three drummers holding bodhráns ["buh-rons"; handheld drums] started to pound a cadence for the entry. Everyone became still and silent while the drummers pounded the rousing rhythm.

Conall rode down the corridor, followed by Teague and Alastar. When they entered the courtyard, they stopped in front of the drummers and other musicians. Conall held up his hand again and the drummers stopped. Everyone watched them and stood silent.

Alastar scanned the crowd for Nola. He found her at one of the many lanterns he saw her hanging in the afternoon. They were unlit, but there was someone standing at each lantern strung around the courtyard. Others manned the three large bonfire piles set inside the courtyard. The bonfires were positioned one on each side of the stage where the band was, and the last was centered on the stage, far off on the opposite side of the courtyard.

Conall addressed the crowd, "Friends, t'night another day passes on. The sun sets before us, and the glowin' night's lull sends its weary eyes inta our hearts. But we say now ta our hearts, it isn't time for slumber! No! For tonight, we welcome a new friend, a new son ta Loch an Scáthain and light the night for his stay. All now, welcome our honored guest, Alastar Duer!"

The crowd cheered, and the people at the lanterns and woodpiles lifted up something cupped in their hands and pointed it towards their stations. They blew a spark from it and lit the fires around the courtyard all at once. Alastar was startled by the sudden glow of light all around them. The sun had already fled beneath the horizon, so the magical glow of the landscape was dominate until the courtyard was set alight.

Conall and Teague cheered loudly as well and the band started to play lively music. "That's it, lad," Conall said to Alastar. He pat Alastar's back at the shoulder. "Time ta meet. . . and dance. Your grebe is waitin'."

They got off their horses and Teague led them away. Alastar and Conall stayed as everyone came forward to meet Alastar. He felt overwhelmed as he greeted and shook hands with everyone. Never did he ever see so many people take interest in him. They were so welcoming; he felt he was part of their family.

All through the greetings he kept looking for Nola in the crowd. Faces and bodies swirled all around him. Some people started to dance, while others began to roast things on the bonfires. After a few minutes, he saw Nola with Ula, Flann, and Mab at the rear of the crowd. They waited their turn to see him. The four of them wore dresses with red, knee-high skirts and white blouses with shimmering, open gold jackets. He noticed many women wore the same outfit.

Some time passed before he saw Nola face to face. She was the last person to greet him. They smiled gleefully at each other, caught in a world of glowing lights and joyous melody that bounced between their eyes. They hardly noticed what was happening around them, when all of a sudden the band started to play a different tune after Conall gave them a signal.

It was a solo violin playing another lively tune. Couples started pulling into a circle formation at the center of the courtyard. Nola tugged on Alastar to join her in the dance. He was reluctant not knowing the specifics of it, though, he had learned to céilí dance when he was younger.

The couples faced each other as they all formed a large circle. When no more people came into the formation the violinist stopped and the whole area fell silent. Then all the musicians stomped their feet repeatedly on the wood stage floor and started to play the tune together. It was a quick, spirited melody that was easy to move to. Everyone in the dance started moving. Couples skipped toward each other, spun around and crisscrossed while they maintained the large circle. Alastar fumbled some steps, but the group dance was simple enough to keep pace. Thankfully the dance had similar steps to what he already knew.

Alastar and Nola danced without taking their eyes off each other. They skipped about to the music for many minutes. It became apparent she was the much better dancer. She never missed a beat, while Alastar was hesitant at first when he was trying to learn the dance. When the music stopped, they stood holding each others' outstretched hands. It was the closest they'd been since meeting, but everyone's watchful eyes kept them from lingering too long on one another.

Nola lowered her hand. "I have ta go."

"Where?"

"Just wait by the rear fire. You'll see." She walked off and disappeared behind the stage. All the women in the red and gold dresses did the same. People started to line around the center of the courtyard, making a large semicircle that opened toward the stage.

"Let Alastar have front center," Conall said. "He'll be wantin' ta see this clear." The crowd moved apart at the center, directly facing the stage. Alastar stepped forward into the gap, while Conall and Teague took positions at his sides. Everyone sat down and waited.

Twinkling white lights started to appear behind the stage. The lights came from the many white blossoms of tree branches that were carried by a dozen young girls who wore pink dresses. The branches were as large as the girls were, and with their every step and movement, the flowers shimmered with light. The girls walked in a procession to the front of the stage and formed a corridor like the one Alastar rode through earlier.

Alastar turned to Conall. "What sort of branches are those?"

"White beam, lad. Just in bloom."

The girls held the branches upwards toward each other, crisscrossing near the tips to make a sparkling steepled roof for the corridor. They stopped moving and the branches stopped sparkling. They held still for a moment, and then the drummers started to beat a rising cadence.

The women in red and gold started to skip through the corridor as the girls shook the branches vigorously. Glowing white dust from the flowers fell onto the women as they passed under the branches. They emerged from the sparkling corridor coated in the bright sparkling dust. About a dozen women, including Nola, skipped toward the center of the courtyard. Their hair and clothes were twinkling with the fine luminescent dust. Alastar was amazed at the beautiful sight. It was like a swarm of starlight had rested on the women.

Then the rest of the band suddenly started to play when all the women entered the courtyard. The dancers started a complex movement of changing formations to the music. They formed circles and stars and many other shapes that burst with color and light as they moved. The crowd clapped in time, and Alastar stared at the performance, mesmerized, like the first time he saw the glowing symbols appear on the cliff.

Teague leaned into Alastar and said, "Never seen a grebe dance like that, have ya?" He smiled and Alastar laughed softly.

After a few minutes, the dust stopped glowing on the dancers, and the girls with branches ran out and surrounded the women in a dance procession of their own. They sprinkled more of the sparkling dust on the women with quick, snappy movements and returned to their former positions again.

"The blossom dust loses its radiance after some minutes," Conall told Alastar. "But it makes for a grand show."

"Certainly does," Alastar agreed.

The women continued dancing for another brilliant set, almost until the dust stopped shining again. They made their exit with skips and twists and disappeared behind the stage. Everyone cheered and clapped for the performance. The girls with the white beam branches then ran out towards the crowd and sprinkled the glowing dust on everyone while the band continued to play music.

"Are we ta dance now?" Alastar asked.

"Amaideach! Ya won't see me dancin', lad," Conall said."That was just for the fun."

"The more ya move," Teague said, "the more the dust'll flicker. Try it out, lad. Do a dance. Your grebe is comin'."

Nola rushed up to Alastar with Flann and Ula. She smiled the entire way she wove through the crowd of people who were dancing and aimlessly flailing about to see the light flicker on themselves.

"What did ya think?" Nola asked Alastar with giddy excitement.

"I couldn't believe my eyes. We don't have dances of that sort where I come from; not even close."

Mab and her husband walked up to them.

Conall greeted them, "Mab, Fionn." Teague and Alastar nodded their heads.

"Conall," Fionn replied. He looked to Alastar. "What does our fine guest think of the céilí?"

"The finest anywhere, sir," Alastar said. "Not just the gatherin', I mean the people as well."

"BAH! Don'tcha be givin' us a siosóg ["shish-og"], boy!" Fionn burst out with a laugh. Everyone but Nola and Alastar joined in his humor and laughed loudly.

"Dadaí!" Nola exclaimed. She looked at Mab. "Mam, tell 'im ta behave." Alastar stood confused. He didn't get the joke.

"*What?!*" Fionn said with a smirk. "The lad gives my girl a dandy dradairín, and I cannot tell a simple kissin' joke? I thought it was a good one too." Conall and the others continued to laugh, but Nola didn't see the amusement when Alastar didn't understand. She took his hand and pulled him away from them.

Conall controlled his laughter. "Right, Fionn. A fine joke, it was, but be easy on the lad. He's not used ta our manner."

"Sure, sure," Fionn responded. "He'll get used ta our manner quick 'nough. A father has the proddin' rights ta lads who wish ta court his daughters."

"It's all well," Conall said. "Ya actually should prod him more. I'd be happy ya run him off so he'd take interest in my Ula."

"Dadaí!" Ula retorted softly and walked off.

"Boys. The whole lot of ya!" Flann said. "Let's just enjoy our time."

"But we *are*," Fionn said.

"Right. The food is ready," Conall said. He raised his hands and the band stopped playing. "Everyone! Help yourselves ta the feast we have. Carry on!" The band continued to play and people started to walk to the tables freshly set with roasts from the bonfires. Bread, fruit and vegetables of all kinds were set out as well.

Nola pulled Alastar towards a quiet place outside the courtyard. Alastar looked around the sky as they walked. "What are ya lookin' at?" Nola asked.

"I'm tryin' ta find the moon."

"Ya won't find it t'night. It's a new moon."

"Right," he said. He felt disappointed the full moon wasn't out like the last night he had in Eritirim. He felt like it would be the perfect setting to tell Nola the poem he had given to Nuala before. Nuala didn't appreciate it. He felt Nola certainly would, but there wasn't even a crescent moon out. He would have to save the poem for later.

They stopped near the lakeshore. The water was smooth and calmly reflected the forest glow all around it. "What was the joke about? A shishog thing?" Alastar asked.

"Dadaí was just makin' fun. Sayin' ya were bein' overly friendly ta win us all over. Pay no mind ta it."

"Sure. Then what's a siosóg?"

Nola fidgeted uncomfortably for a moment. She put her hands on her hips, closed her eyes and leaned forward, puckering her lips far out. Alastar was confused. Was she asking for a kiss? It was hardly the spontaneous, natural first kiss he had imagined. He quickly leaned into her and kissed her on the lips before she released her pose.

"Why'd ya do *that?!*" Nola said surprised. They both straightened back up.

"I thought ya wanted a kiss." Alastar started turning bright scarlet.

"Is that how ya think I'd wanna kiss?" she said irritated and amused at the same time. "I was tryin' ta show ya a siosóg. It's a puckered kiss with a good deal of suckin', ya silly wheatear! Do ya do nothin' without thinkin' first? Everyone's sure ta have seen that!"

Alastar felt even more embarrassed. "Forgive me, Nola. I suppose I was anxious ta kiss ya."

Nola relaxed her face and smiled. "Sure, but I thought ya would've minded manners and asked me what I was doin' first. . . It's all right." She still felt amused he kissed her like that. His inexperience with romance was obvious. "Ya do need a lesson or two in kissin', mind ya."

Alastar laughed. "Right. I was hopin' you'd help me with that."

"Well, it certainly won't be here!" she retorted.

"What about a dance then?"

"What? Here?"

"Sure." Alastar took her hands and placed her left hand on his shoulder while he held her other hand out. He put his right hand at the back of her waist and started moving around in clumsy, exaggerated swooping motions.

"Do ya know what you're doin'?" she asked.

"Not exactly. It's a dance my father showed me and mam. He said they did this in the kings' courts." He spun themselves in quick circles. "Round and round, round and round…" Then he stopped suddenly and made her lean backwards. He looked into her eyes and she giggled.

"Are ya lookin' for a siosóg now?" she joked.

Alastar feigned releasing her to drop on the ground and she squealed. He brought her back up as she giggled. As he lifted her up, he brushed his hand on her jacket pocket and felt something in it. "What's that in your pocket?" he asked.

"Oh, it's just the tine-stone ["chin-neh stone"; fire stone] for lightin' the fires." She took it out of her pocket and showed him. It was a large round agate the size of a thumb. It was polished smooth and glowed with red and orange bands.

"I've never seen an agate so large or brilliant. It glows like fire in the light," he said.

"Here then. It's a gift from me." She handed him the stone.

"I couldn't accept this. It looks like it's worth more than a lifetime of work."

"Nonsense, even enchanted stones are common in Torthúil. The River Bradán holds these stones like the million salmon that run the waters every year."

"Enchanted?" Alastar wondered.

"The stones don't make fire on their own. They work after conjurers in Cnoc na Rí place enchantment on 'em." She looked into his eyes. "Keep it with peace. The dradairín ya gave me is much rarer," she said with a gentle smile.

"Thank you, Nola," he said and smiled back. Alastar put the stone in his pocket. "How 'bout we get some food?"

They went back to the busy noise of the céilí and took food from the banquet tables. Everyone was eating and talking. The band had stopped to feast as well. The melody of instruments was absent, but boisterous singing was heard from scattered parties in the courtyard. Alastar and Nola found their friends and sat down to eat with them.

They dined, talked and joked for a time. The night darkened

the sky completely, but the light of life continued to glow on the land, and the blazing fires of the céilí nearly blotted out the carpet of shining stars overhead. Alastar felt the warmth of friendship and family here like he'd never experienced before. Even the many blunt jokes he received were a welcome change to the quiet, almost solitary life he had for years.

Alastar was sitting towards the northwest and noticed an unusual twinkling spot among the dim stars in the sky. It immediately reminded him of the glowing, shimmering symbols. He stared for some moments when Nola noticed him.

"What are ya lookin' at?" she asked.

"Do ya see that twinklin' in the sky there? Getting' lower and lower."

Nola knew what it was immediately. "Conall!" she cried. "A Greerian comes."

Conall looked up and saw the shimmering movement in the sky. He got up and walked towards it. He stopped a little ways outside the courtyard and waited. As the shimmering spot got bigger, it took on a golden reflection and the wings of a large bird could be seen. People stopped what they were doing and looked toward it and the scanned the horizon.

"Somethin's not right," Teague said. "See there, far off in the hills?" He was pointing out a wide field of moving red-orange dots that swayed about - the torchlights of a large company. They were outside the border, so it meant one thing. The Áiteoir were coming towards them and in large number.

A minute passed and the Greerian reached Conall. He held out his arm and the great eagle landed on his forearm. Alastar never saw anything like it. It was unique, like the Seabhac Azure, but it appeared to be made of mirrored gold. "Is that truly a bird?" Alastar asked.

"It is, but enchanted," Nola replied. "Many patrol our borders."

"Their feathers are like mirrors," Teague said. "They can appear almost invisible if they wish. Normally they are as polished gold like you see before you. It's speakin' ta Conall its report."

The Greerian squawked a few times and then took off to fly southwest. Conall jogged back to them. "The Áiteoir have a large unit marchin' toward us, he said. "I sent the Greerian ta assemble the garrison at Dún Tearmann. Their direction is straight ta Loch an Scátháin." Many people gasped. Conall addressed the crowd, "Everyone, I'm sorry. The céilí is over. Gather everyone ta the mountain refuge. The fightin' men are ta come back here with your arms."

People quickly scattered and left. Conall turned to Alastar. "Lad, have ya told your whole story? It cannot be by accident they come now and Braede's gone missin' after your arrival. The Áiteoir must have an interest in ya. They had never driven towards Loch an Scátháin before and are movin' very fast. They hope ta get here before the garrison at Dún Tearmann."

A look of dread came to Alastar. He did not want harm to come to these people because of him, but he didn't know what to say. "I don't know what else there is, sir. I don't know why the Áiteoir would want me."

"How exactly did ya come ta Loch an Scátháin from the River Valley?" Conall asked. "It's not easy ta wander here unless you're determined ta follow the river upstream. Did the Seabhac Azure lead ya directly ta us?"

"I followed the Azure ta the cap of the valley. Then it turned southeast and flew over the mountains. I aimed ta follow it, but somethin' else led me here."

A look of concern came to everyone's face. "Why did ya not

follow the Azure, lad?" Conall asked.

Alastar started to feel uncomfortable. He remembered how much Éimhín wanted him to go over the mountain to Netleaf. He wondered if he should tell them about the fairy. They must know what it was. "A sort of. . . a fairy in a blue dress showed me a trail that led inta Loch an Scáthain. I thought it was a hummingbird at first because it had a long horn on its head."

"Banger'd scones!" Fionn exclaimed. "The lad is not meant ta be here!"

Nola was shocked. "That can't be," she said.

"Well, not meant ta be here at the moment anyways," Teague said.

"Right," Conall affirmed.

"Lad, I hate ta say," Teague continued. "That was a shadow fairy ya saw. It's renowned for leadin' unwary travelers off the path they're meant ta walk."

"Be thankful ya found us instead of a den 'a wolves," Conall said.

Alastar couldn't believe what he was hearing. He felt certain he was meant to come to Loch an Scáthain and meet Nola. He felt everything was falling into place.

"Lad, there's not much time," Conall said. "I hate ta say it, but ya have to go where the Seabhac Azure was leadin' ya. The king's chancellor will have ta find ya another time. You're meant ta be where the Azure was leadin', and ya *have ta* be leavin' *now*. The Áiteoir are not ta have ya. The Seabhac Azure would've kept ya safe on its path. You need ta bolt back on it, right quick."

Alastar couldn't believe he had to leave suddenly. "But what about now? Will the Azure come back ta lead me?" he asked.

"It's certain, lad," Flann said. "Don'tcha worry 'bout that." She gave him a comforting smile.

"I don't want ta leave ya ta fight alone," Alastar said.

"Lad, there's no choice in it now," Conall said. "Have no worry over us. The garrison will be here shortly. Your path needs ta part from us for time bein'. That's more important. I promised ya my protection, though." Conall turned to Teague. "Teague, take up your pack and arms. I'll have ya escort the lad until he's safe. Meet him at my home." Teague nodded and left quickly.

Conall continued, "Alastar, let's go now. We need ta be speedy."

Alastar hesitated and looked at Nola. She sensed what he was thinking and shook her head. "I can't go with ya, Alastar. I belong with my family. Don't worry about us. If thin's are meant ta be, we'll see each other again." Her eyes started to fill with tears and she swiftly walked towards her parents. They rushed off towards home. Everyone else was gone except for Flann and Ula.

"My dears, ya know what ta do," Conall said to Flann and Ula. Flann took his hand and pressed it firmly. Ula hugged her father.

"Come now," Flann said to Ula. "Ta the refuge. We'll catch ya another time, Alastar. Your travel be blessed. Slán."

"Slán," he replied.

Conall and Alastar ran to their horses and galloped towards his home. There, Alastar grabbed all his things and packed Éimhín up; stocks of wood and all. Conall put on his armor and sword. He had already looked formidable without the soldier's dress, but Alastar was stunned to see him wearing a commander's chainmail, chest plate, and helmet with the mantle he was wearing before. He also had a wood round shield tied to his back that covered his rear like a turtle shell.

All the metal he wore looked to be of golden polished bronze, but it had a bright pearl infused luster to it rather than the yellow-gold or copper hues of typical bronze. *Unusual,* Alastar thought. He never saw anyone have so much bronze nor of the high sheen that Conall's displayed. It was a very expensive metal and once iron and steel became common, fine bronze armor and weapons were only had by the wealthiest of princes and kings. Conall's armor looked magnificent. He stood before Alastar as a pearl-gold warrior on a strong steed.

"Lad, wait for Teague," Conall said. "I must tend ta the men and battle. Pay mind ta your path. Don'tcha worry over us here. The Áiteoir will not prevail. We will meet again." He unsheathed his bronze sword and raised it high up. "Walk brave now, lad. Ride the currents 'a destiny!"

Alastar nodded in acknowledgement. Conall kicked his horse's sides with his heels and he galloped off. Alastar waited astride Éimhín for some minutes. Teague arrived on his horse, fully armed and dressed as Conall was. It was obvious he was also a seasoned commander. He also wore a full array of bronze and leather armor that matched the quality of Conall's, except Teague did not carry a shield. A seabhac messenger also followed him as he came. When he stopped, it rested on a perch that was attached to the rear of his saddle.

"Lad," Teague said. "I saw the garrison movin' swiftly from Dún Tearmann when I went ta get Bress. They should meet the Áiteoir just outside of Loch an Scátháin. Let us leave now and mind our own mission. Conall will have the fight in hand here. Lead the way."

They left galloping and rode down the trail towards the falls. Alastar couldn't believe he was leaving his friends in a time of great peril. What if the Áiteoir broke through? Would Nola and his friends be safe? "Mind our mission," he repeated to himself. *Mind our mission...*

*A*lastar and Teague stood at the ridge of the mountains. They were on their horses and the sky was now completely dark in the height of night. Tall pines surrounded them so the view out toward the coast was obstructed.

"This is where the Seabhac Azure flew straight out ta the coast," Alastar said. "But it kept flying higher and higher till I couldn't see it. I felt it was headin' for our home on the coast."

"Right," Teague said. "Then ya got distracted by the shadow fairy." He paused in contemplation. "Ya should've followed the Azure's course. It must've known ya would get distracted. It flies ta the heights ta set your course till ya need further guidance. Otherwise it would've waited for ya."

"How do ya know so much of the Azure?"

"Never seen it myself, and I'm no scholar, but I've studied much of the Prophecies Glasa ["glah-sah"]."

"The Glasa?" Alastar repeated.

"The Green Prophecies, written in walls a' clear emerald, scattered among mountain cliffs 'n caves. No one knows who wrote 'em, but there's not one error in the tellin' they give. The Glasa are useful knowledge for a scribe and conversin' within the king's circle.

Ya said the Azure was leadin' ya home? I thought ya weren't of this isle?"

"We're not. Not *exactly*. . . but in some ways we are." Alastar hesitated. Would Teague understand where they came from?

"What are ya blatherin' on about, lad? Where did the gateway take ya from?"

"We came from this isle, but I believe the gateway took us far back in time. I know not how far, but from what I've seen of Rathúnas it appears ta be ages and ages."

"Banger me, lad! Ya cannot be *that* Swan-bearer," Teague said with amazement. "I didn't quite put it together till now. Ya came from the valley upon a horse and through ages. . . the Glasa say the Swan-bearer will ride from the heart of the Valley Bradán after crossin' the ages. He will lift the reign of the swans ta its greatest heights and brin' the isle ta union and peace."

"*What?!*" Alastar said in disbelief. "That can't be me! I'm just a woodcarver."

"Face it, lad. All the pieces fit together, and the blessin' of the Seabhac Azure makes it all the more solid. Let us go towards your home. I don't imagine it should be there. There's not a settlement straight off on the coast from here. There's few towns from Lacharan up ta Cnoc na Rí, and they don't hold half the people Loch an Scátháin does. What is your hometown called?"

"Netleaf."

"I've not heard of it. There's only Potaire ["Pot-teh-reh"] and Dún Liath ["Doon Lee-ah"] north of Lacharan." Alastar's heart sunk with the knowledge his home in Netleaf was not here. He suspected as much, but had hoped to find his home and loved ones in Rathúnas. Now he wasn't sure if he'd ever see them again.

"Lacharan is a ways south along the coast from here," Teague continued. "I wonder if you're meant ta go there. The Swan-bearer has somethin' ta do with the Eachraighe, but I do not remember what exactly. Best ta keep ta your set path. We'll head straight ta the coast as ya said the Azure went."

Teague looked up the trees. Their thin branches jutted out from their trunks all the way to the top. "Ya look wiry 'nough ta climb the branches," he said. "Get on up there and see what's beyond the mountains."

Alastar dismounted Éimhín and took out leather gloves from a saddlebag. The pines would be sticky with resin, so he put the gloves on to keep his hands clean. He lifted his way up a tree and used the branches like the steps of a ladder. He was careful not to touch the bark excessively so his clothes would remain clean. Alarmed red squirrels scurried about the branches as he climbed. The smell of pine needles was strong. He went up as far as he thought the branches could hold him and looked out toward the coast.

The landscape was familiar, like the view he saw in the white oak on his last night in Eritirim, except here, anything alive and green continued to glow with dim sunlight. The thick forest on the mountains broke into sparse forests and then to open plains beyond. Alastar could see the edge of the dark ocean in the twilight, but there were no visible signs of settlements along the coast. He turned to look right, far to the south along the coast, to see if Lacharan was visible. *It's one of the largest cities on Rathúnas. It should be visible from this height,* he thought.

Sure enough, there was a faint glimmer of many lights far off where the coastline tucked into a large round bay area. It was some 50 miles away. No doubt, the city lights of Lacharan. Then Alastar saw a few groups of distant, dark dots slowly moving on the plains. They came from both the north and south and appeared to be parties on horses that were coming toward them.

Alastar quickly came down the tree and gave a report. "There are four parties on the plains comin' this way - from both the north and south. I cannot say if they're friendly."

"They wouldn't be friends of ours, lad. The plains and small towns are under Áiteoir control. No one'd be daft 'nough ta travel in the dead'a night there. We're bein' hunted, lad. It's certain the Áiteoir know of your arrival. They wouldn't take kindly ta someone who's ta subvert their power over the isle. There must be a spy in Loch an Scátháin. I don't know how else the Áiteoir could find ya so quickly."

Alastar started to panic. His friends in Loch an Scátháin were in danger as long as the enemy thought he was there. His peaceful life was quickly coming to an end. "I'm hardly a threat ta anyone!" he burst out. "I barely know how ta fight! I can't be this Swan-bearer they seek!"

"Calm down, lad," Teague said firmly. "Good in a fight or not, your place here is needed. Heroes do not make themselves. They're lifted by the currents 'a destiny. Don't fight the current. You're made ta go with it, like the water turns a mill's paddle wheel. The currents are meant ta turn your life's paddle wheel. Trust that. . . Do ya know the sword?"

"I don't, but I'm handy enough with my staff, and I have a dagger and small axe with me."

"Conall thought as much. He told me ta train ya as well as keep my eye on ya. You'll need ta be better than handy in battle. We have ta train ya in warfare and with the sword at that. But that has ta wait. We need ta go where the Azure was leadin' ya first. The enemy patrols are far 'nough away not ta alarm our Greerian. Otherwise, one would fly ta me, like ya saw at the céilí."

Alastar thought about how easy it was to see the enemy parties on the glowing landscape. Teague and him wouldn't be able travel on the plains without being sighted. He noted, "But if we head straight out ta the coast, we'd be sighted with the enemy on both sides of us. Our dark bodies are easy ta see against the glowin' land."

"Then we wait. The glow will be gone in roundabout an hour."

"But then the parties will be close by," Alastar said with worry covering over him.

"That they will. Trust your path is set. We'll slip out quietly under night's cover. Rest now and have somethin' ta eat. Gather strength. The night will be long for us. Next time the Azure comes, just follow it. Remember, ya wouldn't be runnin' like this if ya stayed its course the first time 'round. Goin' against destiny always makes for a tougher journey."

They rested for a time and when the land had almost dimmed into darkness, Teague spoke. "Climb the tree again, lad. Get a report on where the enemy is, right till the land goes dark."

Alastar acknowledged and went up the tree. He saw one of the parties from the north was nearly at the foot of the mountains. The other northern party was far away but following. The southern parties had hardly moved at all. They were still many miles off, in between them and Lacharan.

Soon the whole land became dark and nothing could be seen but faint shimmering on the sea and the glimmers of light in Lacharan. Alastar quickly went down the tree. "A party from the north is near the mountains."

"Right ya are," Teague said and pointed to the sky towards the north. A gleaming Greerian flew toward them. He raised his arm up and held it for the eagle sentry to perch. It landed surely and silent. Teague appeared to speak to it with his mind as Conall did. Only a few moments passed and it took off flying towards Loch an Scátháin.

"The close party numbers a dozen. They're bein' followed by a larger group. The southern groups are camped, larger units, a hundred strong each. No one has torches or fires lit. They must be trying ta hide in the night as we are."

"The Greerian told ya all that?"

"It did. Not in words but with pictures. It appears the southern units are tryin' to block our way ta Lacharan. The Áiteoir know the

Glasa as well as we do. They suspect we'll join the Eachraighe. I told the Greerian ta report our situation ta Conall, but we cannot expect help from Loch an Scáthāin. They have their own battle.

"We need ta get past the closest party and head for the coast. The Áiteoir likely have their Lorgaire scouts runnin' ahead. Our order is ta ride slow and silent as a shadow. The Lorgaire have keen eyes and unnatural trackin' skills. They must have our position pinned ta be headin' square on us.

"Do ya have a cloak? We need ta cover and make us dark as all 'round."

"I have my long coat," Alastar answered.

"Good. Take it out."

Alastar got his coat and put it on. He pulled its hood over his head to conceal himself. Teague also covered his head with the hood attached to his mantle and wrapped the cape around his body to cover his bright armor. Then he went to the rear of his horse and had Bress perch on his wrist. "Fly in waitin'," he commanded the hawk. He lifted up his arm and Bress flew off.

"She'll keep close until I call her back," Teague said. They got on their horses and started down the mountainside.

"Be silent from here," Teague said. "And look for quick flashes 'a light. Lorgaire eyes reflect light if you see them from an angle." He pointed two fingers at his eyes from the side to show Alastar. "There's enough light around us ta help us in that at least. If ya see anythin', get my attention by clickin' with your tongue twice, like this." Teague made a soft, double-click sound and Alastar nodded in acknowledgement.

"Since they expect us ta head for Lacharan in the south," Teague continued, "We'll head north and pass between the two northern groups. Just follow my lead. They won't expect us to head straight ta the coast. The Azure's course appears to be exactly what we need here."

They continued down the mountain and Alastar was grateful the ground was well padded with soil and grass. There were few rocks, so moving silently was not difficult. He constantly looked about for signs of the enemy. Alastar had never felt so tense with fear before. Despite the cool air, his hands were sweaty. Thoughts of Nola, his friends, his home, and being caught by the Áiteoir flustered his mind. *Mind the mission,* he reminded himself to keep calm.

At the foot of the mountain, Teague paused. He raised his arm up and pointed to the right. Alastar could see a few glints of light there – a Lorgaire scout on foot was making his way up to where they had just come from. His dark silhouette was tall and lanky, and he appeared to be carrying a weapon or pack on his back.

Teague started to make a sharper path to the north to avoid being seen. Alastar's heart was racing. He consoled himself by whispering to Éimhín and patting his neck, "Quiet and calm as can be. Quiet and calm…" He looked off to the right and saw more glints of light just beyond Teague's position. He was about to alert Teague with clicks, but before he could, Teague raised his arm and slowly pointed in the direction of the faint glimmers. Teague swung his arm slowly in an arc off to the right to show the enemy's position. The party was just a stone's throw away.

Teague quickened their pace to gain distance from the enemy. There was no sign of the other northern party. They should be coming up soon. Alastar felt the pressure of his pounding heart. It urged him to run. He tried to keep calm and leaned forward to grab hold of his staff that hung from Éimhín's left shoulder. When his hand wrapped around it, he heard quick footsteps start off in a sprint and suddenly something crashed into him before he could take his staff out.

Alastar flew through the air with a Lorgaire gripping his body. Éimhín reared up and whinnied. The entire enemy party knew where they were now. Teague quickly drew his sword and jumped off his horse before Alastar hit the ground. He ran to Alastar and plunged his gleaming bronze sword into the scout.

"Back ta your horse! *Ride!*" Teague yelled.

They both mounted quickly and galloped straight as they could towards the coast. The forest was still thick, so they weaved to and fro among the trees. They focused entirely on pressing forward and could hardly hear the enemy take pursuit. Soon they heard arrows darting past them. Alastar looked back. The dark forms of soldiers on horses and foot chasing them nearly brought his heart to a standstill.

"*Quick!*" Alastar said to Éimhín, and they surged forward with renewed strength. They broke through the forest and galloped full speed into the plains. The enemy party was close behind and blew a horn to alert the other parties. Then a flaming arrow blazed into the sky and landed far ahead of them. It struck the ground and continued to burn brightly.

"The other units have our position!" Teague yelled. "Arm yourself!"

Alastar took out his staff as he saw Teague turn his horse around and take the hood off his helmet. Even in the dark light, his golden armor gleamed like pearls in the ocean depths. He raised his sword and charged their pursuers. Alastar stopped the gallop. He couldn't believe his eyes. Should he charge too or wait? As he hesitated, Éimhín snorted and stomped his forefeet.

"Right. Fight then," Alastar acknowledged. They took off at a full gallop and followed Teague's lead. Teague struck down an Áiteoir rider as he rode into their group. Alastar followed and swiped at another rider who held up a sword against him. The sword nicked and glanced off his staff and sent the sword flying.

Teague was making quick work of the Áiteoir. He cut them down before Alastar could even think about swinging his staff. Their number dropped to half by the time Alastar knocked the swordless rider off his horse. But before he could target another soldier, Alastar found himself surrounded by the remaining foot soldiers – four of them.

Alastar swung at them as they tried to pull him off Éimhín. It wasn't easy for them. Éimhín fiercely protected Alastar by swinging around and rearing up against the attackers. They were held at bay until Teague came back to finish them off.

"Right grand fight, lad!" Teague said. "Catch a quick breath. The large units south 'a us are interceptin'." Alastar looked to the south and saw the hundreds rush toward them in the dim light. They looked to be some minutes away. "I cannot see the other unit from the north. They must still be far off. . . Come now. Ta the coast!"

They rode towards the coast again and saw the southern units change course to intercept. *How are we getting out of this?* Alastar worried. *Teague couldn't possibly fight them all.*

They had continued toward the coast for a few minutes when Alastar saw a white object in the sky directly ahead. It was coming down from the clouds, and he knew exactly what it was. "The Seabhac Azure!" he yelled and pointed his staff at it. Alastar's heart was gladdened to see it. His friends were right. It did come back to see him through the rest of his journey. The southern units were closing on them quickly, though, and Alastar's heart shrunk again when he saw the other northern unit in the distance. It appeared to be half the number of the units in the south.

Teague sensed Alastar's anxiety. "Just watch the Azure and follow!" he reminded.

The Azure circled in front of them and then started to fly south, directly towards Lacharan. Then again, it continued to ascend high into the sky until it disappeared.

"Lacharan, lad! I told ya! You *are* the Swan-bearer! *GO!*" Teague yelled and turned south with his sword still drawn. He galloped ahead, but the southern units were headed straight to collide with them.

This can't be right, Alastar thought. He hesitated again and looked backwards to the north. The northern unit was galloping swift to intercept as well. He closed his eyes and gathered calm and courage. "We're gonna meet the horse riders of Lacharan, Éimhín. Don'cha worry. I won't sell ya ta a breeder." He patted Éimhín's neck and followed Teague.

Alastar raised his staff high in the air and screamed with all his might as they caught up to Teague. Courage welled up in him like he'd never felt before. His fear was pushed aside. He couldn't have felt more ready to fight. When the southern units were close, Teague veered right to ride directly into them. He charged them as he did the first time and proceeded to hack at the enemy.

All the enemy archers were on foot, far behind the cavalry. Their aim was not accurate either, so the arrows flew past them harmlessly. Then Alastar entered into the fighting. He swung his staff as best he could. He didn't dispatch the enemy as Teague did, but he kept out of harm, at least for a time.

The Áiteoir outnumbered them greatly and they started to swarm around Alastar. Éimhín started taking a defensive stance and spun about as Alastar swung at anyone who came near. Teague was many meters away and being swarmed as well. Alastar didn't have time to worry about the urgency of their situation. He just kept fighting until the call of a loud horn came from the north.

Everyone paused to look. The northern unit was very close,

but they didn't appear to be Áiteoir. They were all on horses and wore bronze armor. They carried long, red banners on poles like Alastar saw at the bird cage on the mountain and charged toward Teague and Alastar. *Could they be from Loch an Scátháin?* Alastar wondered.

When the Áiteoir recognized the attacking unit, most of them shifted their focus and charged to attack. Teague quickly broke out of surrounding soldiers and came to help Alastar. "I was wrong, lad. We have friends on the plains tonight! The north unit is from Cnoc na Rí. It looks ta be the party escortin' the king's chancellor."

"We're still outnumbered two ta one," Alastar said. "The other southern unit is almost here."

Teague grinned. "We have the advantage here, lad. The soldiers of Torthúil are the finest." He pointed to the enemy archers who were retreating towards the southern unit. "See, their archers are runnin' ta regroup. Do not pick any more fights, lad. Leave the fightin' ta us."

Teague rode off to charge the remaining Áiteoir unit coming from the south. Many of the soldiers from Cnoc na Rí followed him. Alastar watched in amazement at the battle before him. He was glad not to be engaged in the combat. It was much more fierce and bloody than he had imagined from stories.

Soon the last of the Áiteoir around them were killed and Torthúil's horn was blown again. Alastar now saw the horn was made of polished bronze and curved in a long, slender, graceful S that perched high above the trumpeter's head. At its call, the majority of the Torthúil unit charged ahead to join Teague in the south. Alastar watched the fighting intently and didn't notice a rider approach him from behind.

"You must be Alastar," he said, startling him. Alastar turned around and saw a thin, elder man with brown hair and short beard. He sat atop a white horse and wore a long, royal blue léine that went down to his ankles. It was trimmed with gold designs and ornaments.

"I am, sir," Alastar acknowledged and bowed his head in respect.

The man bowed and extended his hand in a forward wave. "Gilroy Mac Dáithí, Giolla Rí ["Gil-roy Mahk Dah-hee, Gil-la Ree"]. Chancellor ta King Fuar. You are supposed ta be in Loch an Scáthráin, son."

"I was. But we were attacked."

"I know. All the Greerian reports reach my ears. We were headin' ta Loch an Scáthráin, but the Seabhac Azure led us south ta follow the Áiteoir unit out of Dún Liath. We weren't sure why, but once I heard the report given ta Teague tonight I knew we were being led ta ya.

"Brought us right where we needed ta be; and just in time. Ya were at the edge of the enemy's fingertips. You're a mighty commodity, son."

"It appears so, sir," Alastar said. "I can't imagine how all this came ta be. I only know I'm meant ta be here now, and I need ta go ta Lacharan. I thank ya for your timely arrival."

"I had nothin' ta do with it," Gilroy said. "Be thankful you are blessed." Gilroy looked towards the fighting in the south. The enemy was scattering and running farther south where there was the distant twinkling of red-orange dots of light. "We'll be ta Lacharan before dawn. Let us be swift. The Áiteoir will have report of what happened before we reach Lacharan. They're sure ta break the truce there as they have at Loch an Scáthráin. Follow me."

Gilroy signaled the men to go. They galloped south to meet Teague and the rest of their soldiers.

"A large army approaches," Teague said. He pointed southwest to the torch lights that swayed about in the distance. They were emerging from the southern end of the mountains. "Many thousands, and more appear by the minute. We need ta reach Lacharan *now!* They move quickly ta prevent our safe haven."

"How did we not see them before?" Alastar asked.

"They were hidden in the west," Teague noted, "Around the south rim of the mountains, lad. They keep well ta their borders. Our sentries don't consider them a threat till they press toward our borders. We're on their land now, lad. Lacharan is ta be our sanctuary. Their watchmen are sure ta know the Áiteoir advance. They're vigilant, but they know nothin' of our mission. We need ta inform 'em of everythin'."

"That is sure," Gilroy said. "We need their help in this." He looked at Alastar. "The Swan-bearer needs their help, certain as we all need yours, son."

"What help am I?" Alastar wondered.

"All will be revealed in its time," Gilroy responded. "Just keep vigilant, focused, and patient as the tower watchmen. Stay the course shown by destiny's turnin'. You've been shown much already, but its full meanin' will not be known until all the pieces come ta fall in place." Alastar wondered how Gilroy could know that he saw many strange things coming to Rathúnas. Perhaps Gilroy would know how to get him home through the stone archway.

"Right, lad," Teague said. "Mind the mission. Don't go followin' distractions you're not meant ta walk in. Let the currents take ya. Listen and watch for their movin'."

"But if I didn't find Loch an Scátháin," Alastar said, "I wouldn't have gotten your aid. I never would've made it here without your help - from you and the soldiers of Torthúil."

"Not so," Teague reminded. "Remember, if ya stayed in the flow ya saw at first, ya wouldn't have needed my help, nor of the good fightin' men of Torthúil. I imagine ya would've gotten ta Lacharan without much trouble at all. Ya wouldn't have been hunted as ya are now.

"The Áiteoir would've sent a unit from Dún Liath as they did, ta investigate your border crossin', but they wouldn't know who ya were. Never would've caught up ta ya either. You'd pass Potaire on the way ta Lacharan but there's no garrison there. Ya would've traveled safely and be well received, as ya were in Loch an Scátháin. The Eachraighe are anxious as we ta have news of good tidin's."

"True," Gilroy said. "They would've questioned ya in Lacharan, but your dress and horse would have ya seen as one of their own. Mind ya, they would've sent for consultation with me as well. It wouldn't have been long till they found out who you are - who you're meant ta be.

"I would've taken interest in ya square off after ya crossed our borders too. The Greerian would've sent me word of it. . . but what's ta worry of possibilities now. You took a different path, and we need ta set ya on course, and keep ya to it." Gilroy gestured to ride to Lacharan and a soldier blew the horn. Everyone started in a gallop directly south.

They rode nearly an hour across the dark plains with the sight of many thousand torches on their right coming closer at every step. The distinct silhouettes of marching horses and soldiers were now seen among the many points of light. There were also strange shapes running ahead of the main group that Alastar couldn't identify. They leapt forward like running dogs but were much larger. Alastar picked up Éimhín's pace to get beside Teague.

"What runs ahead of the Áiteoir?" Alastar asked.

Teague looked and became alarmed. "BANJAX!" Teague yelled. "The Áiteoir set their fáelshee ["fahl-shee"] on us! They mean ta take blood! *RIDE!* Swift as ya can!"

"Fáelshee?!" Alastar yelled as everyone came to a full gallop.

"The black lion wolves of the Rásúir ["Ræ-soor"] Mountains. Do not speak now, lad! *RIDE!*"

Their group rode furiously toward Lacharan for many minutes. The high city walls were visible, but it appeared the leaping fáelshee would overtake them before they could reach the gates. Gilroy signaled the men to make a stand and the battle horn rung out again. "Ride ahead," he told the flag bearers. "Have them open the north gate for us."

The rest of them stopped and made a double line to confront the enemy. Some men on the front line held long spears outward. Teague was front and center with his sword held out, while Gilroy and Alastar remained in the rear.

The line of fáelshee bounding toward them was twice as wide as their line – more than 20 huge wolves; one for every pair of fighting men in their group. Their dark, hulking shapes were rife with coarse fur and full manes. If the sight of them rushing near with snarling teeth and pale, gray eyes wasn't enough to stop everyone's hearts, the sounds of their howling and growls sent their courage fluttering away, like startled pheasants taking flight.

Their horses were whinnying and fidgeting anxiously. Éimhín remained steady, though Alastar could feel his uneasiness. Alastar pat and stroked his neck to soothe him. "Easy, boy. Easy. . ."

"Hold steady, son," Gilroy told Alastar. "We'll see ya through."

Alastar clenched his staff and held it ready. He noticed Gilroy was unarmed and no one guarded him. "Should we move back, sir?"

"It would not make a difference. The fáelshee would leap on our backs if we run. Better ta face them head on."

The first of the fáelshee leapt high at the soldiers in front to push them off their horses. The dark wolves were nearly as big as the horses. Some were skewered by spears, but their weight knocked every rider down and sent their horses running. Teague was able to kill the first one, but its flying bulk knocked him off his horse as well. Alastar's heart raced and tears started to well up in him as he saw the men being ripped and gored. Their armor was crushed under the massive jaws of the fáelshee.

Teague was just getting up when a fáelshee jumped on him and bit down on his right shoulder. He screamed in pain, and Alastar moved to help him, but Gilroy held him back. "Stand here, son," he said firmly.

Alastar grit his teeth trying to hold back his emotions. He watched Teague and saw Bress come swooping down from the sky. The hawk attacked the giant wolf's face and sent it in retreat. Many of the men were dead and the fáelshee started to break through their second line. Then another battle horn called out. It was from Lacharan. Alastar and Gilroy looked backwards and saw the heavy city gates open. The flag bearers rode back to Gilroy's side and the air filled with the sound of a large cavalry unit charging out of the city.

A fáelshee finished mauling a soldier and ran toward Alastar. Éimhín reared up and kicked at the beast. It was about to leap onto Éimhín's neck when a bright flash of light exploded from Gilroy. It left the fáelshee stunned. The flag bearers quickly moved onto it and killed the lion hound with their swords.

The cavalry from Lacharan rushed through the gates and helped kill the remaining fáelshee. Alastar rode forward to Teague, who stumbled toward his fallen horse. He held his wounded right shoulder and grumbled, "I need a new horse! Bog bean and sickle swifts! The Áiteoir thought ta have us flittin' off like corncrakes from hunt dogs. Amaideach!" He turned to Alastar. "Lad, help me get the saddle off. Bress needs a perch."

Alastar jumped off Éimhín and went to Teague's horse. Teague was grimy and covered with blood splatters. "Are ya hurt?" Alastar asked him.

"Shoulder's well bruised but none of my blood was shed," Teague answered. "Armor did its job."

"Quick now," Gilroy reminded. "The army nears. Everyone! Behind the gates!"

Inside Lacharan, bells rung throughout the city and heralds ran through the streets to call out the coming siege. Farmers and peasants ran through the city gates with their horses and livestock to take refuge from their farms and ranches outside. Alastar had never seen such a panicked commotion of people. The whole city was on their feet to brace against the surge of the Áiteoir.

"They'll be here within the hour," Teague said. "They slowed their march seein' we entered the gates. Their fáelshee push was ta render us corpses before gettin' here. They were swift ta send such a force. The dark wolves are only used ta kill without mercy. It's clear the Áiteoir have no want ta speak with ya, lad."

"You are a grave threat ta them, son," Gilroy said. "The army marchin' here looks ta be twice of any they've dispatched before. It must've been sent straight after they heard of your arrival. The fáelshee come from Áiteoir lands around the Muir Airgid ["Mooer Ar-gedge"]; a hard day's drive from the northwest. The Áiteoir must believe you are *the* Swan-bearer ta send such swift and strong blows ta wherever they think ya stand."

Alastar started to worry about Nola and his friends in Loch an Scátháin. Did they survive the attack there? "How can I stay here?" Alastar said, "When I cause such a threat to people wherever I go? Many have died since I arrived."

"Mind your mission, lad," Teague said firmly. "Ya are here for reasons hidden, but it is for purpose. Runnin' off only delays what's needin' ta be done. Worse calamities will come on ya and everyone else if ya don't keep ta plan. Who'd run in ta take your shoes if ya go skippin' off from your own destiny? Have faith, lad. You're the one ta be walkin' in your path - no other. All of us have our roles ta play. Just know yours and stay the course."

"Right," Gilroy said. "Let's not speak more on the streets. The enemy may have spies. Mind who ya speak with 'n what ya say. I will see Duke Gearóid ["Ger-rudge"]. He is the head of Lacharan." He looked at Teague. "See the lad rests. The city walls will hold for many days. There's no need ta keep wake through the night. I will find ya in the mornin'."

Gilroy rode east into the city toward the coast. Alastar needed rest but he wondered how he could in the commotion and anxiety of everything. It was just the day before he felt the tranquil life around Loch an Scátháin and the bubbling hopes of new life and love with Nola. And the day before that, he was secure in a peaceful existence on Eritirim. It seemed to him the currents continued to thrust him into unfamiliar settings. What good could he do as the Swan-bearer? Was he truly made for this journey?

"This way," Teague said. "The captain is an old friend. He will see ta our quarter." Teague led Alastar to the stables and barracks where they would stay. It was relatively quiet with most of the garrison manning the walls. They were safe, but Alastar couldn't help thinking that just beyond a stone wall was an enemy that was desperate to kill him. They wouldn't turn away from Lacharan unless he was given into their hands.

*A*lastar woke late in the barracks. The bright sun of day streamed through the windows and urged him to move, though his body still felt tired and sore from the night of running through the forests and plains. He sat up and looked around. The handful of beds in the room was empty. He could hear distant shouts of men. No doubt soldiers in the siege.

He grabbed his staff by the bed and went outside. It was late morning. The sun was tucked behind billowy clouds towards the east. People were not rushing about as in the night. If it weren't for the sounds of battle nearby, it would seem the city was in its general state of affairs. There was no worry on anyone's face as they went about their business. Lacharan was no stranger to sieges. She was confident in her walls to hold back the crashing tide of the Áiteoir.

Alastar went to the stables and found Éimhín. "Rested now, boy?" he asked as he pat and stroked him. He saw a large bucket of fodder on the ground in front of Éimhín. It was almost empty. "The stable page feed ya well? Ya didn't finish. I think ya'd be famished after the run last night. Or did ya save room for dessert?"

He took out a few apples and fed them to Éimhín. "Last ones we brought from home. It's the fruits of Rathúnas from here on." Alastar took out his long coat and put it on. "The sky's patchy today. I think a cool rain is in store. Let's take a walk."

Alastar led Éimhín outside and walked down the street toward the east where he saw Gilroy go before. He might find him or Teague this way. People hardly paid any attention to him as they walked along, but anyone who noticed Éimhín's strong build and tall frame stared curiously at them.

"Don't mind 'em," he said to Éimhín. "These horse folk are just figurin' where ya came from. Nola said they'd fancy ya."

The sun broke through a patchwork of clouds strung thin by the wind. Alastar looked up at the golden rays that streamed through and saw the silhouette of a large bird flying down from the clouds. He watched it intently as they strolled down the street. Soon the white and blue of the Seabhac Azure were evident. It was silent as it flew down and landed on the rooftop of a building near them. *The Azure must not want too much attention here,* he thought. Alastar continued to walk toward it. He looked around to see if anyone else saw the Azure, but no one else appeared to notice. When he was closer, it took off again and landed on the top of a building towards the north.

"Our friend wants us ta turn here, Éimhín. Seems we need ta be somewhere again."

They turned right onto another street and continued to walk towards the Azure. When they came near, it flew again going east down a street and then flew once more high into the sky. When Alastar reached the street he looked down its length. It was a long, broad street that led all the way to the sea.

Alastar mounted Éimhín and trotted down the street. At the end of the road he found docks and markets lining the bay, left and right. The broad walkway along the bay was paved with large flagstone of various dark grays and browns. It was a busy area with many sailing ships in port. *Where should I go now?* he wondered.

Merchants called out their goods, but one caught his attention immediately. "Stones and gems! Stones and gems from shores far!" Alastar remembered he needed wood stain and this merchant should have exactly what he needed. He got off Éimhín and led him towards the merchant, who had a table set up under a tarpaulin canopy at the entrance to a long dock. The merchant had many types of stone under glass cases.

Before Alastar looked at the selection, people coming off the ship at the end of the dock caught his attention. Uniformed guards escorted a young blonde woman in a fine, sage green dress and an older woman next to her. The older woman wore a plain white dress and carried a parasol by her side. They hadn't taken more than two steps on the wood dock before a light shower of rain poured down. The woman in the white dress quickly opened the parasol and held it over the other woman as they walked down the dock.

Alastar covered his head with the hood of his coat to keep dry. He wondered who were the people coming down the dock. They appeared to be nobility, but he tried not stare at them. He turned to the merchant's table and scanned the stones on display. There were many stones and gems, uncut and cut, rough and polished – rubies, lapis lazuli, sapphires, agates, pearls and the like. . . as well as what Alastar was looking for - amber stones, except they were large, high quality specimens; too valuable for his purposes.

"Do ya have more rough amber?" he asked the merchant. "Of the kind ta quicken the color in stains?"

"The cast-offs?" the merchant replied. He looked at Alastar closely and wondered why a noble looking man would want to make his own stain. *Shouldn't he simply buy it?* he thought. "Do ya have anythin' ta pay with, lad?"

"I have a selection of rare, dried wood." Alastar pointed to the bundles of wood on Éimhín. The merchant walked from under his canopy and examined the wood. His face tightened into a slight scowl as he was being drenched in the rain.

"The wood is worthless ta me, lad." Then the merchant saw the bundles of sage. "But what are these green branches? I've never seen 'em before."

"Desert sage, sir. Very rare."

The merchant brought his nose to the sage and smelled it. "Excellent. You can have as much of my cast-off amber as ya like for your sage."

Alastar smiled. "Certainly, but give me one of your decent stones for it all. Otherwise, I'll give ya half my sage for the amber."

"Bog bean!" the merchant replied disappointed. He stood a moment to think as the rain soaked him. "Grand thin' for ya I know someone who'd pay finely for this sage. Ya have a deal. Let me get outta this wet 'n pick a fine stone for ya." He took the bundle of sage and went back behind the table to look through his selection in the case.

Alastar turned away from Éimhín and looked toward the merchant. He found the two women were now standing by the table with the guards nearby. He noticed the soldiers wore royal blue uniforms with gold trim similar to Gilroy's léine. The women looked at the merchant's stones. The blonde woman was taller, but still a little shorter than Alastar. Her silvery-blonde hair was bound up in a bun in the back and along the sides it was wound in thin braids, like a wreath crowning her head. Even from behind she appeared very elegant.

"I have one for ya," the merchant told Alastar.

The women looked up at Alastar, and he quickly uncovered his head and bowed to them. "Ladies, Alastar Duer." The rain all of sudden stopped and he blinked several times to get the water out of his eyes. He squinted through the water dripping from his hair and the first thing he noticed was the blonde woman's green eyes gazing large and round at him. Then he saw the large jewel pendant on her necklace and almost took a step back in surprise.

It was a smooth polished amber stone set in gold and suspended by a necklace of round amber beads. The pendant gemstone looked exactly like the image of the round gem with the other glowing symbols on the cliff face. When the rain stopped, the sunlight came to overpower the gray sky and made the amber pendant glow in mottled brown and golden hues. It looked just as the glowing image by the stone arch, except now it was in vivid color and had the depth of real life.

The clouds split apart farther and let more sunlight shine down. Alastar looked up at the sky and saw a huge rainbow arc across his view in front of him. The last two symbols in the puzzle just appeared before him - a brilliant, mottled gemstone and a full rainbow. *Who is this woman?* he thought bewildered. *What does this mean?*

"Amber Lyn Ealaí ["Ahm-ber Lin Ah-lee"]," the blonde woman said with a nod of her head. "And my attendant, Mairéad ["Mah-raid"]." She noticed Alastar staring at the sky and looked backwards. The rainbow was vivid and stretched across the entire bay, like a bridge connecting its two farthest points.

"A grand sight," the merchant said. "Rainbows hide many treasures, but few ever chase 'em with the selfless eyes needed ta find their dreams within. For you, Alastar, lad. I have a splendid emerald."

Alastar brought his eyes back down and saw Amber was not covered by the umbrella anymore. The shadows no longer hid her face and the sun lit up her hair. He could see how bright it was now. It had a shimmering luster, like the polished finish of the fine bronze he noticed in the armor and weapons of Torthúil.

He caught himself staring at her. She had a simple beauty made from the soft curves and crisp projection of her smiling face. He was caught in a moment of silent reflection, like one would stare at the plain beauty of a clover wet with dew. Then he remembered the merchant. He turned to him and looked at the rough, uncut gemstone he held out. It needed to be worked by a jeweler and had a fracture running through it, but it was a good size, almost as large as his small fingernail. "Grand altogether, sir. The exchange is a good one."

"Excellent, lad." The merchant handed the emerald to Alastar. Then he took out a small box and opened it. "Select your amber."

Alastar fingered through the small, rough amber stones. He selected mostly stones of red-orange and deep golden brown. He also collected a few stones of golden yellow. As he looked through them, he thought it was very curious to be finding Amber Ealaí, who wore a pendant of amber, while he was searching for amber stones. And he was led there just at the right time to meet her under the rainbow. The currents of destiny continued to show its intricate threads for him to follow. He obviously needed to know more about Amber.

"It was nice ta meet you, sir," Amber said to Alastar. She looked at the merchant and nodded to him. "Sir," she acknowledged. "We need ta be off."

Alastar stopped looking through the stones and fumbled for words to say so she wouldn't leave. The only thing that came to mind was what he needed for the wood stain. "Would ya happen ta know where I can get linseed oil?" he asked her.

"I have a half pint of linseed," the merchant said. "Two pence or somethin' 'a value."

"Sir, would your linseed oil have gold dust in it?" Amber remarked. "I'll give ya a halfpenny for it. A grand deal that would be for ya."

"Not if the lad gives me two pence for it, it wouldn't," the merchant said smiling. Alastar started to blush and wondered if he was taken for a fool. It seemed the merchant was very keen to make an excessive profit.

"I'm sorry, sir," Alastar said. "I haven't any coin nor anythin' I wish ta trade."

"Don'tcha worry, Alastar," Amber said. She turned to Mairéad. "A halfpenny for the merchant."

"A halfpenny it is," Mairéad acknowledged.

"Thank ya," Alastar said, "But I can't have ya payin' for my things."

"Nonsense!" Amber said. She nodded at Mairéad to continue. She took out a purse and gave the merchant a coin.

The merchant tried to hide his dissatisfaction for having his profit spoiled. "Ya must be locals, me ladies," he said to the girls. "Ya put on quite a flare 'a match for the lad's sake. He's fortunate ta have ya. And I'm glad ta sell ta ya. You said you're of the Ealaí house? Would that be the Ealaí house of Lacharan?"

"There is only one Ealaí house on all the isle, sir," Amber said. "My father was Prince Donavan Ealaí ["Don-ah-vin Ah-lee"]."

The merchant was surprised and bowed to Amber. "I'm honored ta be in your presence, Princess. I'm only a traveler ta your city, but I serve ya nonetheless."

Princess? Alastar thought. He stared at the ground and wondered if Amber was important to his future. The bright sunlight was heating the walkway and made steam rise from the dark stones that were glazed with rain. Then the sound of footsteps approaching them broke his pondering. The guards stiffened up.

"There ya are, Alastar!" Gilroy said. "I see you have met Princess Amber Lyn Ealaí."

The royal guards bowed to Gilroy.

Amber greeted him, "He has, Chancellor. How did ya know I was here? I was about ta send ya word of our arrival. I thought you were in Cnoc na Rí."

"That I was, just yesterday. But it seems thin's have worked out ta bring us all together just in time. I was not expectin' ya so early either. Come. All 'a ya. We must speak with Duke Gearóid."

Amber turned to Mairéad. "Have my thin's brought home."

Mairéad nodded. "Certainly." She waited with one of the guards for the luggage to be brought out from the ship. Amber, Alastar, Gilroy and the other guard left for the duke's palace.

"Lacharan is under siege by a large Áiteoir army," Gilroy told Amber.

"How could they know I've arrived?" she asked.

"They've not come for you, Princess. But if they find you here, they will target ya as well. Let us not speak of these matters here. We will converse with the duke."

"Why would the Áiteoir want the princess?" Alastar asked.

"Son," Gilroy said, "She is the last in the House of the Swans and next in line ta rule after King Fuar of the House of Lorcán ["Lorkh-kun"]. Did ya not gather that from her surname? Ealaí means Swans, just as Alastar means Swan-bearer." Understanding popped into Alastar's mind. The reign of the Swans that the Glasa told about referred to Amber's family reign.

Amber looked at Alastar with intense, curious wonder. She knew she would ascend to the throne someday, but she didn't expect to find the Swan-bearer who would help her to be such a young, uncouth boy - much less, have him in front of her already. King Fuar didn't have any heirs, but his rule had no sign of coming to an end.

Her life was in an upheaval after her father was killed in the war with the Áiteoir and they tried to assassinate her years ago. It was for safety that the chancellor sent her away from the isle, but when she got word from him to come back, she hoped it would begin a time of peaceful reign. The Glasa said the isle would come to be united and peaceful under her family's rule, but things did not appear to be in harmony.

Alastar's thoughts surged about as well. How was he supposed to help Amber? How long would his journey be with her? He had other things in mind for his immediate future. Nola was a part of it and he wished to return to Loch an Scátháin to see that she was safe with the rest of his friends.

They continued to walk down the streets of Lacharan near the coast of the bay. The fighting at the city walls could not be heard from there. It appeared to be a quiet, pleasant spring day, and the calm, blue sea's soft murmuring enhanced the mood, but the events unfolding around them kept their minds and spirits in continual churning.

"Ya have such a fine horse," Amber said to Alastar. "Finer than all in the stables of Rathúnas. What is his name?"

"Éimhín, Ma'am, er. . . Princess," Alastar responded. "He's the very best of horses and friends."

"'Swift,' is it?" Gilroy said, noting the meaning of Éimhín's name. "He surely is quick, and a steady guardian from what I've seen."

"Do ya ride with the Eachraighe?" Amber asked Alastar. "You have the stature of a rider and your horse and fitments are the finest, but ya don't carry our clan's seal."

"I'm not one of the Eachraighe, Princess."

"'He will ride with the Eachraighe but deny being one with them.'" Gilroy said, quoting from the Glasa. "Teague was right. Ya fit the mark of the Swan-bearer exactly. It would be pointless for ya ta deny you are he."

"But I haven't yet ridden with the Eachraighe," Alastar said with a note of denial that he was the Swan-bearer they waited for.

"You'd be wrong about that, son. The cavalry of Cnoc na Rí and I belong ta the Eachraighe. Lacharan has been under the rule of the Torthúil Kingdom for generations; since the kingdom was formed. All our cavalry and most of the royal guard are from our clan."

"I see," Alastar said. "No use in lookin' backwards ta my old life. My future here's somethin' I've come ta accept now. It's hard ta turn away from the facts when everywhere ya look, there they are, repeatin' the message. It was no coincidence I met the princess this mornin'. The Azure led me ta the dock just as she was comin' ta shore. My search for amber stones with the merchant ended in findin' Princess Amber too. Grand things the weavin' of destiny's threads. I do wonder, though. Just how am I ta aid the princess?"

"The Glasa say not," Gilroy said. "But be patient. All will be revealed in its time."

The duke's palace was set near the south end of the bay. Alastar never saw such a large and beautiful building. It was made of white stone blocks and had many roofs of vibrant teal blue that covered its expanse of long wings and towers. The estate was surrounded by a cobblestone wall topped with bronze spears that stood along the entire length. They walked through the main gate, which was also made of bronze, and saw the colorful cultivated gardens that spanned the grounds everywhere.

"Welcome home, Princess. . . Chancellor," the guard at the gate said.

They nodded at the guard and continued to the palace doors.

"You live *here*, Princess?" Alastar asked.

"I do. The Duke is regent of my father's estates and moved here as the head of the Eachraighe and Lacharan after my father died."

Gilroy added, "The palace is used for state business as much as it is a home for the royal family."

A young page ran up to them. "Your horse, sir," he said to Alastar. Alastar gave him the reins and watched him lead Éimhín to the stables.

Inside the palace, they were greeted by many servants. They

were led to a meeting room where Teague sat with Duke Gearóid and another man. The men wore léine tunics, armor, and mantles much like Teague and Conall did. Their dress was less ornate but sturdier than that of Loch an Scátháin, and their mantles were blue instead of red.

"Amber, Chancellor," Gearóid greeted. "Who've ya brought?" Gearóid appeared relatively plain for someone of a royal station. He hardly appeared different than Teague in body and dress; more as a soldier than a royal governor. *They could be brothers,* Alastar thought.

"This is Alastar Duer," Gilroy said.

Gearóid held out his hand and Alastar grasped it with both his hands, top and bottom, in an awkward handshake. "Duke, Lord, sir," Alastar said, uncertain how to greet the duke. Amber found his cumbersome manners oddly endearing. She noticed he was nervous and seemed to be sweating at the brow. She thought, *How can this boy be my champion? He doesn't even carry a sword.*

Gearóid smiled. "Simply Duke, Alastar, but as the minutes pass address me by name. People may look ta me as a noble, but I am as ya are – simply a man with a purpose. I am pleased ta meet ya, Swan-bearer. I believe ya know Teague." He turned to the other man. "This is Conn ["Kon"], Captain of the Guard. We have urgent business ta speak of. The watchmen of Turnmor Tower saw an Áiteoir fleet of siege ships and longboats comin' this way."

"They've never dared ta attack by sea before," Amber said.

Teague interrupted, "They must be driven ta strike down the cords holdin' our future in position - you, Princess, *and* the lad."

"Right," Conn said, "but no fleet ever passed through our catapults surroundin' the bay. They are armed and waitin' as we speak."

"There's no reason ta believe the Áiteoir know the princess is here," Gilroy said. "We saw them move quickly only ta take Alastar.

They spared no effort, and we should expect a fierce fight from land and sea. They only need ta cut one cord ta have our future fall shatterin' ta the floor."

Alastar didn't like the idea that an entire city was in danger because of him. "Can't we negotiate with them? I don't sit well knowin' I'm the cause of sufferin' and death ta so many. If they only seek me, perhaps. . ."

"Strike those thoughts, lad!" Teague burst out. "Did ya not get the Áiteoir want ya *dead?!* The princess as well. What could we possibly negotiate with 'em? Your surrender?"

"Right," Gearóid said. "They'd kill ya before ya could lift a banner 'a truce. And even if ya leave the isle, they'll finish what they started here. Lacharan will be under the edge of their axe until they confirm your death."

"You were sent ta Lacharan for reason," Gilroy said. "You're among many friends now."

"And fighters," Gearóid added. "The time now is ta stand and battle. You've a noble soul ta give yourself up for the rest of us, but that is not ta be. We stand with ya, lad. It's time ya learn we stand together, and we do not give up our ground, not till we've bled dry."

Alastar's spirit lifted with the support of his friends, but he still worried over them. "I'm grateful for your boundless support. What do we do now?"

"I was charged with your trainin', lad," Teague said. "It was Conall's order when we left. Ya have a mean swing. I imagine you'll take ta the sword right quick."

"I must be seein' ta the soldiers," Conn said. "The enemy will be near the bay soon." Conn hurried out the room.

"Where do ya stay, Alastar?" Amber asked.

"We were in the barracks by the north gate, Princess," Alastar replied.

"I invite ya and Teague ta stay at the palace with us. It is secure. You can train without disruption. The servants will show your quarters. I bid you leave now. Is there further business I need attend ta here?"

Gilroy looked at Gearóid and Teague. They showed no signs of needing to speak. "None, Princess," he said. "Only stay at the palace and notify the duke or myself if you need go anywhere. We need ta stay t'gether for the time bein'."

Amber nodded at Gilroy. "Certainly, Chancellor. I leave the defense of Lacharan ta your capable hands. I will settle in. Be free ta ask the servants for whatever ya need." She turned and made a curt bow toward the others.

"Thank ya, Princess, for sharin' your home with us," Teague said. "We are most grateful."

"Most grateful," Alastar added awkwardly. Amber smiled at him with a disarming charm that made him uneasy. She was beautiful and had fair skin like Nola, but like their hair – one dark, the other golden – they seemed to oppose each other. Nola had a simple, unrestrained joy and more obvious allure about her, while Amber had a graceful glow and careful demeanor that gave her unadorned features a more subdued beauty.

Amber turned around and left the room.

"Lad," Teague said with a smile, "I think you've found another grebe in the lake."

"What are ya sayin'? I've already given my heart," Alastar said with firm denial of attraction for Amber.

Gilroy eyed Alastar and was about to speak when Teague cut him off. "I believe it was just a dradairín ya gave Nola, lad." Teague grinned and slapped Alastar's shoulder in jest.

"A potato?" Gilroy said. "The jokin' of ya young folk is beyond me, but set not your heart in stone, son," he told Alastar. "Let the currents and time tell ya who you're meant ta be with before ya go snarin' after a bird. Many restless hearts find themselves trapped in fleetin' love; givin' in ta impressions that fade away. True love, son, etches its colors into our hearts ta change our very soul. Its colors do not wash away in rain nor storm."

True love? Alastar wondered. *Is love not love?* He did not understand what Gilroy was saying. A bewildered look came upon him, but he feigned understanding. "I'm certain I love Nola, sir, but I will be watchful."

Gilroy sensed Alastar's confusion. "Just be patient, son. Do not bind yourself ta see only one or another with a lover's eyes. Your heart cannot see clearly of itself. Be watchful of the signs of true destiny as you've already been given in this journey. Remember where they point ta, so ya can ignore the distractions tryin' ta lead ya stray."

Signs of true destiny? Alastar wondered. *Things and circumstances fitting together inexplicably in an intricate puzzle? Like the grape vines at the stone arch that matched my staff's carving? And how Amber's pendant and the rainbow matched the glowing symbols? But what about Nola appearing to be the Nuala I wished for?* By everyone's reckoning, he wasn't meant to meet Nola as he did. Likewise, he knew they'd say he should see Amber as a potential 'grebe'. *But her importance is of another nature,* he thought. *It couldn't be to build a family with her too.*

"Let's get ta trainin' ya on the sword, lad," Teague said. "Get your head outta spinnin' over destiny and shimmerin' grebes." He turned to Gearóid. "Have ya a spare sword for the lad?"

Gearóid unclasped his scabbard and gave it to Alastar. "Take my sword, lad. Yours ta keep. I've been waitin' for a reason ta go back ta the sword my father gave me long ago. This new one never felt right in my hands."

"I'm honored, Duke," Alastar said, "I accept it thankfully." He held it with both hands. It was longer than his leg from hilt to tip and only slightly heavier than his ironwood staff. The grip of the solid bronze hilt was wrapped in ruddy, brown leather and the hand guard was a simple, thick cross with a disc at its center. The pommel was a smaller disc at the end of the hilt that had raised artwork of gold, silver and jewels on both of its flat sides. One side had a three-leaf clover knot of gold twine with a round opal at its center, while the other side displayed a harp with a body of hawk's eye gemstone and gold strings.

Like the pommel, the larger disc in the hand guard also had designs on both sides. Alastar looked closer at the etching on the large disc. It was a crest. He was surprised to recognize the image of the horse in it. It was the same leaping horse as the glowing symbol on the cliff face. The image was unmistakable. It was set inside the outline of a shield with a crossed sword and spear in the background. He saw similar crests on the banners of Torthúil and on Conall and Teague's ring clasps and other people's uniforms, but he never looked closely until now. "What does this crest mean?" he asked.

"It is the crest of the Eachraighe, son," Gearóid said. "Ya are now an honorary clan member."

"I have no words for this," Alastar said. "Truly destiny is worked as I've never seen before. But why is the crest different than that of Torthúil? The crown on top of the shield and eagle's wings are missin'."

"The crown and wings were added after the kingdom was established generations ago," Gilroy said. "In times before, the Eachraighe were only one clan of many throughout the isle. The first king of Rathúnas united many clans in the east and founded Cnoc na Rí, the Hill of the King, ta be the throne of Torthúil. Since that time, other kingdoms came forth in the north, south and west, but the north and south fell ta the Áiteoir Kingdom in recent years. Now our kingdom stands alone against them, and diminished at that. We lost most of our small towns ta the Áiteoir."

"I must leave this grand history lesson," Gearóid said. "I will be at the north gate ta see that our walls are not breached. Teague, use the common terrace on the roof for trainin' the lad. It's quiet and ya can see if trouble brews in the bay. But first, settle inta rooms. The servants will show your way." Gearóid walked out the room and told a servant to fetch his sword.

"I must send word ta the king and ask for aid," Gilroy said. "I expect the enemy ta force their way inta the bay. The city walls can hold for many days, but if the bay is taken, we'd be pressed against a hammer with none but the sea's mist ta shield us."

"Didn't the captain say no fleet ever passed through the defenses?" Alastar said.

"That he did," Gilroy responded. "But the Áiteoir wouldn't send a fleet if they did not think they could prevail."

Teague added, "I've already sent a seabhac ta Loch an Scátháin for word. I expect we'll hear from 'em by day's end. Perhaps Conall can come with the garrison of Dún Tearmann, if they're not busy enough themselves."

"How do ya think they fare?" Alastar asked with concern for his friends.

"Worry not, son," Gilroy said. "The Greerian have not reported any more border crossin's. It appears the enemy is focused entirely on gettin' to you."

"Right," Teague added. "And Conall is our best commander. The company attacking Loch an Scátháin couldn't have gotten far." He looked at the sword in Alastar's hands. "Come here, lad. The sword is not a staff. You're ta wear it 'n make it a part of your body."

Alastar stepped forward and Teague showed him how to fasten the scabbard around his waist under his long coat. Teague stepped back to appraise the results. Alastar stood tall and the sword complimented his clothing nicely, but he appeared awkward and unconfident.

Teague noted, "We have some thin's ta work on, and your coat needs a seam in back ta let out the sword, but it suits ya well, like horns on a bull. Grand altogether, lad."

"Very good," Gilroy said. "I will find you men at a later hour." He nodded at them and left.

A servant was waiting at the door to show Teague and Alastar their rooms. "This way gentlemen," he said.

They followed him through finely decorated corridors to the top floor. He stopped in a long hallway and opened a door. The servant looked at Teague. "Your room, sir." They looked through the doorway and were impressed to see a gorgeous sea view framed by large windows. The room itself was lavishly decorated in shades of ivory and rose burgundy.

The servant pointed down the hall. "Access ta the terrace is at the end of the hall, through the parlor." He looked at Alastar. "Sir, your room is the next adjacent. This way."

Alastar followed him to the next room that faced the sea. The servant opened the door and Alastar was greeted with another spacious room with a beautiful view of the sea. His room was decorated in hues of gold, green and natural wood. He'd never seen such luxury and felt as if he were a chunk of burnt coal thrown into a bag of brilliant gems.

"Thank ya, sir," Alastar said.

"Certainly, sir. If ya be needin' anythin', pull the rope by the bed a few times and someone will be right up for ya. And so ya know, the princess is in the wing past the parlor and the duke and chancellor have rooms below ya."

"Thank ya, sir," Alastar said. He went into his room and took off his long coat and sword. He sat down in a plush chair by a window and looked out at the bay. It was a sunny calm view that hid the turmoil of the unfolding events, like a pleasant daydream come to distract a weary traveler. This was quite a change from the barn at the Conalls'. He never would have imagined being set in so many different and strange surroundings during the past days. He couldn't help wonder what else was in store for him.

A knock came from the open door. "Bring your sword, lad," Teague said.

They went up to the terrace to begin Alastar's swordsmanship lessons. The terrace on the roof was more like a large courtyard than a balcony. It was paved with stone and exhibited beautiful gardens that matched the palace grounds. A low railing of the same white stone the palace was built with fenced in the terrace and provided a bright underline to the wide bay and deep sea beyond.

The views in Rathúnas keep getting better and better, Alastar thought. The sea was calm; a stunning blue expanse, much different than the continually gray, churning seas at home in Netleaf.

"Have ya seen the sea so beautiful in the bright of day?" Alastar asked.

"Grand surely, but ya haven't seen Cnoc na Rí. It's set in the high mountains at the mouth of the River Valley. The city of smooth marble and granite shines a pearl as the sun smiles on her from the sea each morn. And the royal gardens line the steps of the sea, like an elegant tapestry laid over the whole north of the bay; overflowin' with flowers, trees and shrubs; all colors and shapes. Swans commingle in the ponds and musicians play in the courtyards. I'd say ya won't find a lovelier place ta stroll with one of your grebes, lad."

"I've got only one," Alastar said.

"Right, just one ta end up with. I imagine a time 'a choosin' will come for ya, lad."

Why did everyone think he would have to choose? Alastar already had his mind set on being with Nola, if she'd have him. He felt being with her was a certainty after all the trouble with the Áiteoir would fade away. "Why is it ya have in your minds that Amber and I are ta be more than. . . than, whatever we are; you and Gilroy? Do the Glasa say somethin' more about the Swan-bearer and the Swans Family?" Alastar asked with concern.

"Don'tcha put yourself in bits, lad. Ya look like someone banjaxed your whole life. I don't think the Glasa say anythin' more about the matter. Just pay mind ta the currents. Ya made it here, right where you're supposed ta be." He looked at Alastar and gave him a forceful push to quickly change the subject. Alastar almost fell over. "See how you're top-heavy?" Teague told him. "Ya need ta stand strong and steady with your sword; make a solid base ta swing from. And more sideways, so your frame's a narrow target." Teague turned sideways and pointed his left leg forward. Then he brought his rear foot back and farther out so it was in line with the edge of his hip. He bent his knees slightly and turned his rear foot to point forward and right. "Go on, make your frame."

Alastar mimicked Teague's posture. Teague went to him and shoved him again. This time Alastar hardly moved.

"Can ya feel your base is solid now?" Teague queried as he stepped back to make some distance between them.

Alastar nodded in acknowledgement.

"Now draw your sword and attack me," Teague commanded.

Alastar drew his sword somewhat clumsily and ran forward

with his sword held back, ready to make a big swing. Teague quickly drew his own sword and swung it at Alastar while he moved to the side at the same time to avoid Alastar's swing. He smacked Alastar's left shoulder with the flat edge of his blade before Alastar had his sword halfway toward its target.

"Grand try!" Teague said, "But did ya notice how easy it was for me ta strike ya?"

Alastar gave a look of disappointment. "This is harder than it looks. I think I rather prefer the longer reach of my staff."

"Amaideach, lad! One quick block 'a your staff and I'd be inside your defense ta finish ya. A longer reach doesn't always make for a better weapon," Teague noted. "You need learn the proper manner 'a usin' your sword. It's like ridin' your horse. Would ya try havin' Éimhín jump before he could steer left 'n right?"

Alastar smiled as he remembered how Éimhín lept out of the deep canal. "Éimhín's right grand leapin' 'bout without my help!"

"Sure, that horse *would* be runnin' with hardly a tug 'a the reins. You, though, need learn how ta steer before leapin' with your sword. When ya came after me, ya broke two rules ta remember. First, ya lost your solid frame when you charged me and held the sword high. And two, ya came at me with naught but your skin in defense."

Alastar looked puzzled. "What else do I have ta protect me but my sword?"

"*Right!*" Teague remarked. "Use it in the proper manner and you'll have a defense much better than a full suit 'a armor. We need train ya ta move with your sword first and have it pointed square at your enemy when you aren't swingin' it. The point of a sword boltin' straight at your face will make ya think right quick 'a how ta make defense instead of the other way round."

They spent over an hour in the afternoon sun going over basic use of the sword. Alastar never knew there were so many subtleties in handling it, but he learned quickly and the sword soon felt like a natural extension to his body. They were growing tired of lunging, stepping and parrying when they heard tower bells ring. Teague looked to the right, at the far end of the bay. A number of distant ships were turning inward toward the bay.

"The Áiteoir fleet," Teague said. "They're still too distant for the catapults ta reach."

Alastar tried to count the vessels. They were barely larger than dots on the water. "There must be a hundred out there." Then he scanned the bay for friendly warships, but saw only merchant vessels. "Why aren't there any warships in the bay?"

"Torthúil is a peaceful kingdom. We have few warships and they all dock at Cnoc na Rí. Even those are used mainly ta escort the king. Conquest outside the isle was never of part of our history. Defense from enemy fleets is fought from the shore.

"Fear not, lad. The defenses of Lacharan have fought off fleets larger than this. The Áiteoir must think their siege ships make advantage for 'em. I've not seen any as large as them, but their catapults are still smaller than ours. Lacharan will have 'em in flames before they come close 'nough ta be a threat."

More tower bells began to ring around the bay and the sounds of soldiers preparing were heard coming from beyond the trees in the south. They stood watching the fleet approach for many minutes. Most of the dark ships were lined with large oars that came out their sides in addition to having sails. The dozen siege ships were twice the size of any others and had large paddle wheels in the rear instead of sails and oars.

The fleet came just outside the entrance to the bay and stopped, beyond range of the defenses. Many more minutes passed and the ships did not move.

"They've anchored," Teague said. "What are they plannin'?"

They stared at the fleet a while longer without any further movement from the ships. "Perhaps they wait for the army ta breach the walls," Alastar said.

"They'd wait a long time. Can't be that. If they take us by sea, they could open the city gates from the inside much faster."

Teague and Alastar were watching the fleet when servants came onto the terrace with trays of food and drink. "Cupán tae, scones 'n brisket?" one of the servants said. "Ordered by the princess for you gentlemen." They placed the trays on a table and stood ready to serve.

"Wonderful timin'!" Teague said. "Thank ya." He gave Alastar a soft nudge on the shoulder and said, "See, lad. The princess has ya on mind. Fancy her a grebe or not, you'd be amiss ta bar yourself from becomin' fella from friend ta her."

Alastar replied with agitation, "Are ya gonna be pesterin' about the princess all the while? I've already met someone. Grebes are loyal ta their mates, aren't they?"

"For a season, I'd say. Not that you or Nola have wanderin' eyes, but swans do have the nature ta choose a mate for life. Ya do seem ta have that swan nature in ya, lad."

They walked to the table and had their lunch. All the while they kept watch on the enemy ships, but the fleet held to the same position. Hours passed as they finished eating and went back to sword training. When the sun passed into late afternoon, Teague stopped the training.

"That's enough for t'day," Teague said. "You've learned well, but your sword arm will be sore t'morrow. Still, practice everythin' I've shown ya whenever ya can – stance, footwork, sheathin', unsheathin', parryin'; all of it. Your movements will be more precise and your mind will etch it in with practice. You'll be a master swordsman as ya are a woodcarver in time. Sooner the better. The next fight can come at any time."

"I'm grateful for your help. I'm findin' the sword ta be a pleasant skill. Makes me feel more a soldier than not."

"Grand, lad. Soon we'll get ya armor as well. Get rest now. I'm off ta see if Bress is back from Loch an Scátháin and ta speak with the duke on matters. Stay at the palace. We'll find ya in the evenin'." Alastar acknowledged and Teague left. Alastar turned to the bay again and saw the fleet still had not moved. *What could they be waiting for?*

Fine Threads

*A*lastar decided to walk the palace grounds and headed down to the stables to check on Éimhín. He walked with a new confidence, as if the sword hanging from his hip surrounded his whole body with impenetrable armor. He practiced walking with the sturdy frame and solid footing he learned in training, but he did it clumsily. He walked about stiffly and people around the palace eyed him curiously.

He found Éimhín eating from another large bucket of fodder in a stall. "How ya farin', boy?"

Éimhín looked up at him chewing. Alastar rubbed his coat for a moment and then turned to his side to show the sword. "Look! I'm an official rider now. . . or whatever 'honorary' means. It's all part of the plan woven in the currents. You and I have some work ta do with the Eachraighe and princess 'n all."

He remembered how Éimhín seemed urgent to return home days before. "I'm afraid we aren't returnin' home for some time. Not sure if it's even ta be." He started to feel sad about his mother, who was now home alone. Do his friends and family even notice their long absence? They traveled back in time. What did that mean for everyone in Netleaf and the isle he knew?

"No time ta dwell on those thin's now. Ya finish your meal. I saw a garden in the back of the palace I'll tread about."

Alastar left the stables and walked to the rear of the palace. He was still consciously trying to walk with the gait of a swordsman, and from time to time he quickly placed his right hand on the sword's grip and drew it out with a forward stomp of his foot to keep balance and form. Since no one was around, he walked into the garden like that. However, he didn't realize Amber was on the roof terrace and watched him walk about the garden like a child immersed in a new found trinket. He waved the sword about, parried, and thrust, like a boy who explored the workings of a mysterious treasure. She smiled. His awkward seriousness was a refreshing contrast. Everyone else around her exhibited the well-poised manner of royal society.

She remembered thinking earlier that Alastar didn't even have a sword. Now all of a sudden her empty handed champion had one and was very intent on using it correctly. *He certainly has the determination,* she thought.

"You're a quick hand!" Amber yelled to him from the terrace.

Alastar stopped practicing and looked around. He didn't see anyone. Then he looked up and saw Amber leaning over the terrace stone railing. He stood in shock for a moment when he saw how different she looked. Her golden hair was down, draped about her shoulders, and she wore a light, simple dress of peach silk. It shimmered satin and flowed solid with the pale, rosy color of fresh salmon flesh. Her large amber pendant dangled from her neck in front of her. It reminded him again of the glowing symbols and the currents of destiny. It all made him uneasy to be thrust together with her.

He noticed her cheeks were slightly pink and the way she gazed at him made him blush as well. He felt a rushing tremor in his heart, and he had to quickly look away. "Princess," he answered and tried to continue in the movements of practice.

"You're makin' a fine swordsman," she called back.

Alastar tried not to look at her and was starting to fumble his movements under her stare, so he stopped and lowered his sword. "Thank ya, Princess. Do ya see the enemy fleet?" he yelled back, still not looking at her. She laughed inside seeing that he was trying to avoid eye contact.

"They're still far off," she answered. "Hold on! I'm comin'

down!"

Alastar looked up and saw her leave the railing and disappear into the palace. He didn't realize how tense he was around her just then. He never felt that way before. He sheathed his sword and anxiously paced the garden. He couldn't concentrate and kept telling himself to treat her like any other friend. He shouldn't be nervous around her. Unfortunately, his racing heart and apprehension to look into her eyes made him feel otherwise.

What's wrong with me?! he wondered with frustration. He had his heart set on Nola and put it firmly in his head that he just needed to act normally around Amber. After all, he grew up being friends with Nuala and other girls. *How hard could it be? Just be normal but keep my distance.*

Then he remembered how hurt he felt when Nuala didn't return his affection. He didn't want Amber to feel like that. He couldn't really tell what kind of feelings Amber had for him. He wondered, *Is it more than casual friendliness? She's a good natured, pleasant girl. Her smile could bring warmth to a cold autumn rain. Maybe she always has a radiant charm about her?* Alastar convinced himself that he was exaggerating any attraction between them. *Nothing to worry about,* he told himself.

Amber appeared from a patio door that faced the garden. She smiled and walked to him with a beautiful grace. Alastar returned her smile, but tried not to appear too pleasant. "Princess, ya didn't have ta come down," he said.

"I couldn't stand yellin' 'cross the way," she replied. She tried to point out his avoidance of eye contact. "It's flusterin' ta not speak eye ta eye," she said with a suggestive glance and slight grin.

Alastar smiled at her teasing and looked down for a moment. Then he looked forward still intent on keeping his eyes off her. "Your garden is wonderful, Princess."

"Thank you. I haven't seen it in years, but it looks just as it did when I left. Have ya seen all of it?"

"I haven't."

"Let me show you." Amber started to walk towards the right where a white gazebo was set on a small hill near the shore. Alastar walked next to her and kept his distance. They passed rows of sculpted hedges, and then found themselves in front of many rows of densely planted flowers. They were arrayed in curved rows before the gazebo with a stone path in the middle. The back rows had taller plants that led to the shortest in front.

"These are the radiants," she said.

"Like guelder rose?"

"Right." Amber pointed towards the gazebo. "The guelder rose are used ta circle the gazebo. My mam added 'em for her weddin'. She loved their bundles of flowers. She said they had ringed bouquets all 'round, just in time for their weddin'. My parents were married right there." Amber rushed forward on the path. "Look! They're all in full bloom!"

Alastar ran after her and passed rows of roses, valerian, orchids, forget-me-nots, violets, and daisies. Amber stopped by a guelder rose bush and plucked off a large, puffy bundle of blossoms. They sparkled bright white as she jostled them about. She brought the flowers up to her nose, closed her eyes, and breathed in deeply. A broad smile washed over her face as a memory returned to her.

Amber lowered the flowers. "Mam used to take these bundles and chase me 'round the garden with 'em. She had in her mind they were good for smackin' people in the face. *'A right bit better than a snowball in the face 'n much more fun,'* she'd say. The gardeners used ta get angry at mam for leavin' flower petals everywhere after her guelder rose rampages."

Alastar smiled and remembered how he left the guelder rose bushes on the cliff with fallen petals everywhere. He looked into Amber's deep, green eyes for a moment. She was shorter than him by slight inches. They were nearly eye to eye, and he could see the shimmering dust from the flowers lingering on her face. Then she looked into his eyes and he looked away. Something about her doe-eyed gaze made him feel as if he could not stand to stare back.

"Where is your mam now?" he asked.

"She died about eight years ago, from fever. I still miss her. . . and dadaí." Amber noticed again how Alastar avoided eye contact and wondered why he was so intent on keeping distant. "Have ya someone ya miss, Alastar?" she asked, intending to find out if he had a girlfriend.

"Sure. I miss my parents as well. My father died round about five years ago 'n my mother, well, she must be worried where Éimhín and I have disappeared ta. At least I think she's worried. We were ta be back home a day or two ago."

"Why wouldn't your mam worry?"

Alastar pondered if he should speak frankly. She must know the Glasa better than most, considering her position. She would understand easily. "I'm not so sure my mam notices we've gone this long. Éimhín and I traveled the ages ta be here now. We found a gateway, or rather, we found one prepared for us. It took us back in time, but I haven't a clue if we can get home again."

"Right. I figured that's why you're not quite like anyone I've met. You've only been here a couple days. Ya couldn't be missin' anyone else, could ya? Back at home?" Amber looked at him with curiosity, but Alastar didn't quite understand what she was getting at.

"Ya mean my friends? Can't say I miss anyone else at home,

not terribly. We've only been gone a few days."

"Then ya haven't a mot?" she asked with her eyes brightened in the thought he could be unattached to a girl.

Alastar didn't understand what she asked. "A mot?. . ."

"A *girl*, who you'd be givin' affection ta." Amber looked at him with such a tangible yearning. It troubled Alastar she was showing deeper interest for him. He was finding it hard to tell her about Nola.

"I. . . emm. . . in Loch an Scáthain. Ya could say I miss someone there," he said with difficulty. Amber's bright face washed over with disappointment. Then a thought hit her.

"*Loch an Scáthain?!*" Amber retorted. Her disappointment quickly turned into fiery disapproval. "You were barely there a day! And from what I hear, ya weren't even meant ta be there!" She turned around and started walking past the gazebo towards the shore.

Alastar felt bad. He couldn't say a word; nothing that would bring her the comfort she wanted. He followed her to the stony beach where Amber stood staring at the Áiteoir fleet in the distance. She plucked at the guelder rose blossoms and tossed the petals into the water. They glowed and shimmered opalescent light as she plucked them and dropped them into the sea. Her future was at a precarious balance. What was the enemy planning? Would they be successful? And her hopes of being with her Swan-bearer as she had always dreamt were being cast into the sea and carried away, like the delicate white petals floating in the water at her feet.

The Glasa never said anything about the Swan-bearer and her family becoming more than a working relationship, but since childhood she had dream visions of marrying her champion, even before she knew about her family's destiny. She felt it in her heart the Swan-bearer would be hers. She kept her heart in reserve knowing that destiny could be trampled on if the heart was allowed to stray after things it was not meant to keep, so she didn't let a single boy catch her attention until Alastar came along. Now that he arrived, she couldn't help but feel sorrow that his heart wanted someone else.

Alastar stood beside her and could see she was feeling pain, but he didn't know what to say. He watched the flower petals bob about in the water. They still glowed like the symbols on the cliff face. A thought hit him and he started to scoop up all the petals. Amber stopped plucking at the flowers and watched him.

He knelt down and started to lay out the petals on the beach to make the image of Amber's pendant, like he saw on the cliff and when the sun made it glow on the dock that morning. He tore some petals to make the smaller details. Amber watched him with amazement as she recognized the image of her pendant. "You're an artist," she said softly.

Alastar remained silent and kept using the petals to finish the pendant's image. Then he used more petals to make a rainbow over it. When he finished he said, "See, even the fallen petals are used for the brightness of dawn." He looked up at Amber. "These images were at the gateway that brought me here. I know they speak of ya and that my destiny is intertwined with yours, Princess. But I cannot promise anythin' but my loyalty ta serve ya as the currents show. Is that a fair promise?"

Amber returned his promise with a sweet smile. "It is well. I couldn't ask anythin' else of ya."

Alastar stood up and looked at the guelder rose bundle in her hand. It was mostly bare stems with few petals remaining on it. He took it from her hand and tossed it far out into the sea. "Ya don't want ta keep hold of plucked and frazzled dreams like that. Starin' at 'em just aches your heart. Keep your mind on better things 'n what's ta be done at hand."

Amber gave him an earnest smile. "Ya have more wisdom than your age seems ta carry. Thank you."

"I only know what I know. A friend recently told me ta mind the mission when all I could think about was ta turn back n' see ta my heart's concerns. Some things are too big for us ta handle, but if we just do our part as the currents show, I've found things work out just as they should."

Alastar looked out towards the fleet. "Do ya think the Áiteoir wait for nightfall?"

"I don't know why," she answered. "They couldn't slip past the guard even in the dark. There are many eyes on 'em."

"And what of the enemy at the walls? Aren't ya worried about 'em?"

"The walls held solid for many months the last time they sieged," she replied. "Their supply and resolve ran out far before ours. Gilroy said they sent a much larger force this time, but he and the duke are confident we'll hold strong as before."

The wind began to pick up. It sent Amber's long hair flapping about and the petals on the ground fluttered off. She grabbed after strands of her hair that waved across her face and brushed them behind her. She looked over at Alastar and lingered on the features of his kind face. His light brown hair waved about his head in a tossed mess. She felt the urge to reach out her hand and fix it, but she held back. Would destiny bring her dreams to fruit with him? Or were they no more than the imaginings of a youthful heart?

Alastar sensed she was looking at him and turned to face her. He saw again that yearning gaze pierce through him as if her dewy, round eyes sang to his soul. He couldn't hold his gaze upon her and looked quickly to the right where he saw the radiants shimmer and spark lights of many colors as the wind blew them. "The garden takes on new life when it's tossed in the wind," he said.

Amber looked to the flowers. "It does. I used ta watch the flowers dance with their lights for hours when storms came and in the heavy winds of spring, like now. I always loved the rainstorms. The lights 'n swayin' were more vibrant in the dim tusslin' of thunder 'n heavy rain. It was like the garden put on a cheery show every storm that came. I was always sad when the blossoms left at the end of summer."

Standing on the shore with the swift wind around them reminded Alastar of home. The shores around Netleaf were much like this. He couldn't help feel the warmth of familiar appreciation. "This place feels like home; the sea and wind, I mean. We don't have radiants where I come from."

"I would like to see your home, Alastar. . . if it is ta be. I do hope you see your mam 'n friends again."

"I'd like that too," he said before he realized she might think he wanted her to see his home as more than a friend. "Emm. . . ta see my mam, 'n all."

Amber smiled inwardly understanding his hesitation. "Let me show you the rest of the grounds." She started to walk down the beach and Alastar followed by her side. She showed him the boathouse where she would pretend to sail the far seas when she was a girl. Sometimes she would run out there to hide when she was angry or distraught. It was one of the few places she could find complete privacy until someone came to pry her back into the scrutinizing eyes of palace life.

They explored the rest of the garden. It covered the entire rear of the palace grounds along the sea. Alastar never saw so many artistic arrangements of flowers and bushes. It also had an area of sculpted evergreen bushes that were shaped into the forms of animals – horses, lions, fish, eagles and swans.

Amber paused by a large dense bush sculpted into two swans that faced each other. Alastar immediately recognized them. They matched the first glowing symbol on the cliff wall. "The very first Ealaí was my great, great, great grandfather," she said. "He took the name after comin' here ta build a home with his new wife. He was amazed at all the swans in the river and ponds here. People came ta callin' him Ealaí - Swans - when he'd gift swans or use 'em ta barter. He was the first ta settle here and founded Lacharan.

"He also took ta horse breedin' 'n had many; more than any other on the isle at the time. When Lacharan grew, the swans diminished and the horses flourished. Ealaí became the first chief of the Eachraighe when they united all the families in this part of the isle."

"Did your grandfather Ealaí found Cnoc na Rí as well?"

"His father, Rían ["Ree-en"], built Cnoc na Rí many years after Ealaí built Lacharan. When King Rían died, Ealaí was the rightful heir ta the throne. He was eldest son, but decided ta relinquish the right ta his brother, Lorcán. King Fuar is the last in Lorcán's line. He has no heir of his own. It appears my family is next ta inherit the throne."

Alastar wondered why Amber would need any help to ascend to the throne. It appeared to be set without need for his help. "What would be for me ta do then if you're already in line ta take the throne?"

Amber felt she already knew his place was by her side to reign together, but she couldn't tell him. The Glasa and her dreams implied it. Her family and even the chancellor knew she waited to be with her Swan-bearer, but Gilroy always cautioned her not to jump to conclusions. He told her dreams are often symbolic metaphors and not literal. *Don't take more out of them than what was shown,* he'd say. *Sometimes our hearts want things that aren't meant to be - to marry a certain person or just to marry once for a lifetime. But how often do we see desires whither or our lives tumble when things don't work out as we plan? Haven't you seen many a widow find love again, even more than once? We'd be wonderfully blessed to share a lifetime with one person who is dear to our heart, but still blessed to love again after losing a spouse tragically. Time will tell in the currents what is meant for you. Still, A Chara ["ah kahr-rah"; my/dear friend], your heart is right to be faithful to the one you are meant to be with. Only be certain that faith is set on the right person.*

Amber turned from the sculpture and looked at Alastar. "You are my Swan-bearer, my Champion. I will need your help and I'm grateful you pledged ta me." Her steady gaze and earnest words seeped into his soul. He felt the wholeness of purpose and harmony that he just started to feel when he arrived on Rathúnas. It was ringing through him now, like Amber had suddenly removed a heavy blanket that muffled all his senses.

Alastar started to feel uncomfortable under her eyes again. He mustered a slight smile of affection. "I will do what can, Princess. I do wonder. . . Am I prepared for all I need do?"

"I do not doubt ya," she said firmly. "Neither should you."

The sincerity of Amber's confidence in him sent resolve through him. So many things about her made him feel that he couldn't turn away from helping her. He felt it was the right course for him, but his heart ached to see Nola. He looked away from Amber to find a distraction and saw two interesting sculptures at the far end of the garden. They were two eagles with the body of lions that faced each other to make an arched doorway with their wings.

"What animals make the arch?" he asked.

"Those are griffins of Torthúil. They roost in the highest peaks round Cnoc na Rí. Said ta be guardians for the king. I've only seen 'em from afar when I visited Cnoc na Rí long ago. They were far off, but I could see they were much larger than I imagined. Even a tall mountain pine would have snapped if one landed on it."

"We could've used one or two of 'em last night ta fight off the fáelshee," Alastar said. "I never saw beasts so fierce and great in size. I was afraid Éimhín was about ta have his neck bit straight through before Gilroy blinded the wolf."

"You were blessed ta make it here safely."

"I am grateful for that, but many good soldiers died helpin' me, and the enemy keeps pressin' on. I wish there was a way ta end this bloodshed."

"Don't let your feelin's sway ya from a steady course," she said. "It's a basic lesson they teach ta those who'd rule, but everyone could heed it. Who'd ever get ta a goal if they keep changin' course at every flight of the heart?" Amber smiled trying to suggest he should mind the fancies of his heart. "I'd be tucked out, like a mouse swimmin' against a river's flow."

"I wouldn't say ta go against the currents," he replied. "What if there's a different way ta reach the goal? Sometimes the branches keep us from seein' the outline of a simpler design." He tried using a metaphor from woodcarving, but Amber looked at him puzzled. "Here, I'll show ya. Come ta the stables with me."

They exited the sculpture garden through the griffin archway. The front courtyard was just beyond. They made their way across the front and walked to the stables on the other side. Servants and guards around the palace watched them as they entered the stables. Everyone murmured about Alastar and how Amber finally found her Swan-bearer. Even though a strong siege was upon them, it hardly gave them concern. Their spirits were lifted in many hopes with the currents of destiny showing its flow through Alastar's appearance in Rathúnas.

Inside the stables, a page tended Éimhín and wiped his coat with a brush.

"Takin' good care of Éimhín, I see," Alastar told the boy.

"Surely, sir. He's the mightiest horse I've laid eyes on." Then the page saw Amber next to Alastar and nodded to her. "Princess. But your horse is still the prettiest I've seen."

Alastar looked about the stables and wondered which of the dozen horses was Amber's. "Which is yours, Princess?"

"Muirgel ["Mer-gel"] is just beyond Éimhín," she replied. She pointed to an elegant, slender horse with gold flaxen hair.

"I should've known," Alastar said. "You and Muirgel have the same shinin' hair."

"Sure 'nough," Amber said, "But our best feature is we're quick on our feet. What are we here for now, Alastar?"

"Right." Alastar went to Éimhín's stall to find his bundles of wood. He found them on the ground in the corner of the stall. He looked through the wood and tried to find a suitable piece. Amber and the stable page watched him curiously.

"Why do ya have so much wood?" Amber asked.

"Hold on. I'll show ya," he replied. He selected a stick with gray-white bark and many stubs of branches on it. The main stalk was wider at one end and tapered narrow toward the other. He stood up and held it out for Amber to see. "What does this look like?"

"An alder branch," she said quickly.

"Right," he said, but he expected a different answer. "Do ya see anythin' more in it?"

"It looks like an arrow someone done wrong," the page burst out. Amber laughed and Alastar looked at the boy with a smile. "Sorry, sir, I didn't mean ta interrupt."

"Sure 'nough," Amber said, "An arrow done wrong. Quite

banjaxed the lot of it!" She laughed again and surprised Alastar with her lightheartedness. It was nice to see she was more than the always mindful and reserved royal heir.

Alastar tried to focus again. "The extra branches suggest somethin' ta your eyes. . . like your banjaxed arrow." He smiled. Then he pulled out a small knife and started to cut off most of the smaller branches on the stick so that it was more like a spike. "But once we trim off the things we don't want, it starts ta take a different form."

He started to shave the bark off and tapered the narrow end even more. Then he carved out the large end and its branch stubs to look like a simple half open rose with leaves underneath the blossom. The rough shapes were done quickly, within minutes. He finished by rounding off the tapered end and held out the rough sculpted piece for Amber.

"A rose hairpin for you, Princess," Alastar said.

Amber took the hairpin and examined it. "You've much skill ta do this so quickly. Thank ya for it. It's wonderful."

"You're very welcome, Princess. I am a woodcarver by trade. Passed on from my father."

Amber continued to look at the hairpin and contemplated. "Then you were meanin' ta say a solution ta a goal is not always so obvious."

Alastar smiled. "Quick on your feet, as ya said." He enjoyed speaking with her. It felt like they understood each other without much effort.

Amber grabbed her hair and twirled it about in the back of her head. She placed the hairpin in it and turned around. "How does it look?"

"Grand altogether!" the page answered.

"Splendid!" Alastar said. He thought the pale wood of the

hairpin blended in too much with the color of her hair. A rosy stain would make it a perfect accent. "Only it needs a smooth and final finish. Would ya mind if I use your kitchen ta make a stain for it? I'll have it set for ya tonight."

"Certainly," Amber said. "Only keep out of the way. The servants are busy preparin' dinner for us. That is, all of us – Gearóid, Gilroy, 'n Teague as well." She took the hairpin out of her hair and gave it back to Alastar. "Someone will take you ta the banquet hall when the time comes. I must see ta thin's now. It was a joy ta speak with ya." She gave Alastar a demure smile, then turned to the page and acknowledged him before leaving the stables.

The page waited for Amber to leave before speaking. "The princess has a softness for ya, sir. I've never seen her so comfortable with someone. She was hidin' it just now, under the formal speech. A bright fire she is, not so well with hidin' her feelin's."

"She is a wonder," Alastar said. "Only I have another girl in my heart."

"Are ya a mainidh! . . . er, sir," the boy exclaimed. "Forgive me. But aren't you *the* Swan-bearer? You and the princess are meant ta be together."

Alastar was shocked at the page's directness. Did everyone know he was the Swan-bearer? And now Amber wasn't the only one who thought they belonged together in a way he did not expect. "Sure, sure. We are ta be together. I'm ta champion her ta the throne, but I believe that is all I need do for her."

The boy gave Alastar a look of disappointment and turned back to brushing Éimhín. "I haven't many years, but I'm a fair hand at readin' people. I gather you're one who needs more time ta understand where he's meant ta go."

"You may be right," Alastar acknowledged. "I have felt a lot of confusion of late." He went to his saddle bags that hung on the stall railing and took out his tool kit, amber stones, and linseed oil. "Thank ya, lad, for carin' over Éimhín *and* myself." He pat Éimhín on the shoulder. "And a good night ta ya, boy," he told Éimhín.

Alastar left the stables to find the palace kitchen. A servant led him there where he found many people busy preparing a lavish dinner. He was amazed to see the kitchen was larger than his home in Netleaf. Long tables were at center and it had three fireplaces lined with stone hearths and two large wood burning stoves made of clay along the walls.

Alastar asked to use a small pot and fire. A servant led him to one of the stoves and gave him a pot. He proceeded to pour some of his linseed oil in the pot and waited for it to heat. While he waited, he used his tools to smooth out Amber's hairpin and give it finer details.

When the oil was hot, he selected some red-orange amber stones and put them in the oil. After some minutes, the amber melted and tinted the oil to make a golden rose-red stain. Alastar stirred the stain and let it cool. He continued to finish the hairpin and even sculpted the shaft into a winding spiral.

Many servants watched Alastar curiously as they worked. They minded their jobs, though, and didn't speak to him. Everyone knew he was the Swan-bearer, but most were surprised to find him to be an off-fitting young man who did not seem to know the first thing about war and royalty. However, his amiable nature and noble presence went a long way to give him immediate respect.

After some time, Alastar finished the hairpin and asked for a rag. He used it to work the stain into the hairpin. It was finished in seconds. It only needed to dry out before he could give it back to Amber. Then he asked for a small jar to keep his stain in and went upstairs to his room.

He was tired after a long day of walking, talking, and sword training. Seeing how Amber felt about their future together also weighed on him. If being the Swan-bearer wasn't hard enough for him to live up to, the thought of needing to live up to her expectations kept his mind turning restlessly.

He found solace in thinking only about Nola and the warm relationship they started. But then thoughts of Amber and her patient, joyful demeanor would turn him about again. Swans and grebes and wonders and destiny; it was all hard to absorb, so he just kept simple thoughts pinned to his heart, like he was sure he loved Nola and that it was no useless potato he gave to her. He firmly set his mind on being with Nola.

Almost an hour passed and Alastar had drifted to sleep when someone knocked on his door. "Sir. . . Sir, your presence is requested in the banquet hall." The servant knocked again and opened the door. "Sir!" he said loudly and woke up Alastar. "Your presence is requested in the banquet hall."

Alastar got up and straightened out his clothes. "Certainly. Thank you, sir." He grabbed Amber's hairpin from the windowsill. It was completely dry after sitting in the sunlight.

The servant noticed the hairpin. "Exquisite work, sir. Is it a gift?"

"Thank you. It is a gift."

"Then it should be wrapped." The servant went to a drawer and pulled out a white linen handkerchief and a length of red ribbon. He went to Alastar and held out his hand for the hairpin. Alastar gave it to him and he wrapped it, folding the linen into ruffles. He tied it with the ribbon and gave it back to Alastar. "There you are, sir. Would you like a scripted note with it?"

"I wouldn't, sir. This is fine enough a package. Thank you."

Alastar followed the servant down to the banquet hall where he saw everyone was already seated at the end of a long table. Gearóid and Amber sat opposite each other on the end. Gilroy and Teague were next. Alastar was escorted to take the seat next to Gilroy, opposite Teague and Amber.

"Thank you all for waitin'," Alastar said. He sat down and noticed how radiant Amber looked as he acknowledged and smiled at everyone. He consciously made sure not to give Amber any more attention than the others, but her vibrant purple gown, elegantly braided hair and bright face shined in his vision as if all else was dark. He wondered if he should give her the hairpin yet.

Gearóid spoke, "A grand welcome ta ya, lad, ta all here!" He lifted his wine glass up and toasted. "Princess, ta your safe return home. Gilroy, ta your trusted council. Teague, ta your solid eyes and soldierly hands. And Alastar, lad. . . ta your courage and new membership inta our clan." Everyone acknowledged and drank from their glasses. Gearóid nodded to a servant who started the dinner service.

The table quickly flooded with food of all kinds from servants who brought full platters that were duplicated for everyone – a roast pheasant for each person, bread and fruit and other things also on their own platters for each person. Alastar looked around the table with astonishment. He was very hungry, but who could eat so much food? Amber watched him closely and sensed the feast was a new experience for him.

"Take food as ya please, Alastar," she said. "Ya aren't expected ta eat all of it."

Teague stopped grabbing his food and looked at Alastar. "Right, lad. Feast as ya will. Ya look as if someone told ya ta eat a whole stack'a hay. Whatever ya don't eat won't be wasted. I'm likely ta finish it off for ya!"

"Right," Gearóid said. "Only if I don't get ta it first! Runnin' the walls and shores of the bay have me famished."

"How is the state of defenses?" Amber asked Gearóid.

"The wall is steady," Gearóid said. "The Áiteoir are not makin' a strong push, even though their numbers are far more than I've seen 'em march before. Most of the army stands back. They're just tryin' ta wear us out with soft punches till a certain time. I imagine they hold as their fleet does, waitin' on command. The ships haven't moved since they came ta the bay."

"We suspect they wait for dark of night in the comin' few days," Gilroy said. "Or an advantageous early mornin' fog ta conceal their movement. It's their best chance ta get past defenses."

"Sure 'nough," Gearóid said. "But the season for fog is not upon us. They will attack within a week. Their supplies on ship cannot last long if they hold as many troops as I imagine."

The talk of siege reminded Alastar of Loch an Scátháin and his friends there. "Teague, have ya word from Loch an Scátháin?" he asked.

"Surely do!" Teague burst out. "You'll be glad ta know, the Áiteoir were beat back. They destroyed the longhouse 'n many homes along the way, but Conall and the garrison fought inta the night until they retreated. Many died, but our friends are safe." Alastar wondered if Nola's home was spared, but he didn't want to ask in front of Amber.

"Grand news!" Gearóid said. "Grand altogether! The enemy is hard pressed ta take the good soldiers of Torthúil, like hammers on an anvil. They know our solid defenses. They must truly desire their hands on ya, Alastar, ta be makin' such bold moves now."

"They certainly do," Gilroy said. "All their movement shows a single effort ta take the boy. The Greerian reports show they retreated from Loch an Scátháin soon after Alastar and Teague were found in the plains. The mystery of how they knew about Alastar's arrival so quickly is hauntin', though. I fear Braede's disappearance is key."

"Are ya sayin' he's a traitor?" Gearóid said.

"It is possible," Gilroy answered.

"Braede has been loyal ta Torthúil ever since he came ta Loch an Scátháin," Teague said. "Became the king's emissary and worked with me for years. I wouldn't suspect him of turnin' on us. The Áiteoir ran him from his home and Loch an Scátháin gave him a new one. He wouldn't betray his new family for 'em."

"No one's accusin' just now," Gilroy said. "But we must consider all possibilities."

"Wouldn't the Greerian report if Braede went ta the enemy or sent them word?" Alastar asked.

"They would note his travelin' outside," Gilroy answered. "But he could send a message without our noticin'. The Áiteoir use enchanted bird mimics ta carry messages as we use our seabhac messengers. Their éanshee ["ayn-shee"] are not truly birds but animated figures ta look and act as birds - small crows, forest birds and the like. You'd not know an éanshee till ya caught hold of it. They're hard and cold as rock."

"But most in Torthúil can tell if an éanshee lingers around them," Amber said. "They're not smart as natural thin's and keep ta the same spot until they're needed by their owners. Ya can scare them off, but they'll soon return ta the same place ta await their callin'. A spy would have ta keep éanshee hidden or far from people."

"Are the fáelshee animated like the éanshee?" Alastar asked.

"The lion wolves are enchanted but not animated," Teague said. "They are true beasts. The Áiteoir put enchantments on 'em ta control 'em. They were bred from the wolves of the Rásúir Mountains where the cliffs are sharp obsidian and the forests turned ta burnt pitch from the poison heat underground. The mountains run ta the north shore of the isle there. Vast bog land surround 'em on the east, desert in the west, and like a bright pearl nestled in mud, the gleamin' Muir Airgid borders the mountains ta the south."

"The Muir Airgid. . . Silver Sea?" Alastar asked curiously.

"The brightest bit a water you'll ever see, lad," Gearóid said. "I haven't seen the Muir Airgid for over a decade. Hardly anyone in the kingdom has seen the inland sea since the Áiteoir took control of its borders."

"I remember it," Amber said. "My parents took me many years ago; the last summer mam was with us. Forests of water radiants shined through the waves everywhere. Nowhere else are there so many radiants. It was like the sea glowed with waves and streams of silvery sunlight from below. Even the fish and other animals livin' in the sea lit with light."

"It is a most spectacular place," Gilroy said. "Many people have tried ta transplant the sea radiants and stock elsewhere, but the radiants soon die in waters not of the Muir Airgid, and the animals lose their light if they stop eatin' the radiants." He looked over at Alastar. "Perhaps you will soon see the Muir Airgid when peace has covered Rathúnas."

"It would be a grand sight," Alastar said. The talk of animals eating radiants made him remember how Éimhín liked to eat the glowing guelder rose flowers. "What happens ta animals that eat radiants?" he asked. "Éimhín took ta likin' a guelder rose snack when we arrived here. I thought he'd get a bellyache eatin' the glowin' things 'n tried ta stop him, but he insisted." Amber smiled at Alastar's concern. At times he was a serious and determined person, but it was the moments he showed a soft and nurturing character that made her feel he was the champion she had been dreaming of.

Gilroy chuckled. "Your horse'll be just grand. Won't even glow just a bit. Only certain animals can take the light of radiants inta themselves."

"A shame then," Alastar said. "A glowin' horse would be a grand thing ta see. . ." He looked to Teague. "Unless ya need ta hide in the night that is."

"Right, lad," Teague said amused. "Let's hope we don't have ta do that again."

Everyone continued to enjoy the meal and leisurely company for a long time. When dinner service was complete Amber got up. "Excuse me, gentlemen. I will leave ya ta your social time. My time ta retire has come."

Everyone stood up and acknowledged Amber. She headed for the doorway when Alastar remembered the hairpin. He had kept it hidden under the table the entire time. He picked it up and went to Amber. Everyone else sat back down and continued in the feast.

"I have this for ya, Princess," Alastar said.

Amber looked at the elegant gift wrap and smiled. "What's this?"

"Open it."

Amber opened the wrap and was surprised to see the hairpin very different from the last time she saw it. She could hardly believe he finished it so beautifully. "You did all this? It's wonderful! Thank you so much."

"You're welcome, Princess. Just remember – things can work out in ways you'd not think."

Amber gave him a warm smile and left. Alastar went back to the table where everyone eyed him curiously.

"Did ya carve another grebe for this one too?" Teague asked.

"It was just a prop ta show a point," Alastar replied.

"And gift wrapped even," Teague teased with a smile. Gearóid and Gilroy were amused as well.

"Lad, Amber is like my niece," Gearóid said firmly. "I'm like her only livin' relative. Ya would be kind ta tell me before ya go askin' for her hand. . ." He gave Alastar a very firm look. Then he burst in laughter and everyone but Alastar joined.

"Stub it!" Alastar exclaimed flustered. "The gift wrap wasn't even my idea."

"This grand occasion calls for a foot stompin' song!" Teague yelled. He beat his fist on the table to a constant rhythm and sang out, "A sharp lad came ta the isle; Caught a grebe with none but a smile; He took ta the woods 'n lost 'er awhile; Then ashore he stood 'n caught another bird, quite in style!"

Alastar started to blush and stood up. He had to get away from their teasing. "Right then. I think I've had my fill. I'll be retirin' as well."

"Ahhh! The fun's only began," Gearóid said.

"No harm done," Alastar reassured. "I can take so much slag. I *am* tired from the day as well. My regards, gentlemen." He bowed at everyone and left for his room.

In the long hallway leading to his room, Alastar heard the music of a harp and a woman singing a lovely song. It was coming from the parlor at the end of the hall. He could not understand the song because it was in the old tongue, but the words had a beautiful melody to them. He walked to the end of the hall and looked into the parlor. He was surprised to see Amber sat in a plush chair singing with a harp in her arms. Mairéad sat nearby listening.

The harp was just taller than Amber's torso. It leaned against her left shoulder as she plucked its shiny strings. The harp's elegant, curved frame was made of carved wood, and its gold strings rang with the bright timbre of synchronized chimes. Their vibrant sound matched Amber's voice beautifully. Alastar never heard music so soothing.

Amber stopped when Alastar appeared in the room. "You finished quick," she said.

"I was tired," he replied. "You sing like. . . a harmony of turtle doves, Princess. What was that song?"

"It was just a song my mam would sing ta bring father back from his far journeys."

"It's beautiful," he said. Alastar noticed Amber was wearing the hairpin. It was vivid in her hair, like a bright red rose that floated in a field of gold threads. He wondered if he should stay and talk with them, but decided it best to keep distant. Amber continued to shine bright in his vision. It made him feel uneasy that his gaze wanted to linger on her. He looked away. "Please continue. I only wanted ta see who was singin'. Good night, ladies."

Alastar went to his room and could hear Amber continue to sing and play the harp. She sang soft and warm melodies for awhile as Alastar got into bed and lay there. Her singing carried melodies to his heart, but he kept them from entering and thought about Nola as he drifted to sleep.

*T*he room was dark, but the sound of tower bells ringing nearby filled the air with bright urgency. Alastar quickly got out of bed and looked out the large window that faced the sea. Lacharan's catapult defenses were being deployed. He saw many fireballs launched from both ends of the bay in droves. They flew in high arcs in front of the enemy fleet and landed in the water. They burst and splattered as they hit the waves. Alastar judged there were dozens of catapults on each side of the bay from the great number of firepots being launched.

The exploding oil-filled pots quickly made a thick line of fire across the bay. Alastar squinted to see clearly through it. The enemy fleet approached just beyond the flames. Then all of a sudden a flying firepot struck something huge that flew in the air above the catapults. It was black; invisible against the night sky until the firepot lit it aglow. The large flying form had long, jagged wings, like a bat, a long tail with a ball on the end, and its body appeared to be as big as the largest of the warships. Alastar pondered. . . *a dragon?* It was using its club-like tail to destroy the catapults.

"Take refuge! Take refuge!" someone in the hallway yelled. "The attack comes! Take refuge!"

Alastar's door swung open and he looked behind him to see who it was. Teague stood in the doorway. "Gather your thin's, lad! We need ta assemble!"

"Did ya see out there?" Alastar asked. "I think the Áiteoir have a dragon." Alastar looked back out the window and saw the catapults firing many fireballs at the ships and dragon. Many ships were burning. Others caught fire as they went through the wall of flames that crossed the bay. But the streams of fireballs in the sky had diminished. The dragon was making its way around the catapults and destroying them. Soon there would be none left to fire the defenses.

"It appears they do," Teague answered. "Never seen a dragon on the isle before. They must've waited for night ta cover their dragon's flight. Its hide is dark as night."

Alastar strapped on his sword and grabbed his things. They went downstairs and found the others in the room where they met before. Everyone was dressed except Amber and Mairéad were in their nightgowns.

"We know what the Áiteoir waited for now," Gearóid said. "They had a flyin' beast slip through the night ta turn our catapults ta splinters. But its not quick 'nough ta spoil our defenses. Much of their fleet will burn, but some will reach shore. We have a fierce fight on hand. I suspect that dragon will turn ta our walls next and let their land army in."

"We fear you're not safe, Princess, nor the lad," Gilroy said. "The walls of Lacharan will not hold as long as we thought." He looked at Amber and Alastar. "We must get you two ta safety. Cnoc na Rí is the safest place on the isle for you."

"Sounds like we need ta be hidin' in the night again," Teague said.

"Right," Gearóid agreed. "The Áiteoir have all the main gates surrounded, but you can lead a party with Captain Conn through one of the hidden doors and brin' the young ones ta safety. Swing wide around the enemy along the river, then turn west at the ferry crossin' and ride north behind them ta Cnoc na Rí. If ya go swift 'nough, ya could be in the plains by dawn."

"The Áiteoir are sure ta have Lorgaire trollin' any escape routes," Teague said.

"Still, better ta face a few scouts than their whole army," Gearóid responded.

"If we miss a scout, the army will know and be on us far before we reach the the plains," Teague said. "We'd need ta move slow and cautious."

"What of Lacharan?" Alastar asked.

"I will remain here and see ta thin's, lad," Gearóid said. "Not a soul will give up the fight, but if our shores and walls are breached we cannot keep you and the princess safe for long, nor will escape options for ya be strong when we're surrounded inside our very homes. That beast of theirs won't let any of our defenses hold long."

"We must get you and Amber out, son," Gilroy said. "We cannot risk ya bein' caught with nowhere ta run."

"If the Áiteoir do not know the princess is here," Alastar said, "she can hide safely in Lacharan. They came ta find me alone." He looked to Amber. "Princess, I'd rather cut ta a plan that will lead the enemy away from here. I wish not a soul suffer for me. Let them find me."

"I won't have it!" Amber said firmly.

"None of us will!" Teague added. "Did we not speak of this before, lad?"

"I don't mean ta surrender," Alastar said. "I mean ta run for Cnoc na Rí and let them know it. I want 'em ta follow so they leave Lacharan. From what I've seen, we can outrun 'em just enough, so long as they don't have more fáelshee ta run us down. If we send word ta the king. They can be ready ta receive us 'n meet the enemy on our tail."

"I don't know ta call ya a mainidh or the hardest slab a granite I ever seen!" Gearóid said. "Ya certainly have the fightin' spirit of the Eachraighe." He looked at everyone in the room. "What do you all say of our ailpín's ["æl-peen's"] grand plan?"

"The plot of a stout-headed stick for certain," Gilroy said. "The enemy is sure ta follow if they know the lad runs," Gilroy said. "But whatever troops remain may still enter Lacharan ta see that a diversion was not played. The princess cannot stay here all the same. She would be found out. Countless people have seen you in Lacharan, Princess. We cannot expect your arrival ta be kept secret."

"Just as well," Amber said. "I mean ta go with Alastar. Our paths were brought together not ta be unraveled now." She looked at Alastar. "You did pledge your service ta me. How would ya be doin' that if ya run off without me?"

Gearóid smiled. It warmed him that Amber wished to go with Alastar. She had never displayed such fondness for anyone besides her parents. "Then I will see ta the charge myself," he said. "If ya are ta make a mad rush for Cnoc na Rí, I can ensure your escape ta the plains through the north gate. Our cavalry will shield ya through their lines. I will have Captain Conn escort ya with a hundred riders the whole way. I need the rest of our troops ta fight for Lacharan. I believe this plan will work, but we must go now, before the Áiteoir bring their army closer ta the north gate. They won't stand far off long knowin' that their fleet and dragon are pressin' in."

"Mad as it sounds, it appears ta be our best option for all at stake," Gilroy said. "We'll make the bold dash as the lad wants." He looked to Teague. "Send your seabhac ta rally the king before we go. Everyone, prepare ta leave now and meet at the north gate quickly."

"Right then," Gearóid said. "I will make ready. Be at the north gate quick as ya can." He turned to a servant and told him to prepare their horses. Then he left quickly.

Amber told Mairéad to help her pack and they left.

"I will meet you at the gate," Gilroy said to Teague and Alastar.

"Swiftly now! Prepare your thin's and horses."

Teague and Alastar immediately went to the stables. Servants ran frantically to prepare things. All the horses were being fitted with padded leather armor and blankets that bore the standards for the Eachraighe and Torthúil.

Teague found a new horse and quickly secured his saddle onto it. "Lad," he told Alastar. "I go ta set Bress off with a message for the king. I will see ya at the gate."

Alastar watched servants prepare Éimhín with his saddle and bags. They also put armor on him. It did not conform to his saddle and reins exactly, but they fit well enough. Alastar also saw Amber's horse being prepared. Hers was given much lighter armor than the others since she was not expected to engage in battle. Armor for all their horses was meant to be light and allow freedom of movement. Speed and agility was more important to the Eachraighe than hulking stalwartness.

When the servants finished with Éimhín a page asked, "Would ya be wantin' your wood mounted as well?"

Alastar pondered. He wished to take his wood. He spent so much time collecting it, but then decided to leave most of it. "Leave it," he responded. "I will just take a few pieces." Alastar quickly went through the wood and put some of the best stock in his saddlebags.

Soldiers started to come in with full armor on and took their horses. In the middle of the activity, a servant came running into the stables with a stack of clothing.

"Alastar!" he yelled trying to catch his breath. "Sir, by the duke's order, I have armor for ya."

Alastar stood surprised. "Thank you, sir."

"Quick now! Take your vest off," the servant said. Alastar put his leather vest away and the servant put a leather plate armor vest on him. It was made with thick, diamond-shaped leather patches that were linked together by bronze rings. Its hardened leather shoulder guards had the kingdom and clan crests branded onto them. Then the servant put a thigh-length skirt of bronze chainmail on him and covered it with a shorter skirt of leather blades. The leather skirt was made of vertical leather blades that came to triangular points at the bottom.

Alastar continued to stand and watch as the servant fit the last pieces of armor – hard leather greaves for his forearms and shins. The shin guards went all the way up his knees. Amber and Mairéad walked into the stables as the servant gave Alastar a simple round helm made of bronze and leather. "There you are, sir," the servant said. "You are ready."

Amber wore a simple white léine that hung down to her feet, a light-weight leather cuirass covered her torso, and a royal sapphire blue kinsale cloak with hood waved about her. Leather gloves and riding boots completed her outfit, and her hair was bound neatly with bands. She smiled at Alastar. It seemed that every time they met, he looked more and more the champion. "You do look set ta go," Amber told him. Mairéad walked on to Amber's horse and fastened a bag onto the back of the saddle.

"We're set for a swift run," Alastar replied. He looked at the helm in his hands. "I never had a helmet before."

"Here," Amber said, "Let me put it on you." She took it and set it on his head. She fastened the chinstrap for him and looked into his eyes with the longing that made Alastar uncomfortable.

"Thank you, Princess," he said. He tried not to return her endearing smile, but a slight expression of affection slipped into his stiff lips nonetheless. "It feels odd. . . the helmet."

"Ya look a fine 'n fit soldier," she replied. Loud crashing and screams of people were coming from outside. "Time ta go. Our guard is waitin'.""

Amber and Alastar quickly mounted their horses. He noticed Mairéad was not going. "Isn't your attendant comin'?" he asked Amber.

"Mairéad has duties here," Amber said. "There's little for her ta do where we're goin'."

Alastar followed Amber outside where a dozen mounted guards waited patiently while servants ran about in panic. They were rushing to put out fires from fireballs that the siege ships were launching. There were only a dozen siege ships, but they were firing as much as they could before they crumbled in flames. Their large size allowed them quite a bit of time before they sank. Most of the other ships were engulfed in flames and made their way to shore as quickly as possible.

The princess's mounted guard left for the north gate with Amber and Alastar riding in the middle of them. Amber looked back at the palace as more fireballs and boulders came down on it. She wondered when she would return home again. Would its walls be standing? Would the duke be able to keep Lacharan from being overrun? Lacharan's future troubled her, but she once more needed to find refuge away from home. Seeing her Swan-bearer beside her gave her the hope and confidence that everything was working out as it should.

The last time she fled Lacharan, it was not in a hurry, but she was surrounded with the sorrow of exile; that thick feeling of solitude from having to leave behind everything that was important to her – her friends, her life. Leaving now, though, felt very different. She didn't feel like she was running in sorrow or leaving her life behind. She felt that she was running towards her life now with Alastar.

At the north gate, hundreds of armored riders were making a thick line to surround the royal party. Gilroy was already there with his flag bearers and a couple dozen soldiers who remained from Cnoc na Rí. They took position behind Alastar and Amber.

Teague rode up to them and stopped in front of Alastar. "Fine armor, lad," he said. "Gearóid and Conn will be here shortly. I saw them from the bird keep. They were ridin' from the south bay. Some of the Áiteoir made it ta shore, but they were burnin' awful. Most of their sea army is whittlin' away, but that beast of theirs has near all the catapults done for. If they send more ships, it will be hard ta hold the bay."

"I hope there will be no more fightin' here once we leave," Alastar said.

"Certainly hope that ta be true," Teague replied. "Mind our run now. Do not hide your face, but evade their arrows if any come near. The Áiteoir have the keenest eyes 'round. They're sure ta recognize ya and your horse, but their arrows hardly fly true at distance." He looked at Amber. "They're sure ta know you run as well, Princess. I'd be surprised if they don't send their entire army ta take the both of ya."

"That is why we go, is it not?" Amber said.

Teague smiled and looked back at Alastar. "Ya got a handful in her ta care for, lad. Grand craic ["kræk" like crack] ahead!"

"Grand *craic?!*" Gilroy exclaimed. "Your meanin' of a grand good time needs adjustin', son!"

Gearóid and Conn rode quickly to the head of the gate. Gearóid held a round wood shield and a large spear with a gleaming bronze tip, while Conn only had a sword and shield. The entire courtyard and streets around the gate were packed with armored riders who held spears, swords and shields. Their entire cavalry of a thousand were ready to launch.

"The enemy marches toward the gate!" Gearóid yelled. "We will ride swiftly north ta brin' the princess's party inta the plains. Keep your shields high! Do not engage unless I command. Once the princess is safe off, we swing back ta keep the enemy from followin' and make Lacharan safe!" He signaled and the army's battle horns were blown.

The gate doors started to open. As soon as it was wide enough for the line to go through, Gearóid led the charge with Conn and Teague directly behind him. The enemy was surprised by the swift charge and the thundering of thousands of hooves. The enemy troops already at the walls were quickly run over while the rest of the army began a rush towards them. Arrows started to fly through the air and took down some riders.

They pressed onward as hard as they could. Alastar looked back and saw the walls of Lacharan drift away. Hundreds of Lacharan's foot soldiers and riders stayed back to surround the open gate. They would have to hold it for Gearóid to return.

Soon the arrows stopped flying and only the enemy cavalry was able to pursue closely. Many of their foot soldiers were trying to follow but they fell far behind. Their plan was working. Alastar and Amber were running safely towards Cnoc na Rí with nothing but the bare plains ahead of them.

They rode for many minutes without worry of resistance. The enemy cavalry was not gaining much ground on them. They began to feel at ease and slowed to a steady pace to keep ahead of the Áiteoir. Gearóid looked back at Conn and Teague. "Carry on, men!" He signaled his men to follow him and turned back to charge the enemy. Most of the riders surrounding the escaping party followed Gearóid while the royal escort pressed forward with Amber's guards and Conn's unit of one hundred.

Alastar looked backwards and saw Gearóid engage the enemy. Their advance was completely stopped. Then a sudden rush of air went sideways through their party and many riders in the middle went flying. They landed crippled on the ground. The dragon had swept them with its massive club tail.

"Dragon!" Alastar yelled. Everyone looked up as they continued to gallop forward. It was hard to see the black dragon in the dark sky.

Teague scanned the skies quickly and saw a dark shape blotting out the stars as it flew towards them again. He drew his sword and pointed at it. "It comes! Attack!" Everyone without spears drew their swords and most of the riders followed Teague and Conn to charge the dragon. Only Gilroy and Amber's royal guard remained to surround them.

When the dragon came low, many spears were thrown at it, but they bounced harmlessly off. It swooped low to swing its tail through them again. More riders were crushed. It narrowly missed Teague, but he was able to strike it with his sword. He felt how hard it was when his sword did not penetrate its hide at all. "It's a stone dragon!" he yelled. "We cannot cut it! Back ta the party! Protect them best we can!"

They rode back to the party and Teague signaled them to continue riding forward. They were soon out of sight of Gearóid and the pursuing troops. They tried to scatter their party farther apart and ride in haphazard lines to confuse the flying beast. It started to make its way back to them when Alastar saw the familiar brilliant shape of the Seabhac Azure in the dark sky.

"The Azure!" Alastar yelled. He pointed up to it and noticed three flying shapes behind it. They were dark shapes but much larger than the Azure.

"How can it be?!" Gilroy cried. He recognized the large flying shapes following the Azure. "Griffins of Torthúil follow the Azure!"

Everyone screamed with joy, but Gilroy was puzzled. The

griffins never flew outside the mountains. Only once before did they come out of their home range. It was to save King Rían in the final battle to unite the clans of the east. That is when the legends of the griffins' watch over the king began. After that, King Rían chose to build Cnoc na Rí under their perch at the end of the River Valley. They've guarded the kingdom's throne ever since, but never were they seen so far from the valley.

Everyone watched in amazement as the Azure swooped low over them. Then it flew toward the dragon and hovered near it until the three griffins caught up and attacked the dragon. The griffins' golden brown fur and feathers gleamed in the dark air. The dragon was easily double their size, but it could not withstand their swift attack. The griffins clamped onto its neck and wings and sent it crashing down into the ground where it snapped into many pieces. It soon crumbled into dark dust as the enchantment over the obsidian stone fled away.

All in the party rejoiced as the massive griffins stood watching them. The griffins let out deep, loud screams of victory. They were like nothing Alastar heard before; deafening, as if the eagle cries came from lungs the size of mountains. The Azure flew above them again and headed north. The griffins took off, still screeching loudly and followed it. The Azure flew high into the sky and disappeared again while the griffins kept a steady pace and height flying back to their home range.

"Ta Cnoc na Rí!" Teague said. "Victory was given us, but we cannot linger! The mass of the Áiteoir army is sure ta follow swift. Gearóid and his men are certain ta have a hard battle at Lacharan. We honor them by completin' our mission."

They continued to ride north through the night. An hour went by, then two when the dawning sun broke across the horizon. They could see a large number of troops following them in the south, but they were still a safe distance away.

Teague stopped the party to give the horses rest for a few minutes. He pondered whether the enemy would send their garrison from Dún Liath. It was the only enemy stronghold along the coast before they reached the mountains. The Áiteoir are certain to have sent them word of the party.

Teague asked Gilroy, "How many troops are in Dún Liath, Chancellor?"

"Many hundreds," Gilroy replied. "Not an army, but they could give us trouble."

"Should we round west ta keep our distance from them?" Alastar asked.

"The Azure went straight towards Cnoc na Rí," Teague said. "Our line will be the same. Lad, I've not seen anythin' like I've seen round you. Those griffins had ta fly near an hour before reachin' us. That means they left before we decided ta make our run. I'm dumbfounded by the workin' of these blessin's."

"I've not heard of events like these either," Gilroy added. "The griffins had never been seen so far from the mountains. And the dark dragon. . . never have I seen such a monstrosity animated from stone. The Áiteoir have gained much in their conjurin' arts. I do not know how, but if they continue in this vein the kingdom is in peril."

"Keep your minds from wanderin' fearful tracts," Amber said. "We know the fight will be heavy. We must hold our resolve no matter the sort of beasts and blows we get. If my father taught me anythin', it's not ta fear fightin' ta the death for our friends, family and kingdom."

Alastar looked at Amber with great appreciation. She was much more than the sweet, elegant princess he first met on the dock. Her inner strength shone through when times became difficult. It made him wonder again, why would she need any help from him?

"Right," Teague said. "Mind the mission. Pick up now!"

Everyone started to ride north again. There appeared to be thousands of Áiteoir pursuing them, but everyone in the party focused on pushing forward. As full daylight sprang around them, Alastar got the familiar feeling of riding the plains around his home. This part of Rathúnas looked much like the lands around Netleaf. If it weren't for his many companions and the need to get to safety, it would have felt like another warm spring gallop.

They had pressed forward for a time when Conn yelled, "Dún Liath!" Its gray stone walls appeared on their right.

"Swift now!" Teague said as he pushed everyone to a fast gallop. They could see the thick forest at the foothills of the mountains just miles beyond Dún Liath. They hoped their presence would go undetected, but as they neared the fort, battle horns were blown behind the walls and the gate opened. Hundreds of Áiteoir riders streamed out the gate with their swords waving in the air. They rushed directly toward the party.

"Swords!" Teague yelled and veered right to intercept the charge. Most of the soldiers drew their swords and followed him. They were outnumbered three to one. Alastar felt the urge to rush with them, but he knew he wasn't trained enough to be of much help. Still, he drew his sword.

"Steady, son!" Gilroy cautioned. "Press on ta the forest!"

They rode past the battle in front of the fort and saw more riders coming out to pursue them.

"Faster!" Gilroy yelled.

They all prod their horses as fast as they could. Éimhín broke out in front of them, still running strong after hours on the plain. Amber's horse, Muirgel, trailed just behind Alastar and Éimhín.

"Wait for us in the forest, Princess!" Gilroy yelled when they neared the border. "The rest of ya, stand your ground here!"

Alastar slowed down and saw Amber rush into the forest. He turned Éimhín around to face the enemy. The others had stopped to make a shield for them, but it was only a dozen to the advancing enemy's hundred. Teague and Conn were still busy fighting the hundreds in the distance.

Gilroy stopped near Alastar. "Son, you needn't fight. Join Amber in the forest."

"I'll stand here, sir," he replied. "We need all fightin' hands. We're ready."

"Right then, I will join the princess. Brace and be strong." Gilroy went into the forest to guard Amber.

Alastar moved up to the line with the guards. They all braced for the enemy's charge. Amber and Gilroy watched from the forest. She couldn't believe Alastar would stand the line like that. He had only begun to train with the sword.

The Áiteoir charged with such a zeal in their eyes. They could see victory was to be theirs. Alastar's heart pumped as if it were going to burst. He tried to keep calm by talking to Éimhín and patting his shoulder. "Easy, boy. Just another run for us."

The enemy drew near, galloping as hard as they could. Alastar gripped his sword tight and held it ready to parry. The charging riders shortened the field quickly, then all of a sudden the loud trumpets of Torthúil rung out from the forest and the first row of enemy riders and their horses crashed to the ground. Many arrows had struck them down and the riders behind them stumbled on the bodies or stopped altogether.

More arrows flooded out from the forest and brought down many more of the enemy. Everyone looked backwards and saw the royal troops of Torthúil run out to engage the enemy. Hundreds of soldiers on foot and horseback came out to help the party. The enemy quickly retreated back to Dún Liath and shut themselves in.

Teague and Conn regrouped their party with Alastar. Amber and Gilroy rode out to them as well.

"I had my doubts, son," Gilroy said to Alastar, "But your plan worked. Brilliant!"

"Grand, it was!" Teague said, "And excitin' as fishin' the salmon run up the river with your bare hands! Not what I'd prefer ta do, though!" Everyone laughed in their victory. Amber beamed at Alastar. She knew her champion would be able to carry her through.

"Right. Grand altogether," Gilroy said. "We must keep movin'. The enemy continues ta march. They'll be right angry after chasin' all night only ta have us slip away."

As they were about to turn into the forest, a rider on a heavily armored horse and in a full bronze armor suit rode out of the forest. A gold crown crested his helmet and everyone bowed to him as he passed. He was a tall, middle-aged man with long, brown hair and trimmed beard.

When the party saw him, they bowed as well. "King Fuar," Gilroy said. "We're grateful you answered our call."

"Why wouldn't I aid my young cousin Ealaí and her Swan-bearer?" Fuar replied. He looked over Alastar with keen interest. "The Áiteoir have grown very dangerous in this young man's presence. I see why they're runnin' amuck. Ya look a strong 'n noble lad. Your horse as well."

"Thank you, sir," Alastar said.

Teague quickly whispered to Alastar, "Address him as sire or king, lad."

"Sire, thank you," Alastar repeated embarrassed.

"Very well, son," Fuar replied. "We'll have time for pleasantries later." He looked at Gilroy. "Have your party escort the princess ta the palace. They're prepared ta receive her. I will see ta the enemy here. They would be foolish ta press inta our borders."

Gilroy acknowledged and had their party continue north into the mountains of Torthúil.

*I*n Loch an Scátháin, the burnt remains of homes were a common sight for many villagers. Nola was going through the ashes of her home with her family and the Conalls. Only the charred stone walls were left standing. Most of the homes on the south and west sides of the lake were completely destroyed by the Áiteoir before they retreated.

Nola looked out into the bare fields. Every barn and house in sight was a burnt hull. *At least the cropland is unharmed,* she thought. They were just planted, so their coming harvest was a good promise of renewal in this time of despair. She wondered if Alastar made it to safety and whether he would be back to help them rebuild.

"Your house is the last they turned ta pitch," Conall said. "They didn't get ta Braede's and the rest on the east side. Your family is welcome ta stay at my home till ya rebuild."

"We'd appreciate that," Fionn said. "Is it safe ta rebuild even? The Áiteoir never pressed so far inta our lands. Who'd say they won't be back soon?"

"They seem ta have went on after they found Teague and Alastar in the plains," Conall replied. Nola looked at him with curiosity when she heard Alastar's name. Conall returned her gaze. "You'd be glad ta know I've heard from 'em. They made it ta Lacharan after a mad dash before an Áiteoir army and fight with more than a dozen fáelshee."

Everyone's eyes widened with shock. "*Fáelshee?!*" Mab exclaimed. "Are the lads all right? How could they stand against so many?"

"They had help from the chancellor," Conall said. "Seems the young boy's blessin's never cease. The Azure led the chancellor ta 'em in the plains and then straight on ta Lacharan. They entered Lacharan by the tip of a needle. Still a rough fight, but they're safe. Fared better than we, I'd say, but I'd not expect the Áiteoir back here. Their army tries ta enter Lacharan after the boy, right at this moment."

A look of concern fell over Nola. It didn't sound like Alastar would come back soon, and if he did, Loch an Scáthán would be attacked again. *We can't have a life here,* she thought, *not unless the enemy is gone or we go into hiding for the rest of our lives.* She went over to where her bed used to be and looked through the burnt remains. The wooden grebe Alastar made for her was nowhere in sight. It was lost in the fire. She turned away with a heavy heart and started to walk toward the fields.

"I'll gather the horses and flock ta the Conalls'," Nola said quietly. Ula followed her into the fields to help.

"Right," Fionn said. "Straight ta buildin' then. Pity Braede is not ta be found. He was the handiest at buildin' sturdy thin's."

The rest of them started to clear out the ashes and prepare the grounds for their homes to be rebuilt. The mood over Loch an Scáthán was somber. It was an overwhelming contrast to the joy-filled céilí preparations they had the day before. Now the whole town was filled to bursting with clean up, repair and mourning over their dead. The day passed into night with the fog of war over Loch an Scáthán. No one noticed a lone person on horseback coming from the west as the sun descended low on the horizon. He kept to the outskirts, just before the hills and mountains and made his way to the mill.

Braede got off his horse and entered the mill. "Brónach!" he called.

Brónach appeared from an adjoining room. "Where have ya been!?" Brónach asked firmly. "The Áiteoir attacked last night and everyone's speakin' of your absence. Did ya not make it ta Cnoc na Rí?"

"There's not time ta speak of it now," Braede said with urgency. "Pack your thin's. It's not safe in Loch an Scáthain."

"And where do ya think we're goin'?"

"We'll go ta my homelands in Cloch Lom ["Klukh Lum"]."

Brónach gasped. She realized her husband must be working with the Áiteoir. "*What!* Your home in the north? Your lands were taken."

"It's been arranged, dear," he said stiffly. "We must leave now."

"I won't leave Loch an Scáthain and neither should you!" she said tearfully. "Stay with your friends here. What is left for you in Cloch Lom?"

"Ya must go with me, Brónach! I cannot see ta your safety if you're not by my side! I'll speak none more of it now! There's little time. Take what ya need. We'll not be sayin' our goodbyes ta folk. A quick flight from here is best."

Brónach couldn't believe what Braede was saying. She couldn't leave her family and friends like this. Braede had conspired with the Áiteoir to reveal Alastar and get back his estate. She loved him, but she could not go with him. "I won't leave!" she scolded. She ran out the door and went up the road towards the Conalls'. Braede watched her and panicked. She would tell everyone.

Braede scurried around his house to grab valuable things and money. He quickly left and galloped his horse northwest. No one noticed him going through the land until an eagle sentry reported to Conall.

"The Greerian reported him past the border," Conall told Brónach, "Moving swiftly northwest. I'm sorry. I doubt he'll be comin' back."

Brónach hugged her sister, Mab, with tears in her eyes. "May I stay with ya? I don't want ta see the mill again." She looked to Conall. "I give the mill ta Loch an Scáthháin. You may do with it as ya please."

"Very well," Conall acknowledged. "The mill will belong ta the village so long as you please. You may take it back if ever you wish it. Your sister's family is stayin' here. There's certainly place for ya as well."

"Thank you, Conall," Brónach said. "You've always been as a brother ta our family."

"We've none but family in Loch an Scáthháin," Conall said. "May ya take your thin's tomorrow from the mill, Brónach? There are many families without shelter. The mill can provide them a place till we've all found our green pasture again."

"Surely," Brónach said.

"We'll all help ya," Flann added.

"Right," Conall said. "First thin' tomorrow, we'll all be at the mill ta get your thin's. Time now, though, ta write the king of Braede. Teague and Alastar would be wantin' ta know of this as well." He left the house to go to the bird keep.

The evening settled into dim twilight. Everyone rested uneasily inside the main room at the Conalls'. Braede's talk of Loch an Scáthháin being unsafe etched deeper fear into their hearts after the attack. Why would they attack again if Alastar was not there? Nola thought Alastar must be coming back. Even though his stay in Loch an Scáthháin was brief and undestined, thoughts of seeing him brought warmth to her heart.

Nola sat up in the middle of the night. Everyone was sleeping quietly, but there was a low rumbling sound coming from outside, like distant thunder rolling across wide plains. She quietly got up and went out the front door to look. The night air was cool and still. There was nothing unusual in sight.

She stood listening intently and heard again the distant rumbling. It seemed to come from the west. She walked to the back of the house and stood by the lakeshore. The water was a smooth mirror and a white fog hovered just above it. Everything was still.

Then the rumbling came again, louder, and the lake surface made tiny ripples under its breath. The thundering continued to come closer. She looked left, toward the west where the sound came from. She could tell now it was the sound of many horses galloping. The lake surface appeared to ripple deeply everywhere as the sound grew louder.

The thundering became so intense she had to cover her ears. Then a sudden rush of wind came from the east and overtook the thundering. She looked into the wind and saw a soldier in the bronze and leather armor of the Eachraighe. He led a charge of many horses. Their startling rush past her made her gasp for air.

Nola opened her eyes quickly and sat up. She breathed heavily and found herself in the Conalls' main room with her family.

Mab woke up. "Are ya alright, dear?" she asked.

"Just a dream, mam."

"Right then. Get back ta sleep. There's much ta do tomorra'."

Gilroy led the party into the mountains where the forest quickly became dense with vibrant foliage and color. Alastar rode slightly hunched over. His mind and body were severely fatigued from the night's gallop and intense fighting; the second night in a row, plus many hours of sword training before that and only a few hours sleep.

The adrenaline that kept him going had seeped away and left him tired and limp.

Alastar looked over to Amber who rode by his side. She appeared to be undiminished since the last evening. She gave him a warm smile, just as bright as the sun that followed them towards the summit. They were almost there.

"Let us rest at the peak," Amber told Gilroy. She could see Alastar was very tired. They all were. A short rest in the sanctuary of the mountains was needed.

"Surely, Princess," Gilroy responded. "We'll stop at the Giant's Hammer."

"Grand," Teague said. "I've not seen it from the topside."

"The Giant's Hammer?" Alastar asked.

"A grand big cliff on the south side of the valley," Teague replied. "Shaped like the head of a heavy blacksmith's hammer. Looks as if it struck clear down the middle of the mountain. All the granite is none but smashed boulder 'n rubble beneath the hammer's head. Much of Cnoc na Rí was built from that stone."

"Legend has it," Conn added, "the giant smith carved the River Valley with the hammer in one sweepin' blow 'cross the land."

"Quite a fanciful legend," Gilroy said. "But the cliff does look as if a hammer struck down the mountain and was left sittin' in the middle of it."

After many minutes, the party reached the top of the mountain and Gilroy led them east, to the right. They soon stopped at a clearing on the other side of the mountain where the tall pines and sprawling rowan became sparse. The ground broke into bare, gray-white granite stone where they rested.

Everyone got off their horses and rested. Alastar, Amber, Teague and many others walked to the edge of the cliff to see the view.

They could see the whole mouth of the valley, straight to the other side, over ten miles away. Alastar noticed the valley was much wider here than at the middle. The river also looked to be twice as wide as he saw before. Here, it flowed east calmly into the sea.

The stone of the mountains here was not made of the red-orange agate layers that dominated the center of the valley. The valley's mouth was white and silver granite, marble and crystalline rock. It jutted out in many sheer cliffs that were too steep to hold soil. A quick glance to the west, though, showed the mountainsides became smoother and completely covered by thick green forest.

The floor of the valley around Cnoc na Rí was also green and fertile, except the land was cultivated with many crop fields and orchards sprawled around the bright stone city and large river. To the right, the whole of Bá Rí ["Bah Ree"; King's Bay] opened into the sea where many fishing boats and merchant vessels dotted the water.

Alastar scanned Cnoc na Rí at the other side of the valley. He looked for its defenses but saw none. The city didn't even have a fortified wall. The high mountains and cliffs were its walls. They loomed far above the tall towers and spires of the city, and most of Cnoc na Rí was built on top of the layered cliffs that stepped higher and higher into the mountainside. Alastar did notice a prominent walkway bridge that extended for a mile or more from the palace to the royal garden by the sea. The large garden covered the north shore of the bay just as Teague described. It spread out to the sea like a thick, decorative carpet.

"Where are the city's defenses?" Alastar asked Teague.

"You mean like Lacharan's?" Teague said. "Ya won't find 'em inside the city. The catapults are higher in the mountainsides, all around the bay, hidden in alcoves and behind trees. The king's seat was sculpted ta be as elegant and beautiful as it is sturdy and secure.

No siege ships can come close enough ta fire upon the city, and it'd be a fine bit a tuggin' ta bring siege machines over the mountains inta the valley.

"The enemy would need ta build their siege machines here or take Rían's Gate in the north. None too easy ta crack the anvil 'a Cnoc na Rí. No army has tried ta march on the king here. Can ya blame 'em? Look. . ." He pointed to a far off summit on the other side of the valley where some griffins flew about. "The griffins are always flyin' over the king."

Alastar stepped farther to the edge of the cliff and looked down. The Giant's Hammer was many hundreds of feet high. It didn't look like anything more than a massive, wide vertical wall from the top, but he could see the bottom was a great pile of boulders, just as if the mountain had crumbled under the blow of a massive hammer.

"Don't step too close," Amber told Alastar. "The height can make ya dizzy. I won't go near it."

"I'll just be sittin' down for a spot," Alastar said as he sat and hung his legs over the cliff ledge. The sun bore down its full heat in the open air. Alastar was sweating and took off his helmet. He started to unfasten his armor vest when Gilroy interrupted.

"Leave your armor on, son," Gilroy said. "We'll be in the shade of the forest shortly."

The party was gathering to leave when the scream of a hawk rung out. Everyone looked around and saw a hawk fly across the valley toward them.

"Bress!" Teague yelled. He held up his arm and the hawk landed on his forearm. Teague took a scroll from her carrier and released her. She flew to the perch mounted on his saddle. He read the message. "It's a relay from Cnoc na Rí about Loch an Scátháin. Conall sent word about Braede. He was seen leavin' Torthúil for the north. They believe he revealed Alastar ta the Áiteoir and is fleein' ta his homelands. He tried ta take his wife along, but she refused and told Conall."

"That mystery appears ta be unlocked," Gilroy said.

"Conall suspects Loch an Scátháin will be attacked again," Teague said. "Only because Braede told his wife it was unsafe there. They've no notions why the Áiteoir would want ta come back, but they're watchful. The garrison of Dún Tearmann lost many soldiers. They have but 500 on foot, 100 cavalry." A grave look came upon Teague. "They've lost nearly half the men. If the Áiteoir bring the army we saw at Lacharan, they've got no chance but ta run."

"Conall doesn't look the type ta run," Alastar said.

"Surely not," Teague acknowledged. "But he's an experienced commander. A good soldier knows when he needs ta step back before swingin' the sword again."

"Prudence is a valuable trait, son," Gilroy said. "It's not oft that rushin' through danger is a preferred plan." He was referring to Alastar's plan of pressing boldly through the enemy lines. "Still, reinforcement for Loch an Scátháin may be a need. The Áiteoir may anticipate your return or they may wish to take the entire south region of the mountains."

Amber looked at Alastar when Gilroy mentioned returning to Loch an Scátháin. She wondered how great his desire was to go back. Were his feelings for the girl there strong enough to forget his pledge to her? Alastar didn't reveal any feelings with his demeanor, though.

"The king surely wouldn't let the Áiteoir take more territory," she said. "The kingdom is less than half as it was. Dún Tearmann was built ta house the kingdom's refugees. Where would they go if they flee?"

"I don't believe the king would leave Dún Tearmann and Loch

an Scáthâin ta be lost either," Gilroy said. "It would be a horrible moral defeat ta have only Cnoc na Rí and Lacharan left standin'. We can't continue to stand by now that the Áiteoir have breached the treaty."

"The enemy only used the treaty ta gather their strength," Teague said. "If the king saw what they threw at us durin' the last days he would agree."

"It may be time ta take back our territory," Conn said. "The time ta make our kingdom secure must come near. The Swan-bearer is here now *with* the princess. We should be thinkin' ta *expand* our former borders! The whole isle is ta come under this peace is it not?"

"Surely," Gilroy said, "but do not be rash. What good is it ta build a bridge when ya have not reached the river? We must follow the currents, not try ta out run them. The House of Ealaí does not yet sit on the throne. That must come as the isle comes ta unity and peace."

Amber looked at Alastar again. She knew in her heart he needed to accept a greater role with her than just to be her champion. How could she tell him? Would he be willing? He was a hard working and amicable fellow, but he hardly showed interest in doing more for her than he promised. She had no idea when he would lift her onto the throne either. Would it be months? Years? She had to let the currents flow and not press him before he was ready.

Thoughts of finding out more about Nola and his friends occupied Alastar. He felt bad they were put through trouble after harboring him and that he could be the reason they'd be forced from their homes. He worried over what people expected of him too. It seemed they put a lot of hope in his presence. Why wouldn't they after gritting through so much hard war? But he had no idea how he could bring the great peace they were expecting.

"These matters need discussin' with the king," Gilroy said.

"Let's continue on. We all need a lengthy rest in the city."

Everyone got back on their horses and followed Gilroy down the mountainside. Teague stayed behind to write a quick message. He sent Bress off with it before catching up with the party. He rode up to the front with Conn and Alastar.

"I sent a note ta Loch an Scátháin about our whereabouts," Teague told Alastar. "They'll be glad ta know thin's are well with us."

"I hope they're farin' well, or better than we," Alastar replied. "I'm drained as it is. Some days of rest would be grand."

"Perhaps an evenin'," Teague said. "You need ta resume trainin' ta make ya most fit for the battlefield."

"I'll see the boy has the best instruction," Gilroy said. "The royal teachers will be his for as long as needed. I imagine your presence is best served in Loch an Scátháin. Conall needs all hands there."

"I'll go as Conall calls," Teague said. "He told me ta escort and instruct the lad wherever he goes. But I gather Conall will call me back soon judgin' from thin's. Alastar is most secure in Cnoc na Rí."

The party descended into the valley for most of the morning. When they reached the valley floor, they looked back to the mountains behind them and could see the Giant's Hammer to be a clear depiction of its namesake. Alastar looked all around the valley and craned his neck to see the mountain peaks around them. The mountains on both sides were much higher than they were in the south. Though the valley was twice as wide at its mouth, the higher cliffs and peaks continued to make it appear as a deep ravine of rich, green forest.

"The bridge is just some miles off," Gilroy said.

The party traveled leisurely through farms and orchards. Many residents and workers smiled and waved to them. As they recognized the princess, some people started to gather around the party and

walked with them. Amber had not been seen in the valley for years.
The crowd soon murmured about the young man who rode next to her
on a horse that stood a full head higher than the rest.

"They're curious about you and Éimhín," Amber told Alastar.

"I'd rather they not be," he replied. "We've never had so many
eyes on us, have we?" he said, petting Éimhín. "At least not so many
friendly eyes. This is better than bein' under the Áiteoir's scrutiny."

"Surely is," Teague said. "Still, be careful who ya speak ta. The
enemy knows enough about thin's as it is. You and the princess need ta
keep in close circles."

"Very close," Gilroy said. "I don't want either of ya leavin' the
palace grounds once we set in. The Áiteoir slipped an assassin inta
Lacharan before. They could try it again here."

Alastar didn't like the notion of being confined to the palace.
He wanted to return to Loch an Scáthpáin to see Nola and help his
friends rebuild. He also pledged to help Amber, but it didn't seem there
was much more to do for the time being. What more could he do for
her being stuck in a palace?

By the time the party reached the bridge, a small crowd
was following them. Alastar scanned the road ahead and saw more
people gathering beyond the bridge as well. The gleaming white and
silver buildings of Cnoc na Rí hovered over the scene, still far in the
distance. The large city spanned the entire view and was just as vibrant
and bright as the glowing landscape around them.

As they stepped onto the long stone arch bridge, people greeted
the party with enthusiasm. The clip-clop of the horse hooves on the
cobblestone was still loud enough to be heard over the murmuring
crowd. The curious looks and warm greetings made Alastar remember
the céilí in Loch an Scáthpáin. Their brotherly acceptance made him
feel as if he were returning home, but he didn't like so many eyes on

him.

"Grand crowd," Teague commented as they continued their march to the city.

"They aren't just curious for the princess," Gilroy said. "Word of the Swan-bearer's arrival has spread quickly. The people have much hope for a larger peace ta sweep the isle soon."

Amber looked at Alastar to gauge his feelings. He appeared to be hiding from the attention. His posture was humble. Though he was sitting up, he was hunkered down into Éimhín's sturdy frame. "The palace will be quiet," she said. "I remember the thick walls holdin' no sound at all in the farthest rooms, next ta the mountain face. Even the outside courtyards were usually quiet. The people are kept far from the palace walls and the sea cannot be heard either. I don't know if the palace will ever feel like home for me without the sound of the sea and people nearby."

"I can't imagine livin' in such a place," Alastar added. "I like the quiet of a simple life, but I do prefer to be surrounded by the sounds of the land and sea. The sounds of a few good friends from time ta time is welcome too."

Amber smiled at Alastar's lifestyle inclinations. They were the same as hers. She was used to the busy goings of royal life, but if she could retreat into quiet with a few loved ones, she would. Sometimes she thought of having a life without the many considerations of her station, but the future of her kingdom and people also held great importance to her. She couldn't leave those responsibilities. She didn't want to. Her disposition was woven tightly with her destiny.

After many miles of passing crowds of curious people in the outskirts of the city and through its inner streets, they came to the large gates of the palace. The gate doors were gold and made of long spears and crossbars. The kingdom standard was large in its center and surrounded by flowing designs of grape vines and leaves. The gate's archway was a towering, solid stone sculpture of two griffins that faced each other, much like the garden sculpture in Lacharan's palace. The gate's high wall was also made of large stone blocks. Its silvery granite and white marble stretched far beyond sight in both directions.

Many guards kept people away from the gates and quickly opened them to let the party through. The front courtyard was largely a wide, empty expanse of smooth stone tiles made of the same stone as the palace and surrounding walls. Some areas on the floor were embedded with designs made with colorful stones. The vivid designs swirled about with the elegant gait of wind and flourishing growth.

The only structure in the courtyard was a giant statue of an armored rider on a horse. It was bronze with a base of stone and depicted the horse on its hind legs while the man held a round shield and had his sword pointed to the sky.

"The statue shows King Rían in the battle that united the clans," Amber said as they went pass the statue. It stood high over them, double the size of life.

Gilroy stopped at the steps of the palace and got off his horse. He told Teague and Conn to take the men to the barracks and settle in. Then he looked at Amber and Alastar. "Young ones, come now." Alastar expected to go with the rest of the soldiers, though, and looked at Teague.

"Enjoy your stay in the palace, Sire," Teague told Alastar with a tone of jest. Teague smiled and gave a curt bow of his head. "The fightin' men will be at your feet." Alastar understood his joking. It made him feel better and diminished his uncomfortable feeling of being thrown into a grand palace as if he were a penniless servant given the king's chambers.

"Grand craic for a skint fellow!" Alastar joked in return.

"*Skint?. . .*" Teague questioned, "Hardly. You've much means 'n wealth about ya, lad. But sure 'nough, let it be grand craic for ya." He gestured to the men and rode with Conn to the barracks. The rest of the party followed them while Amber and Alastar got off their horses. They walked up the wide expanse of steps to the palace doors, while servants waited for them in the open doorway.

"You'll be taken ta your rooms," Gilroy said to Amber and Alastar. "Rest for the day. I have thin's ta attend. Just ask for me if need be. Remember ta stay in the palace, and ask for whatever you need. The grounds are yours." He looked at Alastar. "Perhaps you should continue ta stand near the princess. . . ta keep out of trouble. She knows royal etiquette." As he left, he told a servant, "Give them rooms next ta each other and send in their bags."

*A*lastar woke from a long nap in the evening. The room was dark except for faint twilight that came through the windows and glass doors. He got up and looked out a window. His room was high above the ground and had a small balcony that faced the bay. He walked to the glass patio doors and opened it. The air was chill, but he stepped outside to look.

He went forward to the stone railing on the balcony and looked around. Amber was right. The palace was very quiet. There were no sounds of the evening – no chirping crickets or calling birds or the soft murmur of the sea. He could barely hear the cool breeze that swept softly about the mountain.

The bay and twinkling lights of the city were clear, though. It appeared to be late in the evening. Bright stars shone through scattered pillows of clouds. There were few people out. He scanned the palace grounds below and wondered where Éimhín was. He couldn't tell where the stables were, but a building near the wall looked like it was the barracks. Many soldiers were standing leisurely around it.

Then he heard the faint speech of people coming from below. He leaned farther over the railing and looked down. King Fuar and Amber were talking at a table on a large terrace. Many torches lit the area and servants attended them and brought food.

He couldn't hear what they were talking about, but Amber didn't look comfortable in front of the king. She always had a more relaxed elegance whenever he saw her, but now her body and movements were stiff. He couldn't see her face. She had her back to him, but he could see the king's face. He appeared to be agitated but was speaking calmly.

After some moments, Fuar looked up and saw Alastar. A smile came to Fuar and he gestured for Alastar to join them. Amber looked backwards to see who Fuar was speaking to. She smiled when she saw Alastar. Fuar noticed her display of affection and gestured to a servant. He said something to him and the servant left.

Alastar acknowledged the king's invitation with a nod and wave. He went down to the terrace entrance where guards stood watch. They didn't let him pass until a servant came out to get him. As he walked up to the table, he noticed this was the first time he saw Amber look tired. The torch lights flickered in her weary eyes and she gave him a warm smile that continued to glow radiant life despite her fatigue.

Fuar stood up and extended his hand. "Son," he said, "Welcome." Amber stood up as well. Alastar noticed the king now appeared to be very pleasant. He took Fuar's hand with both of his, pressed firmly, and bowed his head.

"Sire," Alastar acknowledged. Amber was impressed that he didn't fumble greeting the king. Alastar looked very comfortable.

"Sit," Fuar said.

Alastar sat at the table in between Fuar and Amber. Servants set down a plate and utensils for him to eat. Fuar and Amber sat down again.

"You must be famished," Fuar said. "I don't believe you've eaten since arrivin'. Slept quite soundly since ya set foot in your room, I hear. Go on, eat."

"Thank you, Sire," Alastar said.

"You seem quite popular since comin' ta Cnoc na Rí," Fuar said. He looked at Amber. "You as well, Amber. The city missed her princess and is glad ta see the Swan-bearer. In fact, word of your bold flight through the largest Áiteoir army anyone's seen is flyin' circles through the city, like that dragon bitin' at your heels. Impossible grand thin's! I've not seen the people rejoice as this for many years. Perhaps we should honor ya with a céilí as they did in Loch an Scátháin?" He gave a slight smile and chuckled softly.

Amber looked at Alastar. "They gave ya a céilí?"

"They did," Alastar said. "I think it was Conall's idea. It's not something I'd prefer, but I admit they put on a grand show with the music and dancin'."

"Conall," Fuar said. "My best commander in the south region. Fights like a ragin' fáelshee, and smart, but he's a soft heart. Not surprised at all he gave you a céilí." His words flowed like thick bitter juice that mixed with thinly sugared water. Alastar got the impression he did not approve of the céilí in Loch an Scátháin. "And the people there, they must've loved ya as they do here."

"They treated me as family," Alastar said. "Wonderful folk at the mountains' mirror. Do ya think they're in danger?"

"That's ta be seen," Fuar answered. "But worry not over them. Losing Loch an Scátháin cannot come ta pass. The lake nurtures the life of the valley, from loch ta river ta sea. The enemy cannot be allowed ta tamper with it."

Gilroy stepped through the terrace doors and came to the table. "Sire, Amber, Alastar," he greeted.

"I called ya for discourse with the boy," Fuar said. "Sit with us."

Gilroy sat down across from Alastar. He waved away servants who tried to give him a plate and utensils for the meal. "There *is* much ta speak of."

"There is," Fuar said. He looked at Alastar. "You would be glad ta know the army pursuin' you did not wish ta engage us at Dún Liath. Their envoy met with me, and they saw no good in pressin' on after seein' you escape inta the mountains. Instead, they refortified Dún Liath and sent the rest of the army back ta Lacharan."

Gilroy added, "Reports from Lacharan say the entire army retreated back to the northwest where they came from. Lacharan stands safe. Your bold plan did work, son, but we fear the enemy rounds the mountains ta march on Dun Tearmann and Loch an Scátháin."

Amber looked at Alastar after Gilroy mentioned Loch an Scátháin could be in danger, but he still did not show emotions.

"Son," Fuar said, "Have ya reason why the Áiteoir would press inta Loch an Scátháin? You're not there, and all their movement of late has been ta move against you."

Alastar got nervous and hesitated. He didn't want to discuss his feelings in front of Amber, but he had little choice. He avoided looking at her and said, "Perhaps Braede told them of my interest. . . there." Amber perked up to listen further.

"Let me guess," Fuar said with a roguish smile. "A *girl?*"

Alastar didn't want to answer. He felt Amber's stare and sensed her heart was holding its breath as if it expected to be stabbed through.

Gilroy looked at Alastar. "You mean, the 'grebe' you lads were jokin' of?"

"Right, sir," Alastar acknowledged. He was blushing and couldn't look at Amber. He asked Fuar with a voice of concern, "Are reinforcements ta be called for Loch an Scátháin? Many lives were lost and I'm certain they couldn't stand another attack."

"We're preparin' units ta leave in a day's time," Fuar said.

"You mean tomorrow?" Alastar asked.

Fuar returned Alastar's question with a look of annoyance. "I mean tomorra' evenin'. As early as we can."

Gilroy looked surprised. "Sire, shouldn't they be dispatched at day break? The Áiteoir could be in the hill country by mornin'. They have no concerns over the truce. We aren't bound by it any longer. We should send swift force ta be ahead of their march."

"I've no concerns, Chancellor," Fuar said. "They spent the night chasin' ya here and the rest of today runnin' back. They march as if their feet never left the mud of their bog lands. The lot of 'em looked worse than scangers beggin' for crumbs on the market floor. They didn't have the strength ta fight me at Dún Liath. They certainly won't have the strength ta march inta Loch an Scátháin tomorra'. That army may outnumber us by five, but I've yet ta feel an ounce of threat from 'em."

Gilroy still didn't understand why Fuar wouldn't send their troops as soon as possible. "Sire, they nearly breached the walls of Lacharan and their army outnumbers Conall's men by a hundred ta one. It would be a prudent precaution ta send troops early in the mornin'. Perhaps…"

Fuar cut him off. "I've decided! There's not need ta hurry here," he said firmly. He looked at Alastar. "It also gives time for ya, boy, ta train before your friends leave. The chancellor told me our best teachers are ta school ya, and so you will have 'em, but I imagine ya'd like Teague's instruction as long as he's here. He and Conn will go south with their men ta refortify Dún Tearmann and Loch an Scátháin along with my soldiers tomorra'."

"I appreciate that, Sire," Alastar said. "I will be ready ta train first thing in the mornin'."

"Good then," Fuar said. "You may stay in the palace and train as long as ya need. In fact, you're free ta go and do as ya please, in my city and outside. I wouldn't be one ta lock ya here."

"I wouldn't let him outside the palace, Sire," Gilroy said. "The enemy knows the boy is here. He isn't safe outside these walls; nor is the princess."

"Nonsense!" Fuar retorted. "There's not a safer place than the whole of my valley and its mountains." He looked at Alastar. "You're a strong, sensible lad. You may go as ya please. You got everyone safely here, did ya not?" Then he looked to Amber. "But you, Amber. I would ask that you stay in the palace. It is the customary way."

A look of concern came over Amber's tired, heartbroken face. She did not want Alastar roaming about, certainly not without her and a company of guards. "I understand, Sire," she responded. "I have no plans ta go elsewhere. But I ask you ta keep Alastar inside the palace for his safety."

"I'm very grateful the boy brought ya here," Fuar said. "But his duties with ya are fulfilled. The Swan-bearer has brought the 'Swans' ta the throne of Torthúil, and now here you sit. He may go as he pleases."

A feeling of dread came over Amber and tears started to well up in her eyes. She rose up and turned to walk away. She moved so quickly that she bumped her wine glass and made it spill, but she walked away without concern for it. Alastar and Gilroy were troubled as they watched her leave, but Fuar sat without showing emotion. A servant rushed to the table and cleaned up the spilt wine.

"What was that?" Gilroy asked Fuar.

"The flight of a woman, I imagine," he said nonchalantly. "Who knows which way they go?"

Alastar wondered what bothered Amber. He never saw her upset before. Was it her concern for his safety?

"Amber isn't known ta go off without consideration," Gilroy said.

Alastar felt he should talk to her and started to get up. "I should. . ."

"She's tired," Fuar interjected. "She had little rest all day.

Leave her be. Finish your meal, son."

Alastar sat back down and continued to eat.

"Chancellor," Fuar said, "See that the boy starts trainin' early as he wishes. That will be all."

"Certainly, Sire," Gilroy acknowledged. He got up and left.

Alastar felt uncomfortable being alone with Fuar. The king appeared to be appraising him in every movement. It felt like the first night in Rathúnas when Conall and Braede inspected him closely. However, Fuar did it in silence with the strong eyes of distrust.

Some minutes passed before Fuar spoke. "I know you wish ta see your friends ta safety in Loch an Scáthain. It would be a grand thin' for them ta see ya return with many horses and swords. You're not a great warrior yet, but my instructors can have ya ready ta fight with the rest of your friends by day's end when they leave. They may keep ya ta the rear, but you'd be in the fight, if even there is one."

"I *would* like ta return ta Loch an Scáthain and help," Alastar replied with interest. "But I gave the princess my word ta help see her through whatever she needs."

"And ya *have* helped her in grand fashion!" Fuar exclaimed. "Amber is safe here, and her throne will not escape either. Where will it go?" He laughed. "What more can ya do for her here, son? Go on with your friends. The enemy will be tired and spent anyways. It will hardly be a fight if they attack."

The thought of coming back to Loch an Scáthain with the troops was appealing to Alastar. He felt bad having to leave them the evening they were attacked. Going back to help fight and rebuild would be redeeming. "Thank you, Sire. I *will* join the troops tomorrow. I believe the princess is well cared for here."

"Grand, grand!" Fuar said. "I wish I could march with you, Swan-bearer, and see the Áiteoir flee before our brilliant fighters." He got up. "Have a fine day of trainin' tomorra', son, and don't speak of leavin' ta Amber. She appears ta be most sensitive ta the subject. Let me tell her."

"Certainly, Sire. Thank you," Alastar said.

Fuar walked away and Alastar sat silent at the table and finished his meal. He was happy to know he could return to Loch an Scáthháin soon and see Nola. He had to find out how her and his friends were faring after the battle.

Alastar soon finished eating and got up. He clumsily thanked the servants and went back to his room through many hallways lit by oil lanterns. He could barely see anything in his room with the door to the hallway closed, so he lit some lanterns and candles that were arrayed around the room with the tine-stone Nola gave him. The ivory and blue décor of his room glowed in the slowly moving flames. Their soft shadows danced in every corner.

Alastar noticed all his bags and staff were in his room. They were brought up when he was sleeping earlier. He looked at his staff and then at his sword set by the bed. They represented different parts of his life – one of a simple, peaceful past and the other of complex turns and sharp edges. He never could have expected his life to change so much, but he hoped to still make a simple and peaceful life for himself. He would soon be back in Loch an Scáthháin and hopefully free soon to live a quiet life with Nola after the enemy was thoroughly run off. He fell asleep with many daydreams of a triumphant return to the south of the valley.

*T*he night passed swiftly for Alastar in the deep sleep of new hopes. He got up before dawn and started to get ready. He wanted to go into the city to sell his staff. He was fond of it, but he didn't need it any longer. He noticed it got in the way of swinging his sword while he was riding, and he didn't have need to wield both a sword and long staff. His staff would fetch a good price with the right merchant.

Alastar put on his sword but left his armor. He would return to gear up for training after this errand. He left his room carrying his staff in its leather riding holster. Then he found a servant and asked where the stables were. They were just beyond the barracks.

He went outside and walked toward the east where he saw the barracks from the balcony. The rising sun was just peeking above the palace walls. It made the white polished stone around him glisten in bright gold streaks of sunlight.

Alastar continued toward the barracks. Soldiers were just starting to move about in the early morning. Most of them waved and acknowledged him cheerfully. He stopped by the entrance to see if Teague was there, but a soldier said he had gone.

Alastar proceeded to the stables where he found the horses. Éimhín was next to Muirgel at the far end. The stables were packed full with the additional horses of Lacharan. There must have been almost two hundred all together in the stables.

"How ya farin', boy?" Alastar asked Éimhín. "You're packed in here like beans in a bag." He walked around Éimhín and rubbed his hide. "Ya look grand. All our quick runs haven't worn ya at all. I'm off ta do somethin', but I'll see ya later today. We've more runnin' ta look forward to. Back ta Loch an Scátháin."

Alastar turned to Muirgel and stroked her fine coat. "My you're a fine mare. Don'tcha let Éimhín be eyein' ya. He's not used ta bein' round girls pretty as ya are." Éimhín let out a snort and nicker of discontent. Alastar laughed softly and left the stables.

He went to the palace gate and walked outside. The guards showed him where the markets were. They pointed him towards the bay. "Cnoc Seamair ["Kruk Shæ-mer"; Clover Hill] straight off ta the bay," one of them said. "They'll just be startin' their day 'bout now."

The city streets were still very quiet. Cnoc na Rí felt like an abandoned city after seeing all the people the day before. Alastar walked through miles of closely packed houses and buildings. They were all built on top of the mountain's hard granite rock, which served as the pavement for the streets as well. Everything looked exceptionally sturdy and clean compared to the structures of Lacharan.

Most of the houses in Lacharan were built of wood and thatch, but Cnoc na Rí was built largely of the same granite and marble that the palace was built with. Even the roofs appeared very sturdy, layered with thick, rounded clay bricks of reds and browns. They were overlaid like ruby scales that accented the tops of silver white fish.

As Alastar got closer to the shore, the terrain turned to green with short, thick grass and clovers covering the ground everywhere. The structures continued to be solid stone, but the houses were not so densely packed on the hill. Soon he saw the beginning of the market district where many colorful signs and canopies hung in front of the buildings.

Alastar looked for a shop that specialized in carved wood. He found one near the end of the street. Its sign was a carving of a mermaid basking on rocks with the text – Woods and Trinkets. Beyond it he saw the docks full of sailing ships. Sailors and merchants were busy loading and unloading, while royal guards stood watch.

Alastar turned back to the shop and walked in. He found a heavy-set old man arranging wood figurines on a shelf. He turned around and greeted Alastar. "Early are we?" he said. "Or is twilight yet? Could've sworn mo bean ["bæn"; wife] come back ta have a right áirneál ["ahrr- nya-ul"][5] with me."

Alastar looked at him with a curious expression. He didn't understand the words the merchant used.

"Not from here, are ya lad?" the merchant said. "Well, come along now. Ya needn't stand there in bits. Call me Murtagh ["Mer-tah"]."

Alastar approached him. "Grand ta meet ya, Murtagh. I *am* new ta Rathúnas, sir, but your choice of words alludes me. What were ya sayin'?"

"Curious," Murtagh said as he eyed Alastar keenly. "Ya have the right look of an Eachraighe Brother. Ya carry a sword with their standard. Are ya not a Rider?"

"Surely. I am with the Eachraighe, sir."

"Then how could ya be *new* ta the isle?" Murtagh said with confusion. Then a sudden look of comprehension came to him. "*Rapid!* You came in with the princess yesterday, didn't ya? *HA!* Grand day! Grand day it is! Hardly anyone comes ta my corner so early. Yet here now the Swan-bearer stands before me! Forgive me, son. I thought ya were a local. I was only makin' jest when ya walked in; it bein' so early. I was only sayin' how I thought your steppin' through my door could be my wife come back for a friendly night visit. Pay no mind ta that. I'm at your service. What brin's ya ta my little shop?"

Alastar put his staff in front of Murtagh. "I came ta sell my staff, sir. Would ya give a fair price?"

---

[5] 'ny' is an 'n' + 'y' sound like the Spanish niño, pronounced "neenyo"

Murtagh took the staff out of its holster. He examined it and grinned wide. "Exquisite, son. Where was this worked?"

"I carved it myself, sir."

"Banjax that! Did ya?" Murtagh looked at him with surprise. "You're an expert woodcarver too?" He continued to look over the staff carefully. "Beautiful carvin'. . . Rich gold texture. . . Just a few nicks. . . It appears ta be. . . chestnut?"

Alastar shook his head. "Much harder than chestnut."

"Not the right texture or color ta be cherry or pine," Murtagh pondered. "Wait. . . I have ya! It's from a strawberry tree! Exact right texture and grain."

Alastar smiled. "You do know your woods, but its desert ironwood, sir. You'll be hard pressed ta find anythin' harder and ya won't find any wood like it on Rathúnas. It comes from the desert valley near my home."

"Ahhh, I don't know ironwood, son, but I've heard of wood axes and blades from the dry Réalta ["Ree-ahl-tah"] Mountains beyond the south seas. Wood so heavy it sinks. And when hardened by enchantment, it's just as hard as our cré-umha ["kray-oo"] armor and blades."

"Crayyy-ooo?" Alastar tried pronouncing.

"Cré-umha draíochta ["kray-oo dree-ehkkta"], our Enchanted Bronze, son," Murtagh said. Alastar looked at him without a clue. Murtagh waited a few seconds before filling him in. "Your sword, lad. It'd be made of cré-umha draíochta – a trademark of Torthúil – made from rock mined in our mountains and forged by our conjuring blacksmiths."

Now Alastar understood why most of the armor and weapons he saw was made of bronze. *Iron and steel must not be common or not in use here,* he thought. Cré-umha was enchanted bronze that was even harder than the best steel and did not corrode like iron or steel did.

"I see," Alastar acknowledged.

"May I test your staff?" Murtagh asked.

"Certainly."

"Follow me ta the back." Murtagh went to a back door with the staff and exited the shop. He walked to a long trough full of water in a rear fenced-in yard. He set the staff on the water's surface and it quickly sank to the bottom. "Sinks like a stone. Ironwood, it is," he said with satisfaction. He grabbed it out of the trough and walked back inside. They walked back to the storefront as Murtagh dried the staff with a towel.

"I trust ya know the staff is of the highest quality," Alastar said. "How much would ya pay for it, ridin' holster included?"

"Your staff is fit ta adorn the palace, son," Murtagh said. He pondered a moment. *If I have it hardened as the wares of Réalta, it would fetch a kingly price. At least 50 quid,* he thought.

"*Buuut. . .*" Murtagh said. "There are some mars on it. I'll give ya 15 quid."

Fifteen quid (pounds) sounded low to Alastar. He thought he could get at least twenty. "15 pounds?" he repeated with hesitation. "You can't be serious, sir. Let's make it 30. Ya don't know how far this staff has traveled ta come here."

"Right, lad. It does have special origin, and it would be the most valuable item here," Murtagh said. He hesitated to give Alastar the full price. "Staffs are easy ta sell. . . Sure, sure. 30 quid for ya, son."

Alastar gave a pleased smile. "Grand!"

Murtagh went to a backroom where he rummaged through many coins. He soon came back with a small bag of coins and handed it to Alastar. "30 quid solid."

"Thank you, sir." Alastar looked in the bag and noticed all the coins were the same 2 pound pieces. He needed smaller coinage if he was to buy a variety of things. "Only, could ya break the coins? Make half of it smaller coin?"

"Certainly, son. I'll save ya a trip ta the banker." Murtagh took the bag again and left the room. He came back with the bag packed full. "There ya are. Two-quids, quids, bobs, coppers and halfpennies."

Alastar looked in the bag again. He selected a pound piece and gave it to Murtagh. "For your trouble, sir."

"Are ya *gone* in the head?!" Murtagh burst out. "Most of the thin's here cost less than half this quid! Let me give ya somethin' for it." He started to look around the shop.

"That's alright, sir," Alastar said. "Your help is worth the coin. I must be returnin'. Thank you!" He left the shop in good spirits. He felt he was starting to settle into a life in Rathúnas. He had plans. He had friends. He had money. He felt a new home and family of his own would come swiftly now. Thoughts of returning to Eritirim were far from him.

Alastar returned to the palace with clouds moving in to canvas the sky. It made the palace appear cold gray, like the bare cliffs of the mountains surrounding it. A servant at the front entrance told him to meet Teague at the stables. He needed to begin the day's training.

Alastar quickly went up to his room and put on his armor. He put most of his money in a saddlebag and kept a handful in his pants. He separated a halfpenny and put it in a different pocket than the rest.

As he dressed, a knock sounded at his door. "Come in!" he answered.

The door opened and Amber walked in. He noticed she was wearing the rose hairpin he made for her. She was dressed in a fine but simple emerald green gown with a short, tight collar and high neckline fastened by three buttons. She still had a tired look about her. It looked like she hardly slept during the night.

"I tried you earlier, but you'd gone already," she said.

"I was just in the market by the shore. I sold my staff for a handsome price." He walked to her and took out the halfpenny from his pocket. "Here ya are, Princess. For your trouble on the docks the other day." He gave her the coin.

"Trouble?" she wondered. Amber gave him a puzzled look.

"For the linseed oil you bought me."

Amber smiled. "Nonsense. It was a gift." She gave the halfpenny back to him. "Besides. . . if you remember, you gave me a splendid thin' ta remember for my trouble." She turned her head slightly and touched the hairpin with her hand.

Alastar finished putting on his armor and grabbed his helmet. "I'm expected for trainin'."

"Right," she said. "I only wished ta apologize for leavin' so suddenly on the terrace." She gazed at him as if she had sent a love letter to him years ago and still waited for his reply. She took his helmet from his hands and put it on him like she did in Lacharan. "I don't know what came over me."

Alastar looked up and over her head to avoid eye-contact, but he could feel the warmth of her hands on his cheeks as she tightened the chinstrap. His heart turned a few steps, like it had stumbled on a loose stone on the road he paved towards a life with Nola. He thought he was walking solidly on it, but whenever Amber came close, it reminded him of the feeling he got in the garden with her – that wholeness of purpose. His breathing became strained as he felt he needed to step back from her.

When she finished tightening the strap, Alastar stepped away from her and looked into her eyes. "You needn't say sorry, Princess.

We thought you were terribly tired, shattered from all the runnin'." He turned and grabbed his bags. "I hope ya find grand rest t'day."

"Thank you. I may walk the gardens later," she said. She hoped he would find interest in joining her.

"Wonderful! Slán!" Alastar replied quickly and rushed out the door. He wanted to avoid speaking too much in case she might ask about the troops leaving. He didn't want to let on that he would be leaving with them later.

Alastar found Teague getting his horse ready in the stables. "Get Éimhín set ta ride, lad," Teague said. "You're ta learn some Eachraighe swordsmanship. We'll make ya ready ta meet the enemy chargin' on horseback!"

After Alastar left, Amber went to her balcony to watch him go to the stables. She saw him walk swiftly with the saddlebags over his right shoulder. He appeared very focused and seemed to go straight to the stables without taking notice in anything else. Many soldiers with their horses were busy gathering in the area. Most of them were making their way to the training grounds outside the palace walls in the east. *I can watch them from the sky bridge,* she thought. *They'll just be starting when I get there.*

Amber left her room. "If anyone needs me, I will be headin' ta the gardens," she told a servant in the hall. She made her way through long corridors toward the east side of the palace. Even though, she hadn't spent a lot of time in Cnoc na Rí, she remembered the layout of things. Her memory was nearly perfect for most everything. It often helped her learn, and she put it to good use in music and singing as well as her official royal affairs.

In a few minutes she came to the door that connected to the sky bridge and continued walking. The bridge was a long, raised walkway of stone arch bridges that connected many round towers the entire way to the garden by the shore. It was over a mile long and three stories high, while the towers were double the height. The bridge was used by the palace to look over the city and gain access to various points at the towers. It allowed royalty to walk to and view the inner city without having to pass through the streets.

Amber walked for many minutes along the bridge as it descended from the topmost parts of the city to the lower areas. She stopped inside a round tower near the training grounds. There, she went into a small room with a balcony and sat on a couch to watch.

Many groups gathered in the field below and made mock charges at standing posts that stood in the place of foot soldiers. She found Alastar and Teague in a smaller group with the royal instructors. They were telling Alastar how to swing his sword on horseback. Soon he was making charges at the straw-stuffed targets with other cavalry riders.

Amber was glad to see Alastar honing his soldier's skills. He was a ready and eager student. She watched him for a time and hoped he would look up and see her in the tower, but he never did. *Always immersed in what he's doing,* she thought. She fell asleep on the couch wondering when he would turn his eyes and heart to her.

Some time had passed and Amber woke to the loud trumpet of a commander's battle horn. She sat up and looked down at the training field. Everyone gathered in front of Fuar and Gilroy who were also on horses. She looked about the sky to see how much time had passed. She felt like she slept for hours. Her body was numb in deep slumber. The sky was darker than before, so she couldn't see the sun anywhere behind the clouds. The wind was moving swifter too. A storm seemed to be building.

She turned back to the assembly below her and tried to listen, but she was too far away to hear what the king said. Then before she could wonder what was happening, the horn blew again and all the soldiers on horseback started to gallop west, back toward the palace. Something was happening.

Amber ran down the stairs of the round tower to catch the king and chancellor before they left. When she burst through the door, everyone had gone except Fuar, Gilroy and a small company of guards.

"Sire!" she yelled. She stopped running and tried to catch her breath.

Fuar turned to face her. "Leave me ta speak with her," he told Gilroy and the guards. They all left as Amber approached.

"Sire," she said. "Where is everyone goin' so swiftly?"

"I called the troops ta leave for Loch an Scáthain immediately. The Greerian reported the mass of the Áiteoir army entering our hill country."

"Why did Alastar leave trainin' as well?" she asked. Her earnest eyes looked up at Fuar high on his horse. "He isn't goin' with the troops is he?"

"He is, Princess. Bein' part of our grand charge gave the boy some bolt. The chancellor did not approve, but the lad made his choice. He'll flare a grand fight. Worry not over the boy."

Amber's heart flittered into tatters hearing that Alastar was leaving. Amber pleaded, "He's not ready ta fight with the army, Sire. I ask you. Keep Alastar here. His presence in the battle won't affect its outcome."

"Nonsense," Fuar retorted. "The troops are quite uplifted ta have the Swan-bearer with 'em. He may not decide the battle, but his enthusiasm rides with the others. His friends in Loch an Scáthháin will be very glad ta see him as well." He held out his hand to Amber. "Come. Ride back ta the palace with me."

Amber bowed respectfully. "I decline, Sire. I will take the sky bridge back. Thank you."

"Very well then," Fuar said with a look of disappointment. He turned his horse and rode off with his company of waiting guards.

Amber rushed back to the round tower and ran along the sky bridge. She hoped to get back to the palace before Alastar left. Maybe she could convince him not to go. Her feet began to hurt in her slippers, so she took them off. The guards along the bridge watched her curiously as she ran past them. She couldn't remember running so hard before. Her breath nearly gave way when she reached the door into the palace.

But before she could open the door, she heard the horn sound again. *Oh no!* she worried. She ran to the side of the bridge to see what was happening. There was a large cavalry unit assembled outside the palace gates. At the horn's call, they all rode forward on the west road into the River Valley.

It was too late to reach Alastar. She saw him ride away in the rear with the last of the troops. There must have been only 600 riders. Too few to match the tens of thousands they rode to meet in battle. Amber's spirit started to shrink in distress. How could the king not send more troops? How could Alastar leave without telling her?

Tumbling Compasses

*C*onall assembled his remaining troops to face the Áiteoir that came from the northwest. They were centered in the fields between Loch an Scátháin and Dún Tearmann. A cool rain started to lash down on them. Conall sat atop his horse at the front and faced the hills. He could see the enemy's wide line approach them slowly.

So this is the army that almost took Lacharan, Conall said to himself. *Why did they come back?* He looked around at his unit of almost 600 men. They were the last of his fighting men. They stood silent in the rain and looked solemn, as if they attended a grave burial. His men had no spirit of cheer left in them after losing half their number in recent days.

"Stand easy!" Conall shouted to his men over the sound of a few bodhrán drummers who beat a rhythm to rally their spirits. "The king promised ta send force from Cnoc na Rí. They will come in time ta fight beside us!" He drew his sword and lifted it high towards the enemy. "Their axe head is broad and heavy. . ." Then he hit the side of his sword's blade hard against his round shield many times. "But they meet the anvil of Torthúil, lads! We are the hardened of the hills and mountains and fear not what blows come! Strike tiresome fear, lads! Strike it down with our enemy!"

Conall lifted his commander's horn from his saddle and blew a long note. It was a slender, bronze, semi-U-shaped horn with its sounding hole on one side of its narrow end. The men raised their swords and spears with a great shout in response. They knew the odds were against them, but they resolved to stand firm. As the enemy approached, Conall rode out forward, left and right to survey the land. He tried to spy the king's reinforcements without letting his men see his weary appeals for help. They would come from the east, however, the hills and fields toward Loch an Scátháin stood empty under the dark clouds.

The rain kept falling in slow waves that swept across their faces. The wind sent cold water through every crack and crevice in their armor as if it resolved to empty their spirits completely. Its piercing chilliness rushed to void their determination, but the men simply stood firm with gritty resolve tightening over their brows.

Conall returned to the front and center of his unit. A half hour passed as the rain continued to soak through them. The enemy was close enough to charge now. Their line covered the horizon in front of them.

Conall ordered his foot soldiers, "Make a thistle, lads!" The men formed a large, tight circle, four to five men deep with the spearmen behind the swordsmen. They pointed their long spears outward as they stood shoulder to shoulder. The outer men hunched below the spearheads and stood ready with their swords and shields up. They would fight in this formation until they could no longer hold it. It would help them resist the great numbers against them.

The Áiteoir battle horn called out through the gray, wet plain. Its dark iron funnel created a low boom, like the deep bellow of a huge bull. Their entire line charged forward with the cavalry going first. The foot soldiers behind them quickly split into two fronts – one headed southwest toward Dún Tearmann while the other went toward them and to Loch an Scátháin. All their cavalry rushed toward Conall.

Conall wanted to draw them away from Dún Tearmann because all their friends and family took safety behind its high timber walls. Loch an Scátháin and its hidden mountain refuge were empty. They couldn't trust that the refuge remained a secure secret after Braede betrayed them.

Conall rallied his cavalry and they rushed toward the left to break the line going to Dún Tearmann. Half his riders held long spears that they pointed forward. They aimed level to take down the Áiteoir riders that came toward them. In less than a minute, they came close enough to see the Áiteoir cavalry wore heavy, black armor of different design than they'd seen before. It glistened smooth in the rain, and even their horses were fully covered.

When Conall's riders met the enemy cavalry, many of their spears broke under the impact of the charge. They dislodged many of the Áiteoir from their horses and continued to hack at them as the large number of infantry on foot advanced. Conall waited until the infantry drew closer, then he ordered his riders to charge them. They left the remaining enemy riders behind. Most of them gave chase, but they were slower under their heavy armor. Conall's men kept ahead of them as they cut down the infantry. They kept moving swiftly so they couldn't be overwhelmed and taken off their horses.

Conall's foot soldiers held strong as well. They were able to stop most of the heavy cavalry that came at them and were holding against the infantry. They were losing many men, though, and their thistle of spears and swords continued to shrink as wave upon wave of attacks punched into them.

The battle went on for a long time and large numbers of the enemy continued toward Dún Tearmann and Loch an Scátháin. The rain fell the whole while. Conall and his men began to fatigue. At times he looked to the east for a glimpse of help from Cnoc na Rí, but the horizon remained a dark empty expanse.

After near an hour, many of his riders were pulled off their horses. They could no longer hold up the speed and agility they needed to keep from being swarmed. His foot soldiers, too, were very tired. They lost half their number and continued to fall, yet they kept their tight thistle formation against the thousands continuing to attack.

Just beyond the battlefield, Conall saw the Áiteoir commander on his horse. He wore a dark, stony suit of armor like his heavy cavalry. His suit had more ridges and ornamentation, though, and his flat topped, round helm was capped with spiky frills on its sides. The commander struck the butt of his spear into the ground and picked up his battle horn. He blew a long note and held up his spear into the air. A long orange and black banner at the spearhead waved in the windy rain. He pointed it to the east.

Conall looked where the commander pointed and saw many dark dots coming out of the hills in the northeast. It was a cavalry unit. He quickly burst out of the soldiers that were attacking him and shouted, "Torthúil!" He took chase of the enemy commander and riders who went to charge the new troops. Conall's remaining riders joined him. They barely numbered thirty from the hundred that began the fight.

Conall's cavalry rushed through the wind and rain. They were catching up with the enemy even though they were much worn from fighting. Soon they heard the call of a high pitched horn from Cnoc na Rí's riders. It surged their spirits through and they all let out a shout. They chased the hundreds of Áiteoir riders until they all clashed together in great clouds of bronze against dark metal.

The 600 riders from Cnoc na Rí found it difficult to cut down the Áiteoir heavy cavalry, but they had more soldiers and fresh vigor. The Áiteoir riders started to fall in greater number, but their infantry was moving in from both directions of Loch an Scátháin and Dún Tearmann. The troops coming from Loch an Scátháin were already very close. They had found the town empty and were coming back to the battlefront.

Conall was so busy fighting he didn't notice Alastar was in the rear and holding off the enemy admirably. The Áiteoir commander quickly identified Alastar, though, and led a surge of riders to him. They cut toward him like a great sickle thrashing a path through a field of grain. When Conall saw where they were going he yelled to Teague who was directly in their path. "Shield Alastar!" Conall urged.

The dark hulking Áiteoir commander was bent on reaching Alastar and pushed past everyone. Teague was overwhelmed by many attackers and no one else could help push them back. Conall saw their advance to Alastar and broke free of the battle. He rode as swiftly as he could around the perimeter, but the infantry had come in and slowed him down when he needed to slice through them.

Before Conall could reach Alastar the enemy commander made his way close to him. Alastar was busy hacking at attacking foot soldiers and didn't notice the commander lift his spear. Éimhín saw the threat and reared up to defend Alastar, but the commander's aim was good. His spear flew swift past Éimhín and struck Alastar in the left shoulder. He gasped as the force of the heavy spear threw him to the ground.

Conall gave out a great shout of torment and rage when he saw Alastar fall. He rushed toward him and jumped from his horse with his sword out and shield ready. He ran through the infantry like a battering ram and cut down whoever tried to overcome Alastar. Conall hovered over him like a great white bear protecting its cub.

Alastar struggled on the ground in pain and tried to get up. He called to Conall, "The spear's pinned me ta the ground!"

"Be still, lad!" Conall yelled as he continued to fight off attackers.

The Áiteoir commander got off his horse and drew the large sword that hung from his back. The great long sword was dark as his armor and almost double the size of everyone else's. He walked toward Conall with a slow and confident gait. Conall stood firm to meet the commander. As they engaged in swordfight, Teague worked his way to Alastar with a few other soldiers. He never saw the Áiteoir wear such heavy armor or fight so fiercely as they did here. They were like the menacing fáelshee and even harder to kill under their bristling armor.

The rain was coming to a stop, but Conall hardly noticed as he fought the commander. He was so fatigued from fighting for the past hour that the heavy blows from the commander sent his frame buckling. Soon Conall's wood shield splintered and split under the hammering of the heavy sword. Conall threw the shield at the commander when a large chuck of it if fell away.

The commander stood enraged. He charged Conall with a shout and swung his armored forearm at Conall's head. The side of Conall's helmet crumpled and the commander quickly gave another hard blow with the butt of his sword. Conall fell back in a daze and the commander pierced his stomach through with a mighty thrust. The heavy sword broke through Conall's chainmail and he fell flat to the ground near Alastar.

Teague rushed harder to reach them but he was still too far to help. The commander stepped forward and raised his sword with its point towards Alastar's chest. He plunged it down, but Conall mustered enough strength to strike it with his sword. The commander's sword deflected from Alastar's chest and plunged through his left thigh instead. Alastar screamed in pain.

Conall tried to get up but his strength was gone. He quickly fell back down and life left him. Teague shouted as he ran hard at the commander and tackled him to the ground. The commander was a hulking man, the same size as Conall, and fell to the ground with a solid crash. Others rushed to defend Alastar and Conall from further attacks.

The commander got up quickly and lifted off his helmet. His long dark hair was wet with sweat. Teague was just getting up. An angry scowl came over the commander's tan leathery face. He used his helmet to batter Teague's head with a long arcing swing. Teague went flying backwards and the commander ran for his horse. There were too many soldiers around them, so he commanded his troops to regroup at Dún Tearmann.

The Áiteoir retreated quickly with their commander. The soldiers of Torthúil shouted in victory and grouped around Teague and Conn. It was a vicious fight that took many of their lives, but their unit stood strong and ready.

Teague looked at Conn with stricken relief. "Grand fight, Captain. Go now ta save Dún Tearmann. I will tend ta Conall and Alastar."

Conn acknowledged and led the troops to chase after the Áiteoir. Teague turned to Alastar and found Éimhín nuzzling his face. *That Éimhín is a loyal one,* he thought. Alastar was awake but couldn't move. Teague saw Conall motionless too and ran to them hoping that Conall was still alive.

Teague knelt down and took off Conall's helmet. When he realized he was dead, grief struck his heart. He couldn't believe Conall was gone. They had spent a lifetime together as friends and soldiers. He always thought Conall would be the last man standing after a battle.

"Conall's left us," Teague told Alastar. "Laochmarú ["Lee-ukhk-mahr-roo"] didn't leave ya much better."

"Laochmarú?" Alastar asked gritting through pain. He felt cold and dizzy from the loss of blood and damp spring air. It stopped raining, but the sun was not shining its warmth on them.

"General Laochmarú. He would've killed ya if not for Conall. Gave his last for ya."

Tears welled up in Alastar. He remembered how Conall pledged to protect him. He had hoped to help Conall rebuild Loch an Scátháin and that his return would be a joyous victory. He wanted to help his friends with all he had, but many had died. He blamed himself for it and wished to make amends, but he couldn't even get up. Both his shoulder and leg remained pinned to the ground with Laochmarú's spear and sword in them.

Teague went to the sword in Alastar's thigh and quickly lifted it out. Alastar groaned and wanted to clutch his leg in pain but he couldn't move his upper body. Teague ripped fabric from a dead soldier and used it to bind Alastar's leg. Then he looked at the spear in his shoulder. The long spearhead had gone almost all the way through. Then he looked around and took a belt off another dead soldier.

"This'll hurt, lad," Teague said as he placed the belt in Alastar's mouth. "Bear down."

Alastar gripped the grass tightly with his hands and clenched his teeth into the belt. Teague put a foot on his chest to hold him down and yanked hard on the spear. He lifted it clear and threw it aside. Alastar never felt so much pain. The shock sent his vision white and he almost lost consciousness.

Teague took the belt out of Alastar's mouth and more fabric to pack Alastar's shoulder wound, front and back. "Your armor fared well, but it wasn't meant ta stop spears and arrows. A chain shirt would've helped. Too bad that sword missed your chain skirt. Banjaxed your leg."

He lifted Alastar up onto his shoulder and carried him to Éimhín. "Can ya ride?"

"I'll try," Alastar muttered. Teague helped him onto Éimhín.

Alastar was very weak and dizzy as he tried to steady himself. He picked up the reins, but the world quickly faded to gray-white and he passed out.

Nola, her family, Flann and Ula were huddled in an underground cellar in Dún Tearmann. They hid there when the Áiteoir broke through the walls.

"Hold silent," Flann whispered. "Hope we're not discovered."

They breathed nervously in the dark pit. Shifting shadows broke the slivers of light that came through the cellar doors above them. People were running about and shouting outside. Then they could hear the distinct crackling of burning wood through the many screams and sounds of shattering glass.

"They're burnin' us out!" Mab said quietly.

"Lay calm," Fionn reassured. "We may yet walk free if we remain hidden."

Suddenly the doors opened and the faces and swords of enemy soldiers surrounded them.

"Get out!" an Áiteoir threatened.

Everybody came out and was bound together with rope. Nola blinked in the bright light trying to see. When her vision cleared, she saw the Áiteoir everywhere. Everyone in Dún Tearmann was being rounded up and forced to march out. They set fire to everything once they gathered the people.

Nola gasped to herself, *We're being taken as slaves!*

Outside the fort, Nola saw her friends and neighbors being carted away in caged wagons; hundreds of people. She looked around for Conall and their fighting men, but only saw a few with their hands bound and being loaded into the wagons. The enemy stood numerous around them; many thousands. To the east, she saw the large Áiteoir commander approach with his cavalry.

Laochmarú rode up to Dún Tearmann satisfied. All of Conall's soldiers were dead or being round up and smoke rose from Dún Tearmann and Loch an Scáthháin. He saw the cavalry of Torthúil in the distance and ordered everyone to move out with haste. Then he blew the horn to rally his infantry and rode to the northwest toward their territory with his cavalry. There was no need to fight any longer. He had only come to take the people and kill Alastar. He wasn't sure if Alastar would die of his wounds, but his troops needed to regroup and rest after much marching and fighting.

Nola and her family were the last to be round up. The enemy prod them into a wagon and locked them in. Nola looked through the bars to the east and saw many more riders coming. The sun was breaking through the clouds and she could tell they were from Cnoc na Rí. Their bronze and leather armor was unmistakable.

"The Eachraighe come for us!" Nola exclaimed with hope.

The wagon started to move as Conn and his riders collided with the Áiteoir infantry. They were holding off the cavalry from reaching the wagons. The prisoners' hopes drained away as they saw the mass of soldiers preventing their rescue. Nola started crying as the wagon drifted farther away.

Conn saw the many wagons full of people, but there were hundreds of soldiers blocking the way forward. He looked right and saw their line thin out hundreds of meters away.

"Rally with me!" he shouted to his riders. He retreated backwards and rode up towards the thinnest part of the Áiteoir line. Some of his men were able to break free with him. They rode in a giant round arc to burst through the enemy.

Nola sat up after she saw their riders run through the infantry. Only a dozen were able to make it past the line, but she was inspired to hope in a victory. People in the caged wagons murmured quiet gasps for their riders.

Conn ordered his men to the nearest wagons. They cut down the soldiers who guarded them and tried to open the locks. Conn went to the last wagon and struck the lock with his sword. The cage door opened and the people rushed to get out.

Conn held out his hand. "Quickly! I can carry someone!"

Fionn pushed Nola and Mab forward. "Ride with the captain!" he yelled.

Nola looked at Conn as she took his hand. A feeling of familiarity came over her as she climbed onto the back of his horse; he was the Eachraighe rider in her dream. Her mother clamored onto the front of Conn's horse as if she was trying to climb over its shoulders.

"Hold tight!" Conn said without waiting for Mab to sit securely. He rode off just as the infantry came to secure the wagons.

Conn's men were able to save handfuls of people, but the majority of them were captured and carted away. Conn rode as swift as he could toward Loch an Scátháin and had his men retreat with him. He stopped for a moment to have Mab sit up on his horse so she didn't bounce uncomfortably on her stomach.

They looked back at Dun Tearmann. It was engulfed in flames and the enemy was not pursuing. Nola continued to cry. Most of her friends were not saved. Where was Ula? Her father? Brónach and Flann? She held on tightly to the back of Conn's saddle as they continued on. She had never seen war so close before. Her sorrow intensified when they passed the fields where Conall and his men lay.

"Stop!" she screamed and jumped off the horse when it slowed.

She recognized Conall and ran to his body in the field. There were hundreds of bodies strewn about, but Conall's polished armor gleamed in the brightening sun. It made him easy to identify.

Conn rode to her and Mab jumped off to join Nola. She looked over Conall with Nola and they wept together.

"Ladies," Conn said. "Conall was the best of us. Loch an Scátháin lost her favorite son, but we must get you ta safety."

"We'll not be leavin' our sons and brothers," Mab said. "Help us carry them home."

Conn looked back toward Dún Tearmann. There was no sign of the enemy. "We'll get 'em home, Ma'am." He commanded his men to carry their dead soldiers on the horses. They would all walk back to Loch an Scátháin. He picked up Conall and placed him on his horse. Mab came over and unfastened the ring clasp from Conall's shoulder. She took the clasp off him so it could be given to Flann and Ula.

While they were gathering bodies, Teague came riding back with a wagon behind his horse. "Dún Tearmann?" he asked Conn.

"We could only save the few here," Conn answered. "The enemy was too many. They captured everyone else and burned the fort. Strange that Laochmarú already left when we arrived. They were makin' their way back north and didn't wish ta pursue us."

"We must've made a banger of their aim ta kill Alastar," Teague surmised. "Laochmarú went straight after him when we arrived, like he knew he was with us."

Nola was surprised to hear Alastar had come back. "Where is Alastar?" she asked quietly.

"I put him up in the refuge," Teague replied. "He's slumped like a sack'a taytos. The general struck him down. Would've killed him right off if not for Conall. Conall gave his last for the boy."

"Right that," Conn affirmed. "Conall stood like a lion over the lad. But Laochmarú was rent with fury. I'd not seen the Áiteoir fight with such frenzy, and their cavalry's heavy armor is new. We didn't notice it the night we fled Lacharan."

"It makes 'em slow," Teague added, "But they were hardened as the stone dragon they sent on us."

"*Dragon!?*" Mab exclaimed with concern. "What times have come on us?"

"I don't know what things the wind carries," Teague said. "I only know Alastar is *the* Swan-bearer ta set thin's right on the isle. The currents carry him and the Áiteoir are keen ta put an end ta it. Things are movin' ta put Princess Ealaí on the throne as the Glasa foretold."

Nola grew concerned about a future with Alastar. Could they have a life together with all that was happening? She desperately wanted the war to end and begin a quiet life with the warmth of family around her. "Is the princess here too?" she asked.

"We brought her ta Cnoc na Rí," Teague said. "She remains there."

"What of our brothers and sisters?" Nola asked. "The Áiteoir took Flann and Ula. . . Dadaí and Brónach. We have ta get them back."

Conn was taken by Nola's fighting spirit. Her will to not give up rose through the tears in her eyes. "Your friends and family aren't lost," he reassured. "We'll mount a rescue."

"*After* word from the king," Teague interrupted. "Our small number give little hope ta break through ta our friends. I will send word when we've done here." His heart was full of solemn duty now that he took Conall's place as the head of Loch an Scátháin. He ordered everyone to take care of the dead and find more wounded. They filled the wagon he brought many times over as they worked through the day to gather their clansmen from the fields.

The sun had broken through the dreary clouds and sent

them away in light wispy threads, but everyone in Loch an Scátháin struggled with the heaviness of death and despair. They felt as if the cold rain that soaked the land earlier had seeped into their bones and lingered. They worked all the day to gather and bury their dead. Others tried to gather the scattered flocks that strayed during the attack. At night they retreated to the mountain refuge that was set in the mountainside above the mill. They had nowhere else to go after the enemy left every home and building in flames.

*F*or Amber the hours passed as slow as sticky resin seeping from a tree. She spent the day in her room with the weight of Alastar gone sitting square on her heart. How could he join the cavalry so soon? She was sure he would get hurt, yet the king reminded her that he was fit and ready. Gilroy didn't want Alastar to leave either, but he said Alastar agreed to go and the king stood behind it. Alastar was quite enthusiastic to leave and his friends pledged to keep him safe, so there was little else to be said that could keep him in Cnoc na Rí.

Amber stared out the window for hours as the rain spattered upon its panes. The cold gloomy view made her miss home where she would have watched the radiant flowers blink in the garden. The palace of Cnoc na Rí felt a chilly shadow of her home. She felt no warmth there, especially since Alastar left.

As evening set in, she resolved to help Alastar somehow. Maybe she could convince Fuar to send more troops and call him back to Cnoc na Rí. She set out to find Fuar. He would most likely be in his state room mulling over kingdom affairs.

Amber made her way to find him and saw Fuar far down a hallway. He ducked into the library and closed the door. She followed him there but was surprised to find no one in the room.

"Sire," she called out. "Sire. . ."

There was no answer. There were no other doors to the library. Where could he have gone? She looked about the room for a minute. The library was a large round room with two stories and a center atrium. Tall bookshelves lined the outer walls, while the center was a comfortable reading area. There was no trace of Fuar anywhere. *He must've gone somewhere,* she wondered perplexed.

Amber decided to wait and see if he would come back. She climbed to the second level of the library on a spiral staircase. It wound around a huge stone pillar at the outer edge of the atrium area. Then she found a dark corner to hide in and waited. The dim gray light from the atrium ceiling barely lit the room. It would be easy to remain hidden when he returned. . . if he returned.

Many quiet minutes passed. She started to feel foolish hiding in the corner, as if she were a child ready to pounce on an unsuspecting passerby. She pondered leaving, but then she heard a heavy door open. It came from the lower level.

Amber slipped quietly to the railing on her hands and knees and peered down. She saw Fuar come through a hinged bookshelf door with a lit lantern. *A hidden door,* she thought. She watched him as he pushed the door shut and quickly left the library.

She got up and ran to the bookshelf door. She tugged at the end but it was so heavy it barely moved. She struggled and pulled harder. "Why isn't it opening?" she whispered.

She looked the bookshelf up and down wondering how it opened. She ran her hands around the bookcase to search for a lock mechanism but couldn't find anything. Then the door to the library opened suddenly. Amber was startled and jumped. She hoped Fuar didn't find her examining the secret door. She turned her head to look behind her.

A servant peered inside the library. "Princess," he said. "There you are. The king requests you in his state room."

Amber breathed a sigh of relief. "Certainly," she replied. "Thank you."

When the servant left, she stepped backward to rest against the metal railing in front of the bookshelf. She misjudged the distance and hit her foot on one of the vertical railing bars. She felt it move.

Curious, she thought.

She turned around and pushed the bar forward. It hinged on the floor and when she pushed it as far as it would go, a loud click came from the bookshelf. She looked back and the shelf door had popped open slightly. She went to it and opened the door completely. It swung easily. *It must've been locked before,* she thought.

The door hid a long, dark stairwell that went up. It went so far up she couldn't see the end. There wasn't time now to see where it went. The king was waiting for her. She quickly closed the hidden door and went to the state room.

When she arrived, Fuar greeted her and told her to sit down by his desk. He went to the door and closed it. "There is an important matter I want ta speak of," he said. Amber was distracted about finding the secret door and what it might hide, but she looked at him with polite interest.

Fuar continued, "You know my wife died years ago and left me with no heir. I haven't chosen another bride all this time." He walked toward her and sat on the front of the desk and faced her. He held a determined gaze on her eyes. Amber started to feel uncomfortable. She knew what he was going to say.

"It's time I marry again," he said. "I've selected my bride."

Amber tried to stay calm and played innocent. "A grand thin', Sire. Who would be this woman you honor with your love?"

Fuar smiled. "She's the finest of our clan, and its fine time she fulfilled her destiny ta take the throne... with me. I've chosen you, Amber."

Amber sat silent for a moment. She knew he was going to make this proposal. Since they arrived, he had been trying to get close to her; uncomfortably close. She wanted to simply refuse and leave, but she couldn't disrespect the king.

"I'm honored by your request, Sire." She bowed her head in respect. "I respectfully decline. My place is with the Swan-bearer."

"What, the *boy?!*" he scoffed. "He's fulfilled his duty with you. Lifted ya ta the throne by bringin' ya here and under great opposition. A valiant young man, but what more do ya think he can do for you or the kingdom? His time is finished."

The dread that filled Amber the night before when they were on the terrace came back. She wanted to get up and run away again, but there was nowhere to go. She knew in her heart that marrying Fuar was not how she would fulfill her destiny. *Alastar is the one to help me,* she thought with firm resolve. *His time with me isn't done.*

"I'm sorry, Sire. I cannot marry you," she said with a quiet but unslacking rigidity.

"I'm not askin', Amber," Fuar said firmly. "It is my right as king ta choose my bride, and you are the most logical choice. We will brin' the isle ta union and harmony together. That *is* our destiny. You have no further business with Alastar."

Amber's eyes started to well up with sorrow. What could she do? Fuar had a reputation for doing things as he wanted, but he wasn't known to be overtly forceful. Perhaps he would change his mind if she refused again. "Sire, I won't marry you. I. . ."

Amber was interrupted by a knock on the door. "Sire," Gilroy said from behind the door.

Fuar stood up and gave Amber a look of resolve. "We *will* wed. Don't try ta leave. I've told the guard ta hold you in the palace. I will announce the weddin' tomorra' and the ceremony will be in three days. You may call any of our aids ta help you prepare." He turned away from Amber and called to Gilroy, "Come through."

Gilroy entered the room and saw Amber sitting with a look of despair. "Princess, is all well?" he asked.

"I've just given her a start," Fuar said. "What do you have?"

"I just received word from Loch an Scátháin. The Áiteoir destroyed every building in Dún Tearmann and Loch an Scátháin. Most of the residents were captured. Conall is dead and Alastar is severely wounded. Teague is now the area's commanding governor. He's asked for aid ta help rescue our clansmen."

Amber flushed with grief. Her fears were coming true. Alastar was gone and hurt, and the king was forcing her to marry. She tried to keep focus and remembered how she wanted to help Alastar. Her face turned steadfast. "You must send help, Sire, and give Alastar our best physician," she said bravely.

"I will consider matters," Fuar said. "I will decide in the mornin' what ta do."

"Sire," Gilroy said with earnest. "Time is essential. We cannot let the Áiteoir carry our people far inta their territory or there will be little hope of a rescue. And I agree with the princess. We must send Alastar a physician. We should send them an aid party with nurses and extra workers. There are many wounded and they need help ta rebuild. All of Conall's men are dead or captured and we lost many of the cavalry we sent."

Fuar walked behind his desk and sat down. He thought hard for a moment and with a tense brow he answered, "Very well. Send physicians and servants as you see fit, but no more soldiers will leave. We will deal with the captives diplomatically." He looked at Amber. "If you please, Amber. Let me speak with the chancellor."

Amber nodded her head. "Sire," she acknowledged and left the room.

"I have another matter ta speak of," Fuar said. "I am announcin' my marriage ta Amber tomorra'. We will wed in three days."

Gilroy was shocked. It was a sudden proposal and he remembered Amber's dreams of marrying her Swan-bearer. "Sire, is that the right course? We have yet to see how the currents show our headin' from here. I believe Alastar is still important ta the kingdom. We should. . ."

"It is *my* kingdom, is it not?" Fuar retorted. "I've no need for the boy. He did a grand thin' ta bring the princess here, but his duties are finished. I've decided Amber ta be my bride and make good the promise of union and harmony for our future. There's no other way she will sit on my throne. Make the necessary preparations. Announce the weddin' tomorra'. That will be all."

Gilroy was deeply troubled. The king's directions were not prudent. It made societal and political sense to marry Amber, but the Glasa implied the Swan-bearer would bring the isle to union and harmony with the Ealaí house. Fuar's marriage to Amber did not fit with anything shown in the currents. "But, Sire," he tried to persuade. "We should wait on the weddin'. Perhaps a different course will show itself. It is a precarious thin' ta go against destiny."

Fuar glared at Gilroy with disapproval. "I've *decided.* That will be all." Gilroy nodded in acknowledgment and left to prepare a relief party for Loch an Scátháin.

Amber left the state room feeling overwhelmed with the forced marriage to Fuar. She tried walking as fast as she could, but the long hallways felt like they extended forever in the dark, cold palace. It felt as if the entire place was trying to swallow her whole. She longed to speak to her mother and father. They wouldn't have been able to stop the marriage, but they always gave her the warmth and comfort she needed.

The only person she felt comfortable speaking to in Cnoc na Rí was Gilroy. He was often with her family as she grew up. He was like an elder uncle to her. His experienced counsel was always thoughtful and helpful. She would have to speak with him about things.

As Amber approached the library again, she remembered the secret door. She looked about to make sure no one saw her and went into the library. She grabbed a lantern from the reading area and lit it with the tine-stone that was set in place next to the lantern's wick.

She opened the hidden door and closed it most of the way as she went into the tunnel. She left the door slightly open. She didn't want to lock herself in not knowing how it opened from the other side. She turned around and looked down the tunnel. It was roughly carved out of the mountainside. On the right, above her head, there was a metal lever that pulled down. She pulled on it and heard the same click that opened the hidden door. It was another lock release mechanism.

Amber pulled the door shut so it would not look out of place if someone came into the library. She turned around and held the lantern high to illuminate the long stairwell that went up. It was narrow and very steep. Even with the lantern light, she couldn't see the top. She started to ascend the stairs. There were cobwebs and dust everywhere. She never walked in such an eerie place. The air kept getting chillier as she went up and the low howl of wind began to fill the passage near the top.

It took over a minute to reach the end where there was a wood plank door. She pushed it open and a sudden gust of cold air sucked her breath away. Outside, she found herself standing inside a large shallow cave near the mountain summit. She stepped out farther to peer out the cave's opening. The sound of crunching was under her feet. She looked down and found the floor covered with seeds scattered everywhere.

Then suddenly a bird the size of a hand flew down and landed near her feet. She brought the lantern toward it. It had a blue-gray head, white back and orange underbelly. *A rock thrush,* she recognized. It stood motionless for a moment and then went about the floor picking at the seeds, though they all appeared to be empty husks.

Amber brought the light up and around to examine the cave walls. There were many more thrushes that nested and slept in the nooks. She looked again at the thrush on the ground. *Why isn't this one sleeping?* she wondered.

She looked around the cave again and saw a bucket nestled inside an alcove on the ground. She went to it and pulled the bucket out. It was full of seeds. She set her lantern down near the alcove and saw something else tucked deep inside the hole. She brought her head down to the floor and looked inside. A wood box sat in the end of the hole.

She took the box out and opened it. It had three compartments – one with small pieces of blank parchment paper, the next had parchment with writing on it, and the last compartment had a writing slate, ink and pen. *A messenger kit,* she recognized. *These birds must be message carriers, but we only use seabhac messengers in the kingdom. I've never seen thrushes used before.*

She took the parchment with writing on it. It was the only message in the box. It read: You promised slaves and the Swan-bearer in exchange for the safety of your kingdom but your men prevented us from taking him. We will only hold to our agreement if you deliver the Swan-bearer or prove you've killed him yourself. – G. Laochmarú

Amber gasped when she understood that the king made a deal with the Áiteoir to hand over Alastar. That's why Fuar didn't want to send any more troops to Loch an Scátháin. He didn't intend to rescue the captives. The king gave them as slaves to the Áiteoir. He wouldn't have even sent help to Alastar if they didn't press him for it.

Her heart sunk farther as she realized Fuar must have been communicating with the Áiteoir in secret for some time to have these things in the cave. But there was only one message here. How long has this been going on? She didn't know who G. Laochmarú was, so she had to make sure it was the Áiteoir the king was communicating with. She had a hunch how to find out.

She took the lantern and went back to the thrush on the floor. It was still acting peculiarly by picking at empty seed husks. She approached it slowly and held out her palm to it. It immediately hopped onto her hand. She closed her hand around it and felt it was hard as a rock. "An éanshee!" she exclaimed. *This is an Áiteoir messenger. The other birds must be real thrushes used to hide the éanshee in their midst.*

She wondered how it carried messages. There were no carriers around or on the bird. She looked closely at the éanshee and touched its white speckled back. A small door opened on the top of its back. She looked inside and the bird was hollow. Parchment would fit inside easily.

She closed the door on the éanshee and set it back down. Then she tried to sneak over to the many dozens of nesting thrushes to examine them. They seemed to be behaving like real birds. When she got close to a nest they startled and flew about the cave and went outside. She let out a scream as they as flew about her, but she quickly covered her mouth to keep quiet. She couldn't be discovered.

After a few moments, all the birds were gone, including the éanshee. Amber quickly put away the messenger kit and bucket, but she kept the parchment message. She had to show it to Gilroy. She tucked it in her dress and ran back down to the library.

She slowly opened the hidden door and looked inside. The library was pitch black. She quickly came out and closed the bookshelf door. She had to find Gilroy. Was he still in the state room with the king? She wanted to avoid Fuar, so she made her way around the state room by going to the lower floor.

After going back upstairs, Amber came to Gilroy's chamber door and knocked. "Chancellor," she called.

"Come in," Gilroy answered.

She was relieved to hear him inside. The importance of what she discovered was a burden she couldn't bare alone. She entered the chamber and greeted Gilroy.

"There's an urgent matter I need speak of," she said in one quick breath.

"Certainly. I know," Gilroy said. "The king told me. Sit, sit. Calm yourself. You look in bits and mad off all at once."

Amber gave him a confused look. She closed the door and sat in a chair. "What has the king told ya?"

"Your weddin' of course. I understand why you're anxious. . ."

"I'm not marryin' Fuar!" she interrupted with fire in her eyes. "But that's not why I've come. The king has been conspirin' with the Áiteoir. He intended ta send Alastar ta Loch an Scátháin ta die!"

A grave look came on Gilroy. He'd never heard accusations so serious. "How do you know this?"

"I saw him use a secret passage in the library. It faces the mountainside and goes up inta a cave on the summit. When he was gone, I looked there and found an éanshee and this message." She gave him the parchment.

Gilroy read it. His face turned pale as he realized the truth. "This message is from General Laochmarú. He killed Conall today. It puts us in a dangerous position, Princess. If the king finds we know, our future is grim. He would replace me, or worse. . . and he would still force you ta marry. I don't know that we can stop the weddin' as it is. We have no grounds ta refuse it."

"I won't marry him! Not before, nor after I found of this," she said with passion. "I know who I belong with. You must help me escape! The king has ordered the guard to keep me here."

Gilroy looked at her with sympathy and sighed. "I don't believe you should marry Fuar either, child. But you know what it means ta deny him."

"I do," she replied quietly.

"You will be in exile and hidin' till it's your time ta take the throne. You must return the message where you found it. It's safer if the king doesn't know his secret is loose. I will help you flee. Return ta your room afterwards. I will send ya instruction soon as I can."

Tears started to flow from Amber's eyes. She never thought things would come to this. "Thank you, Chancellor. You were always kind ta me and my family. I only ask, bring me ta Alastar as well."

"I don't know how we can do that safely. The king knows Alastar is in Loch an Scátháin and will be very keen ta be aware of his whereabouts. It appears Fuar negotiated away a siege of Cnoc na Rí by givin' away Alastar and our clansmen. I'm afraid both you and the boy will be hunted without aid from the kingdom. Both the Áiteoir and king want their hands on the both of ya."

"I understand the risks," Amber said. "I must be reunited with Alastar and see ta his safety as well."

Gilroy gave the parchment back to Amber. "Go quickly now," he told her, "And don't speak of these thin's ta anyone. We don't know who ta trust." Amber mustered a slight smile of courage, but her face carried deep concern. He gave her a reassuring smile. "Go now, child."

Amber left remembering how she felt when Gilroy sent her into hiding after the Áiteoir tried to assassinate her. She was awash in all the same feelings. Where would she go? How long would she be in hiding? She wanted desperately to simply return home and live in peace, but things were more complicated than they've ever been. She walked back to the library with tumbling hopes watered in the spring of anticipation. Would she be able to reach Alastar? Would he recover from his injuries?

She took the long way around the palace again to avoid passing by Fuar's state room. When she got to the corner of the library's hallway, she paused to listen for anyone. It was quiet, so she peeked around the corner and saw the hallway empty. She started a brisk walk to the library door when all of a sudden it opened. Her heart skipped and she ran back around the corner as quietly as she could.

She tried to catch her breath and stood with her back flat against the wall. She had to know who was in the library. It sounded like they were walking away from her so she peered down the hallway again. Fuar was walking away with a lantern. A gasp struck her. *He must've went to the cave and saw the parchment missing,* she thought. It would do no good to return the message now.

Amber headed back to her room with her nerves flying in circles. What would the king do? Who does he suspect? When she returned to her room, she collected resolve and got her things together. She dressed in the same traveling clothes that she came with and expected to leave in the night. *But how? Gilroy will come through,* she thought.

She was fortunate that she had very little to pack. The bag she brought from Lacharan only held a few simple dresses and undergarments. She remembered having much more luggage – many chests worth – when she went into hiding before. But that exile was expected to last many months and they had packed for Mairéad as well.

She looked around her room to make sure she didn't forget anything. The only thing left was the hairpin Alastar gave her. It sat on a dresser near the bed. She picked it up and looked at it with fond memories of him. Then she twirled her hair in the back and stuck the hairpin in.

A knock came from her door. "Princess," someone called. It startled her. She was dressed to travel with her leather cuirass, cloak and boots on. That would look out of place in the middle of the night. She jumped quickly under the covers of her bed. She pulled out the hairpin and slipped it under a pillow.

"Come in," she replied as she fluffed her hair to make it tidy.

A young maid with auburn hair tied neatly away came in holding clothes. She wore a plain white dress with a gray wool cloak. "Princess, we're leavin' for Loch an Scátháin. The chancellor said ta be *quite* discreet 'n have ya go as a nurse, same as me. The enemy has many eyes, he said, and we'd be needin' ta take care. We'll leave as soon as ya put on this nurse's gown and cloak."

Relief came over Amber and she got up from under the covers. The nurse was surprised Amber was already fully dressed. "I see you're set ta head out as it is," she said.

Amber put the hairpin back in her hair and took the clothes from the nurse. "You can be certain I'm set ta leave right quick," Amber commented. She took off her kinsale cloak and put on the nurse's gown and cloak over her clothes. She also packed away her hairpin. "What is your name?" she asked.

"Áine ["Æn-yeh"], Princess."

When Amber had dressed and packed away her cloak, Áine gave her a sealed letter. It was from Gilroy. She opened it and read:

A chara, Amber. See to Alastar's welfare and gain the confidence of
Teague and Conn about the king. They appear to be most loyal to you
and Alastar. I will charge them with your protection and care, but be
careful with words. No one else need know why you go to Loch an
Scátháin other than to aid their recovery. I will send Gearóid a message
about these affairs and advise him to be discrete with the king. My efforts
remain with you and the kingdom. My duties to serve the king may be
at odds with helping you, but we will have advantage so long as the king
keeps me as chancellor. Be in good cheer. You go not alone and perhaps
the king will see reason to accept you and Alastar after some time of
persuasion.

Amber finished the letter with a bright spirit. She would see
Alastar soon and be with many friends. She stashed the letter in a
pocket and stood ready to go. "Let us leave now," she said.

Áine held up her hand to note something. She noticed Amber's
large amber pendant stuck out like a beaming torchlight on top of her
many layers of clothes. "Best ta tuck your necklace under, Princess.
And cover with the hood. Your fair countenance is hardly discreet."
The nurse covered her own head with her hood and picked up Amber's
bag.

Amber took the bag from her. "A nurse carries her own bag,"
she said.

"Right," Áine acknowledged. "A servant's habit ta do the
carryin'."

They went to the stables cautiously. Gilroy had guards along
their route repositioned or distracted so they would not question the
princess. They arrived in the stables without incident. The rest of their
party was there preparing their horses. They numbered two physicians,
four nurses including Amber and handfuls of craftsmen and laborers to
help rebuild.

Amber found they covered up Muirgel with blankets to disguise her as well. Once they had everything ready, they all rode to the front gate with their hoods on so Amber would be inconspicuously concealed. Gilroy was already there to see that the party went without hindrance. He gave Amber a look of steady reassurance. "Your errands and journey be blessed," he told them.

Secret Errands

*T*he party of physicians and workers took the west road
out of Cnoc na Rí as quick as they could. Their speed wasn't to get
distance for Amber's safety. None of them knew Amber's real reasons
for leaving the palace. Gilroy only gave them enough information to
ensure Amber be kept hidden.

They made a fast departure into the valley to take advantage
of the diminishing light from the glowing landscape. It would only be
another hour before complete darkness surrounded them. They had to
make their way through Gap Dearg ["Jair-reg"] where they could cross
through the mountains easily and enter the hill country. From there
they could make a fast gallop through the fields instead of the slow
pace through the thick forest of the valley.

Gap Dearg cut the time for their journey to Loch an Scátháin in
half. It was a winding fissure in the north side of the valley just a few
miles west of Cnoc na Rí where the mountain rock turned to red and
orange. The path through the gap looked like the mountains split apart
just enough to make a narrow path through them.

Amber had never ventured so deep into the River Valley
before. Its dense forest felt like a plush wool sweater compared to the
thin fleece of the plains and forests around Lacharan. She'd seen no
other forest as thick as that of the valley. Even the large, sprawling
forests around the Muir Airgid did not have the lush variety that was in
the valley.

Soon they were passing through Gap Dearg. Amber looked up
the steep cliff walls on both sides of her. It was much darker inside the
fissure where the vegetation on the cliffs was sparse. Long vines and
thick, crooked roots hung from the cliffs. They made it look as if giant,

faintly glowing nets held up the walls.

At the end of the gap they saw Rían's Gate. It was a massive stone wall and watch tower that closed off the gap and valley from the outside. When the party came near, the gate door was opened for them. The guard already knew they were coming.

Once they passed through the gate, the lead riders picked up the pace and rushed out into the plains and sparse forests of the hill country. The land was very dim as they turned southwest towards Loch an Scátháin. Soon they rode only by the thin light of the crescent moon.

Alastar forced open his eyes despite a heavy feeling of numb aching that slogged through his entire body. Someone wiped his forehead with a wet rag. He was so tired, his eyes barely opened halfway. The blurry face of someone familiar smiled over him.

"Amber?" he murmured.

"Hush," she replied. "You've a brutal fever."

Alastar tried to get up but he slumped back down in great pain. He moaned. "Are we safe? How?. . ."

"Don't move!" she warned as she rubbed ointment on his shoulder wound. "The physician has ya well sewn up. I'm packin' your wounds with honey daisy ointment. It'll speed your healin'."

"How did you get here?" he asked with a scratchy voice. His throat was dry, but his vision began to clear. He found himself in a large cave with many wounded people lying on low cots and blankets.

"We came from Cnoc na Rí soon as we heard what happened," she replied. "Been here almost a whole day. We're safe for the time bein'. Just rest now." She held a cup of warm tea in front of him and lifted his head. "Drink. This sage teasel root tea will help your fever. I added a spot of lavender and honey ta help soothe your sores."

Amber finished rubbing ointment on Alastar's shoulder and leg wounds and bound them with clean fabric. She stood up. The mountain refuge was a small network of caves near the cliffs of the bird keep. It could shelter more than a hundred people in times of war. Now it served as an infirmary for their wounded. The rest of the soldiers and people camped in the fields at the foot of the mountain below.

She walked out the cave and looked down to the land below. The day was bright and the sun's rays gave the workers and soldiers a resurgence of strength. She could see the mill being rebuilt and everyone's tents scattered beyond it. Their temporary shelters of animal skins and fabric dotted the grounds, like white and gray blossoms had sprouted after the heavy rains the day before.

Amber saw Teague below and went down to him.

"Alastar woke," she reported. "He wanted ta get up right quick, but I had him be still. His fever still needs pass."

"Grand," Teague acknowledged. "I hope he has strength ta move soon. I don't know how long the both of ya can stay here. You're exposed without any high walls and every enemy knows your whereabouts."

"We've nowhere else ta hide," Amber said.

"Perhaps returnin' ta Lacharan would be best," Teague suggested. "Your city's defenses are better than here despite the loss of the sea catapults."

"We cannot return ta Lacharan so long as the Áiteoir seek us. The king may even march in ta steal us away. If Lacharan remains safe while we are away, then we will remain outside."

"Just as well," Teague added. "I have a feelin' Alastar would say the same thin'. A pair of hard blocks ya are." He thought a moment and looked out toward the north hills where the enemy would usually march in. "I heard from Gearóid. He has pledged loyalty ta ya, Princess. Lacharan is yours after all. If he must stand against the king, he will. You have my support and Conn's as well."

"I am grateful," Amber said. "Thank you. But it is a sad time when the kingdom stands ta be divided. If there were a way ta have the king relent on his course and help us, I would be very glad."

"I hope that would be," Teague said. He remembered the excitement when Alastar first arrived. "Conall was so sure the king would embrace Alastar. He knew the lad meant mighty thin's were ta happen. I felt it too, but we never thought it'd be like this. At times, life flows as thickened blood and sweat. We may not know the end of it, but ta not pick up and fare on, well. . . ya might as well dig your grave on the spot. Thin's may seem ta be unsettled, but we'll see thin's right, Princess."

Amber looked beyond Teague and saw Conn approach with Mab and Nola. She remembered Nola was reluctant to leave Alastar alone in the care of the nurses. "Who does the captain walk with?" she asked.

Teague looked behind him. "That is the wife and daughter of Fionn – Mab and Nola. They live in the next parcel down toward the fields. The rest of their family was taken prisoner."

Conn approached them and greeted Amber, "Princess." Then he turned to Teague. "Sir, the Fionns' home will be the first ta be fit again. The roof will be lashed tomorrow."

"Fine progress," Teague said.

"Any word of the prisoners?" Amber asked Teague. "Has recourse been made?"

"Gilroy said the king has no plans for 'em," Teague said. "Our scouts track 'em goin' ta Loch Chnámh an Áidh ["Lahkh Kroww an Eye"][6]. They will likely be taken from there ta work the mines in the old Méine ["Meen-yeh"] Kingdom and the deserts of the Áiteoir homeland. We would need ta move swiftly ta prevent 'em from bein' scattered throughout Rathúnas."

The dread of never seeing their family again shook Mab and Nola. "We must do somethin' for 'em!" Nola pleaded.

"Chnámh an Áidh is a large walled city," Amber said with concern. "We cannot breach their walls without layin' siege."

"That was my concern," Teague added. "We have no siege weapons, and if the king hears we attack 'em, he would know we work against him. Rescuin' our clansmen has great risks."

Amber saw the despair in Mab and Nola's faces. She wondered if a rescue was possible. "What are the chances we can rescue them if the walls are breached?"

"If Laochmarú's army remains with 'em, I have better chance ta carry 'em out with not more than my bare arms," Teague quipped.

"Right," Conn added. "We've barely over three hundred riders. They still number more than ten thousand with hundreds of heavy cavalry."

"We've more than three hundred," Amber said. "Lacharan is with us. Gearóid commands two thousand."

"Is it wise ta move Lacharan against the king's wishes?" Teague asked. "Gilroy suggested you show your strength with Lacharan on your side, Princess, but I fear the king would move heavily against us if ya give a flare of match."

Gilroy hadn't told Amber about using Lacharan's strength, but she recognized why he suggested it to Teague. "Gilroy knows we must

[6] 'oww' in pronunciations is the "ow" sound as in cow and plow

persuade the king ta see reason," Amber said. "The king must realize I found of his dealin's with the Áiteoir, so whether he knows of our movements is not the concern. He must be made aware the kingdom will split if he continues his course against his own people. Lettin' him see Lacharan move without him will be a strong signal ta heed."

Everyone was impressed with Amber's resolve and political acumen. She would stand with what was right even though there was great risk. If the king allied with the Áiteoir, they would not be safe anywhere on the isle. Nola, especially, found great respect with Amber. She wasn't just heir to the throne but was also worthy to lead the kingdom.

"The king would stand up 'n take notice if he saw Lacharan go with us," Conn said, "but we still haven't any siege weapons nor do we have the time ta build 'em."

Amber remembered Loch Chnámh an Áidh. She traveled there many years ago with her parents. It used to be part of the Méine Kingdom that often traded with Torthúil before the Áiteoir conquered them. "We may not need ta tear down their walls," she suggested. "Chnámh an Áidh is like Lacharan. It sits surrounded by waters on one side. The loch is shaped as a broken wishbone, and the city nestles inside the lake's northern crescent. Its walls only stand ta the north and east while the loch acts a moat ta the west and south."

"I see what you're gettin' at, Princess," Conn said. "We could enter the city by crossin' the lake, like the Áiteoir tried ta do in Lacharan's bay."

"We could only ferry a handful 'a men across the lake," Teague said. "And their army stands between us and openin' the gates. Lacharan's troops avail us little if we cannot get more men inta the city and open the gates ta carry our people away."

Amber remembered Alastar's plan to lead away the enemy

from Lacharan by acting as decoys. "Then we should carry out another ailpín plan," she said. "Use me ta lure the army out of the city, so our men can enter and open the gates."

Mab gasped. "We cannot put ya in danger, Princess!"

"You're just as stout-headed as Alastar! A grand pair 'a ailpín!" Teague remarked with unbelief. "I agree with Mab. We can't have ya at such risk. Laochmarú would press ta take ya as they did the lad. It was difficult ta hold off their heavy cavalry. Conall died tryin'."

"You said yourself," Amber replied. "I can't stay here long nor can Alastar. We are safest where the bulk of our soldiers are and seein' our people need us at Chnámh an Áidh, that is where we will be. Send word ta Gearóid ta assemble a march for Chnámh an Áidh quick as a seabhac flies. We will meet him south of the loch."

Teague acknowledged, "Certainly, Princess." He turned to Conn. "Assemble our men." Then he left to go up to the bird keep.

Nola felt concern over Alastar leaving again. *They can't move him,* she thought. *He's still unable to ride.* "Princess," she queried. "Would Alastar be leavin' as well?"

Amber didn't want to depart from Alastar again, but she didn't see how he could join them. She had to see that her people were rescued. "He isn't well enough," Amber said. "He will stay with enough guards ta keep him safe. If we're successful, we'll be back before he recovers from the fever. Then we can see him ta a safer place."

Nola gave a look of disappointment. *See him to a safer place?* she pondered. *Alastar won't be staying in Loch an Scátháin.* A quiet life with Alastar was quickly dissolving into muddy puddles. Nola couldn't do much about it, but she was glad he would be safe. "Thank you, Princess," she said. Amber gave her a reassuring smile and left to go back to the refuge.

Conn turned Nola and Mab around to head back to their house. "I'll see that your home is roofed in before we leave," he told them. He looked up at the sky. The sun had made its best efforts for the day and was well to retreating toward the horizon. "I'll pull workers from the mill ta finish it swift off."

Mab and Nola gave him looks of appreciation. "Thank you, sir," Mab accepted. "Thin's have been a jam since all the fightin' started again. We're grateful you came ta help us."

"We truly are," Nola added. She gave Conn a warm smile. "I don't believe I ever thanked ya for rescuin' us. Thank you, sir. You Eachraighe are brave heroes worthy of the clan's name."

He smiled. "We're not known ta be bouzzies," he joked. "Just doin' the best we can."

Nola laughed quietly. "Not one a bouzzie among all a ya."

"The finest lads 'round," Mab added.

Hours passed as Loch an Scátháin moved restlessly to rebuild and prepare for another long ride across the country. The physicians, nurses, builders and a dozen soldiers were to stay behind while everyone else packed to leave for Loch Chnámh an Áidh.

Alastar woke and found Amber hovering near him. His head and body still ached. "Nurse!" he called to Amber in jest.

She turned to him and smiled. "Found your strength have we?"

"An ounce," he said with a dry rasp. "Water please?"

Amber brought him a cup of water and helped him drink. "You appear better," she said. "Are ya peckish? We've some colcannon and nettle soup for you."

"I *am* hungry."

"Here, let me help you sit up." Amber lifted him slowly and rotated him so his back leaned against the cave wall. "A moment," she said. She went to get a plate of food and brought it back.

"Did you make this?" Alastar asked as he looked at the potatoes, kale, and green nettle soup.

"Áine made the colcannon; one of the nurses. I managed the nettle soup. It's a simple healin' broth I know. I'm afraid my cookin' skills are limited ta boilin' water. More than that, I wouldn't know. I never came ta learnin'. Mam told me, 'Beauty doesn't boil the kettle, but since I'm not a grand hand at fixin' meals, I'll teach ya how ta fix the sick 'n wounded.' Grand thin' for ya. Mam and I spent much time in camps of battle carin' for our soldiers. We'd dress wounds, prepare medicine, and sing for their healin', hours on end."

"You'd sing?" he asked wondering.

"Sing 'n make music," she said cheerfully. "Music helps ta heal." Amber looked around pensively. She wasn't sure if she should sing in the refuge. It had been years since she sung for the sick and it wasn't the custom outside of Lacharan to sing for the injured. She looked at Alastar and he stared at her with quiet interest. He didn't ask, but she felt he wanted to hear her sing. "We haven't any musicians here, but I'll sing a spot. Somethin' mam and I sang together." She started singing in a slow and smooth melody - 'The Fields Call Home':

"The fieeelds, caaall hommme↗, tooo youuu↘, todaaay↘
The fieeelds, caaall hommme↘, forrr youuu↘, to staaay↘

Your aaaches↗, yourrr paaains↗, wiiill waaash↘ aawaaay
Graaass so↗↗ greeen↗ and riverrrs↘, so-- bluuue↘
Your liiife reeenewww↗, yourrr liiife↗ reeenewww↘

The fieeelds, caaall hommme↗, tooo youuu↘, todaaay↘
The fieeelds, caaall hommme↘, forrr youuu↘, to staaay↘

Your rrrest, yourrr souuul↗ wiill fiiind↘, theirr plaaay
Hiiills↗ so↗↗↗ greeeeen and flowwwerrs so bluuue↘
Your liiife reeenewww↗, yourrr liiife↗ reeenewww↘

[The lyrics repeat in Irish…]

Gleeen na ha-hee↗, orrrt↗, in-new↘
Ear-run na ha-hee↗, orrrt↗, fan-nokt↘

Glan-herr↗, da vrohn↗, iss da↘ feeon-ta-wuet↘
Fair kohh↗ glahs↗, ahgus ev-nyahka, gal-horrum↘
Da vah-haa ahnew-eee↗, da vah-haa ahnew-eee↗

Gleeen na ha-hee↗, orrrt↗, in-new↘
Ear-run na ha-hee↗, orrrt↗, fan-nokt↘

Da shkeee, iss dah-num↗, bay shed↘, lahn da-hahs↘
Kriiik kohh↗ glahs↗ ahgus bla-hahna gal-horrum↘
Da vah-haa ahnew-eee↗, da vah-haa ahnew-eee↗

[The fields, call home, to you, today]
[The fields, call home, for you, to stay]

[Your aches, your pains, will wash away]
[Grass, so green, and rivers, so blue]
[Your life, renew, your life, renew]

[The fields, call home, to you, today]
[The fields, call home, for you, to stay]

[Your rest, your soul, will find, their play]

[Hills, so green, and flowers, so blue]

[Your life, renew, your life, renew]

[Glaonn, na hachaidh, ort, inniu]

[Iarrann, na hachaidh, ort, fanacht]

[Glanfar, do bhrón, is do, phianta uait]

[Féar chomh glas, agus aibhneacha, gealghorm]

[Do bheatha, athnuaigh, do bheatha, athnuaigh]

[Glaonn, na hachaidh, ort, inniu]

[Iarrann, na hachaidh, ort, fanacht]

[Do scíth, is d'anam, beidh siad, lán d'áthas]

[Cnoic chomh glas, agus bláthanna, gealghorm]

[Do bheatha, athnuaigh, do bheatha, athnuaigh]"

Everyone listened in the soothing calm of her singing. The words seeped into their souls like a warm healing balm. They felt their spirits comforted and invigorated. Alastar was surprised how her voice cut through the weariness and pain in him. When she stopped singing, they gave her applause and asked for more.

"Cheers!" someone yelled. "They don't give us singin' nurses in Cnoc na Rí, Miss! Lend us another melody!"

Amber laughed and continued to sing for a time. Alastar ate his meal in the company of her music and then lay down again. Her sweet voice reminded him of the night he spent in Lacharan when he heard her singing to the harp as he lay to sleep. He felt that harmony of wellness come to him again. Its heavy peace covered him through and he drifted into a deep, healing sleep.

In Cnoc na Rí, Fuar was in fits of anger and anxiety. *Who found my secret dealings with the Áiteoir? Where did Amber go? Was the secret why she left or did she leave because of the marriage plans? Who could know about the secret passage into the mountain?* He pondered the questions day and night.

The hidden passage was a secret that few people knew. Only the royal family closest to the king was aware of it. Fuar didn't think anyone living knew about it. He was sure he and his wife were the only ones. The passage was built with the palace to be an escape route in case an enemy overtook the city. Fuar turned it into a roost for the birds and éanshee after he started secret communications with the Áiteoir years ago.

They gave him an éanshee after he personally sought to cut out the normal diplomatic channels that involved the chancellor and envoys. He felt it was a better way to conduct affairs with the Áiteoir. It pleased him to eliminate debate with his advisors and quicken the resolution for urgent business.

After Fuar found the parchment missing from the messenger box, he immediately questioned Gilroy, but the chancellor gave no sign he knew anything. Fuar didn't suspect Amber until he found her gone the next day. He ordered search parties to bring her back, so he could complete the marriage with her.

He knew he couldn't continue with the people's support if he did not unite with the House of Ealaí. Everyone knew she was a key to the union and peace told of in the Glasa. There was no other living

Ealaí and Alastar's sudden appearance with her cemented the turning of destiny. Fuar wouldn't let himself be set aside, so he resolved to be pivotal in the kingdom's great future by marrying Amber and bringing the promised prosperity himself.

Fuar told Gilroy to send messages that ordered Alastar to go to Lacharan. He also sent a special envoy to Loch an Scátháin to make sure Alastar got the order and escort him there. He didn't want Alastar to stay in the mountains because he would get warning of an attack by the Greerian. But the Greerian did not patrol Lacharan. The Áiteoir could slip in an assassin there much easier.

Fuar stood in the hidden cave and wrote a message to send out: I will send the boy to Lacharan where you can reach him in secret.

*A*lastar woke the next morning to a quiet camp. Dim oil lamps cast shadows around the dark cave. Everyone appeared to be sleeping in the refuge. He slowly got up and noticed he felt much better. His fever was gone. His wounded shoulder and leg were still very sore, but the pain was bearable enough for him to move. He took a step forward and sharp pain went through his left thigh. Walking was painful. He limped toward the cave entrance where daylight cast down its bright light on the gray rocks.

Outside he saw the sun was rising above the east end of the lake. In the fields below, he saw many workers already pressing to rebuild the mill early in the morning.

"Sir," someone called to him from behind. It startled him and he turned around. A soldier from Amber's royal guard stood there. A dozen more stood behind him among the rocks near the cave entrance. They had come with Alastar and the troops from Cnoc na Rí.

The guard continued, "We've orders ta guard ya till our forces return from Chnámh an Áidh, sir."

"Chnámh an Áidh?" Alastar repeated. "Why've they gone?"

"The commanders seek ta free our clansmen, sir. Most of the residents here were captured."

What about Nola and his friends? Were they taken? Alastar thought with sudden alarm. "Where is the princess?" he asked.

"She's gone with the commanders."

Gone? Why did she go too? Was there anyone he could talk to for more information? Alastar wondered. "You wouldn't happen ta know which residents remain, would ya?"

"I wouldn't," the guard replied. "But the only house we rebuilt so far shelters 'em. Just a handful. It's the next house from here." He pointed past the mill to the southwest tip of the lake.

Nola's house! Alastar recognized. He had to see who was there. "Where's my horse? I have ta see who remains."

The guard turned around and gestured to the others. They left and ran down the mountainside to get their horses. "We'll fetch your horse, sir, but the princess said ya ought ta rest. I suggest you make the visit a quick one."

Alastar didn't feel the need to rest. He wanted to find out what was happening and help if he could. He wondered why Amber left with Teague and Conn. *Why did she put herself in danger by coming to Loch an Scátháin and now going to Chnámh an Áidh? Isn't she safest in Cnoc na Rí?*

When they arrived at the house, Alastar saw Mab and Nola across the road. They were helping to rebuild the barn and fences with workers. He was glad to see they were safe, but he didn't recognize anyone else from Loch an Scátháin there. *Was everyone else taken prisoner?* he wondered.

Nola saw them coming and went to greet them with Mab. Alastar got off Éimhín and limped toward them. His eyes were fixed on Nola who approached him with a reserved smile.

"Ya shouldn't be up!" Mab screamed. "We were goin' ta visit ya before the sun hit its peak. Why'd ya come out so soon?"

Alastar smiled wide. "It's a grand thing ta know you're safe," he said with cheer. He waited for Nola to give a warm smile, but her expression didn't change. He noticed she wore a gold fibulae clasp on her shirt, though. It gleamed bright as it hung from the top buttonhole on her blouse. It was the kind of clasp the soldiers used to secure their mantles to the left shoulder. He noticed only the commanders and royal guard used the gold clasps. Other soldiers didn't have mantles or used simple fasteners for their garments. *Why was Nola wearing it?*

"We're gobsmacked ta see ya standin' strong," Mab said. "We thought you'd be laid down for days with that bad dose 'a fever."

"I'm sore, but I feel I could have another run at the Áiteoir," he replied. "Do ya know they killed Conall?"

Mab started crying. "Terrible thin'. Flann 'n Ula don't even know. They're prisoners along with the rest of the town and Dún Tearmann. Hundreds of our people. We buried Conall and our brothers at the ferta yesterday."

"The ferta?" Alastar asked.

"Our burial grounds on Cnoc na Raithní ["Kruk nah Ræh-nee"]," Nola answered. She looked to the mountains in the south."On the highest summit of the south cliffs."

"I'm so sorry for everyone," Alastar said. "I feel responsible for all your troubles."

"Cut that out!" Mab retorted. "Don't make yourself heavy for the thin's darkness brin's. We mourned through war many years before ya came here."

"Still," Alastar said. "I must do what I can for all of ya. Do ya know when everyone will come back?"

"The captain said two or three days if their plan went ta accord," Mab said. "Many more if they can't get Laochmarú's army ta leave Chnámh an Áidh. The princess thinks they'll leave the city unprotected ta grab after her."

Alastar got worried. He remembered how Laochmarú pushed quickly through everyone to attack him in the battle. "Are they gone in the head?! Amber can't just sit in the field for 'em!"

"You did 'bout the same thin'," Nola noted to him. "When ya ran out ta save Lacharan with her."

"Don't worry, dear," Mab said to Alastar. "Lacharan's army

will be with 'em."

"They're still far outnumbered!" Alastar responded uneasily. "The king needs ta send his army too."

Mab looked at Nola with concern. Alastar didn't know about the king's plans to send him to his death. "Dear," Mab said. "The king won't send help. He let you come back here with the troops ta hand ya ta the Áiteoir."

Cold, grim disbelief went through Alastar. He couldn't believe the king would do that. "Are ya sure?" he asked. "Why?"

"It appears the king made a deal ta hand ya over so peace would be kept with the Áiteoir," Mab said. She looked about to check if anyone was near enough to hear them. They were isolated, so she continued, "Few people know. We are ta be discreet. Respect the king, but try ta keep you and the princess safe away from him and the enemy. Most of the soldiers do not know. Teague and the commanders know, as does the princess and your guard."

Alastar stood in a confused cloud. What was he supposed to do? He was part of a conflict much bigger than he could deal with. He looked at Nola and wondered how he could be left alone with her to live a normal life. "Would ya walk with me, Nola?" he asked.

Nola turned to walk with Alastar when the royal guard trotted up to them. "The king's riders come!" a guard yelled. They looked down the road to the north and saw a group of riders galloping toward them. "Quickly! Ta your horse! We must hide ya before they see you're here."

Alastar strained through pain to mount Éimhín as fast as he could. Most of the royal guard stood in a line to block the view of the approaching riders while Alastar left with two guards to escort him. They disappeared around the bend of road as the king's men approached Nola's home.

"I seek the lad, Alastar!" the envoy yelled as he examined everyone around. He had a pleasant appearance about him, but his face was very determined. "Where is the boy?"

"We don't know where he's gone," Mab responded. "The injured stay near the mill up the road."

The envoy looked at the royal guards suspiciously. "Why is Lacharan's royal guard here?"

A guard responded, "We came from Cnoc na Rí with the king's riders, sir."

"And what of Princess Ealaí?" the envoy asked. "Has she been here?"

"The *princess?*" Mab said feigning surprise. "My that'd be a charm! We'd certainly know if the princess came ta us. Is she comin' here, sir?"

The envoy gave a look of disappointment and rode down the road with his riders. There were a dozen of them intent on finding Amber and Alastar.

Alastar had led the guards to the cave that overlooked the waterfall. They sat on the cliff top near its entrance and watched the road. It didn't appear they were being pursued. They sat for a time in the bright sun and pondered what to do.

"What are your names?" Alastar asked the guards.

"Bearach ["Bæ-rahkh"], sir," the head guard said.

"Niall ["Neel"], sir," said the other.

"Grand," Alastar said. "We've found a bit a craic today, haven't we?"

They laughed at their circumstances. Alastar noticed the gold clasps on their uniforms and remembered Nola had worn one in her shirt. Niall and Bearach didn't have penannular ring clasps like the commanders. Only a single fibulae clasp fastened the two ends of their mantles near the center of their necklines. "Do ya mind if I see your clasp," he asked Bearach as he pointed to his fibulae.

"Certainly, sir," Bearach answered. He unfastened the clasp and gave it to Alastar.

Alastar held it up and examined it. It appeared to be solid gold and was U-shaped with large ends that flared out like the cone funnel of a trumpet. The funnel ends were bent slightly inward to hold the fabric secure as its weight tugged on the clasp. The ends were made to be held in buttonholes or fabric loops, like two connected buttons that fastened things together. The clasp's arc was engraved with slanted stripes that showed the soldier's rank. Nola was wearing a fibulae like it.

"Is there any reason a woman would wear one of these on her shirt?" Alastar asked curiously.

"It's custom for a soldier ta give his clasp ta his bird," Bearach said. "Ya know. . . ta show they've agreed ta be with one another."

Alastar's heart shrunk into a withering mass. "You mean like an engagement ring?" he asked.

"Right that," Bearach replied.

"Like a pre-engagement-engagement," Niall said. "Before ya ask if she wants ta hang her wash with yours."

"Hang her wash?" Alastar wondered.

"It's how we ask a girl ta marry, sir," Niall said. "A girl that wants ta wash her clothes with yours is in your house for the run of it; with ya for life."

"I see," Alastar said with despair. Nola was pledged to someone. The pain of rejection hit him like a pale reflection of his experience with Nuala. Nola turned out to be more like her than he had hoped. *How could Nola do that?* He returned the clasp to Bearach.

The sun was getting higher and its rays made the mist of the waterfall sparkle. Alastar watched the water and listened to its roar. He remembered finding Nola, Flann and Ula there just days before. The hopes of new life and unexpected surprises surrounded him when he thought he'd come here to find Nola, but things weren't turning out as he expected.

Alastar remembered Gilroy told him to let the currents reveal who he should be with and not to set his heart in stone. *Isn't love, love?* he had wondered to himself. Gilroy talked about true love and fleeting love, but he didn't understand the difference. His heart beat heavily for Nola because she seemed familiar and was very attractive to him. He let the natural responses of his heart override everything else that said she really wasn't the one he should pursue. Everyone had said he wasn't even meant to go to Loch an Scátháin.

Then they all suggested he should see Amber differently. He resisted, because he held tight to his desire for Nola, like a child with his heart set on going to the fair. Now that Nola set herself apart from him, that wish faded quietly away as if he had never loved her. Was his heart in numb shock or was his "love" for her simply not the kind that permanently etched its color into his heart's chambers? - fleeting love. How could he know?

He stared at the light rays that pierced through the misty waterfall. They were like shimmering threads that broke through a heavy cloud. Then a rainbow appeared in the rising mist and Amber came to his mind again. He promised he would help her. She was actually why he came to Rathúnas. It wasn't to be with Nola, but to be part of something bigger. He stood up and looked north into the hill country. It was vibrant, alive and green, and that feeling of being connected to the land came to him again. It was the same feeling he got when he was with Amber; more than once. He knew what he had to do.

"I have ta go ta Amber," Alastar said.

"Ya think ya can ride?" Bearach asked. "It's a hard day's press ta meet 'em at Chnámh an Áidh. You were supposed ta rest this whole time."

"Sure," Alastar responded, "but it's more important I'm with the princess. Can ya get my sword 'n armor? I can wait here."

"That's not a problem, sir. Only thin' is, we'd be needin' ta go northwest, straight through the fields in plain view. The search party is bound ta be rootin' through every corner 'a town. I imagine they'll be comin' this way shortly."

"I can hide in the cave here if anyone comes near. It's well hidden. Go gather my thin's as quiet as ya can. We can take the cave ravine here ta bring us ta the plains east of the mountains. Perhaps we can catch up with Gearóid's march out of Lacharan."

"It's a long way round the mountains, sir, but it's a sound plan." Bearach looked down the road toward Loch an Scátháin. There was still no one coming. "We'll be back quick as we can."

The guards left. Alastar went to Éimhín and stroked his neck. "We've got more runnin' ta do, boy. Our home'll be on the hills and plains and forests till our seat is shown." Éimhín gave a reassuring nicker. Alastar mounted him and rode down to the river.

"I see now why ya didn't have such a care for Nola. How would ya know such a thing, ya stubborn beast?. . . Ahhhh, never mind. I'd be the stubborn one. Never did let go of my wishin' for Nuala. Jumped straight on ta Nola with hardly a thought."

Alastar brought Éimhín to the river's edge. "Have a good drink. We'll not be stoppin' for rest this day." Alastar looked up the high waterfall and admired its strength. The roaring waters gave him comfort like the sounds of the churning sea. It made him feel at home, but he wondered would he ever return to Netleaf again. Where would he settle down here? Would he even get the chance to?

As he drank from the river, he remembered people were looking for him. The loud waterfall masked the sounds of anyone who approached. "Let's get back up the cliff, boy. We need ta keep watch."

They went back to the cave entrance and stood watch over the road. Soon three of the king's riders came galloping toward them. Alastar wasn't alarmed until he saw some of the royal guards were also coming down the road a distance behind them.

"I don't think the guard knows the riders are comin' here. Ta the cave," Alastar said as he dismounted and led Éimhín into the cave. He hoped there wouldn't be a conflict with the king's men. What would the king do if he found the people were helping him?

Alastar disappeared behind the thick curtain of vines as the king's riders approached below. He couldn't hear anything but the raging waterfall. He sat for a minute in the dark green veil of the cave. Then he heard shouts and metal clanging. *The guard!* he thought.

He burst out of the cave and looked down. He couldn't see the conflict below, but on his left he saw one of the king's soldiers coming up the path on foot. He had his sword drawn and started to charge Alastar. "Hold there, lad!" the soldier yelled. "Don't ya move!"

Alastar barely did anything before Éimhín burst out of the cave and stood between him and the soldier. Éimhín reared up on his hind legs and kicked at him. The man lost his footing and fell down the cliff.

"Thank ya, boy!" Alastar told Éimhín. "Come on, back here!"

Alastar took Éimhín back to the cave and walked down the trail to see what was happening. The noise of fighting had stopped. Then he saw six royal guards ride up the mountain trail to meet him.

"They won't be a bother any longer," Bearach said. "We brought your thin's. Dress quickly. Don't know when more men'll come this way."

Alastar strained through his pain to put on his armor and things. "Niall," he said, "Stay with the rest of the guard in Loch an Scátháin ta watch over the people. Bearach will accompany me alone ta Chnámh an Áidh. I don't want the king's men ta do any harm ta the people here. We'll return with everyone else quick as we can. Do the best ya can ta keep peace."

"Right then," Niall acknowledged. "Hopefully they'll leave peacefully when they've found no trace 'a ya."

"Best be rid of the bodies," Bearach said. "Let their horses run off." He turned to Alastar. "Let's hope this conflict doesn't reach the king's sight. We're ill fit ta fight a rebellion *and* fend off the Áiteoir all at once. Let's hurry now!"

Alastar and Bearach led their horses through the cave while the rest of the guard attended to their orders. Inside the mountain crevice, Bearach stopped as he remembered something. "Sir," he said as he pulled out a small leather pouch. "A nurse told me ta give this ta ya. Herbs in honey. Half now, half later, with water."

Alastar took the medicine and they continued. He felt very weak and sore after walking some distance. It made his wounds flare up and he started to breathe heavily. He mounted Éimhín and lay on his shoulders and neck to rest as they made their way out of the ravine.

"Just a short way ta the plains," Alastar said.

Gilroy had received reports from the Greerian when Amber left Torthúil with the troops and when Alastar entered the plains with Bearach. *What do they think they're doing?* he wondered. *I told them*

to be discrete. One goes north while the other goes in the opposite direction? Both in enemy territory.

He didn't tell the king what was going on but thought furiously about the consequences of their actions. Could they avoid a rebellion? How long would it take the king to find out about their movements? He had to try and keep events from unfurling into a chaotic conflict, but Amber's push into enemy territory suggested they were mounting a rescue effort. The king was sure to find out about that one way or another.

Gilroy went about palace business uneasily. He felt conflicted trying to keep loyalty to the king and supporting what was right. *This could bring the kingdom to ruin,* he thought. He needed to remain in the king's confidence, so he had no choice but to tell him about Amber's actions. He decided to try and persuade the king to support Alastar and Amber, so the kingdom would not be thrown into rebellion.

"Sire," Gilroy addressed Fuar. "The Greerian have reported the princess movin' with the troops you sent ta Loch an Scátháin. They appear ta head for Chnámh an Áidh."

"*What!?*" Fuar exclaimed. "What is she doin'?" He wondered if Alastar was with her. "Anythin' about the boy? Is he with her?"

"Alastar was not seen with them, Sire. I imagine he is still very wounded."

"Very well then. Let me ponder. Thank you, Chancellor. Leave me."

"Sire," Gilroy said firmly. "You *must* consider leavin' the princess alone ta be with the boy. The currents brought them together and it'd be right for ya ta support 'em. You see she holds the loyalty of her people."

"It is *my* people and soldiers she is commandin'!" Fuar said with anger. "Assemble my army! We will march ta Earraigh ["Ah-ree"] within the hour."

"Cnoc Earraigh?" Gilroy questioned. "What could we possibly do in the hills east of Chnámh an Áidh? Aren't we ta negotiate for the captives *at* Chnámh an Áidh?"

"Simply carry out my orders, Chancellor!" Fuar rebuked. "That'll be all."

Gilroy was flustered. The king appeared to be planning something other than to aid the princess and free their clansmen. He desperately grasped for something to hold off the king from making a rash decision. "Sire, it would be best ta meet the princess on the field at Chnámh an Áidh. The Áiteoir are certain ta attack them."

"I understand the circumstances, Chancellor," he said with cold resolve. "I appreciate your counsel, but your constant retorts have me at my end. Where is your allegiance?"

"I serve you and the kingdom, Sire."

"Then make the preparations!"

Gilroy left to prepare the king's army. Fuar immediately went to the secret cave and wrote another message to send: The princess moves to free the slaves from Chnámh an Áidh. Bring her to me unharmed at Earraigh. I will be camped there. The boy still rests in Loch an Scátháin. I will see he leaves for Lacharan.

*T*eague and Conn looked south from the top of a high hill near the forests of Loch Chnámh an Áidh. "There they are," Teague said. "Looks like Gearóid brought the whole lot." He saw a distant group of cavalry and infantry approaching. There were two thousand, half on horseback and half on foot. Most of the soldiers held long spears with blue banners that jutted into the sky. They approached like a bristling cloud that floated over the smooth green hills.

"That *would* be the lot," Conn affirmed. "The Áiteoir heavy cavalry stand like heavy hills of ash, but they number far less than our riders. Our thousand on the hoof move as a sea of swift, sharp timbers and flashin' blades, crashin' wave on wave. I feel we'll have Laochmarú runnin' much faster than our last encounter in Loch an Scátháin."

"We can't discount the rest of 'em," Teague noted. "Their infantry and light cavalry may look just out of a hard famine, but their numbers can overwhelm us. We'll have a rough fight ta keep the princess safe. I hope your group will free the captives far before we see Laochmarú's cavalry press on us."

Gearóid's troops soon joined them in the foothills near the River Seascannach ["Shæs-kon-nahkh"] that ran north into and through the waters of Loch Chnámh an Áidh. Amber greeted Gearóid and led him to meet with Teague and Conn.

"Lads!" Gearóid said to them with cheer. "We've got a grand céilí assembled. What sorta dancin' are we ta step to?"

"A fast jig that'll be over before we know it, I hope," Teague said. "We've a set dance ta march to. Conn will cross the river ta the northwest with his men. A dozen of 'em will swim the loch ta enter the city secretly, locate our clansmen, and open the gate.

The princess and my men will approach the city gate from the south for Laochmarú ta see and draw his army out, while your men remain hidden in the hills just south of us. We'll offer negotiations, but Laochmarú isn't likely ta be diplomatic. When he engages us, you'll charge 'n scatter 'em ta defend the princess. We hope they'll be distracted in the fight so Conn's men can ride from the north, take the gate, and bring our clansmen out. We regroup here once our people are taken away from the city."

"Quite a jig ya planned," Gearóid said with appreciation. "I fear it may not be a quick dance. Do we have 'em unaware?"

"Our scouts reported the city ta be quiet, sir," Conn said. "Their army rests within the city and the gates are open for travelers. There's no sign they suspect anythin'."

"Grand then," Gearóid said. "And what's the dance if they'd not take the bait?"

"They're sure ta come for me," Amber said. "But if they don't, we haven't choice but ta wait. There's chance Conn's men can open the gates from inside once they've shut, but with their army inside, it could be a long wait for an opportunity ta take the gate."

"Waitin' we've done before," Gearóid said. "But we're use ta bein' on the other side of the walls. And even if we *can* open the gates, freein' our clansmen will fail if Laochmarú's army bars our way."

The screech of a hawk broke their discussion. "Bress!" Teague recognized. He raised his arm for the hawk. It carried a message. A surprised look came over him as he read it. "The scouts report Laochmarú movin' his army outside the walls. They take a battlefield formation there."

"They must know we're here!" Conn exclaimed. "They're makin' ready ta attack!"

"Can't be!" Gearóid said. "They'd get ta marchin' straight for us if they wanted ta attack. Why'd they form lines on their front steps? What's the thinkin' in it?"

"Right," Teague acknowledged. "If they expect an attack and don't wish ta fight, they'd stay behind the walls. They know we have no siege machines. They must want ta engage in battle. If they plan a march somewhere, they wouldn't form lines there."

"Does it matter what they're doin'?" Amber asked. "We want them out of the city. This is what we wanted them ta do."

"Sure 'nough," Gearóid said. "We came for a fight. We'll give 'em that, but now that they're out, we don't need ta have ya at risk, Princess. You should stay in camp."

"That'd be wise," Teague agreed. "But we need ta act now. They may be plannin' ta move the captives. Conn, lead your men accordin' ta plan quick as ya can. We'll go ahead all the same, except the princess will remain in camp."

Conn led his unit of a hundred across the river and then north into the forest surrounding Loch Chnámh an Áidh. Teague moved his cavalry of three hundred to the hills in plain view of the city and Laochmarú. Amber remained in camp with a guard of fifty while Gearóid marched far behind Teague to remain hidden in the hills.

When Teague crested the last hill he stopped to survey the view. The day was bright and cloudless. The large mass of the Áiteoir army lay as a huge dark stain across the green fields below him. The army stood motionless and waiting. He saw the city gates were shut tight behind them.

Teague squinted to see the army across his field of vision. It appeared they had strengthened their numbers since the last battle. *Must be near twenty thousand,* he thought. *Not the sort of céilí I enjoy. Good thing the princess and Alastar are far from here.* He rode forward with an aide who carried a flag of parley. *Would Laochmarú honor negotiations peacefully?* he wondered.

Conn rushed his men north through the dry forest. Most of the trees were yellowing and parched. Only the trees closest to the lake and river remained a healthy green. He stopped near the narrowest part of the lake to send off the soldiers who would enter the city covertly.

"Cathal ["Kah-hul"], Rónán ["Roh-nahn"]!" Conn commanded. "Take your men across the loch here. May your task be blessed." Cathal and Rónán acknowledged and dismounted their horses. A dozen other men did the same. They took off most of their armor and uniforms and stowed it with their horses. They needed to enter Chnámh an Áidh inconspicuously, so they armed themselves only with bows and swords. When they were ready, they ran forward to reach the lakeshore.

"Brin' their horses!" Conn ordered. His party continued through the forest to position themselves north of the city gate.

Cathal's party crept up to the lake on their stomachs to avoid being seen. He slowly rose up and peered through the reeds along the shallows. There was an island off to the left with a lot of driftwood caught around it. He noticed the water flowed swiftly. "It's not gonna be a spash 'n wade, lads," he said. "Looks ta be a mile across, deep waters 'n the current's flowin' strong." He tried to see the far end of the bank. There were houses and towers of all kinds.

"Rónán," Cathal said. "Take your men straight off from here. Come ta shore between the watchtowers. Appears ta be quiet there. Head ta the gate 'n find a way ta open it after Laochmarú engages

Teague. I'll land downstream n' find our people. They should be in the markets in the north district. We'll help ya secure the gate once we find 'em. "

"Right then," Rónán affirmed. "Let's have at it, lads!" he ordered his men. His group broke off hollow reeds near the shore and entered the water. They swam deep underwater as much as they could and used the reeds to breathe through without breaking the surface. Cathal watched them disappear into the waves.

"Those lads swim like seals," Cathal said. "Don't know how they do it."

Cathal told his men to break off reeds too, but they weren't adept swimmers as Rónán's men were. They needed to swim to the nearby island and use it for cover. There, they found a large floating log they hid behind as they swam to the other side of the lake.

Cathal peeked up from behind the log as they tried to guide it to shore. They were floating right past a watchtower where he saw a guard keeping watch. "Stay under!" he whispered to the others. "A guard is near."

"Grand thin'," a soldier said sarcastically as he panted to keep his head above the water. "Eachraighe turned ta selkies! Do I look like a murúch ["mur-roohkh"; mermaid]?"

"Amaideach, Neese, ya scanger!" Cathal told him. "You'll be a mermaid for the time bein'! Get under!"

Cathal scanned ahead to see where they were drifting. He found a quiet bank to land on. "There, lads," he said. "Kick ta the boathouse. We'll come up behind it."

Neese struggled to swim quietly and kept grabbing at the others and the log to keep afloat. He made them bob and splash up and down. As they drifted by the watchtower, his face turned an excruciating red, but he managed to keep quiet. They made it safely past the watchtower and landed behind the boathouse. It concealed their movement perfectly as they got up from the water.

Neese was livid. He jumped out of the water and screamed, "Last time ya have me skimmin' water like that! Somethin' bigger than my leg brushed me! Some sea monster, kelpie somethin' or another! It was desperate, I'm sayin'! Couldn't scream an ounce till now!"

"Cop on!" another soldier told him. "If ya weren't such a grand archer, we wouldn't have needed ya here, ya babby ["bah-bee"; baby]!"

"Quit your coddin', lads, "Cathal said. "We've business ta attend." He looked around. The grounds appeared to be part of a wealthy estate. There were clean, open fields and cultivated gardens just beyond the tree line."Not a bit a skint in this corner," he joked. "And just in time for the wash." He pointed to clothes that dried on many lines past the trees. They snuck up to the hanging clothes and quickly patted themselves dry with them.

"We'll be dry quick as a bolt in this sun," one of them said.

Suddenly they heard someone in the distance yelling. A maid ran angrily toward them and called for help.

"We're not invited for a cup, lads," Cathal said. "Quick! Ta the city!"

They ran into the surrounding woods and headed toward the inner city. Chnámh an Áidh quickly turned from grassy forest and fields into busy streets full of people. Chnámh an Áidh was a hub between many cities. There were travelers everywhere. Cathal was relieved they could blend into the crowd easily. Despite their wet clothes, no one paid any attention to them.

The city was packed with ragged buildings, homes and dirty markets. One street was so full of the stench of blood and rotting meat, they had to hold their breath as they walked through. "This place is right manky! Too many butchers," Cathal noted. "Why would they have so much meat out? It's well inta midday."

"It must be for the Féile Plandála ["Fay-lah Plahn-dah-lah"]," a soldier said. "Most of it'll be gone by sundown. They celebrate the plantin' 'a their crops with a festival and feastin'. One fine, huge meal ta hold 'em over till harvest. I'd say they're peckish most of the time otherwise."

"How would ya know that bein' a horseman?" Cathal wondered.

"My mam came from the north kingdom, sure 'nough. Lived the lean farmin' life till my ole man swooped 'er off ta Lacharan 'n made her a fat rancher's wife."

Cathal laughed and noted the soldier's chubby features. "Sure 'nough! And she made many a fine fat lad in Lacharan! Stocked the lot 'a ya full 'a rashers 'n hash every morn'!"

The men laughed as they walked into a large clearing by the city wall. There were many wood cages, wagons and pens full of people and animals. They found the slave and livestock market. Cathal noticed more than a dozen caged wagons that he recognized from the battle at Dún Tearmann.

"Our people are here," Cathal whispered. "Too many guards. We'll need Conn ta free 'em. Just keep walkin', lads. We'll see how Rónán is farin' at the gate."

They continued to walk past the slave market trying not to gather attention to themselves. Cathal counted over fifty guards in the area and others manned the top of the city wall. Some of the guards stared at them with interest. Small groups of lightly armed men were not unusual in the Áiteoir Kingdom. Thieves and the like roamed the wilderness, but Cathal's men didn't appear to be from the kingdom. Their clean, sturdy garments and well-made weapons suggested they were not poor wanderers from the area.

"You there!" a guard yelled at them. "Come forth!" More guards shifted their attention to them.

Fionn and Brónach were caged just behind the guard who called to them. When he heard the guard yell, he lifted his head and took notice. "Brónach," he whispered. "Those are riders that tried ta rescue us at Dún Tearmann. I'd recognize their swords anywhere."

"Ya think the Eachraighe came ta save us from here?" she responded. She tried to sit up to pay attention but Fionn held her down with a hand on her shoulder.

"Keep still," he said softly. "We can't reveal 'em."

Cathal and his men approached the guard warily. They looked about slowly and assessed the situation. Many guards watched them closely and a few archers on the wall held their bows ready. A fight here would not bear good fruit.

"What's your business here, strangers," the guard asked.

"Simply walkin' the market for thin's 'a value, sir," Cathal replied.

"Right big place ya 'ave here," Neese added. "But we've empty hands! Where'd ya keep the poteen 'n honey wine?"

The guard gave Neese a scowl. "Quiet, lad! I'll be speakin' ta your mate. Where do ya lads come from?"

"We're just on the doss from our ranch upstream," Cathal said. "Strollin' your fine city ta pass time away. Where would your local be?"

Fionn jumped up and yelled at Cathal, "I know you! Bouzzies and chancers, the lot 'a ya! Good fer nothin's! Get back ta your farmin' before your master find's ya ran off ta roll in the sun!"

Then the sound of Laochmarú's battle horn was heard just beyond the walls. The guard waved away Cathal and his men. "Run off with ya!" he told them. They walked away with great relief and continued down the street.

"Remind me ta thank our clansman once we get 'em outta here," Neese said. "Quick thinker."

"Surely," Cathal said. "Step *quick* ta the gate! The battle's startin'!"

They made a fast walk toward the gate and looked around. Many people were around the gate but they didn't seem to care about what was happening outside the walls. Most of the soldiers on top of the walls were looking outward, though.

Cathal looked for Rónán and his men but didn't find them near the gate. The gate was an enormous door of solid oak and bronze crossbars. The gate tower above it was high and there wasn't access to the winch room from the ground. Only people on top of the wall could get to it. *How can we get up there?* Cathal wondered. Then a bell started to ring and he looked down the wall to a nearby bell tower. Rónán and another man were climbing it while his other men shot arrows from the ground.

"There they are!" Cathal told his men. "Help 'em take the gate from here!"

Cathal's archers started to shoot down soldiers on the wall while Cathal and others ran forward with their swords. They struck down guards at the gate and waited for Rónán to reach the winch in the tower.

"Cover Rónán!" Cathal yelled. "More comin' from both sides!"

Dozens of guards ran toward them from all directions on the ground and on top of the wall. Cathal's archers soon ran out of arrows and drew their swords, while Rónán's other men climbed the bell tower to help fight along the top of the wall. Rónán needed protection as he worked the winch.

"Come together!" Cathal ordered. His men regrouped and

stood in a semi-circle in front of the gate to face attacking guards. Rónán started to open the gate as his men fought off guards around him. They fought fiercely, but Cathal and Rónán's men fell one by one as the gate slowly crept open. Eight of them were left when Rónán finally locked the gate open.

Cathal looked out through the gateway and was dismayed to see a unit from Laochmarú's army running to the gate. At least a hundred infantry bore down on them just fifty meters away. He looked about desperately to see if their men were near, but Conn and Teague were nowhere to be seen. *Where is Conn!* Cathal worried. *We can't hold the gate much longer!*

"Lower the gate!" Cathal yelled to Rónán.

Rónán and his men were too busy fending off guards to lower the gate. The infantry outside charged furiously. They were barely ten meters away when all of a sudden they stopped, faced to their right, and braced themselves.

Conn's riders burst over the top of a hill with swords and spears floating ahead of them, like the glistening edge of a cresting wave. His cavalry quickly washed over the infantry and trampled them. Relief came over Cathal as he saw the enemy smothered and scattered, but he was growing weary fending off many attackers at the gate. They were being pushed farther and farther outside.

"Captain!" Cathal yelled. He hoped Conn saw they needed immediate reinforcement.

Then they heard a horn blast from behind them and dozens of Conn's riders flooded through the gate. They overtook the guards there and soon Cathal and his men stopped to breathe.

Conn rode up next to him. "Well fought!" Conn told them. "We have the gate!"

"A minute sooner would've been grand," Cathal remarked with

a weary smile.

"Right!" Conn acknowledged. "The river crossin' took more than we thought. The Seascannach's current nearly swept us all off, 'n the bog land 'round it swallowed some of us whole. The river's true ta her name. She was *murder!* A downright hard neck!. . . Where are the captives?"

"Just ta the north," Cathal said.

"Grand," Conn acknowledged. "Hold the gate!" He blew the battle horn again and led his men to rescue the prisoners. There were few enemy guards left to hinder their success, but as Cathal surveyed the scene, he worried about the lack of resistance. It was too quiet. Where did Laochmarú's army go? The fields outside the city were barren; only dozens of the enemy's dead were scattered about. Where were the many thousands?

It didn't take long for Conn to gather their clansmen from the city. They took the wagons to transport the people back to camp. Their party left Chnámh an Áidh in a long procession of overjoyed people rejoicing over the victory, but Conn was cautious. He had seen Laochmarú's army charge south at Teague when they came to take the gate. It was the same direction they had to go. Their camp was some miles away due south.

Conn led everyone as close to the lake and river as possible. He hoped Laochmarú's army was farther to the east where Teague and Gearóid stood against them. As they passed over many hills, he grew concerned. There was no sign of the armies or battle anywhere near. *The battle should be visible from the high hills, he thought. Where is everyone?*

*A*lastar and Bearach rode for hours around the perimeter of the mountain forests. They tried to keep the pace up, but Alastar's wounds made the journey painful. He needed to stop for rest almost every hour.

"I think my cut's splinterin'!" Alastar yelled. He stopped Éimhín and looked at his left thigh. Blood was soaking through his clothes.

Bearach came over to him and looked. "Best ya take the rest of the honey-herb now. I'll wrap your leg. How's that shoulder?"

"Sore but not banjaxed as my leg," Alastar replied.

Bearach tore a long section of fabric from his horse's blanket covering and tied it tight around Alastar's wound. Alastar winched in pain and a shock of dizziness rushed to his head. He leaned forward slightly and steadied himself on Éimhín's neck.

"How far do ya think we've gone?" Alastar asked.

"We've been ridin' north almost an hour now," Bearach said. "Maybe half the distance." He looked forward along their trail. There was no one in sight; just the mountain forests on their right and endless green fields and hills ahead and to their left. "Not a sign 'a Lacharan's men, but the grass here is well trampled. It's certain Gearóid took this path. . . or some well-sized army anyhow."

Alastar took his remaining medicine and they continued. The mountains disappeared behind them as the hours passed. Then the hill country surrounded them with smooth rolling hills. The lush green terrain would have been a soft and easy ride if Alastar was not injured, but he continued to strain with pain.

The sun was midway to receding from its highest point when

Bearach held up his right arm and stopped. "There's a large group ahead," he said. "Not an army. Maybe a hundred light riders. . . but they're Áiteoir. Must be garrison from Túr an Tairbh ["Toor ahn Tahr-rev"]; just west 'a here."

"A tower?" Alastar asked as he recognized the word, túr.

"Right," Bearach said. "Tower of the Bull. The largest round tower on Rathúnas was a watchtower for the Méine Kingdom, when they still had a kingdom. Now it's an Áiteoir fortress guardin' the mouth of the River Seascannach. The Áiteoir must know we're gatherin' at Chnámh an Áidh. Those riders look ta be headin' straight there."

"We shouldn't get too close," Alastar suggested. "If they take chase, I don't know how long I could outrun 'em before falling over in pain."

"Right. We can't overtake 'em anyways. They're too far ahead 'n movin' fast. We're less than an hour ta findin' our clansmen. No time ta go round 'em. Best we hang back and rest for the comin' fight."

Amber stood on a hill that overlooked the river. Their soldiers left hours ago and she anxiously waited to see them return. The River Seascannach flowed toward Chnámh an Áidh like a thick muddy serpent. She watched the water flow north to the city and wondered how it became so dirty after coming from the clear waters of the Muir Airgid. The inland sea sparkled with silver and light, but the river was usually brown and muddy as it crawled north across Rathúnas. It seemed to splay out into all the land it touched and created mucky bogs everywhere.

As she stood on the hill with her guards, no one realized there was rustling far down near the river bank. A Lorgaire scout was watching them. He crouched behind thick grass and dry reeds. The surroundings blended perfectly with his ragged clothes of green and brown. He was one of many scouts that Laochmarú sent out to locate Amber's party after he heard she was coming.

The scout had traveled down from Chnámh an Áidh for hours. The slow trek was tedious, but now he was delighted to find his mark. He slowly took out paper from a pocket and wrote on it. Then he opened a leather pouch and took out a small éanshee to relay the message. He released it and it flew towards the city.

Outside Chnámh an Áidh, Laochmarú watched Teague approach his army to offer negotiations. He had no interest in debate over the captives, though. He only set out to find Amber and Alastar and was waiting for his scouts to give him word.

Teague stopped in the field just out of reach of Laochmarú's archers and waited for Laochmarú to respond. Every man stood silent and still. Minutes passed without a response. It made Teague feel like the bright sun had baked them all into solid statues. No one moved in the warm, dry air.

Teague watched Laochmarú carefully the whole time. Then he saw a small bird fly up to him and land on his shoulder. *An éanshee,* he recognized. Laochmarú read the message it carried and brought his dark battle horn up to his lips. He blew the call and his army lunged forward.

"Retreat!" Teague told the aide. "They have wind of somethin' ta turn their feet swift on us!" They raced back to their unit and made ready to lead the enemy into Gearóid's soldiers who waited just out of sight behind the hills.

Teague watched them charge. He had never seen such a mass of movement come toward them before. The enemy surged like a massive black tide that covered the land around them. As they drew near, he yelled to his men, "Ta Gearóid!" and they took off toward the hills behind them.

When they joined Gearóid, everyone waited for the enemy to crest the hills. Gearóid sounded his horn as he saw them flood over the hilltops. He lowered his spear and pointed it forward. Everyone else did the same and they charged full ahead into Laochmarú's army.

The armies quickly clashed, but when Laochmarú saw Gearóid's troops he blew his horn and separated his army. His other commanders took half of the men to the southeast, while he continued to blow his horn and urged his men to press forward, directly south. His heavy cavalry punched a channel through Lacharan's men and they continued forward while his infantry followed. The hills were filled with his men running and attacking, but they focused more on following Laochmarú instead of fighting.

Teague saw what they were doing and yelled to Gearóid as they fought off the enemy all around them, "They're pressin' on ta the princess!"

"Run 'em down!" Gearóid acknowledged. He blew his horn again and rallied his men to chase after Laochmarú. They turned around quickly, but the enemy was all around them. They couldn't catch him easily. Only a few riders closest to Laochmarú were able to take chase freely.

Teague noticed half of the enemy was running off field to the southeast. *Where are they going?* he wondered. He didn't have time to ponder. The princess needed to be secure, so he worked to lead his men after Laochmarú in the south.

Laochmarú continued unhindered for miles with more than a hundred of his heavy cavalry. Only small pockets of Eachraighe were able to catch up, but the Áiteoir's heavy armor made it difficult to dislodge them from their line of attack. The chasing riders could only kill a few with well aimed spears that slipped in between links of armor.

Teague was able to break free of the battle with more riders, but they were far behind Laochmarú. Over a mile separated them. He urged his men forward as fast as they could go. After many minutes, Laochmarú slowed to conserve strength, but he could see Amber's camp far ahead in the hills. Amber's guards saw them approach.

"Laochmarú comes with heavy armor, Princess," a guard said. "Near two hundred riders. I wouldn't recommend we wait for 'em. I don't see many of our men chasin'."

"Where can we go?" Amber asked. They looked around for somewhere to hide. When they appraised their surroundings, they were surprised to see another large group of riders approaching from the south. They were so focused on the north that no one noticed the enemy coming up behind them.

"We're bein' surrounded," Amber said. There was nowhere to hide in the hills and plains. The closest shelter was the forests around Chnámh an Áidh just northwest of them. "Can we make it ta the forest?"

"We haven't a choice," the guard said. He ordered everyone to mount their horses and head to the forest.

The Lorgaire hiding near the river saw them take flight down the hill. They would gallop right past him. He couldn't let them escape, so he took out a small pouch and poured half a dozen small clumps of black powder on the bog peat around him. The lumps quickly soaked up the peat, water and things nearby and grew into scaly, long-legged lizards. They looked like lean, hairless wolves with scales of moldy yellow-green and brown. Their breath gave off a visible plume of yellow mist that turned the scout's head away. He covered his mouth and waved them off toward the princess. The giant lizards leapt toward Amber's party and started to scatter them.

"Lagharitshee ["lye-irtch-shee"] !" a guard yelled. "Swords! Do not breathe their smoke!"

The lagharitshee leaped onto many soldiers and spewed their noxious breath at them. Soldiers and horses alike fell fast unconscious. Amber held her breath as she urged Muirgel to gallop into the forest, but a lagharitshee chased her down and jumped onto her back. She fell hard to the ground and when she landed, a gasp broke through her lungs. The lizard hovered above her and blew its sleeping fumes around her. She fell unconscious.

Most of the guards were taken under by the lagharitshee's sleeping fumes. A few remaining guards cut them down and tried to gather to Amber, but Laochmarú arrived and surrounded them. The other Áiteoir unit from the south also arrived. Amber's guards were killed quickly as the camp filled with enemy troops. Not one soldier of Torthúil was near. None of the chasing Eachraighe survived their attack on the heavy cavalry, but Teague was quickly approaching with more men.

Alastar and Bearach were also coming close to camp, but they couldn't see what was happening by the river. The high hills around it hid the river and forests beyond, but they knew the enemy had reached their camp.

"I hope no one was in camp," Alastar said. "It looks like everyone's gone." They pressed forward harder but tried to keep far enough away so they wouldn't draw attention to themselves. When they came near, they left their horses hidden behind a hill. "Stay here, boy," he told Éimhín. "We'll just have a look."

They crawled to the top of a hill to look over the camp. Alastar groaned in pain as he tried to move.

"You should stay with your horse, sir," Bearach suggested. "You're not aidin' your wounds."

"I have ta see what's goin' on," Alastar said. "I'll be grand. There'll be time for healin' later."

When they reached the top of the hill, they surveyed the area. There were many small tents and fire pits strewn about, but no one was in view. Then they saw Laochmarú and his men appear from behind the highest hill and ride across their view to the right; hundreds of them. Alastar felt a tinge of pain seeing Laochmarú and his heavy cavalry again. His last memory of battle had Laochmarú tower over him in dark armor with a spear and sword pinning him to the ground. Then Alastar noticed one of the riders had a woman hanging limp in front of his saddle.

"Amber!" Alastar screamed. He almost stood up, but Bearach held him down.

"We can't do anythin' now," Bearach said.

"Where are our men?" Alastar wondered. "We have ta follow 'em!"

"Sure thin'."

They waited for all the Áiteoir to leave, but were surprised to see half of them split from Laochmarú and go south. Laochmarú led his other men with Amber to the northeast. "Why are they separatin'?" Alastar asked.

"The garrison must be returnin' ta Túr an Tairbh," Bearach said.

"Some of their heavy cavalry go south too, though. We only followed light riders on the way here."

"They're plannin' some maneuver, sure 'nough," Bearach acknowledged. "One of the heavy riders is a commander. What should we do?"

"We have ta stay with the princess," Alastar said. "Find out where they're takin' her."

They crept back down the hill and mounted their horses. Alastar's wounds were flaring up with pain again. He was pale and felt weak, but he grit through the pain and weariness to go after Laochmarú. It felt strange for him to chase after the enemy when they had spent so much time running from them in the past days.

Alastar pat and stroked Éimhín on the neck. "We're on for another run," he told him. "We'll have ta rest another day." Éimhín whinnied and they took off. When they crested the highest hill in the camp, they saw Teague chasing Laochmarú's group with many riders.

"There's our men!" Bearach yelled gladly. "And it looks like Gearóid's army just beyond, but there's a whole army of Áiteoir runnin' after 'em."

They galloped hard to meet Teague. He was surprised to see them chasing Laochmarú as well. "Lad!" he yelled to Alastar. "Ya look ready ta sleep for a month! What are ya doin' here?"

"We left Loch an Scátháin after the king's men tried comin' for me this mornin'. We saw Laochmarú leave camp with Amber so here we are."

"Right then," Teague said. "Grand ta see ya safe. Keep ta the rear so the general doesn't see ya."

Alastar acknowledged and they continued to chase Laochmarú. Gearóid's men were catching up as well. The mass of the infantry for both armies was left far behind as the chase went on. The rolling hills smoothed out into fields filled with vast patches of blue and white flowers. The sun was on their backs as it moved lower on the horizon. Behind them, the sky dimmed to colors of orange and violet and the fields of flowers appeared to glow brighter around them; rambling lakes of bluebells and ramsons dotted the emerald green grass everywhere.

The scene of natural beauty was cut off farther up the horizon where Laochmarú's men stood in dark contrast to the vivid colors around them. They were getting closer to Laochmarú, but they soon realized the darkness on the horizon was expanding. They were running straight into the half of Laochmarú's army that split off at Chnámh an Áidh. Laochmarú had ordered them to wait for him in the east. He anticipated needing a blockade to help him carry Amber to Earraigh where Fuar waited.

When Teague came near, he ordered everyone to stop. They saw Laochmarú disappear with Amber through his thick wall of cavalry and infantry. They stood there waiting as Laochmarú carried Amber farther away with most of his riders.

Alastar rode up to Teague. "What do we do now?" Alastar asked.

"Wait for Gearóid to join us. We need all our riders ta punch through that line. Laochmarú's takin' the princess somewhere."

"We can't lose sight of her!" Alastar said.

"Hold tight, lad," Teague reassured. "They don't seem ta wish harm on her. They would've killed her already if they did. I don't know why they carry her this way, though."

Alastar looked at the enemy line. It extended across their whole view. Many thousands of soldiers, but their lines did end. "Why don't we just go 'round?"

"They'll charge us wherever we try to break through. It's best we pierce 'em straight quick with the mass of our floatin' spears. We'll need the sharp of Gearóid's men ta break 'em swift."

When Gearóid came near, Teague left to intercept him quickly. They planned to break through the enemy's center as Teague suggested - with the mass of their many hundreds of spear carriers charging in a concentrated line. The charge would be like they did out the gate of Lacharan - with Alastar in its center, so he would be carried through under their shields.

"Ride straight through 'em!" Gearóid told everyone. "We aim ta retrieve the princess, not batter their army." He raised his horn and rallied the men.

They charged quickly with spear carriers many riders thick in front and to the sides. The enemy archers started launching arrows as soon as they came near. Riders fell here and there from the arrows, but their spearhead remained intact. Alastar hunkered low on Éimhín and mustered his strength to hold tight. His wounds gave him intense pain as they galloped. When they crashed through the enemy, he lifted up to see ahead. Their plan worked. They were riding straight through the army, but it was hard to see Laochmarú.

Alastar tried to stand on his stirrups to get a better view, but his leg hurt so much he couldn't hold himself up for more than a few seconds. He did see a distant group of riders far ahead. They galloped as fast as they could toward them.

He leaned back down on Éimhín and reassured him. "I know ya ran all day, boy; just another hot run for Amber. Give her all ya got!" Éimhín understood and lowered his neck farther. His stride became even swifter and they surged forward toward the front of the line. Alastar had to hold on with all his strength. His wounds struck with pain at every pound of the gallop and his brow was wet with the sweat of pain and effort.

The chase went on for many more minutes. They were gaining on Laochmarú, but as the colorful plains flew underneath them, they saw something else draw near on the horizon. It was another camp settled on a hill with the ruins of a castle on top - Cnoc Earraigh. The camp was very large and bright with many torches and fires burning around it. They pressed onward to catch Laochmarú, and were nearly on his heels, but when they saw the large camp was the king's army, Gearóid and Teague stopped their charge.

They saw Laochmarú enter King Fuar's camp. "What is the king doin' here?" Gearóid asked with dismay.

"He must want the princess," Teague suggested. "Laochmarú is deliverin' her right ta him."

Alastar joined Teague and Gearóid in the front. "What have we here?" he asked.

"Laochmarú brought the princess ta the king," Teague said.

"The king is openly conspirin' with the enemy," Gearóid added. "Have we any choice but ta fight 'em both now? The king brought his whole army 'n the rest of the Áiteoir will be comin' on our back soon."

The soldiers of Torthúil stood confused on both sides. Most of them didn't know the king was working with the Áiteoir. They certainly didn't expect to be facing their own clansmen on these fields. Whispers of betrayal, honor and loyalty ran through their ranks. Many men wished to be loyal to the king and kingdom. He was still their leader, but others were loyal to Amber and held on to the honor of siding against the enemy. Soldiers on both the king and Gearóid's side stood questioning what was happening.

"Why would they bring Amber ta the king?" Alastar asked.

Teague replied, "The king wishes ta force her marriage ta him. He plans ta secure his reign with the prosperity foretold for the House of Ealaí."

A desperate shock went through Alastar. He worried over Amber. He knew she didn't want such a union with the king, and he struggled with his own feelings for her. He felt a fierce loyalty to her, but was it romantic love? He didn't know. He only felt he had to get her out of there.

"What can we do?" Alastar asked. "Can the king force marriage on her?"

"It is the king's right," Gearóid said. "There is no wrong in the marriage, even if Amber does not wish it. It's the willful trade for you and our clansmen's lives that have the king at odds with what's right. Now that everyone sees he works with the Áiteoir, there's bound ta be rebellion. Amber did not wish it, but we must attack ta save her from the king's plan. If the marriage goes through, a rebellion'll be messy. It will be hard ta resist the king, because those loyal ta Amber 'n Lacharan will be forced ta side with him once they unite in marriage."

"The chancellor is against the king's plan," Teague added. "But I'm sure he'll be forced ta perform the marriage as soon as can be; right on these fields, I imagine. The king isn't likely ta risk any more complications by waitin' on a grand ceremony in Cnoc na Rí."

As they talked, Fuar and Gilroy rode forward to meet them in the open ground between their troops. Two flag bearers rode on each side of them.

"It's time ta speak with the king," Gearóid said. "Teague, come with me."

"Right," Teague acknowledged. He turned to Alastar. "It may be too late ta hide ya, but keep yourself in the rear, lad."

Alastar nodded and quietly went to the back of their lines. Behind their troops, he became alarmed as he saw the enemy infantry running towards them. They would soon be surrounded.

Gearóid and Teague rode forward to meet the king. "Sire," Gearóid acknowledged.

"You are commanded ta leave these fields and return ta Lacharan," Gilroy said. "Your acts are treasonous, but the king will forgive this if you leave with your men peacefully. Any more advance on the king will have you and your men sentenced ta death for treason."

"We only wish ta retrieve the princess, Sire" Gearóid said to Fuar.

"She is in my keepin'," Fuar said. "I have no other terms for you. Do as I ask, and you may go home in peace."

"Sire," Gearóid replied. "We cannot leave Amber with the enemy around us."

"She is safe with me," Fuar said firmly.

"And with the Áiteoir in your ranks?!" Gearóid fumed. "Their army marches on us this very moment!"

"That is not your concern, Duke," Fuar said with agitation. "Leave now and I will see the Áiteoir will not hinder your passage as well."

Gilroy moved uneasily on his horse. He didn't like having to side with the king in this confrontation. He worried that the armies of Torthúil would shed each other's blood before the day's end. The kingdom that King Rían founded generations ago was ready to splinter after so many years of solid kinship. Soldiers on both sides shared his concerns. Everyone worried they would have to fight their own clansmen.

Gearóid and Teague knew what had to be done. They held their resolve to rescue Amber immediately. The king had more than double their troops, but his army was mostly infantry. They might succeed in the battle with their larger number of cavalry, but the advancing

Áiteoir worried them. How could they win if two armies were against them?

*G*earóid gave Fuar a respectful bow and backed away. He returned with Teague to their front line and started to inspire the men to stand firm. Fuar and Gilroy also returned to their camp. The king told Gilroy to secure the princess in his tent while he ordered his men to prepare for battle. Everyone took their positions. Units of men moved three large machines of timber logs and rope and pointed them towards the center of the Eachraighe line. The three ballistae were like giant crossbows that launched spears the size of tree trunks. They lay ready to launch, hidden behind the soldiers.

Fuar went to Laochmarú who was waiting with his riders for the battle to begin. "The boy is in their ranks," Fuar told him. "Do what ya will. Only help me crush the traitors 'n I will share the riches of Lacharan with you."

Laochmarú affirmed with a nod and led his riders to the front lines. Their dark armor and horses were an odd contrast to the rest of the king's army, which was bright and gleaming in hues of gold bronze, white and red. Many of the king's soldiers fidgeted with anxiety. They couldn't believe they were standing with the Áiteoir and preparing to attack their own clansmen.

Across the field, Gearóid rallied his men with the sound of many bodhrán players drumming a beat to rouse their hearts. He yelled out to his troops, "The princess *needs* ta return home, lads! We cannot stand with the king on this. He threatens the kingdom by sellin' off his own people n' throwin' the Swan-bearer ta the enemy! He would make the princess a slave and brin' Lacharan and the Eachraighe ta shame! Stand up for her, lads! Stand up for the city your forefathers came out of! Stand up, lads! You all bear the mark of the Eachraighe! You carry

Lacharan's banner!"

All their soldiers gave a great shout across the vast field, whether they had come from Lacharan or Cnoc na Rí. Their bewilderment over loyalties disappeared as they understood what the king had done. They were ready to take back Amber and uphold the kingdom's honor.

Gearóid planned to charge into the king's lines and disperse them. He hoped to do it quickly so they could take Amber before the rest of the Áiteoir arrived. Laochmarú's army was fast approaching behind them.

"Lad," Teague said to Alastar. They stood with Gearóid at the center of the front line. "This time ya stay near me. Remember your sword lessons. None of us will have rest t'night."

Gearóid blew the battle horn and pointed his spear forward. Teague and Alastar drew their swords and everyone surged forward together; nearly a thousand horses bristled with bronze spears and swords as they galloped toward the king's line. When they approached, Fuar ordered his three ballistae to fire their giant spears at the advancing riders. The huge bolts took down entire lines of soldiers from front to back.

"Faster!" Gearóid yelled. "Before they reload!"

Then the king's archers loosed their arrows and many riders fell under the raining darts. Alastar surged ahead with Teague and Gearóid close behind. When Laochmarú saw Alastar clearly, he ordered his riders to intercept. Nearly two hundred of his heavy cavalry fixed solid onto the spear point of the charging Eachraighe. Laochmarú aimed to stop their charge by swiping them hard from the side with his heavy horses.

Gearóid and Teague recognized the threat from Laochmarú and began to veer away from him. Gearóid tried to press even faster to break the king's line farther down the field before Laochmarú reached them, but there was not enough distance to make their charge successful. Laochmarú's men pounded into the front of their line and broke their formation. Horses went tumbling and riders flew through the air.

Most of the Eachraighe coming from behind rode around the mess that Laochmarú's heavy cavalry made at the front. They continued to charge the king's soldiers but lost much of their speed and cohesion. The men in front, including Alastar, Teague and Gearóid, were caught in a tight battle with Laochmarú's heavily armored soldiers.

The king ordered his soldiers to advance into the charging riders and soon the entire field was a disheveled array of fighting. After losing their momentum, Gearóid's riders failed to break through the king's lines, but they continued to battle hard. The field of fighting men moved like a great lake of thousands of dying fish that flailed about in shallow puddles of water. The soldiers fought and gasped like fish trying desperately to find the safety of deep water.

Laochmarú went after Alastar as quickly as he could. He slashed through many riders to reach him. This time Alastar saw him coming and stood ready. He could barely feel the pain of his wounds with his adrenaline surging hard. Alastar thrust and parried with all his strength as Laochmarú swung his sword at him. He was surprised at the power behind Laochmarú's swings. He felt as if he was being struck by a falling tree with every blow. Alastar's speed helped him, though, and he maneuvered Éimhín deftly around Laochmarú to keep a safe distance. Alastar held him off, but he couldn't harm Laochmarú either. He was quickly tiring of fending off his strong blows.

Teague saw Alastar being attacked but he was busy in his own fights. Many of Laochmarú's men stood between them. He managed to kill some of the heavy cavalry with pinpoint sword thrusts through their links of armor, but it took time to place the killing blows. He knew he had to get to Alastar quickly. He let out a fierce yell and burst forward to charge Laochmarú.

Teague swung quickly at the general. He struck his sword and armor many times, but he couldn't find a killing blow. Laochmarú used his size and strength to push Teague off balance. He came close and swung hard at Teague with a forearm. The blow knocked him off his horse and Laochmarú turned back towards Alastar.

Just as soon as he turned around, though, Laochmarú saw Gearóid run at him on foot with a spear. The sharp blade pressed into his belly, but it didn't break through the chainmail. Laochmarú fell to the ground flat on his back.

"Ride outta here!" Gearóid ordered Alastar. "Find a way ta Amber!"

Alastar broke out of the fighting with Laochmarú's men, but quickly found himself clashing with the king's soldiers. Their infantry was easier to handle, but their numbers kept pressing him backwards. All the Eachraighe were being forced farther and farther away from the king's camp. In between fighting, Alastar scanned the camp to look for Amber. He couldn't see her, but he saw Gilroy stand with a handful of guards by the king's tent at the top of the hill. It was in front of a crumbling wall that was part of an old castle there. *Amber must be there,* he thought.

The Eachraighe's strength was faltering. They continued to be pressed back by Fuar and Laochmarú's men. There were too many strong soldiers for them to handle. As the battle went on, they heard Laochmarú blow his horn. He had signaled his approaching army to charge into the fight.

Everyone looked backwards. The Eachraighe were attacked by

thousands more soldiers from behind. Their courage pressed into tight pockets of resistance, but their strength began to falter with so much force against them. Many of them lost their ardor for the fight and some began to retreat any way they could. Gearóid and Teague tried to urge their men to continue fighting, but the numbers were so great against them that there appeared to be no way to survive the battle.

Alastar was still fighting off the king's men, trying to get through their line. The Áiteoir reinforcements didn't reach him yet, but he saw the Eachraighe having trouble. They were losing the battle.

Just when Alastar began to lose heart with the enemy closing in on every side, he heard a familiar call ring out from the distance. He looked up and saw the Seabhac Azure perched on top of the wall above the king's tent. The sight renewed his hope. *I have to get to Amber!* his heart screamed.

"We have ta do somethin', boy!" Alastar told Éimhín. He turned Éimhín around and went back a distance from the king's line. The Áiteoir were charging fast at him from behind too, but he steadied himself and took a deep breath. "Remember the canal?" he whispered to Éimhín before they charged forward.

They rushed like the gale of a storm toward the king's men. The men formed a solid line but it was only a few men deep. They ran as quick as they could at them and just before colliding, Éimhín leapt high over their heads and landed securely behind them. They kept galloping forward with nothing to hinder them. Before anyone could react, they bound up the hill to the king's tent and stood before Gilroy. The Azure flapped its wings vigorously again. The guards were about to attack Alastar, but Gilroy ordered them to stand down. "Get the princess," he told them.

Everyone now had their eyes on Alastar and saw the Azure. They were dumbfounded. Everyone stopped in their tracks. Shouts of triumph came from the Eachraighe. The grand sight of Alastar standing on the hill with his sword held high and the Azure over him brought their fighting spirits back.

Fuar yelled orders to seize Alastar, but then the Azure flew down and settled on his right shoulder. A guard brought Amber outside the tent and Gilroy cut the rope that bound her hands. They all gazed at Alastar and the Azure. The great bird flapped its wings hard behind him and all of a sudden, bright light shone all around them. The Azure's wings grew gigantic and Éimhín reared up. They appeared as a radiant winged horse and glowing rider with his sword held high. Everyone stood stunned and had to shield their eyes from the intense light.

When Éimhín came back down on his feet, the bright light diminished and the Azure took off flying high to the west. Amber stepped forward and looked up at Alastar. He smiled wide at her and held out his hand. She was so glad to see him that her eyes dampened with new life, like a refreshing morning dew had rested on her. She jumped up onto Éimhín and they rode fast together down the hill outside the battle lines. Gilroy rushed to his horse and followed them.

"With the Swan-bearer!" Gearóid yelled. "Victory!"

All the Eachraighe stopped fighting and rode out of the battle to follow Alastar to the west. The sun had already set and no one chased them into the night. The enemy was too stunned to absorb what just happened and needed to regroup.

Alastar and Amber galloped where the Azure had flown, back toward Chnámh an Áidh where they had made camp. Alastar held Amber securely in front of him with his right arm. She had lost the feeling of complete security around her after her father died and throughout the years of exile, but now that warmth of safety and love seeped back into her, like warm honey filling her heart.

Gilroy and the rest of the Eachraighe followed well behind them, but they all felt the great joy and gratitude of being saved from destruction. They rode towards the waning sunlight on the horizon with not a flicker of gloom over the crumbling of their kingdom under King Fuar.

Soon Alastar saw a group of riders and many more soldiers on foot in front of them. He stopped to look harder and waited for the others to catch up. The army in front of them didn't look like Áiteoir.

"It's Captain Conn and our men," Amber said.

"That's a relief," he responded. Alastar looked backwards and saw Gilroy, Teague and the others riding swift to join them.

Everyone stopped around them and gave shouts of joy and victory. "Grand rescue, son!" Gilroy told him.

"Ya always surprise me, lad!" Teague added. "You 'n that Éimhín. I imagine no one will underestimate ya again."

"Let us continue," Gearóid said. "We don't know if they pursue."

"Were the captives freed?" Amber asked.

"We don't know," Gearóid answered. "All day we were engaged with Laochmarú's army 'n chasin' after *you!* Let's ask who should know." He turned to Conn who approached them.

"I see you've brought the princess back," Conn said. "We found the camp full of bodies and ya missin', Princess. But I'm surprised ta see it's the Swan-bearer carryin' ya." He gave Alastar a keen smile. "Didn't we leave ya moanin' sore in a cave?"

Alastar smiled. "That ya did! I couldn't help but run back ta ya, even sore as I was."

"We've all bled a cut or two," Teague said. "Never had I seen a day of battle as hard as this."

"What of the captives?" Gearóid asked Conn. "I don't see 'em with ya."

"They're all back at camp. We took the lot of 'em from Chnámh an Áidh, and other prisoners who were in the slave market. They're from all over Rathúnas. All were glad ta be out of there. Your coaxin' Laochmarú outside worked the trick. Quite a set dance we had today!"

"You hadn't seen the half of it!" Teague enthused. "We near had our dancin' feet cut straight off at Cnoc Earraigh! The king had his army there, ready ta receive the princess from Laochmarú. We were bein' strangled by two armies on all sides till the lad gave 'em such a flare 'a match. Everyone stood senseless! Jumped right over their lines 'n crested the hill ta take the princess!" Everyone cheered, but Alastar felt humble. He didn't feel he did anything except what he needed to do. "I only did what I thought I had ta," Alastar said. "Éimhín deserves more credit than me, and the Azure for certain. Who couldn't see the light comin' from it?!"

"*What!?* What happened?" Conn asked curiously.

"Ya had ta be there!" Gearóid said. "The Azure gave such a grand vision! Turned the lad and steed inta a winged pillar 'a victory!"

Conn was confused. "A winged what?"

"Never mind, Captain," Gearóid said. "We need ta press back ta camp and leave enemy territory."

They all marched back to camp with their army reunited and flying with stories of hard fighting and grand unexpected victory. It took hours to return to camp. They were all exhausted, but they had to pack up and leave before an attack came.

Amber found Muirgel unharmed in camp. She quickly helped prepare to leave but noticed Alastar was strained from his wounds and exertion. He limped about trying to help people gather things.

"Quit pullin' your socks up!" she told Alastar. She led him to a wagon where she had him lay down and rest for the journey. "You'll not be gettin' up till I say so!" she said firmly. She covered him with a blanket.

"Would ya have any more of that honey sage tea?" he teased. "My sores came flarin' back."

Amber smiled. "You need only know when ta rest now. Just sleep." She went to Éimhín and stroked his mane. She told him, "Thank ya for your hard work. Ya ran the whole day and hardly look any worse for it. Quite a sturdy boy." Éimhín nuzzled her and gave a soft nicker. She led him to Alastar's wagon and tied him to it. Then she took off the saddlebags from him and placed them in the wagon. "You'll just be strollin' along with us. Alastar always has ya carryin' everythin'!"

She mounted Muirgel and everyone left in the middle of the night when the last glow of the landscape dimmed into darkness. They traveled all night by torchlight. Despite being deep in Áiteoir country, no one came to bother them. However, Gearóid, Gilroy and Teague pondered what the king and Áiteoir's next move would be. They had victory, but they also knew more days of restless fighting were sure to come.

Amber looked up at the crescent moon and bright stars. The sky was completely clear and the air was warm as during the height of summer. She wondered about the vastness of everything around her. How so much was out of her control, and yet in her small part of existence, she had a part to carry out that could affect so much more than she could imagine. All the people around her were part of a current in destiny that she could only grasp from afar. Where would it take them and her kingdom?

*T*he long caravan of soldiers and refugees returned to Loch an Scátháin some time after dawn. They were all fatigued after traveling through the night, but the joyous cheers of welcome from everyone in town gave them glad hearts.

Mab and Nola came running to find Fionn, Flann, Brónach and Ula. "Where are Flann and Ula?" Mab asked Fionn and Brónach as they climbed out of a caged wagon. "I don't see 'em anywhere."

Brónach started to cry and hugged Mab. "Flann and Ula were sold off with other young men and women," she said in muffled cries. "We don't know where they were taken." Nola and Mab started crying too and hugged Brónach tight.

Their cries woke Alastar and he got up to walk over to them. As he approached, he saw Conn and Amber reach them first. Conn gave Nola a light hug and said, "We'll do all we can ta find 'em. Conall's family needs ta return ta their land of heritage."

Amber tried to comfort them too with assurances that their friends and family would be found. When Alastar made it to them he consoled, "I'm very sorry. I'll do what I can ta help find them." He saw Nola sobbing and felt he wanted to give her more comfort somehow, but then he noticed Conn's mantle wasn't fastened by a fibulae clasp on his left shoulder anymore. Instead, he secured his mantle through the fabric loop made for the clasp and pinned it fast with a bent needle.

Nola gave her heart to the captain, Alastar realized. She still wore the gold clasp in her shirt. Conn wasn't being overtly close to her, but it seemed right to Alastar. *Why else would he hug her and stand with her?* Alastar felt dejected Nola had shifted her attention away from him so quickly, but he didn't blame her or the captain. It was now obvious in all the events that she was not meant to be with him. Many things drew them apart, while many more things kept bringing him back to Amber.

He looked over to Amber who was at his side. She looked back at him with a warm, steady reassurance. He wondered what his feelings were for her. *Do I love Amber?* he pondered. *What does the true love that Gilroy talked about feel like?*

Before Alastar could muse any more, Teague came and gave his comfort to them. "These are sad times," he said. "But the good news is we're missin' just a handful that were taken. We'll try ta locate 'em, but we've more pressin' matters ta attend now." He looked to Amber, Conn and Alastar. "Princess, Captain, we need ta speak of what we do from here. The king branded all of us at Chnámh an Áidh as traitors and would put us ta death. We must expect troops ta come, whether they be the king's, Laochmarú's, or both. We can't stay in Loch an Scátháin. It has no place ta make defense against the armies we face."

Gearóid and Gilroy approached them. "We've a hard road ahead," Gilroy said. "Our best refuge is ta return ta Lacharan."

Amber was about to disagree when Gearóid spoke. "We know how much ya don't wish harm on our people, Princess, but it seems we've little choice. We need the supply of Lacharan. Cnoc na Rí is closed ta us 'n these fields are barren. Most of the grain was burned with the mill. Our high walls in Lacharan will stand many months against attack. . . so long as they don't brin' any more monsters, like that stone crushin' dragon."

"I'm afraid you're right," Amber conceded. "I would roam the wilds forever if it would keep Lacharan safe, but the choice does not appear in the currents for us."

"We'd roam the wilds with ya, Princess, if that was your wish,"

Teague acknowledged.

"Right!" Gearóid added with the chime of others.

Amber looked over at Alastar. Nola saw again the yearning
Amber had for him when she first came to the refuge. Amber had went
straight to Alastar when she arrived. Her love for him shimmered like
an iridescent curtain that she longed to part so that her feelings could
be seen in full. That was why Nola decided to pull away from Alastar.
She was very fond of him, but she knew her feelings were not set
in her heart. She had only felt the jitters of new attraction that soon
drained away when absence replaced nearness.

Alastar looked back at Amber in appreciation, but he was
silent. His mind contemplated and was confused about where destiny
was taking him. All the events of the last week swirled about him,
like a rushing river that carried him away from the quiet life he grew
accustomed to in Netleaf. He remembered their first day in Rathúnas
and how fast and fierce the river in the middle of the valley flowed.
He felt as if he had jumped in and was letting it carry him wherever it
went.

"It's best ta swim with the current, is it not?" Alastar said. He
turned his gaze from Amber and looked up to the sky. It was another
clear, bright day. "Fine day ta make another journey," he said with a
smile.

"Then it's Lacharan," Amber said. "But you'll be layin' in the
cart again," she told Alastar. "I don't believe the word, 'rest,' ever
settles on ya without someone pinnin' ya down with it."

Everyone chuckled. Teague added, "She got ya there, lad! The
boy had Laochmarú's spear 'n sword stuck him ta the ground and still
he wrestled ta get up!"

Alastar blushed. "*What?!*" he remarked. "Can I help it if there's
things ta be done?!" They all laughed.

"Right, lad!" Gearóid said. "We've another march ta set! Everyone rest as much as ya can. We leave in half hour's time."

"What about us?" Mab asked. "Are we ta remain?"

"The king had given up everyone here as slaves ta Laochmarú," Gilroy said. "We can't assume he'll protect anyone in Loch an Scátháin. Everyone should come with us ta Lacharan, but the choice is yours. You were not judged as traitors as the rest of us."

"Shame," Conn said. "We rebuilt some fine houses just ta leave 'em now."

"Strike 'em dead!" Fionn asserted. "I'd rather walk the bogs and wastelands for the ages than be carted off ta market again! My family goes with you, Princess." All the residents agreed and decided to leave as well.

Amber looked to Gilroy. "Chancellor, ask the workers from Cnoc na Rí if they'd join us. Make rounds ta everyone for the choice."

"Certainly," Gilroy answered. "But I am no longer chancellor. That station left me as soon as I left the king in the fields of Earraigh."

"Then I would be grateful if you would remain in my service as chancellor," Amber requested.

"It would be my honor, Princess," he replied and bowed his head to her.

"Grand altogether!" Teague said. "We've an old dog for the hard road. Your wisdom won't be wasted on us, Chancellor." He thought for a moment and turned to Gearóid and Conn. "May we set eyes for our lost kin as well. They need ta be found. Who are your best scouts?" he asked.

"Cathal and Rónán are my most capable," Conn said.

"Let's set 'em ta track our lost clansmen," Teague said. "We need two others ta send off in a pair - one team ta travel northwest, the other northeast. The north provinces have the highest demand for slaves."

"Bearach, one of the royal guards was a most capable countryman," Alastar said. "He escorted me from here ta Chnámh an Áidh."

"Grand," Teague replied.

"Who's the archer with the keenest of eyes?" Gearóid asked Conn. "He's a sharp mark for the task."

"That'd be Neese, sir," Conn said. "So long as he doesn't have ta swim, he makes a grand scout."

"Right then," Gearóid acknowledged. "Set Neese with Bearach."

"Have 'em go ta the bird keep and take a seabhac each," Teague told Conn.

Conn acknowledged and left to give the men their orders. Everyone made preparations to leave Loch an Scátháin. Not one person wanted to stay or return to Cnoc na Rí. They felt the king had abandoned them and that Amber represented the rightful line to the throne. Gilroy and Amber had hoped the king would embrace a united future with her and Alastar, but he could not see things that way. Fuar wanted his line and influence to remain as strong on the throne as he could make it.

Everyone and everything in Loch an Scátháin marched out in a long procession - soldiers, townsfolk, horses and livestock. They all set out in a melody of bittersweet footsteps. The people were happy that most of their clansmen returned safe, and they rejoiced that the currents brought the hopes of a glowing new kingdom with Amber and her Swan-bearer, but their beloved Torthúil was divided and many of her sons and brothers had already died in the conflict.

Many looked back as they marched southwest to round the mountains. The pastures, hills and forests of their heritage continued to call for them. Their hearts wept, but the many bare crop fields reminded them that new growth would return. They wondered, though, would the harvest be in their hands or would others come and claim their land? Would they be able to return? Their tears sprinkled along the trail and made puddles they trod upon, but it was hope that carried their bodies forward. The promises of a good future, whether it was in their homes or elsewhere, held secure in their hearts.

Hours passed by before they reached the end of the Torthúil Mountains. The forests at their foothills broke away in sporadic clumps and jogged Alastar's memory. He was sitting up in a cart trying to rest, but his body felt anxious. He started to talk in breathless sentences to Amber, who rode Muirgel next to the wagon. "We passed these forests when we followed the trail up ta Chnámh an Áidh. Went boltin' fast as we could round the edge of the mountains here. I could hardly hang on with my wounds achin' so. We had ta ride the long way round, south of the mountains after takin' the pass ta avoid bein' seen by the king's huntin' party in Loch an Scátháin. Never pushed Éimhín so far 'n fast as we went yesterday. Did we, boy?" Éimhín gave a soft affirming nicker. "Early mornin' and through the day chasin' after *grand* fair folk! 'N then on through the night, *hours* on end. . ."

Amber smiled. Alastar was obviously feeling better. He had been quiet as he rested in the cart all day but was now very talkative. "And were ya as chatty as all this through the day's chase?" she interrupted jokingly. "I can't imagine poor Éimhín toleratin' such a chippy wheatear." Teague and Gearóid who rode in front of them couldn't help being amused. They chuckled softly without turning their heads around.

"Flittin' wheatear!" Teague added. "Fits the lad exactly!"

Alastar laughed, but he didn't understand the reference to a wheatear. He remembered Nola had called him a wheatear as well.

"Not afraid ta give me slaggin', Princess," he commented. "But why would ya call me a wheatear? What is that?"

Some people in the cart with Alastar held back muffled amusement over his question. Amber looked at him with a warm smile. "They're little birds with white bottoms," she replied. "Round here, they're famous for bein' the most restless thin's on two legs." She giggled. "But I think, you've got 'em beat!"

Gilroy rode up to them from the rear of the caravan. "Teague!" he yelled. "You'll be seein' a Greerian soon. Troops are movin' inta the hills just north of Loch an Scátháin. They appear ta be both the king and Laochmarú's men, headin' straight for Loch an Scátháin!"

"You still get report from the Greerian?" Teague asked.

"I do," Gilroy affirmed. "Unfortunate for the king, the Greerian are linked ta me unless I relinquish them to a new chancellor. Fuar will be blind ta our movements in and out of the mountains."

"I suggest we send swift riders ta Lacharan," Gearóid said. "Prepare for our arrival and quick entry in case their armies pursue."

"That would be prudent," Gilroy acknowledged.

Gearóid looked to Amber and she nodded her head in approval. "I will send Conn," he said. Gearóid rode back to Conn and gave him the orders. He gathered a few other riders and flag bearers and they galloped ahead. When Gearóid returned to the front, he saw a Greerian perched on Teague's raised arm. The golden eagle was a relieving sight. It was good to see some resources of their kingdom still supported them.

The day continued to pass into evening. They were still many hours from Lacharan, but soon Conn returned with his company. He approached them with a sour face.

"Ill report," he told them. "Lacharan would not open ta us. The king ordered 'em shut and named us all as traitors." Gasps of despair went through them.

"The king moved with speed ta secure Lacharan," Gilroy said. "He will send his army there next ta ensure it."

"At least Lacharan will remain safe from siege," Amber said. She felt sorry they could not take refuge in her home, but the safety of her people was more important.

"Surely, Princess," Conn said, "But where does that leave us?"

"Desperate!" Gearóid said with disbelief. "Are we ta wander the wilds now? You may have what ya wished for, A chara Amber."

More murmurs of difficulties and lost hope went through the crowd. Their choices were few and they worried about where they could go. "Armies pursue us!" someone lamented. "Where can we find supply now?" another said.

Then Alastar remembered the River Valley and all its fruit and dense forest. *Surely we could hide there,* he thought. He tried to stand up and speak, but the crowd was heavy with anxious words and the moving cart jostled him around. Teague saw him and ordered them to stop and listen.

"Have ya somethin' ta say, lad?" Teague queried.

Alastar stood up, but his legs were wobbly and sore, so he sat on the railing of the cart. "If we can cross the kingdom's borders without notice, "he said loudly, "then let's turn ta the River Valley. Its center is full of fruit and its thick forest will hide us well."

"Hide right under the king's nose?" Gearóid wondered.

"How long could we hide there before the king searches the valley?" Teague asked.

"Amaideach!" someone yelled. "There's reasons no one settles deep in the valley! Frightful thin's haunt the nights of that forest!" People started to murmur and argue again. Alastar wondered what they were afraid of.

Gilroy raised his arms and spoke loud, "Surely! Surely, there are thin's not ta scoff at in the valley forests. It is why no one stays there. Everyone passes through the ease of Rían's Gate and leave most of the valley untouched. But it makes a perfect place for us ta hide."

"But what of the wild thin's!" someone scoffed.

"Are ya so afraid of sprites 'n fairies now, that you'd rather be hunted down in the open fields?" Gilroy rebuked. "The valley will provide cover for our heads and fill our bellies. That we need abundantly! The other thin's we should not worry over." He looked to Amber. "It is your decision, Princess. Shall we heed another of Alastar's plans?"

Amber gave Alastar a look of warm appreciation. She knew his idea was their best option. "We'll take refuge in the valley. Would I be mistaken ta think ya already have a place in mind?"

He smiled and looked at Teague. "We can cross at the valley's head and go downstream from there. We won't be able ta take the wagons, but the path is a quick bolt for all else and the river and forest will see ta our needs. I saw all the cliffs lined with fruit in the middle of the valley."

"Grand then," Teague acknowledged. "Let us continue before any army or scouts find us."

Gearóid and Teague led them north to the place where Teague and Alastar had crossed into the plains the first night they fled Loch an Scátháin. They hid their carts and wagons in the forest there and continued on foot and horseback. The march up the mountainside was relatively easy despite their need to carry many wounded. They were able to make enough stretchers to carry everyone who couldn't walk or ride a horse.

It took them some hours to reach the head of the river where Alastar saw the shadow fairy. The sun had set behind the west side of the mountains as they continued through the valley and into the forest. They hardly noticed the sky dim because they were submerged in the thick glowing forest. Some people worried over what the night would bring, but their trek into the valley had most of them filled with hope. They felt the nearness of Loch an Scátháin just over the cliffs, and the colorful splendor of the forest saturated them with life.

Alastar told them to make camp when he saw the cherry tree far ahead. It was the tree where the Azure first appeared to him and the only cherry tree he saw in the valley. It still had most of its vivid pink blossoms on its branches. He kept everyone a good distance upstream from it so that no one would stumble on the arch gateway. He felt its location should remain hidden, because disturbing it might ruin his chances to return home. It would also create a chaotic mob to trample the forest and cliffs around it. They needed to remain quiet in the valley.

"Make camp toward the foot of the mountain," Gearóid ordered. "Keep under the cover of forest and make no large fires. Remember we are here ta hide. No one is ta travel under open sky, nor climb the cliffs without permission."

"Grand," Gilroy said. "I will ride the perimeter ta see that no ill lurks near." He looked at Alastar. "Son, ride with me."

The forest quickly filled with the noise of people settling into its many warm alcoves and sturdy boughs. Some people made lofts and hanging beds in the trees, but most spread their tents and blankets on the soft ground. Everyone marveled at how beautiful and lush the forest was. No one but Alastar had been in this part of the valley during the last generation. The legends of odd happenings from travelers long ago had kept everyone from venturing there.

"What sort of ill things could be here?" Alastar asked as he rode with Gilroy.

"There are many enchanted bein's in this world. Some care not for the presence of man in their realms, while others seek us out ta make mischief."

"Like the shadow fairy I saw?" Alastar said.

"Right, son," Gilroy affirmed. "Tales of the forest have many chillin' details, but who's ta know which are true? Let's hope our great numbers will ward off any strange creatures. I don't believe any party a tenth as large as ours ever camped in the valley." He looked about the forest and tried to find anything out of the ordinary, but everything stood out in vibrant color, like an explosion of paints and dyes covered everything. It was impossible to find anything in the plethora of color. The vast forest appeared similar in every corner. "It would be easy ta get lost here. How did ya find your way in all this, son?"

"I knew I could find the river and follow it easy 'nough," Alastar said. He looked about to see if anyone was near. The closest people were far off to their left pitching tents. "There's somethin' I want ta show ya." Alastar led Gilroy to the right, farther down the valley and headed toward the valley wall. In about a mile he stopped at the guelder rose bushes by the arch. "The gateway I came from is here," he said.

"I was wonderin' if it was near," Gilroy replied.

"Up this way." Alastar led him up the cliff and past the guelder rose bushes. He noticed most of the white fallen petals were still scattered about the floor. Gilroy hardly noticed the bushes. His gaze was fixed on the gateway ahead of them. He'd never seen any structure like it.

"Magnificent," Gilroy said.

"You should see it without all the vines covering it. It's bare rock, cut smooth and elegant where I came from."

They rode through the gateway and stopped at the edge of the cliff just beyond to take in the view. The sky was dark blue and the stars were starting to flicker into sight. The valley's misty glow kept most of the stars hidden. Alastar looked backwards toward their camp. The forest canopy hid all signs of the thousands of people there, and no sounds from camp reached them. They could only perceive the calm of the River Valley - the faint rustling of wind through the trees and many chirps and calls of insects and wildlife.

"It couldn't look more peaceful," Alastar said. "I can't imagine harmful creatures ta worry of here."

"I would venture ta say this view is the most splendid in Rathúnas," Gilroy remarked. "But what soothes the eyes and heart can hide dangerous thin's for the soul. Keep your wits about ya when the dark of night overtakes the forest. I don't know what may lurk, but it's best everyone stay close together."

"Right," Alastar acknowledged. "I was wonderin' somethin' else too. Would you know if I can return home through the gateway? I was able ta open it with symbols on the cliff wall, above the bushes there. But in Rathúnas there are no symbols. . . though, the guelder rose here glows like 'em. I couldn't find any way ta open the gateway again."

"I'm afraid I can't help, son. No one in our history has ever seen a gateway. The stories of them come from lands far off, past the sea, but what I know is that they tend ta have a mind of their own. They open only for those meant ta travel in them, and only at the right times."

Alastar's heart sunk into a deep chasm. "I may never see my home again."

"Fear not, son," Gilroy said with reassurance. "If you're meant ta see home again, you will. . . so long as ya heed the currents leadin' ya back. Many folk wander about aimlessly without a care set on the thin's tryin' ta guide us and they miss their windows 'a opportunity. Destiny does not always wait on our meanderin'."

"I suppose that's true," Alastar said. He didn't think he missed any windows of opportunity, but knew he had a problem letting go of attraction to Nola. "I've had other problems 'a destiny ta deal with. More of the sort 'a settin' my eyes right. Sometimes we look ta clutter that spin our hearts ta no avail. It keeps our eyes off the currents. I understand now why ya told me ta not set my heart in stone."

Gilroy gave him a big smile. "Now you're learnin' some thin's, son. Have ya finally seen where the currents want ya?"

"Well. . ." Alastar said with hesitation. He thought Gilroy was wondering if he wanted to be with Amber, but he still wasn't sure where his heart was for her. "It took some hard knocks ta let go of some things I set my heart on. I have ta admit, I wanted ta return ta Loch an Scátháin ta see. . emmm. . . that grebe. I thought I should've stayed with Amber in Cnoc na Rí, but my heart and mind were split. Ran off ta ease my heart 'n ended up getting' some skewers stuck through me! More than the wood 'n metal sort 'a skewers too." He meant that Nola had pierced his heart as much as Laochmarú's spear and sword cut through his flesh.

"The grand thin' about hard lessons is we don't soon forget 'em," Gilroy replied. "Just don't keep rubbin' your wounds. Your mistakes shouldn't remain sore. Let 'em heal over and set your walk and eyes forward."

*G*ilroy and Alastar soon returned to camp and saw tents, canopies and fires sprawled throughout the forest as far as could be seen. Some people huddled around fires in small groups, but the busy hustle of setting up camp was over. Most people rested and slept in their shelters. The soothing quiet of the forest quickly seeped back into its air.

At the camp's center, the doctors and nurses had set up a large tent near the cliffs for the wounded. They found Amber and the commanders settled nearby. Amber was boiling water in their campfire and putting herbs into the pot.

Gearóid and Teague stopped talking to each other as they approached. "How was your survey?" Gearóid asked.

"Lovely forest everywhere," Gilroy said. "But the dense color made it impossible ta find anythin' out of place."

"We've seen nothin' ta worry of here," Teague added. "The biggest danger may be large fruit droppin' on our heads." He looked up at the round, orange fruit that hung from the trees around them. "Some kind of melon. They look 'n smell ripe, but we tried a few and they were all bitter. The grapes, berries 'n other common fruit were grand eatin', though. Odd the forest has fruit in all seasons here, while spring blossoms still cover most trees elsewhere."

"I imagine the melon needs a fair bit 'a cookin' with honey," Áine said as she approached. She went to Amber with a tray of empty cups. "Like guelder berry, bitter vetch, and sloe."

"Ah, sloe wine was a favorite import from the north kingdom," Teague said. "Been years since we tasted a glass. It was one of Conall's favorite drinks."

"The tea is ready," Amber said. She ladled portions from the pot into the cups. She took one of the cups while Áine took the rest into the infirmary tent.

Amber walked to Alastar and gave him the tea. "How can ya keep movin' about with the nicks 'n sores ya have? Drink this and get straight ta bed. I'll be retirin' for the night as well." She bowed her head and acknowledged everyone, then went to her tent.

Alastar sat down slowly next to Teague. He made quiet groans of fatigue and pain. "She's right. I'll be needin' a fair bit 'a rest. But first, what's ta eat round here?"

"Grab one of 'em melons," Teague said. "Fill ya right up if ya can stomach the taste. I was so hungry I took two down my gut. Followed 'em with honey stout. Right grand meal!"

"Stout?!" Alastar wondered. "Where'd ya gather that?"

"I travel with a barrel or two," Gearóid said. He handed Alastar a mug of stout. "A good soldier needs a flush 'a foamin' brew after battle. . . and sometimes more if the fields haven't a fair nurse with tea 'n honey ta coax the pain outta your wounds. You've got *some* square deal with Amber carin' for ya, lad. And I hear, she even sang for your healin'. The richest of princes could only dream of care so grand. You've best have the mind ta see that, lad. Amber hadn't sung for the sick since her mam died." He leaned into Alastar and held out his mug. "Ya mean somethin' special ta her for her ta do that. Sláinte ["slan-cheh"; health/cheers]."

Alastar tipped his mug to Gearóid. "Sláinte." He felt blushing warmth come to his face. He was never comfortable talking about romantic affairs. "She is the kingdom's brightest gem," he acknowledged. "I can't imagine any man would turn away her affections. I know my future is inseparable from hers, but who's ta know what our hearts wish for? It'd be foolish ta rush inta another, emmm, what did Conall say about the lake grebe? A courtship dance."

Teague gave Alastar a quick slap on the left shoulder to give him a tender sting in his wound. "*Grand*," he said sarcastically. "The lad is both a mainidh *and* ailpín! Stout-headed 'n brave but where'd ya lose your head?! Are ya still eyein' the lake grebe when Lacharan's swan bares her heart ta ya?" He looked about to make sure Amber wasn't near. He said quietly, "I do believe Nola has flown ta her own grebe, lad."

Gearóid and Gilroy laughed in affirmation. "Sure 'nough!" Gearóid said. "Never seen the captain pay mind ta a girl before. It's 'bout time for him. . . for the both of 'em."

Alastar smiled at their prodding. "I'm not mindin' the lake grebe!" he burst out. "She was hardly a prick in the heart! It's grand Nola 'n Conn found each other. I've just. . . I just don't want ta rush headlong inta any, emmm, dances." He got up and plucked a bunch of grapes from the cliffs behind them.

He sat back down and started to eat the grapes. Half chewing and speaking, he said, "What's the rush anyhow? We're all stuck here together. And don't we have other matters ta consider? We can't hide in the valley forever. We need a plan ta get the kingdom in sorts."

"There's time ta act and time ta wait," Gilroy said. "Since we've no clear direction from here, it's time ta wait for the currents ta show what we need do. Useless ta build. . ."

"A bridge before we reach the river," Alastar completed. "Right. I remember ya said that. Then what are we ta do here?"

"Do we need ta stick ya with Laochmarú's spear 'n sword again?" Teague said. "We left 'em in Loch an Scátháin, but I'd be glad ta run over the mountains and fetch 'em if ya can find rest with 'em stuck in ya! Just do what the princess told ya. *Rest!* Then a day or two we'll see about returnin' ta your soldier's lessons."

They talked for a time more around the fire and then went to their tents. Teague and Alastar shared a tent while Gearóid and Gilroy had their own. The camp fell into silence as the glow of life from the forest dwindled out.

Alastar had barely slept an hour when a commotion outside their tent startled him. The tent was pitch black, but all of a sudden a lantern lit up and filled the tent with yellow-orange light. Teague got up with the lantern and his sword. "Stay here, lad. Somethin' at the far end 'a camp."

Alastar moved to get up, but his muscles and wounds ached like he was beaten with a paddle for days. He let out a groan and moved slowly. He groped for the tent's opening and peered outside. The forest was nearly as dark as the deepest cave. Only very faint light from the sky snuck through the heavy layers of leaves in the forest canopy.

There were faint shapes of people running toward the river where shouts and screams were heard. He could see moving lights and shadows in the distance there. Loud squealing from some tormented beast echoed through the trees. People started to light candles and lanterns everywhere around camp.

Alastar ducked back into the tent and grabbed his sword. He made a swift hobbled walk toward the loud commotion. Soon the shadows of men with spears and swords came into sight. They were sticking their weapons into a monstrous beast that was covered in thick plates of armor along its back and sides. When Alastar got there, the animal was bleeding to death on the ground. It was a huge, humped monstrosity with thick coarse red fur and a short snout. Huge curved tusks the size of large harvest sickles were on either side of its head.

"A monstrous armored boar," Teague said.

Alastar stared at it. He never saw anything like it. It was more than twice the size of the largest hogs he'd ever seen and only slightly smaller than a fáelshee. Most of its hide was a patchwork of thick rectangular plates over an inch thick. He saw one of the ruddy plates on its back had large claw marks gouged into it and touched it. It felt like hardened leather. "Quite a hardchaw, this beast," he said.

"We had ta stick it through the belly," Gearóid added "Only soft bit we could find. Its meat'll give a mighty feast for us tomorra'."

Conn drew his sword from underneath the boar's shoulder. "A sinewy monster," he said. "Larger than the thousand pound hogs 'a Clochán na Láimhe ["Kluhkun nah Læveh"] but hardly any fat under that hide. A full hand 'a soldiers had ta fell it. It seems ta have wandered inta camp for the melons fallen on the ground. It woke us with its noisy snortin' and eatin'."

"I thought I told ya not ta wander," Teague reminded Alastar. Alastar gave him a wry smile. He was about to say something when more screams went through the forest. They looked about. The noise came from behind them.

"By the infirmary!" Gearóid yelled.

The men ran toward the infirmary tent. When they got near, they saw giant bat-like creatures swooping down from the tall melon trees. They hung from the highest branches. No one had noticed them before because they looked like the large melons that hung from the trees. Dozens of them unfurled their wings from around their short plump bodies and attacked people everywhere. They were like a swarm of writhing vultures flying swiftly, and at times they disappeared and reappeared short distances, even going through trees and obstacles in front of them. Some of them flew right into tents by transporting themselves past the fabric walls. They clawed silently at everyone in sight. The only noise they made came from the flapping of their wings.

The whole area was filled with people screaming and fending off the creatures. Gilroy was trying to hold them off with his bare hands, looking like he was trying to make an invisible shield around him. They barely touched him, but the effort clearly made him tired. The strange bats saw more men coming and attacked them aggressively. Soldiers with swords and spears tried killing them, but they disappeared and transported short distances before any strikes could land. Alastar limped and jumped as fast as he could to reach the area. Many armed soldiers came with him, but the bats hovered around them like a dark, silent, stinging cloud. The men only managed to strike down a few.

Gilroy tired from the attacks and started to kneel down. Amber came running to him with a wood round shield and swiped at the creatures with it. She moved to cover Gilroy with the shield, but in the respite of her aid he collected himself and uttered something. A blinding flash of light burst out from him.

Alastar was behind many others and couldn't see what was happening, but the light flooded through everything and he shielded his eyes. The forest was lit for a brief second with blinding white. It went through the air like a violent shockwave of electricity. Alastar remembered Gilroy made the same flash outside Lacharan to save Éimhín from the fáelshee.

Everyone stopped in their tracks and all the giant bats flew off in a blind daze.

"Sciathánshee ["skee-hahn-shee"]," Gilroy said in gasps. "Night fliers of story. I've never seen them before." He put a grateful hand on

Amber's shoulder and thanked her.

"Sciathánshee hadn't been seen near our homes for generations," Gearóid commented.

"Will they come back?" Amber asked.

"I imagine so," Gilroy responded. "But we can avoid them. Legend says they avoid light and won't fly through large walls. They dare not fly where they cannot see inta."

"Those thin's flapped straight inta my tent!" someone said.

"Our tarpaulin canvas is thin 'nough for them ta see through," Gilroy said. "We need ta shelter behind walls of stone or wood or pad our tents with thick furs."

"Where are we ta get enough furs?" Conn wondered. "We don't even have 'nough tents ta shelter everyone."

"Right," Teague added. "We need walled shelter, but cobblestone is scarce here, and we've no lime or pitch for mortar. Mud and clay may have ta do, but wood planks don't simply grow either."

"Can we take supplies from Loch an Scátháin?" Alastar asked.

"The king is sure ta have a watch there," Teague said.

"We can't risk bein' seen or leavin' trace," Gilroy added. "They're sure ta notice if we take any large amount of stone or wood."

"Who could ferry such amounts inta the valley anyhow?" Gearóid said. "We have no roads for our carts."

"But we have the kingdom's best tradesmen and their tools," Amber commented.

Alastar knew what she was thinking. "Right! And the forest has plenty 'a wood. We can make wood planks enough ta shelter everyone."

"Buildin' wooden shelter as ya suggest is much work, even with the skilled labor," Gearóid said. "Are ya suggestin' we build homes here?. . . found a new city? The amount 'a work needed ta make wood shelter would be wasted on anythin' but permanent homes."

There was silence as people thought about the idea of settling into the valley. No one had thought their refuge in its forests would be a long-term solution. They still had their homes in Loch an Scátháin and Lacharan fresh in their hearts.

"We didn't come here ta build homes!" a soldier said. "Aren't we here just ta hide for a time?"

"I don't care ta live among the wild beasts here either!" someone else added. "Those sciathánshee were foul 'nough! What other monsters does the valley hide?!" People started to argue and replaced the soft murmur of the forest with the cacophony of restless discussion.

"Keep your heads! Stand in your wicks!" Gilroy reminded loudly. "The forest can be tamed, and we can't assume our stay here will be only days or weeks, or even some short months. We must look ta our safety and comfort for much time ta come."

"We all agreed ta follow the princess, did we not?" Gearóid added. "Whatever she decides, we will do. If anyone cares not for our plans, you are free ta leave 'n make for yourselves what ya can in the countryside."

"But I would be most grateful if we all stay t'gether and work t'gether," Amber said. "A kingdom is not a kingdom if we go all our own. Did we not leave the ways of the myriad clans in the dead past?"

"Céad míle mar aon ["Kayd meel mar een"]," Gilroy announced.

"A hundred thousand as one," Teague translated. "Remember the triumph of King Rían long ago? Are we ta undo the unity of the clans under one kingdom now? There is great promise under the House of Ealaí, and we can have the triumph King Rían had - the currents will forge it new for us."

"We are all of the Eachraighe!" Conn yelled and lifted his

sword high. "We go t'gether! Céad míle mar aon!"

Everyone came to agreement and shouted for a time, "Céad míle mar aon! Céad míle mar aon!" Amber was relieved they all showed solidarity. She knew the road ahead would be difficult and many things lay uncertain. How were they to make peace with King Fuar and the Áiteoir? How long were they to hide in the valley? Would they be found out? She wrestled with many questions, but when she saw Alastar by her side she was calmed and reminded that destiny was working for them.

The next day they sought to gather and make building materials - stones, clay and mud for foundations, wood planks for frames and walls, reeds and thatch for roofing and rope. The whole community was busy and the leaders planned how to layout their new homes to be both a functional village and inconspicuous from eyes that might look upon the River Valley. The thousands of people quickly moved and made the resources they needed to build.

They took down and trimmed many trees but were careful to leave the forest canopy intact. It remained a thick covering for them to hide under. They were also careful not to build near the river or any place that didn't have the natural covering of the forest. Their work at the river or under open areas was most cautious. The Greerian were not a threat to them, but the Áiteoir could send flying sentries to find them.

The days passed under continual sunshine in the valley as they worked. New homes and buildings were erected in a matter of days. They didn't have any more problems with the sciathánshee since the first night, though there were many encounters with more timid beasts. The valley was as abundant with deer, boar, and pheasant as it was in fruit. Other predators, such as bears and wolves wandered the forest too, but they kept their distance from the noise of the community.

Alastar got back to sword training in between times of building and woodworking. He made his woodcarving skills useful for everything from making tools to decorating their new homes. Most homes were simple log cabins and wood cottages. The majority of the stone and clay was used to make hearths and fireplaces. The only structure made with stone walls was their new longhouse where the leaders planned and the community could assemble.

The longhouse was a large building that had four giant oak trees in its corners. The stone walls were built right up to the tree trunks. The oaks provided support for the two stories of the longhouse, like massive pillars, each at least three meters wide. From the gabled roof, there was access to spiral staircases that went up the two trees in the rear of the longhouse. Perches were made at the top of the stairs high up in the trees, so they could serve as lookout towers.

Alastar was in the front of the longhouse carving designs into the thick wood doorframe. He made long Celtic knots up the doorposts and was finishing the engraving along the top beam when it occurred to him their town's name should be put over the door. No one had mentioned a name for their settlement before, so he went to Amber.

He found her and Gilroy inside the main floor preparing the area to receive the wounded. The spacious longhouse would serve as their infirmary until the wounded were well enough to care for themselves. The entire main floor of the longhouse was open except for a few small rooms in the rear and beams along the sides that held up the second floor. Besides the two staircases on either side at the rear, a large fireplace was the only other notable feature on the main floor. The second story was open and visible clear up to the roof since its floor only ran along the outside walls, like a large balcony that circled the inside.

The high roof towered far above their heads about 50 feet. It was still less than a quarter the height of the massive oak trees around them. Alastar could see their trunks in the four corners of the longhouse and outside the many windows, but he strained to see inside the dim interior. "How can ya work in here?" he asked them. "There needs ta be more windows, lamps, or somethin'. It's like a huge cave in here, dark as the forest in slumber."

"We've only just begun with the longhouse," Amber said. "There'll be light enough when we've finished."

"I'm well satisfied with it," Gilroy said. "It hasn't been two weeks and we've managed ta shelter everyone *and* frame up this longhouse. Never has a village gone up so quick."

"Would this town of ours have a name?" Alastar asked. "I was finishin' the doorposts when I thought a name for our settlement should be set along top. What do ya think?"

"I think it's right time for a namin'," Gilroy acknowledged. He looked at Amber. "Wouldn't ya say, Princess, since Alastar chose the location for our fine camp, he should be the one ta name it?"

Amber gave Alastar a smile of appreciation. "True, we wouldn't be here if it weren't for you," she said. "I wouldn't have led everyone inta the valley. May you select a grand name for our new home?"

"What?!" Alastar replied with surprise and hesitation. "I can't name a town? I'm just a woodcarver."

"A fine woodcarver, at that," Gilroy commented. "But you've come ta a higher station in our eyes, son. Have ya forgotten all you've done with us? All you've learned? Ya came ta us a lost lad, but found the direction 'a your current. Need I remind ya, in less than a month, ya became an Eachraighe, ya rescued Amber *twice*, rushed ta battle still new ta the sword, faced the strongest of armies, gained the loyalty 'a everyone here, *and* led us ta make home in the most unlikely 'a places. I'd not be amiss in sayin' the Swan-bearer has exceeded my expectations."

Alastar started to blush under the complements. He didn't feel he earned a place of honor. Everything had been such a blur of activity to him since arriving on Rathúnas. He hadn't put any thought into how much he accomplished. In his mind he was only doing what he thought needed to be done in the moment. He didn't realize each step he took, however large or small, added up to a place of immeasurable height. He could never have planned the destination or how the journey changed him, but it was in following the currents towards true destiny that brought him to become the steadfast and capable champion that he was meant to be.

"Thank ya, Chancellor," Alastar acknowledged. "I suppose I'm not who I was just some weeks ago."

Amber remembered how Alastar seemed an unprepared and silly image of a champion in the first day of their meeting. But since then, he continued to grow into the Swan-bearer that she had always dreamed about, and even more than she wished for. His unassuming kindness and straightforward sensibility and humor was endearing to her. She smiled at him and said, "Ya can turn scarlet all ya want. It won't get ya out 'a namin' our town."

"Sure. . ." he muttered softly. "Emmm. . ." Thoughts of his home in Netleaf came to him and then the brilliant colors of the valley forest, especially the bright, red cherry tree where he encountered the Azure. "What is Coral Leaf in the elder tongue?" he asked.

"Duille Coiréil ["Dul-yeh Kor-rel"]," Gilroy said.

"That's it then," Alastar said. "For all the vibrant life in the valley."

"Grand!" Gilroy remarked. "We must honor this formality with a celebration. What would ya say, Princess, ta Duille Coiréil's very first céilí?"

"A dandy idea," Amber said. "We've all been workin' so hard these weeks. A social would be welcome by everyone."

"A céilí?" Alastar said with reluctance. "The last céilí I had ended in me runnin' from the Áiteoir through the night. Chased by men and beasts alike, all the way ta Lacharan."

"And wasn't it in Lacharan that we met?" Amber reminded.

"*And* where ya found the currents carried ya?" Gilroy added. "The boy who became an Eachraighe overnight."

"Right then," Alastar said. "A social is fine, so long as I'm not the center of attention. Let it be for the fellowship of the people under renewed hope."

Amber appreciated Alastar's modesty, but she hoped he would soon realize his role by her side would need a more open show of leadership with her. "That's all well for our celebration," she told him. "But ya can't stand in the shadows for every turn of our path t'gether. Would ya at least sit with me at center, with the rest of our leaders?"

"I'd be glad ta," he replied. "Where else would I be?" Alastar gave her a warm smile and went back to the front door.

"The boy is findin' his gait," Gilroy said. "Don't worry over his duckin' inta the brambles. He'll find the royalty in his steps yet."

"He's more than I hoped for," Amber said. "Only some thin's are most difficult ta wait on. . ." She was thinking about the closeness to Alastar that her heart yearned for. They had grown much closer since leaving the fields of Earraigh, but Alastar still held back romantic affection for her. She felt she was in constant waiting for him to part the curtains that her love hid behind. "Would you make all the needed preparations for the céilí?"

"Certainly," Gilroy replied. "We'll even have grand music ta dance ta. More than a few people carried their drums and fiddles inta the march."

*T*he next day the whole camp bustled with enthusiasm for the céilí. They were ecstatic their quickly built village was going to be named. Alastar had already carved the name into a wood plaque, but Gilroy told him to keep it a secret until the celebration.

Scores of people worked to clear the area around the longhouse of brush and small trees. Others built a stage with a high wood canopy along one side of the longhouse. Still others prepared the food and decorations. Small hunting parties went out to gather deer and boar for the feast. The many preparations went swiftly with their workforce of hundreds and thousands.

Alastar finished his woodcarving duties and sword training for the day. The camp was so busy with activity that he sought refuge by the river. He found a quiet place and sat under a large hazel tree that faced the water. The constant sound of the water rushing by soothed him as he carved a small finger-sized object out of a piece of hopbush. It was one of the ironwoods he had in his private stock from the desert valley.

His concentration broke from the sound of someone approaching from behind. He looked backwards and saw Amber carrying a large bundle of fabric. "There ya are!" she said. "Sometimes you're a difficult one ta seek out."

Alastar quickly hid the object he was carving under his bag of tools. He got up and greeted her. "The village was so noisy. I had ta find quiet for some time."

"I know," she said in a tone of familiarity. "I sit by the river as well ta sort out my thoughts." She gave him an affectionate smile and handed him the bundle. "I brought ya somethin'. Seein' as the céilí is t'night, I made ya somethin' ta wear. You've been wearin' the same torn up clothes since we came here."

"Thank ya," he said as he grabbed the bundle. He unfurled it and held it up. It was a long léine tunic much like the other men wore, except his was made with two colors of fine fabric while most were coarse linen of a single color. The top of his léine was white and from the waist down it was royal sapphire blue. He recognized the blue color. "It's the same color as your cloak, Amber."

"You've keen eyes," she said. "Your léine shows the colors of my clan, the same as Lacharan's - white and blue."

"It's wonderful!" he said as he closely looked over the well-made léine. The long shirt had a simple design with finely crafted folds and subtle decorative trim. He noticed it didn't have any seams or needlework visible anywhere. "Curious. There's no stitchin' or overlappin' pieces; looks as if it was knit whole as one piece. Did ya make it?"

"I did the large part of it. Áine and others helped find the fabric, but the cuttin' and sewin', or fashionin' really, I did. The seamless sewin' art is a family secret from my great, great, great grandmother - Mother of the Ealaí family. She was the first ta use pine and strawberry tree resin with mendin' stones. Go on, put it on," she said anxiously.

Alastar looked about. "What? Here?"

"Where else would I mean? There's no one 'round. Go on!" She went to the other side of the tree and waited for him to change.

Alastar hung his léine on a branch and took off his sword belt and leather trousers. His pants were patched up and stained with blood on the left thigh where Laochmarú's sword had pierced him. He looked at the unraveling patch he had sewn and thought it was good time he got new clothes. Then he took off his shirt, which also had a ragged and stained hole where his shoulder was wounded.

He stood nearly naked under the shadow of the tree, but the air was warm in the bright afternoon. He reached for the léine when Amber asked, "Are ya dressed now?"

"Hold on," he answered. "I've just gone bare."

"You're slow as cold sap in autumn," she commented. Amber remembered how Alastar stood with his helmet in Lacharan for the first time, like he didn't know what to do with it. "Do ya need help, Alastar?"

"This is my first léine, but I think I can manage ta dress myself." He quickly slipped the tunic over his head and fixed it over his shoulders. He looked down and found the bottom hung down to his feet. "Done!" he said loudly. He spread out his arms and looked at the long, hanging sleeves. The cuffs went just beyond his elbows and hung down to his knees, like thick ribbons alongside his body. "Ya gave me wings!" he commented.

Amber came around the tree and looked him over. "Wings, sure 'nough," she said with a smile. "And the sleeves have pockets for your odd stashin' habits. Only you're not done." She picked up his sword belt and tightened it around his waist. "Léine aught ta be fastened by a belt. They *are* war shirts, after all. Ya don't wear it as if it's a nightgown."

After she fastened his belt, she pulled the léine up through it so that folds of fabric hung over and hid his belt. She stopped pulling and tucking the léine when it hung at knee level. "This is how ya wear it most of the time. Just use the full length in the cold 'a winter." She finished fixing his clothes and stepped back to look. "Perfect!" she said. "Your vest and armor will wear fine over it."

Alastar lowered his arms. "Thank ya so much for this. It's so nice I'm afraid ta soil it."

"Just keep it clean 'nough for the céilí t'night." She picked up his old clothes and folded them. "I'll wash 'em for ya and mend 'em nice. You've many sharp skills, but sewin's not one of 'em."

"You don't have ta mend them," he said. "Your gift is more than I need."

"Nonsense! Ya don't expect ta run 'bout bare while your léine is washed and dried, do ya? I'll make your old clothes grand, as they were the first time ya wore 'em."

"Thank ya," he told her with a deep look into her eyes. She hesitated a moment under his admiration and hoped he would show more affection, but he stood silent. She turned away with a smile and went back to the village.

Alastar sat back down and continued to work on the object he hid earlier. *Good thing she didn't see this, he thought.*

Teague and Conn walked slowly near a mountain summit with spears held ahead of them. They were tracking a deer through the tall pines and bushes. "There," Teague whispered. He pointed toward the tips of giant curved antlers that poked up from behind distant bushes.

"*Deadly!*" Conn exclaimed under his breath. "That thin' must stand heads higher than us!"

"Be wide," Teague shushed. "You round on the left."

They separated to circle the giant deer. Conn went toward its back while Teague tried to sneak towards its front. As they came closer they realized it was a monstrous elk. Its antlers were like broad plates with huge curved spikes along the top instead of the sharp branches of a deer's antlers.

Conn's heart raced when he got around the bushes that hid the elk. He could see how massive the animal was now. It lazily ate leaves and blossoms that were far above Conn's head. *This thing is bigger than that tall Éimhín!* he thought in amazement. He took the slowest of steps as he tried to get into range.

Conn saw Teague appear behind the elk. It turned its head to look at Teague and froze. Both men stood still and held their breath, hoping it wouldn't bolt away. A brief second passed and the giant elk turned and ran from them. Teague threw his spear, but it flew past the elk's neck harmlessly. Flustered, he drew his sword and ran after the animal. It was just some meters away, but it leaped and ran quickly despite its great size.

Conn ran toward it with his spear held ready. The elk had not seen him when Teague startled it. It ran in Conn's direction and quickly came close to him. He threw his spear with a grunt and watched it hit the elk's shoulder. The great elk let out a bellow of pain and reared up on its hind legs. When it dropped down, it shook its body violently and made the spear drop to the ground. Then it lowered its head and charged at Conn.

He stood in shock as the huge animal raced toward him with its antlers ready to strike. He looked around for the closest tree to hide behind and started to run, but the elk was too fast. It almost caught up to him when Teague yelled, "Lay flat!"

Conn dove to the ground. The hulking antlers narrowly missed him as the elk swiped its head at him, but Conn was run over. He let out screams as the heavy animal trod on his back. Teague kept running after the elk and picked up Conn's spear along the way. The elk turned around after it trampled Conn. It was still enraged and began another charge at Teague.

"Stay down!" Teague yelled. He quickly moved to the side and lifted the spear. He swung it backwards and launched it as he jumped farther to the side of the elk's charge. The spear landed firmly in the elk's neck and the animal stopped. It stood dazed but did not fall.

Teague drew his sword and yelled to Conn, "Banjax it! Get up! Get up 'n stab it down!" He continued to sprint toward the elk before it ran again.

Conn tried to get up but intense pain shot through his back. He fell back down exasperated. "Stalled, man! My back's done for!"

When Teague got close to the elk, it swung its antlers at him, like giant axe heads the size of large shields. The animal stood so tall, though, that Teague was able to duck under slightly and keep charging underneath it without a stumble. He plunged his sword through its chest and fell it on its side.

"Bog bean!" Teague yelled. "Brutal beast! Are ya well banjaxed, Conn?"

Conn slowly picked himself up. "Nearly cracked my spine! A bit of a crook, but I'm grand; shoulder well bruised too. I'm just glad the thin' didn't fall on my head!" He looked at the massive beast. "How do we get it home?"

"I'll get our horses and we'll drag it back on splints," Teague said. "Stay here and protect it from bears and such."

Teague ran down the mountainside and soon came back with their horses. They spent a lot of time cutting small trees to make a splint carrier for the elk. They slowly fashioned it by tying long, sturdy branches underneath the carcass. The animal was so heavy they almost considered cutting it up and bringing it back in pieces.

"We have ta brin' it back whole," Teague said. "A trail of blood might bring wolves and bears inta camp. Besides, everyone needs ta see how big it is."

"Sure," Conn acknowledged. "But I'll snap my back for certain if I keep tryin' ta lift this thin'." He wiped sweat off his forehead. "The day's heat isn't an aid for us. This is the hottest spring I can remember."

"We haven't had a lashin' 'a rain since Conn died in the fields," Teague remembered. "The sun's been out with hardly a cloud since then." They finished tying the elk to the wood frame. "Right altogether," Teague said. "I hope the carrier 'n ropes hold. Here, tie this lead ta your horse."

They tied the lead ropes to their saddles and mounted their horses. They tried to get going, but their horses strained to get the elk's bulk moving behind them. They urged their horses harder and with many grunts and whinnies, they started to drag the elk down the mountain on its carrier.

"Good thin' camp isn't more than a few miles," Conn said. "Our horses aren't used ta pulling such weight."

"A good Eachraighe steed is grand ta work 'n plow as much as run inta battle," Teague remarked. "But once we get down inta the valley, we'll rest 'em and lead on foot for the remainder. It's a hot day."

It took them a couple hours to drag the elk back to camp. The large carcass often got stuck in bushes and trees along the way. Conn and Teague spent almost as much time pulling on the elk as the horses did. They slumped back into camp dripping with sweat.

Nearly collapsed, Conn complained, "Brutal! Next time we cut up the kill! Or hunt a fawn!"

"Sure 'nough," Teague said. "But this kill is grand fortune for the céilí tonight. The antlers will adorn the longhouse nicely as well."

Gilroy walked up to them with many others who admired the result of the hunt. "Where did ya find this beast?" he asked.

"On the summits just north 'a here," Teague said.

"How did ya fell such a fabled beast? One of this size is rare as a blue clover and harder ta kill than a chargin' fáelshee. Only the griffins hunt them when they've grown so large."

"Its hide was tough," Conn said. "But the elk was a grand blessin' for us."

Alastar followed the commotion and found everyone gawking at the giant deer. "I've never seen a bull as big as that," he said. "The valley has more surprises than I could dream of."

"Bulls, bears and boars. . . Let's hope the bears here aren't so big," Teague quipped. He noticed Alastar's new léine. "Haven't ya found somethin' grand in the forest t'day as well?! How is it that day by day ya look more the noble Eachraighe than I?" he said admiring Alastar's finely made léine tunic. He gave Alastar a big smile. "Was it a swan that dropped that fine thread on ya?"

"Wouldn't ya care ta know?" Alastar replied with calm. Everyone gave Alastar amused grins. They all knew Amber made the léine for him.

"I knew the princess needed ta give ya somethin' grand for that little wrapped *finery* ya gave her in Lacharan," Teague chided. He was talking about the hairpin Alastar had wrapped and given to Amber at the dinner feast.

Alastar started to blush. "Slag me, we're onta the wrappin' again! It was, emmm. . . it was. . . just, ahh, never mind that."

"Not a dradairín?" Gilroy said smiling. "Amber gave ya no small, useless potato today either!"

Laughter rang out around them as Amber came to see what was happening. "What's the craic?" she asked.

"We were only reminiscing days past, Princess," Conn said. He stretched to try and sooth his aching muscles. "I'll leave ya folk ta your craic. There's a few hours yet ta the céilí. I need ta get a kip in.

Draggin' that beast for miles has me bushed." He left to get rest.

Amber noticed most people were looking at her with cheerful glee. She looked to Alastar. "What is everyone delightin' in?" she asked him.

"Right grand kill!" Gilroy interrupted. "Take the deer ta the longhouse and prepare it," he told Teague. He also left to continue preparations and everyone started to scatter. They left Amber and Alastar standing alone at the edge of the village.

Alastar still flushed red with embarrassment over their joking. Amber continued to wait for him to say something. "What was everyone smilin' about?" she asked.

He tried to skirt her question and started to walk back to the longhouse where he was carving designs onto the stage. "It was a grand kill, that deer. No one will walk off peckish tonight."

"About t'night," she said. "Be sure ta wear your vest and sword. It's customary for the chief men ta wear their best at formal affairs."

"Sure, I will," he acknowledged. "I'll dress as soon as I've done with the stage. . . and maybe after a little kip as well. Conn had the right idea. The day's heat and bustle has me tired."

Amber walked alongside him and wondered about his feelings. "Conn and Nola are farin' well t'gether," she commented, trying to see if he still had any attraction for Nola. She often wondered if Nola was the girl Alastar said he missed from Loch an Scáthàin. No one had told her it was Nola, but it seemed obvious enough.

"They *are* grand," he said without a hint of regret. "They plan ta marry as soon as Lacharan is open again. He wants his family ta attend the weddin' and settle near 'em. Maybe even take over his family's ranch."

"Their engagement is a wonderful thin'. Only I'd hope they

can return ta Lacharan before their eyes grow old."

"What about you?" Alastar asked. "Don't you wish ta return home too?"

"I don't miss the palace or Lacharan, really," she said. "I'm very happy ta be where I need ta be; with the people and friends wherever I am." She turned her head to look at his face. Alastar kept his eyes forward, though he felt her gaze on him. "I'm well content ta be by your side," she added.

Alastar held back a smile. He knew she was trying to get him to acknowledge feelings for her, but he continued to hold back. "I'm well fond of ya as well," he said calmly. "I couldn't have imagined a more interestin' path with ya. Do ya think Gearóid will find a way ta open Lacharan?" he asked trying to shift the subject.

"I imagine not," she replied. "He's only sneakin' in ta speak with friends; anyone who could help us."

"I hope he'll find it easy."

"The plan will work," she reassured. "We've many friends in the farms and ranches 'round Lacharan. They'll smuggle him in. Let's just hope the king doesn't have too tight a hold on the city ta prevent our aid."

They reached the area around the longhouse stage. It was nearly ready for the céilí. The forest was completely transformed into a huge expanse of cleared ground. Only the largest trees and grass were left untouched. They built many benches and tables out of the trees that were cut, and high balconies were built on the standing trees for people to watch from. Half of the nearly two and a half thousand people would be able to fit in the area. Torches and lanterns were strung about everywhere, and a large pile of wood was made ready at the far end opposite the stage for the bonfire.

Amber went into the longhouse to continue care for the injured while Alastar set his attention to carving the stage's trim. A swarm of people worked to make everything ready. As the hours passed, the sky and forest grew dim and the torches and lanterns were lit. The great bonfire blazed underneath the huge oaks with many kettles, pans and spits of meat cooking on it.

People started to gather at the tables and seats all around the longhouse when they heard the musicians play on the stage. The band was a handful of drummers, trumpeters, fiddlers and harpists. Their tune carried a joyous melody all through the forest that sent most people's spirits skipping toward the céilí. However, Teague and Alastar sat at a long table on the stage with Gearóid and Gilroy, somber in bittersweet memories of the the last céilí they had with Conall in Loch an Scáthóin.

It was just a couple weeks ago that Conall led them with a firm and steady resolve in the hopes he saw come with Alastar. They had much hope still, but wished that their lost friends could be a part of the future's promise. Teague raised his mug. "Let's grant joy in the memory of Conall and our gone kin t'night. Their lives were not taken in vain, but spur us on ta celebrate our victories and keep on in the fight."

"Sláinte," the others at the table agreed and drank from their cups.

"Their spirits won't be forgotten," Alastar added.

Soon Amber approached their table and everyone stood up and let her sit at the center. She wore the same emerald green dress she had brought to Cnoc na Rí and her hair was bound into an elegant bun with the rose hairpin Alastar made for her. Alastar sat by her right and Gearóid on her left. Teague sat on Alastar's other side and Gilroy was next to Gearóid. They faced out at the gathering crowd and waited.

Everyone in the village came and the seating areas quickly

filled with people. When the tables filled, everyone else gathered around the outskirts and sat on the bare ground. Even the sick and infirm were carried out and given seats next to the stage. The thick wood and vegetation around the longhouse was replaced by a dense mass of people.

When the crowd gathered, Gearóid stood up to speak and the band stopped playing. "Welcome friends and kinsmen Eachraighe! We've gathered t'night ta celebrate, because though we are deep in a forest, we are not far from home. And though we are exiled, we are hopeful of heart. And though our kin have fallen, we build new. We joy t'night for the undying spirit of our lost brothers and sisters and bring a name ta the small community we built here." He looked to Gilroy and introduced him, "Chancellor."

Gilroy stood up with something hidden underneath a cloth. He walked to center stage and uncovered the plaque Alastar made. It had Baile ["Bwhy-leh"] engraved in small letters at the top and Duille Coiréil spanned most of its face. "We name our village Duille Coiréil." He raised the plaque up over his head and translated the text on the plaque, "Town of Coral Leaf."

Everyone gave a shout of acknowledgement as Gilroy set the plaque in a small stand on the stage. The band started playing music again and the celebration started. People brought food from the preparation areas to the tables and groups of people that sat everywhere. Dancing, singing, and feasting spread throughout the camp, but no sooner than the celebration began did bells ring from the watchmen high up in the oak trees that helped frame the longhouse.

Everyone stopped what they were doing and listened. A watchman yelled over the low, worried whispers of the crowd, "Huge beasts fly this way from the east! Three of 'em!"

Gasps went through the crowd and words of the Áiteoir dragon sent their hearts into panic. The camp filled with a confused roar of fear, but Teague remembered their run out of Lacharan and the three mighty griffins that came to save them. He stood up and shouted to calm the crowd, "Keep steady, everyone! Be in your wicks!" He looked up and yelled to the watchman, "Do the beasts beat their wings as eagles?"

"That they do!" the watchman yelled back. "They draw near!"

Then just as the watchman reported, the unmistakable deafening call of the griffins roared through the forest. Their cries shook the giant oak trees as if they were spindly saplings.

"Griffins!" the watchman yelled. "Big as barns for a hundred cows! They flew overhead and turned ta perch on a peak over us!"

The crowd was relieved and gave out shouts of joy and promise for the griffins over their heads. "Surely we're blessed!" everyone said. They continued celebrating in high spirits. The camp was so full of cheer that the dimmed foliage surrounding them appeared to take on new light and life to carry the bright echoes of promise through the whole valley.

When Alastar had his fill of food, he waited for a good time to talk to Amber privately. Their table was full of news and plans. From Greerian reports, Gilroy said King Fuar had returned to Cnoc na Rí after coming from Lacharan. Their scouts also found Loch an Scáthháin was under guard by a small watch left by the king. The location of Laochmarú's army, though, was unknown.

They also heard from their two scouting parties who tried to find their kinsmen sold into slavery. Both parties followed trails into Cloch Lom and found each other far in the north mining district. The parties converged there after Bearach and Neese's search in the west found no slaves had come from Chnámh an Áidh, but Cathal and Rónán heard that a few wagons of slaves entered Cloch Lom from the south. They still needed to find the slaves exact whereabouts, though.

After the conversation dwindled into idle talk, Alastar asked Amber to go away from the party. They took to their horses and Alastar led her to the cliffs of the stone arch. When they broke through the forest canopy, the dark air and warm breeze of the mountains surrounded them with the rustling of hopeful dreams. It was as if the tinkling of the windblown leaves shared in their bond together.

"Where are ya takin' me?" Amber wondered. "This place is beautiful."

"Just wait till we reach the top," he said. The stars were out in a cloudless sky and the bright, full moon lingered over the center of the valley. When they reached the stone arch, he said, "This is the gateway I came ta your isle from."

He got down from Éimhín and went to help Amber off Muirgel. "This way," he said as he led her to the edge of the cliff beyond the arch.

Amber could hardly take in the beauty of the view. The moon's silver light reflected on the gleaming leaves of the forest everywhere, and the river rippled its bright form along its whole length. "I've never seen anythin' so wonderful as the valley here," she said.

Alastar gazed at the full moon and remarked, "It's perfect." He took from his vest the object he carved near the river bank that morning and placed it in her open palm. He kept it covered with his hand and recited a poem as he looked into her eyes, "When the moon is high and shinin' bright, it lights your eyes, like stars in the night. Their radiance pulls me ta heaven, where beauty is all and true. That is the beauty, I see in you." He uncovered the object in her palm. She saw it was a wood fibulae clasp and knew what it meant. "Will ya reserve your heart for me?" he asked her.

Amber flooded with joy and her eyes dampened with tears of

promise. The destiny she held in her heart since she was a youth was now standing in front of her, ready to give his full attention. "You were always the dew that covered my heart in delight," she replied. "I already reserved it for you."

Alastar returned her loving smile and took the fibulae from her hand. He unbuttoned the top button on her dress's neckline and inserted the fibulae into the empty buttonhole. Then he drew close to her and they kissed. They lingered in embrace under the moonlight. It was a quiet and serene moment that bound their souls together like neither of them felt before. Alastar felt her love reach into his heart as if she had the key that unlocked its chambers. He realized then that his love for Nola and Nuala was immature and never truly fit the keyhole of his heart. That was only fleeting love as Gilroy had said, which only covered the heart for a time and washed away.

When they stopped kissing, Alastar asked, "Would ya forgive me?"

"For what?" she wondered.

"I didn't let you touch my heart, because I had fancies I couldn't let go of. But the currents led me ta ya in so many wonderful ways, and yet I still clung ta what I thought my heart wanted. It took some time for me ta see that and. . . emmm. . . I know how bad it feels ta love and not have it returned. I know now, it's painful empty business ta let your heart go after things it wasn't meant for."

Amber shushed him and kissed him again. "Ya needn't feel that way again," she assured him. "I love ya despite your awkward chatter and strollin' 'bout. You're not the mightiest, nor fairest, nor most noble of men. Oft times you're downright stubborn and most aloof! A right ladhb ["lyyb"]!"

"Grand," he said sarcastically. "Am I so awkward?" Éimhín gave an affirming nicker behind them. Alastar looked at him and said,

"You would know, boy, wouldn't ya? Mind your own and get back ta nuzzlin' Muirgel!"

Amber laughed. "Éimhín knows ya well as I. You're an odd wheatear never mindful 'a rest, but you're the perfect man for me." They sat down at the cliff's edge and watched the moon continue its rise over the valley. Over their reminiscing of all that's happened, Alastar noticed the trees along the mountain peaks were withered and sparse of leaf. He remembered all the trees in the valley were full and thriving when he first arrived weeks ago.

"The forest along the peaks are dryin' out," he said.

"It hasn't rained for ages," she acknowledged. "I can't remember the last lashin'."

"I do. I was pinned ta the ground in the fields of Loch an Scáth.in durin' the last rain. I won't soon forget that day."

"How do your wounds fare?" Amber asked.

"They're sore at times, but hardly a bother now. I had the best care," he said with appreciation.

"I hardly had a choice," she joked. "No one else could stop ya from moanin' the whole time!"

"Sure 'nough," he mumbled.

"We should get back ta camp," she said. "Everyone'll be speakin' of our runnin' off in the night as it is."

"Right, we'll not mar your reputation as a proper lady," he said as he stood up. He gave his hand to her and helped her up.

*A*ir rushed past Alastar and he opened his eyes. His body flew across the land and quickly came to a sea that was alight under the waves. He plunged down into its water and saw huge, glowing forests of kelp and seaweed. Brightly illuminated fish of different colors swam all around him. Then suddenly he rose above the water and found himself in a small, flooded prison cell made of dark stone walls. In the corner, a young boy huddled in cloudy water that went up to his ankles. He called to Alastar for help, but Alastar kept rising up and away. Then there was darkness.

Alastar opened his eyes. The morning light came through the window of the shack he shared with Teague and Niall. They were still sleeping in their bunks. Alastar wondered about the dream he just had. *The glowing sea must be the Muir Airgid,* he thought. *But where was the boy? Who was he?* Alastar felt he had to help him.

He got up and put on his léine and belt. He remembered to pull the léine up through the belt like Amber showed him before. He fumbled about with the folds of fabric and wondered how they should settle. *I'll have to get used to dressing in this thing,* he thought.

He went outside. The sky of another bright day shone through the breaks in the forest canopy. The village was very quiet for the time of morning. Usually people were busy already, but the céilí had everyone up late. Duille Coiréil was spent in slumber. He walked toward the longhouse thinking about the dream and wondered if he should make a journey to the Muir Airgid.

At the longhouse, Alastar walked to the side with the stage. The quiet area stood in bare contrast to the bustling party they had. The only movement he saw in the vast cleared forest were thin wisps of

smoke that rose from the large pile of cinders where the bonfire stood.

He turned to the stage and took the town plaque. He brought it to the front door of the longhouse and found the pegs he made for fastening the plaque above the doorframe. As he lightly hammered the plaque into place, Gilroy came by.

"Do ya know the village sleeps yet?" Gilroy said. "Your hammerin' will brin' grumbles for certain."

"I was tryin' ta be quiet as a tricklin' brook," Alastar noted. He finished hammering the plaque and got down from the ladder.

"A brook?" Gilroy scoffed. "Sounded more like thunderclaps from across camp. I was hopin' the rains were approachin'."

"You noticed the valley is dryin' up too?"

"That I did," Gilroy affirmed. "But I've not seen a witherin' as this. The valley has had droughts many weeks longer and never did the trees fade before; certainly not the evergreens. The pines and rowan on the summits appear worse than a faintin' oak in the last throws of autumn. The witherin' appears ta descend farther into the depths of the valley each day."

"Does it mean anythin'?" Alastar wondered.

"The only thin' I can compare is the anbobracht ["ahn-boh-brahkt"] of Rathúnas's west lands."

"Anbobracht?" Alastar questioned.

"A wastin' sickness," Gilroy said. "Awful curse. In ages past, the west of the isle were vast plains, hill and forest country, but the land turned ta smolderin' ash and desert in but a few generations. It is the heart of the Áiteoir Kingdom where there is not but dry sand and black stone everywhere now, all the way up ta the shores of the Muir Airgid."

"The Silver Sea?" Alastar recognized. "I just had a dream of the Muir Airgid. But I flew over green land ta the sea and saw the glowin' forests in the water's depths, but then I rose above the water and saw a boy held captive in a flooded cell. I could not make sense of the dream."

Gilroy pondered. "It may be significant. I believe ya saw the east coast of the Muir Airgid that used ta belong ta the Méine Kingdom. Those shores are still lined with vast forest and plains. The coasts of the Muir Airgid everywhere else have withered inta barren rock and desert."

"The boy in my dream asked for my help," Alastar noted. "I feel I need ta go and help him."

"That may be," Gilroy noted. "But when ta do that remains ta be seen. Little use. . ."

"Ta build a bridge before ya reach the river," Alastar completed. "I know. Sometimes I'm too anxious ta build. I think I've learned my lessons there."

"With dradairín and grebes, ya mean?" Gilroy noted.

"Right, a few too many birds and useless potatoes," Alastar agreed. "My heart had a fancy or two that came ta naught."

"Surely there are pursuits we ought not ta have," Gilroy said, "but havin' a desire in your heart does not make it wrong all at once. It's when we let our desires blind us ta what is right or ta what is meant for us, then it becomes wrong. We can't let our wants overtake our sensibilities. We ought ta live by waitin' on the tunes sung by the currents. They carry the melodies meant for us ta heed. Tryin' ta make your own destiny is wrought in futility and tempered in disaster. The king has seen it in his attempts ta bind his throne ta Amber's future. The kingdom is split upon his choices. I'm certain you see the bad choices you made as well."

"I do," Alastar acknowledged. "I had somewhat of a handful of things I should've done different or not at all since I came ta Rathúnas.

Bein' a flittin' wheatear isn't the most grand of traits."

"We all have our traits, son. Ya ought not ta be ashamed. Ya simply need ta be more mindful of rest and patient temperance. It is a challenge and lesson of the wise that is not learned in the blink of an eye."

Alastar put away the ladder and stepped back to view the plaque.

"Grand," Gilroy said. "Did ya ever think ya would help found a town two weeks inta your adventure?"

"Never. I hardly knew what lay behind the gateway when it opened. I just knew I had ta go."

Niall joined them by the longhouse with a pair of fishing poles in his hand. "So it was you boxin' off the hammer! I woke ta this tap, tap, tap 'n looked ta your bunk. Seein' ya weren't there, I figured it had ta be that lad with his bagful 'a tools." Niall lifted the fishing rods to show them. The poles were made of two sections, a base of hazel wood and thinner tops of juniper. The fishing lines were each sixteen feet of braided horsehair and ended with a crimson fly lure. "I finished the rods yesterday. The grilse ["gril-sheh"] are ready ta hook! Let's say we have a bit a leisurely fishin'," he suggested to Alastar.

"Grilse?" Alastar asked.

"The summer run 'a salmon," Niall said. "They're just comin' round. I see 'em jumpin' for flies more 'n more every day."

"Remember ta keep out 'a sight," Gilroy reminded.

"Sure 'nough," Niall said. "The lines are long 'nough for us ta cast under the trees."

"Grand then," Gilroy said as he walked away. "Catch a fair few for the rest of us, would ya?"

"We'll give it our best lash!" Niall said.

Alastar and Niall went to the river and settled under some trees that overhung the water. Niall handed Alastar a pole and showed him how to unwind the line by twirling it off the pole.

"What sort of fishin' are we doin'?" Alastar questioned. He wasn't familiar with fly fishing. "We haven't any floats, weights, or anythin'. Are we ta bait with worms on these lures?"

"Where have ya been ta never fly fish for salmon?" Niall wondered. "They come ta spawn every year in all the rivers connected ta the sea; snatch up morsels tossed onta the water, like kittens jumpin' at butterflies in a field." Then he remembered Alastar was not native to Rathúnas. "Emmm. . . nevermind. I forget you're a new arrival ta our shores."

"I've heard of salmon runs. I mean, we fish with floats of cork and feathers and use bait mostly on our isle," Alastar said. "The fishermen use nets and traps in the sea, but I only fish once in a while. Salmon don't run along our rivers either, but our river minnows are grand bait for cold fish and crab in the sea. There's hardly anythin' else respectable ta eat from the few rivers we have." Alastar looked at the simple fishing pole in his hand. The line was tied to the end of it. "I never fished without a reel before," he commented.

"A reel?" Niall asked.

"A spool and handle ta wind the line," Alastar said. "Like a winch ta pull rope."

"Ah. . . we needn't anythin' fancy as that," Niall replied. He stepped farther from Alastar to show him how to cast. "I like ta cast overhead, but since we've tree cover, we'll cast sideways." He quickly waved his rod back and forth, sideways, a few times to make the line loop in the air. "Make the line wave like this," he demonstrated. Then he made a final flick of the rod forward and let the fly land on the water in front of him. "Now you try. But step off a bit. I'd rather ya not hook me."

Alastar stepped farther from Niall and started to wave his rod sideways. Niall watched him as he awkwardly waved the pole back and forth. "Keep it low," Niall said. "Ya don't want ta hook the branches either." After some flicking back and forth, Alastar's line wasn't taking flight like Niall's did. "Faster rhythm!" Niall encouraged.

Alastar waved his pole faster and the line started to fly and loop like Niall showed. He cast the line onto the water with a final point of his rod outward. Just as Alastar's fly hit the water, a fish jumped at Niall's fly lure. Niall yanked slowly on his rod and pulled the line toward him. As he brought his rod low to grab hold of the line with his hands, a fish snapped at Alastar's lure and pulled hard.

"I've got one!" Alastar yelled.

"Mind your own!" Niall said as he struggled with the fish on his line. "Just take hold of your line 'n pull easy! Don't tug hard or the line'll snap!"

Alastar mimicked Niall and they both landed silvery salmon longer than their forearms. As Niall unhooked his fish, he said, "What would ya need floats 'n winches for when a line 'n jig'll get the job done?"

"Right," Alastar said. "These are grand altogether! It'll be roast fish tonight!"

They tossed their catches to the side and continued to fish through the morning. As their pile of fish grew, Niall skewered them onto thin ropes so they could be easily carried together. They had caught dozens of salmon when someone came running to them.

"Scouts approach!" the man yelled. "Inta the forest!" He was one of the watchmen stationed at the east end of the valley near the border of Cnoc na Rí. He continued running upstream along the river to look for more people to warn.

"The king finally saw ta search the valley," Niall said. "Take in your line 'n wind it round the pole!"

Alastar and Niall quickly secured their rods and picked up the lines of fish. They ran back toward the center of the village and warned everyone along the way. Everyone in camp already knew what was happening. They ran around to make sure their shelters were covered with branches and foliage. Most structures were hidden in this way.

The only thing they could not hide was the longhouse and its large area of cleared forest. They hoped its position deeply inset next to the mountains would keep it safe from searching eyes. Some of their horses were penned in the open behind the longhouse, but most of the herd was tucked into a large alcove nearby that sunk into the cliffs. It made an ideal natural enclosure to stable the horses and keep them hidden.

Everyone scurried to hide in their shelters or climb the trees to keep watch. Many archers settled into the trees and soldiers hid in the ground brush everywhere. If Duille Coiréil was discovered, the prying scouts would find it difficult to escape the hundreds of hidden soldiers around them.

Niall and Alastar threw down their catch of fish near the longhouse and ran inside. They found all the women, the young and the elderly inside guarded by many soldiers. Amber was comforting a little girl with Gilroy next to her.

Teague greeted them, "Arrivin' late again?"

"We were fishin' at the river," Alastar said. He looked about for Gearóid, but didn't see him. "Where's Gearóid? Aren't we all ta shelter here?"

"Gearóid and Conn left for Lacharan," Teague said. "Everyone's here that needs ta be."

"Grand then," Alastar noted. He walked to Amber. The girl was clutching Amber and he pat the girl on the head.

"Are your hands clean?" Amber asked. "Ya smell like a fisherman! I hope ya brought us a fair catch smellin' as ya are."

"Niall and I caught grilse with hardly any effort," he answered. "Couldn't have been easier if they jumped straight inta our laps!"

"Quiet everyone!" Teague hushed. He stood at the doorway and peered outside. The forest was a dead still. After many days of people working ceaselessly everywhere, the quiet of the village felt as if it was deep in night sleep. He ran outside to get a better look.

He went toward the river and saw a far off group of people on horseback. Many dozens of them wandered loosely in the forest and looked about. Most of them kept towards the river, but a few started coming towards the longhouse. *The search party is coming this way,* Teague thought.

If they came too close he knew their archers would shoot them all. But he didn't want the suspicion of a missing search party. The king would surely send more scouts or a whole unit of soldiers to search the valley again. He had to find a way to keep them away. Then a thought hit him and he picked up a few rocks. He sprinted through the forest and went upstream to get ahead of the search party. His men hidden throughout the forest watched him in bewilderment. Why was he running toward the search party?

Teague ran west and kept out of the party's sight by hiding behind trees and bushes. When he came near enough to the head of the search party, he threw one of the rocks he picked up. It landed far ahead of them with a rustling thud after going through a thick bush. The party looked to the sound and turned their focus forward.

Teague ran again and moved farther upstream, well ahead of the party. He found a large melon tree and climbed it. Then he stood behind its massive branches and waited for the riders to approach with another rock in his hand. When they came near, he threw the rock at a hanging sciathánshee above them. Most of the bat creatures had settled into trees farther upstream after they were scared off from the activity in Duille Coiréil.

The rock hit the sciathánshee square center and shocked it awake. It flapped and gave a high pitched shriek. The commotion woke the entire colony of sciathánshee around them. Hundreds of them took flight in a massive cloud and descended on the scouting party. Teague huddled against the tree and peered downward.

The scouts' horses were startled by the attacking sciathánshee and bucked off many riders. The sight of the large leathery creatures disappearing and appearing around them pitched fear into their hearts and the entire party ran back downstream. They waved their swords and arms around frantically to ward off the giant bats. The men's screams echoed through the forest as they retreated from the dark, toothy swarm of flapping wings. The cries of the retreating men were heard far down the valley.

When the forest came to quiet again, everyone came out and gave shouts of victory. Their village would remain secure from the king's searching for now.

The days in the valley went by without a hint of rain and the forest along the mountaintops continued to wither and crumble. They became so dry that the very ground turned to dust and blew away. Alastar noted spots here and there of exposed red rock where green forest once lay just weeks before. Areas of red-orange agate layers expanded day by day. They protruded along the high forest line, like open sores that scabbed over. If the anbobracht continued, the valley would turn into the desert valley of his home and he wouldn't need to go back through the gateway to see the bare dust of Eritirim again.

Alastar wondered if it was his group of Eachraighe who dug out the canals in the desert valley. Was their newly founded home doomed to wither and blow away in the generations to come? Despite their concerns over the anbobracht, the community continued to build Duille Coiréil. They erected a tall palisade stake wall of stripped trees around the village and concealed it with vines and brush. It would help them defend against attack if Fuar sent another group of soldiers.

They also completed the longhouse and built a smithy, armory, bakery, storehouses and other community structures to anticipate the needs of war and hold supplies. They planned to spend the changing seasons in the valley, but continued to hope for a return to their homelands every day.

Summer threw its intense heat upon the valley and made the drought an unbearable stretch of simmering heat. Most activity in the village ceased as everyone rested in the shade during the hottest times of day.

Amber and Alastar were drinking at the river's edge with their horses when they decided to go up to the cliffs of the stone arch. They often went there to sit and spend their free time together. The breeze higher in the mountains would also be a welcome relief. They mounted Éimhín and Muirgel and rode fast to the cliffs. The rush of wind from riding through the forest gave them some respite from the heat, and they joyed in racing one another as they weaved to and fro between the trees.

During the weeks in the valley, they became adept in quick maneuvers and leaping over obstacles with their horses. Their proficiency made them the most agile of riders and horses. Éimhín was always in the lead too, but barely by a head's length.

"One day Muirgel will have her turn at front!" Amber yelled. "She was the fastest in the kingdom before Éimhín came along."

"Éimhín is barely at a trot!" Alastar replied. He leaned down slightly and pat Éimhín on the neck. "Give 'em a fair chase!" he told him. Éimhín sped up and kicked his hooves even faster. They pulled ahead farther as they reached the bottom of the cliffs. They hardly slowed as Éimhín leaped onto the trail that went up.

At the top, Alastar dismounted as Amber came up just behind them. "I suppose it's not Muirgel's turn today," Alastar said. He went to Amber and helped her off Muirgel.

"Muirgel hasn't hit her prime," Amber noted. "She'll give your Éimhín a surprise yet!" Éimhín gave a snort of disbelief.

Alastar stroked Éimhín on the shoulder as they walked past him. "Ya may let the ladies win a time or two," he whispered to him. "They fancy that."

"Do we now?" Amber questioned. "Isn't it you who jockeys Éimhín? I'd think you rather enjoy me chasin' ya 'bout!"

Alastar blushed at her statement. "I think you're right!"

Amber huffed and hit him on the shoulder. "I knew you were a bouzzie the second I saw ya on the pier!"

"Ya mistake me for another, I'm afraid," Alastar said with calm. "That lad on the pier hardly knew what he was doin' there." He tugged on Amber's hand and turned her toward him. "But the one standin' here knows where his heart belongs." He kissed her with a simple passion. It was like their spirits were tied together with a silver thread that radiated between them at every little glance or feather touch.

They never did anything more than sit together and kiss. Their love for each other was not bound by carnal desires. They felt an invisible harmony together that could only solidify when they both put away the barriers that held them apart - for Alastar it was his preconceived ideas of who and what he wanted in life, and for Amber it was the curtain that hid the love she held in reserve for him. Neither of them could be saturated in each other's love until those barriers fell away.

Amber pulled away from him and sat down at the cliff's edge. "Did I ever tell you how our harps came ta be?" she asked.

Alastar followed her and sat next to her. "I don't recall ya ever sayin'."

"It's a grand story of musical heritage and devotion," she said. "There was once a husband and wife who spent their days in quarrel. Her fiery temper'd claim a broken plate or few. They'd argue over the most trivial thin's - spilt soup, a lost trinket - but most of all, the husband's slothful nature had her eyes *flarin'!* He was quite a fallsáin ["fæl-sine"] really and oft woke well after dawn. His lazy ways had their house in desperate times.

"When they were right skint, the husband thought he'd gain the bread 'n honey by sellin' their last bit 'a livestock - their milkin' cow. When he came home with a handful 'a quid ta show his wife, he thought he'd done somethin' well for a change. But after she found he sold their cow for half its worth, she steamed out the door and said she'd never come back. She traveled through the isle seekin' comfort, but not a thin' helped her calm, and she went from field ta forest and stream ta sea with a sour face. She was not able ta sleep a wink the whole time.

"The husband loved her so much, he couldn't stand ta leave her out 'a his sight, so unknown ta her, he followed as she went through the countryside and onta the north shores of Carraig Mhór ["Kar-rig Wor"]. There on the rocky beach, she sat and looked out ta sea with a heavy frown.

"There was a right whale skull not far washed up on the beach. The wind was swift that day and blew through the tooth threads hangin' in the whale skull. It made such a beautiful sound, the wife was soothed and a grand smile warmed her face. She fell sound asleep there.

"The husband, of course, was not far and saw how the wind's music made his wife happy. He wanted ta soothe her in the same way, so as she slept, he went inta the forest and made the first harp by carvin' wood inta a likeness of the whale skull. He strung it with the whale's tooth threads and sat beside his wife playin' his newly made instrument.

"When she woke and saw him playin' wonderful music, tears of joy wet her eyes. She was so happy ta see him, she hugged him fiercely. She promised never ta leave him again and they went home in the best of spirits.

"He became a musician after that and was the most acclaimed harpist ever ta grace the isle. They never had want of anythin'. People paid well ta have him perform. But he saved his best music for his wife, who never gave him a sour face again."

Alastar smiled. "Sounds like the husband was a woodcarver. Is there any truth ta the story?"

Amber gave him a slight scowl. "Have ya ever seen a right whale skull? You'd notice it matches the frame of our harps *exactly!* How could it not be true!" she said defensively. Then she caught herself raising her voice and calmed down. "Well, I suppose the story may have a bit of fanciful horse's hoof, but our harps do match the whale skulls perfectly."

Alastar was used to her occasional outbursts of energy and ignored her irritated tone. He gave her a look of appreciation. "Right, well. . . horse hoof or not, the man turned his banndaire ["bahn-dehreh"; disappointed person] of a wife inta a woman well sorted out. I could only hope ta make ya so well pleased."

"Despite bein' quite stout-headed, you haven't given me much ta complain," she said.

As they talked in the sunlight, a large shadow flew over them. They looked up and saw a griffin swoop to the peak above them. "Looks ta be a pair of griffin made roost," Alastar noted.

"I think they're nestin'," she said. "The larger one hasn't moved for days."

"Let's say we get a closer look?" he suggested. "They never made a menacin' move toward us. Can't be any danger in visitin' their roost."

"Did I remember ta say you're a right mainidh as well as stubborn?!" Amber retorted. "Who walks up ta a beast the size of a house? Much less two! And the peak's hundreds 'a feet up! We'd faint from heat not half way there!"

Alastar stared at the cliffs around them. "The first cliff's only a skip on the vines," he reassured. "Once we're on top, it's a slow walk the rest of the way."

"Are you coddin'!" she exclaimed.

"Serious!" he replied. Alastar got up and took Amber's hand. "I'll climb first and pull ya up." He led her to the base of the cliff behind them and found a sturdy vine that reached to the top. He tied it around her waist and started to climb the vines. "Wait till I get up top!"

As Alastar climbed, he heard Amber struggling below. He looked down and saw her trying to pull herself up, but she could barely make it a few meters before tiring. She lost her foothold and hung tight to the vine.

"Hold on!" he told her and climbed as fast as he could. The

cliff was over a hundred feet high, but Alastar made it to the top without too much trouble. He quickly went to Amber's vine and started to pull her up. Her weight was more exertion than he expected. He quickly tired and thought he should've rested before pulling her up. *It would a help if she pulled too,* he thought. "Pull up on other vines!" he yelled down.

"I thought ya said it'd be an easy skip!" she chided.

Alastar continued pulling as she grabbed vines to ease her weight on him. It took some minutes of sweat and grunting from both of them before Amber set her feet on the cliff top. Alastar slumped down on the ground and tried to catch his breath. Amber untied herself and looked toward the griffins. The massive beasts eyed them curiously but did not make a sound. They appeared to be more focused on eating something rather than the couple's climbing.

Alastar got up after a short rest and they walked leisurely the rest of the way. The mountainside was rocky, but it provided an easy path to the summit for them. When they breached the peak with their heads, they could see the carcass of a small whale lay between the two resting griffins. The one that flew in had brought it from the sea to feed his mate.

Amber and Alastar continued up and made a slow approach. The griffins were many meters away, but their great size and focused stares made Amber uneasy. She slowed and tugged Alastar backwards. "Are ya sure this is a good idea?" she whispered.

Alastar didn't feel any anxiety and tightened his grip on her hand to reassure her. The majesty of the griffins kept him in awe. They stood like tall towers before them. Their presence gave him a feeling of security more than fear. He tugged back on Amber and helped her continue forward.

"I think this is close 'nough," Amber reminded him in a quiet voice.

"They rest easy," he noted and continued to tug on her to go forward. "Grand altogether."

They were barely twenty feet away from the closest griffin when all of a sudden it stood up and gave a deafening cry. Alastar and Amber covered their ears and crouched slightly in fear. The griffin flapped its great wings and they could see its underside feathers were white. It took off flying toward the sea and the force of its beating wings almost blew them flat to the ground. As they watched it fly away, Amber collected herself while Alastar began to laugh at the startle. Amber didn't think the surprise was funny and pushed Alastar so hard, he fell backwards.

"Grand altogether!?" she screamed at him in sarcasm. "Is that your idea of craic? If I weren't so spent in fear, I'd throw ya off the cliff!"

He got himself back up. "Nothin' ta fear," he said. "They'd snip off our heads already if they thought ill of us."

"Right then," Amber huffed. "I'll wait for ya back at the cliff! I'd had 'nough 'a griffin watchin'!" She started to walk back the way they came when another raptor's cry rang through the air. Alastar recognized it immediately and looked around to find the Azure. It was flying toward them and going west, straight in the sun's path into the horizon.

When the Azure came, the nesting griffin stood up and cried back in reply. Amber and Alastar looked back at the griffin and saw an enormous egg under its belly. Both of them could have crouched inside its massive shell.

"It's a mother!" Amber noted.

"For certain," Alastar acknowledged, but he quickly turned his attention back to the Seabhac Azure. He watched it fly overhead and continue due west in the familiar ascending flight high into the sky that Alastar knew meant he needed to follow. *The Muir Airgid,* Alastar remembered. *It's time to go.* He looked to Amber and said, "I have a journey ta make. The Azure calls me ta the Muir Airgid."

"What?" she asked with confusion. "Are ya certain?"

"I am," he affirmed. "Gilroy and Teague believe it as well. We've been waitin' for the time ta go."

"And you haven't told me till now!?" Amber said angrily.

"We didn't want ta worry ya. I don't feel you're meant ta go. Gilroy thinks Teague and I are the only two ta go," he said trying to ease her. "Teague had a similar dream of the Muir Airgid as I did. It appears we're sent on an errand of mercy."

Amber grew worried. She didn't like the idea of Alastar venturing through Áiteoir country without an army around him. She disliked the idea of him leaving without her even less. "Just the two of you ta cross enemy lands? Don't ya remember how much the enemy wants ya dead?!" she fumed and wondered if there was a better way for them to make the journey. "We must speak ta Gilroy before ya go."

"Surely," he reassured her. "But don't worry over us. I've found that in the most perplexin' and dangerous of times, if we just trust the flow with the currents, fear is a waste of effort. Remember our flight out of Lacharan? I thought we were done for when the dragon came on us and the Áiteoir army just behind."

"Would ya also recall the sword 'n spear that stuck ya through?" Amber reminded.

"I admit ta makin' some mistakes, but I'm sure of my path ta the Muir Airgid as I'm sure of my love for you." Alastar gave her a long kiss and then walked toward the nesting griffin. "Wait here," he told her.

He moved toward the cluster of branches and leaves that the

griffin sat in. It had sat back down on the egg and watched him closely. Not a sound came from it as Alastar went for a large, white down feather caught in the edge of the nest. He kept his eyes on the griffin's stare as he made a slow, tip-toe walk to the feather. The griffin simply watched him curiously.

Alastar climbed over the edge of the nest and grabbed the huge feather. It was bigger than a soldier's breastplate. Then he saw he was close enough to touch the griffin and reached out his hand, but the griffin gave a disapproving squawk that startled Alastar backwards. He tumbled onto his back, but kept hold of the giant feather.

Amber jumped when the griffin called out, but her feet remained planted in fear. "Are ya hurt?" Amber asked meekly from a distance.

Alastar stood back up and smiled at the griffin. "No touchin', right then," he acknowledged. He jogged back to Amber who was grateful to see him unharmed. Then he gave her the feather with a low bow. "A gift for my mot." She took it and he straightened back up. Alastar gave her a silly smile and added, "I'll be leavin' soon. Ya may need it ta remember me by."

Amber didn't find his humor funny. She tightened her brow and said tersely, "I'd be more apt ta remember ya fondly if you'd tell me everythin' before it comes ta leave me flat on the ground!"

Alastar gave her a loving smile. "I'll do my best," he said.

They left the griffin's roost and made their way back to the village. The sun had disappeared under the mountain ridges when they were back on the valley floor. They found Gilroy and Teague to discuss the journey west.

"Shouldn't you go with a unit of men?" Amber suggested.

"Hidin' so many men on the journey would be too difficult," Gilroy noted. "Supplyin' a force for the duration would be a hard road as well. We've no idea how long the trek will take." After noting they might be gone a long time, he saw more worry come to Amber's face.

"We need remain stealthy," Teague added. "The lad and I are well seasoned now in flights through the night. Thin's are well in hand. We have Bress ta send word if need be. Ya won't be completely cut off from the lad," he encouraged. Amber wasn't reassured and kept thinking about going with them.

Gilroy felt her apprehension and said, "Sometimes life takes us from each other for a time. We know how much you want ta go with Alastar, but we can't have you journeyin' among the enemy without need. Your presence is needed among your people here. Sometimes separation is a test of love. Your love is not perfected if you fear separation. Let this time test your love."

Amber understood and let her concerns fall under the weight of duty and reason. She conceded to their plan and looked at Teague. "Then promise me, Teague, that you'll watch him close. Don't let him get odd notions, like pettin' griffins."

Teague reassured her firmly, "I've sworn my life ta protect his. I won't return without the lad."

His confidence eased her spirit and she left to get something. Teague and Alastar fit their armor and packed their horses to begin their journey as soon as possible. Alastar was putting his saddlebags on Éimhín when Teague noted his excessive packing.

"Do ya truly need *all* your bags?" Teague asked. "Best ta be light. No tellin' how swift we need ride."

"Right," Alastar acknowledged. He removed his large bags and tied a smaller one to the rear of his saddle. "Still, I'll brin' my tools. What good is a woodcarver with nothin' ta carve with?"

"Sure then," Teague acknowledged. "You're a right useful lad. Remember ta wear your long coat over your armor as well. We'll be needin' ta be discrete."

Amber found them packing and went to Alastar. She gave him a bundle of clothing. "I mended your clothes," she said. "I imagine you'd need a change 'a clean clothes." He took the clothes and thanked her. He packed them in the bag as she waited silently next to him. He tightened the bindings on Éimhín and looked about trying to remember anything else he needed to do.

Teague looked over at them and smiled. "Lad, even a wheatear knows when his bird waits. Kiss the girl already so we can leave! The sun has set 'n we'll be ridin' only by moonlight once we exit the valley."

Alastar and Amber blushed. Alastar turned around and faced her. They held each other tightly and kissed with the anticipation of separation. They lingered in each others' presence until their love for one another filled their hearts for the absence.

Alastar then stepped back and touched the fibulae clasp that hung just below her neck. "Remember the soldier's clasp is also a vow ta return ta his love." He mounted Éimhín and rode with Teague out of the village.

*C*athal, Rónán, Bearach and Neese peered over the top of a high hill. They looked down into a large limestone quarry that lay next to the sea coast. A small inlet of the North Sea stretched ahead of them. Its cold waters churned gray and white throughout the narrow channel. The other side of the bay was barely a half mile away.

The beach below them was enclosed by great stone cliffs and thick forests of silver birch. They lay flat on their stomachs wearing only their léine war shirts and weapons. They had packed away most of their Eachraighe uniforms and armor to appear inconspicuous during their tracking expedition.

"There must be hundreds 'a people down there," Neese said. "Is this the right mine? How are we ta find our kinsmen in that?"

"This is it," Cathal affirmed. "It's the only mine with a kiln house on the sea." He pointed out a stone building along the beach that had a large plume of smoke rising from it. "The gatekeeper said the slaves were taken ta the mine that baked its stone along the sea."

"What do they kiln the stone for?" Rónán wondered.

"They cart in rough rock and bring out piles 'a white powder," Neese observed. "Barrels 'a somethin' too."

"They kiln the stone ta make lime and limewater," Bearach said. "The barrels must be for the limewater."

"Right, limewater," Rónán acknowledged. "My granddad used ta wash his hair in limewater. Made his fair, long locks thick 'n rough like that of a horse's mane."

"I've not heard anyone do that for generations," Bearach said. "Who wants their hair full 'a chalk? The lime's more useful for mortar 'n such."

Cathal noticed ships docked near the kiln house. "They must ship the lime everywhere from here."

"Grand for 'em," Neese said. "Now how are we ta find our kinsmen down there?"

"We need ta query the slaves," Cathal said. "Someone ought ta know."

"Just how are we ta do that?" Neese said with disbelief. "Should we just walk inta their midst?"

"Exactly!" Cathal replied. "You and Bearach go down 'n slip in among the slaves. Make like you're one of 'em and start askin' 'round. Be quiet 'n discrete 'bout it. We don't want the slave masters ta take notice."

"Let me go in place 'a Neese," Rónán suggested. "I'm a fair hand at diggin' for news."

"Grand plan," Bearach said. "Neese oft runs the mouth wild. Take 'em weeks ta find anythin' useful!"

Neese grumbled. "Quit the slag! I'd root out our clansmen in not more than a hop 'n skip!"

"That ya would," Cathal said. "But I'll let Rónán go. Your keen archer's eyes may be more useful here. We may need your skills in case they get captured." He turned to Bearach and Rónán. "Leave your swords 'n dust yourselves. Just keep a dagger hidden. You can walk inta their camp there." He pointed down to the right where slaves worked near a patch of trees. "Come back here by day's end or when ya find our kin. Get 'em ta stay t'gether in the night so we can mount a rescue."

Bearach and Rónán rubbed themselves with dirt and removed their swords so they would blend in with the slaves. Then they made their way into the forest to get close to the quarry. They looked out from behind the birch trees and spied where the miners dumped large rocks and boulders to be crushed. A few slave masters lingered at different points around the quarry, but they hardly paid attention to the slaves. They seemed content to sit leisurely under canopies as everyone worked around them.

"The slave masters are barely awake," Rónán commented. "Except for that one in the high tower. He looks about like a cat figurin' where his next meal would be."

"Sure, we'll need ta slip in while he's lookin' off," Bearach said. He watched the miners come to the pile of limestone in fragmented groups. Most of them carried stones with their bare hands while others used small carts to bring larger stones to the pile. There, men with hammers pounded the large stones into small chunks, so other slaves could shovel the broken stone into horse drawn carts that took them to the kiln house.

"We can slip in one at a time behind the last in line," Bearach noted.

"Right then, you can have the first go," Rónán said. "Keep eyes on each other. If ya find our clansmen, signal with a fist ta your chest and find your way back ta the hill."

Bearach waited for an opportune time to go. When a break in the miners came, he ran off to stand behind the last person in line. After he snuck behind him, he looked about uncomfortably. He just realized he jumped into a line of men holding large rocks and he was empty handed. He fidgeted about wondering what to do. All the stones were well ahead of everyone. He couldn't just grab one in front of everybody and get back in line.

Rónán watched him from the forest and sighed. "Grand báthlach ["bahh-lokhk"; awkward clown]!" he said gobsmacked. "What's he doin'? Pick up somethin'!" Rónán whispered anxiously.

As the line moved forward, Bearach knew he couldn't stand

there empty-handed for long. He saw the young man in front of him was standing stooped over with a very large stone, so he fell forward and knocked it out of his hands. "Pardon!" Bearach said stumbling. "Pardon! Let me help ya carry that."

The tired slave looked at Bearach with a timid frown. "Sure, glad for the help," he replied quietly. Bearach helped the young man and they carried the boulder together.

Rónán sighed in relief to see Bearach infiltrate the mine without incident. *I think I'll hide under the dray,* he decided as he pondered how to get into the quarry. He crept through the forest to a place where he could approach the horse drawn dray that carted away the broken rock. He waited in the trees for some time before he snuck out. Bearach had already left with the group of slaves and went back into the quarry's depths to haul more boulders out.

Rónán moved swiftly in between the activity of the people who loaded the wagon. When their backs were turned, he slipped underneath the dray and waited. Soon the loading was done and they moved the dray to the kiln house as Rónán hung to the bottom of the carriage. When it stopped, he slipped out and entered the kiln house.

Inside, he saw dozens of people working. Most of them were women. They sifted the rock by selecting larger pieces for the kilns. Men shoveled the selected rocks into large furnace kilns made of clay and bricks. Then they layered the limestone with wood and peat to fuel the fire. Other men brought the fired stone out so it could be smashed into powder.

Rónán went to the huge pile of coarse limestone near the entrance where women sifted through it. He tried to keep hidden by staying behind the side of the pile that faced away from most of the activity. A young, blonde girl knelt there and monotonously picked stones from the pile. She placed them into a bucket and hardly noticed

Rónán when he knelt down next to her.

"Far off from Loch an Scáthain, this place," Rónán commented trying to get a reaction from the girl.

Ula looked up at him warily and wondered if he was a threat. Her soiled face and dress mirrored the torn up condition of her spirit. She wasn't going to speak to him, but when she saw kindness in his eyes and that the style of his léine was familiar, she decided to trust him. "You're not from Loch an Scáthain. I know everyone from there," she said.

Rónán smiled. Finding one of their clansmen was easier than he thought. "You're right on that. I was hopin' you were from there." He looked about cautiously to see that they were still safe. "I'm an Eachraighe scout. We've come ta take our kinsmen back ta Torthúil, errr. . ." He flustered with his words when he remembered the kingdom was split. ". . . Back home. Do ya know where the rest 'a ya are?"

"We're all here," she replied. "A dozen 'a us. My mam's just over there." She pointed to Flann at the other end of the kiln house where she stood covered in white dust with other women. They were crushing the fired limestone in hand-turned mills that sent white powder flying everywhere.

Rónán heard the men outside. They almost finished unloading. "We haven't much time. Can ya get everyone t'gether?"

"They take us all inta camp at the end of the day," she said.

"Right then, let all our kinsmen know we will try ta free ya in the night. Keep t'gether. We don't want ta miss anyone." Ula acknowledged with a look of appreciation.

Rónán got up and quietly went to the door. The men outside were still shoveling the stone from the cart. They threw it from the back of the dray onto another pile on the ground. Their backs were turned, but there was nowhere for Rónán to flee or hide. They were next to the seashore and the forest was a long ways away. Tall cliffs enclosed the quarry, and his escape into the forest had nearly half a mile of bare ground through the quarry's activity.

Rónán crept along the wall of the kiln house to see if there was somewhere to hide behind it. He noticed Bearach still carried boulders with the group he had met before. Bearach looked about frequently to see if Rónán was around and saw him leaning against the kiln house. Rónán signaled that he found Ula and they should get back to Cathal. Bearach gave Rónán a quick nod of acknowledgement and kept working with the other slaves.

Behind the kiln house, Rónán found the area busy with people loading ships. There was nowhere to go there, so he went back towards the men unloading the dray. He tried to go around behind their backs and slip back under the cart again, but one of the men turned around and saw him. The man froze wondering what Rónán was doing.

"Who are ya ta wander 'bout?" the man asked Rónán.

"Right!" the other man added. "None 'a us get a rest. Get back ta your station!"

The commotion caught the attention of a nearby slave master. He stood up from his chair and looked toward the kiln house. Bearach watched anxiously as he saw attention going to Rónán. He thought quickly and dropped the stone he was carrying. He fell down and screamed in mock pain to draw attention away from Rónán. As everyone looked towards Bearach, Rónán ran for the sea and dove in quick as he could.

The frigid water made him gasp. The water chilled him like he had spent a night buried under a mountain of snow, but Rónán was an excellent swimmer and disappeared into the sea. No one noticed him dive in, but a slave master went to see what was wrong with Bearach. He continued to scream in pain and held his ankle.

"Who's twistin' hay?!" the stout slave master questioned. He stood over Bearach with a club.

"Me ankle's knackered!" Bearach shouted through gritting teeth.

The slave master hit Bearach's shoulder with the club. "Get up! Let's see ya walk!"

Bearach got up and feigned a limp. The slave master pushed him and tried to knock him over, but Bearach instinctively caught himself from falling.

"You're a right aindeiseoir ["æn-jeh-shor"; an unfortunate person], ya are!" the slave master scoffed sarcastically. "A proper poor soul might get my pity, but there's hardly anythin' wrong with ya. Get back ta work!" He struck the back of Bearach's waist with the club and noticed it hit something hard underneath his clothes. The slave master raised his club high in the air and yelled to his men around him. "Grab this one!" he ordered.

Bearach knew the slave master struck the dagger underneath the folds of his léine. What could he do? He looked about weighing his options as two men came to hold him. *Should I fight back? Run?* he wondered. As the men came he decided to let them take him. *The lads have things in hand,* he thought. *Rónán got away. The plan will go on. No use in alarming them any further.*

The men grabbed Bearach's arms and held him secure. The slave master walked behind him and felt under the hanging folds of fabric at Bearach's waist. He found the dagger and pulled it out. He noticed it had the Eachraighe seal on its hilt.

"From the south are ya?" the slave master questioned. "What are ya doin' here? This is no common knife."

"I came only ta find my clansmen, sir," Bearach answered.

"Thought ya could sneak in here 'n take what ya want?" the

slave master sneered. "Let's show 'em what we do ta those who twist the hay!"

They led him to the watchtower and hung him from his hands on one of the tower's beams. The slave master struck him several times on the back and stomach with the club. "Where are the rest 'a your friends?!" he interrogated and struck him further.

Bearach grit through the pain and answered, "I'm alone."

The slave master hit him again. "Sure then, are ya that stupid?" He ordered everyone, "Let this one hang a few 'n get him workin' again! He'll be happy ta join his clan in the pit. Back ta work, all 'a ya!"

Rónán labored heavily as he swam across the bay. The water was much colder than he was used to. He could barely breathe in the icy sea. *Amaideach! I didn't bring my seal skin for this!* he thought as he fought the rough waves and chilling water. If he wasn't such a strong swimmer, he would have been lost to the sea.

He made it to the other side of the narrow bay and crawled onto the stony beach. His body made a crunching thud on the wet pebbles as he collapsed with fatigue. "That was a hard swim!" he muttered to himself. Then he turned around onto his back and looked up into the sunny sky. The bright sky warmed him as he lay there to catch his breath.

After some time he got up and took off his léine. He wrung out as much water as he could and put it back on. Then he took off running to the left and made his way back around the bay to find the hill where Cathal and Neese waited. It took him over an hour to run through miles of hills and forest, but he finally made his way back.

"What took ya?" Neese asked Rónán. "We couldn't see where ya went."

"Had a right swim in the bay!" he exclaimed. "Remind me never ta swim the North Sea again! Not much better than jumpin' inta a frozen lake dead in winter! Have ya seen Bearach?"

"They found 'im out," Neese replied. "Strung him up and put him back ta work."

"Ya must have good news ta be here now," Cathal queried.

"Surely," Rónán said. "I made contact with a girl. She'll get our clansmen ready ta flee t'night."

"Grand work altogether," Cathal said. "We'll keep watch. Grab a kip 'n bite. We've a long night ahead."

The men watched over the quarry until work ceased soon after the sun touched the horizon. The slaves were rounded up and marched out on the west road through a gully between the hills. Cathal and his men followed the caravan carefully as everyone but a few guards left the mine.

Ula had already spread the word of their rescue among the slaves who worked in the kiln house. Throughout their march, they anxiously looked about the hills for signs of their kinsmen liberators. However, Cathal and his men kept out of sight as they rode their horses far behind the group and among the trees that bordered the road.

"No sign 'a Lorgaire 'round here," Neese commented as they tracked the slaves. "Hadn't spied any since comin' thirty miles a Cloch Lom."

"The North is far from Torthúil," Cathal replied. "Little use ta post sentry scouts so deep in your own land. I expect we have no worry 'a bein' spotted till we get back down towards Chnámh an Áidh."

"That boggy river town?!" Neese remembered. "You'll not catch me swimmin' those murky waters again!"

"You must be slaggin'!" Rónán laughed. "That swim was a charm compared ta the North Sea! I would've had ta float ya in a babby's pram ["prahm"; baby carriage, stroller] t'day if ya were with me!"

Neese huffed with urgency. "A *pram!?* You'd be in the pram if ya spied the serpent swimmin' in that river!"

"Banjax ya Neese!" Cathal retorted. "You goin' on 'bout that sea monster again? Nobody else saw a thin'! I would've had a right fine swim if it weren't for your kickin' 'bout like babby!"

The men laughed over the teasing they gave Neese, but he continued to hold a stern face and stuck to his story. Their joking stopped when they saw the people turn left off the main road.

"They made camp already?" Rónán said. "Hardly a mile from the quarry."

Neese was riding at the foremost point and looked closer to the left. He suddenly stopped his horse and told the others to stop. "Quick! Get deeper inta the trees. They're marchin' straight inta a ring fort!"

Cathal peered ahead to see the fort. "Right, a big one too! Inta the forest before their watchmen see us!"

They went deeper into the trees and found a way up a hill that overlooked the fort. They hid among the trees there and contemplated what to do. The ring fort was a large circle of stone that surrounded many buildings inside. Its outside wall was meters thick and almost 30 feet high. Guards were positioned on top of the wall, but they were relaxed and languid. They hardly moved or showed interest in their duties.

The small village inside the ring fort had a large stone building set towards the wall opposite the gate. It was a two-story house that was decorated more elaborately than the other small cottages and buildings around it.

"The fort looks ta protect someone's estate," Cathal noted. "The buildin's 'round the mansion are for servants 'n soldiers. Don't see a market or any other village houses down there."

"How are we ta make rescue?" Rónán wondered. "They'll close the gate at sundown, right quick now. We can't hope ta scale that wall or breach 'em once they shut."

"Right," Neese affirmed. "We need ta find our way in before the gate closes."

Cathal pondered. "There are a few guards at the gate, but the slaves are housed near it. If we could get in and gather 'em quick 'nough, we can rush them out. The guards don't look ta be hardened soldiers. Doesn't look ta be a single hardchaw among 'em. Not one has forged armor 'n only a few have swords. We can break out 'a their ranks if they put up a fight."

"How are we ta carry off a dozen of our clan?" Neese asked. "Even if we break out of the pursuit here, they could have the garrison from Cloch Lom on us with armored riders ta run us down."

"We'll need ta take more horses then," Cathal surmised. "The stables are near the gate as well." He looked up to find the sun. It threw long shadows through the forest and was already moving under the hills to the west. "Millie up!" Cathal ordered. "We've not much time. Get all your armor and arms on. No use in hidin' our mark in this fight." He looked to Rónán. "Get back down ta the road and ride in from the quarry. Let 'em see ya. We'll hide in the forest near the gate till ya have 'em distracted. Then we'll charge the gate and mount the rescue."

Rónán and Neese acknowledged the orders and got ready to put their plan into action. In a few minutes they made their way to their respective positions - Rónán went back to the road and trotted toward the ring fort while Cathal and Neese waited in the forest with Bearach's horse in tow.

"Wait for Rónán ta distract 'em with a gallop," Cathal said. "Take down their archers before they do any good."

Neese acknowledged. They could see Rónán coming down the road. He was still at a leisurely trot. Everyone at the fort already had their eyes on him. They watched him curiously but were not alarmed. From the distance, they could tell he was a soldier, but they could not tell he was an Eachraighe. None of the rescue party had the distinguishing mantles and bronze armor of the commanders, but their chainmail and leather armor made it obvious they were respectable soldiers.

Rónán watched the guards carefully as he approached. A handful lined the wall and two stood at the gate. *It's time,* he thought. "Give it a go!" he yelled to his horse. He hunched down on his horse and they jumped quickly to a full gallop. The archers on the wall quickly lifted their bows and aimed for Rónán.

"Now!" Cathal ordered. He charged out of the trees and went straight for the open gate. Neese came out slightly slower with Bearach's horse on a line trailing him. Cathal took the guards at the gate by surprise and struck one down as he entered the ring fort.

Neese stopped near the foot of the wall and brought up his bow. He quickly fired arrows at the archers trained on Rónán. His perfect aim disarmed the threat in barely a handful of seconds.

Neese yelled at Rónán to hurry. "Bolt! Will ya!? They're closin' the gate!" He slung his bow on his back and waited for Rónán. Rónán picked up his pace and drew his sword. He soon joined Neese and took the lead. They charged the gate together. Rónán cut down the remaining guard at the gate and they entered the fort unhindered.

Cathal rallied the slaves and escorted them to the stables.

Guards ran at them from every direction, but Cathal handled them with ease. The fort's unprepared defenses were hardly a match for well trained soldiers.

"Cover us with your arrows," Rónán told Neese as he grabbed the reins for Bearach's horse. "I'll find Bearach."

They went toward the house where the slaves were kept. The area teemed with slaves running everywhere. Some of them even made it outside the fort before the gate closed, but Bearach was nowhere in sight.

"Where is he?" Rónán wondered. He turned toward the stables to join Cathal when he saw Bearach there. He was close to Cathal, but had a dagger to his throat. The slave master held Bearach firm and threatened to kill him.

"I knew you didn't come alone," the slave master said to Bearach. "Stop!" he commanded Cathal and the others. "Ya wouldn't want ta see your kinsman spilt all about, would ya?"

Cathal ordered everyone to stop. They reluctantly ceased the rescue and stood silent with their eyes on the slave master and Bearach. Some of them were already on horses. Flann and Ula were jumping onto a horse together when everyone stopped around them.

"Get off your horses!" the slave master commanded. "The gate's closed. Nowhere ta go."

More guards came to surround them as they dismounted their horses. Cathal, Rónán, and Neese continued to wield their swords and defended themselves from being captured. The remaining slaves gathered behind Cathal and waited to see what would happen.

"Put your swords down!" the slave master urged. "Put 'em down or your lad'll meet the dust!"

Neese and Rónán watched Cathal for cues. Cathal didn't lay down his sword though. His eyes were fixed on the slave master and

Bearach, but he noticed someone in stately and colorful clothing approach from behind the crowd.

The slave master grumbled impatiently and pressed the dagger farther into Bearach's throat. The blade drew blood, but Cathal and his men stood firm. Just then, the man in fine clothes broke through the people.

"What's the ruction here?!" Braede asked loudly.

Flann and Ula immediately recognized Braede and went forward.

"Seems we have a band 'a Eachraighe aimin' ta free our slaves, Master," the slave master said.

Flann and Ula rushed forward into the open. Their presence surprised Braede when he recognized them.

"Flann, Ula? What are ya doin' here?" Braede said innocently.

Anger flared on Flann's face. "If ya cared ta see your slaves, you'd have known we were here long ago!" she fumed. "Ya bought a lot 'a us from Laochmarú's plunder 'a Loch an Scátháin!"

Shocked remorse gripped Braede. He had no idea he had enslaved his friends. "I'm very sorry, Flann. I sent my servant ta buy slaves in Chnámh an Áidh. I never knew anyone had come from Loch an Scátháin."

"There's good reasons we have no slaves back home," Flann retorted. "Your mind would tell ya the right course."

Braede felt guilty for enslaving his friends, but slavery was simply a way of life in the north. He didn't think it was wrong to have forced labor in his mines. "Slaves are a matter common as leaves on trees here," he said. "But. . ." he pondered. "I do value my friends and my time spent with ya." He was careful not to mention Torthúil out of fear that his servants would rebel against him. Their kingdom loyalties were mixed after the Áiteoir conquered the north, but he didn't want to take the chance of being viewed as a traitor among them. He needed to have loyal servants under him.

Braede turned to the slave master. "Let them go," he commanded. Then he addressed everyone, "Any slave that wishes ta go with them may go. Any who wish ta remain as my servant may stay. I will no longer keep slaves but pay a reasonable wage for any who want the work."

The slave master released Bearach. He turned around to face the slave master and held out his hand. "I've no ill for ya, sir," Bearach said, "but I'd be havin' my dagger back. I'd leave it ta ya if it weren't that my da gave it ta me."

The slave master frowned and gave Bearach his dagger. Bearach joined Cathal and the others who were mounting their horses.

"Before ya go," Braede asked Flann with concern. "Have ya word of Brónach?"

"She mourned your leavin' up ta the day we were taken," Flann answered. "We don't know what happened ta her after that."

"I often regret leavin' as I did," Braede said. "I meant no harm ta anyone. I only wanted ta return ta my homeland. I hope ya understand. I wish ya well. May ya go in peace."

Flann put her hand on Braede's shoulder. "Thank you, Braede. May you fare well. Ádh mór ["ah more"; Good Luck]. Slán." she told him with a comforting smile.

Cathal and his men led their clansmen out of the ring fort without resistance. Most of the slaves elected to remain as workers, but a few handfuls joined the party. They set out under darkening skies to make the long march back to the south. Most of them were on foot, but they were all glad to start their journey home. They would have to travel over a hundred miles through enemy country to make it back to the River Valley.

"We camp in the silver birch till the land shows no light," Cathal told them. "Then we travel under cover 'a night and among the shadows of the hills during the days till we reach home. Be silent and mindful. We don't want ta attract the enemy."

*T*he sun sunk low in the western sky with layers of wispy clouds strung around the orange-violet glow of sunset. The River Seascannach stretched parallel to the horizon with clusters of trees strewn about its boggy shores. Teague and Alastar rested inside a small grove set atop a high hill. They had spent days traveling from the River Valley, carefully moving under the cover of night and thick forests. Now they rested in a grove of trees by the River Seascannach waiting for the dark of night to travel again.

"Do ya think the drought covers the whole isle?" Alastar asked as he watched the sun sink into the horizon. "This area appears dry. The anbobracht may cover the whole isle."

"Our last pelt 'a rain was in Loch an Scátháin," Teague noted. "We were covered in gray damp that battle with Laochmarú."

"Ya needn't remind me of that day!" Alastar cringed. "It was the last nawful cold day I remember! Been right rank with heat since then."

"Surely, and the full height 'a summer hasn't even come 'round. But it seems the whole isle is not witherin' away. Gearóid spoke of heavy rains in Lacharan when they came back. Had him and Conn soppin' wet under a cartful 'a hay when they were smuggled out of the city. Even meters 'a straw over their heads did not shield 'em from the rain that day!"

As they talked, the loud screech of a hawk went through the trees. Bress tilted her head toward the sound's direction and made some low agitated squawks.

"A wild seabhac?" Alastar asked.

"That was no hawk," Teague replied. "A good mimic, though."

He got up and went to Bress's saddle perch. He lifted her up and gave the command to hunt. Bress took off flying and soared about the river. Teague came back and sat down with Alastar. "Watch the skies 'round Bress," he said. "You'll soon see what made the call."

Alastar watched a large group of trees and saw Bress fly toward them. When she came near, a colossal cloud of small silvery birds took off from the branches as if all the leaves suddenly jumped into the air and turned into a swarm of fluttering, flashing tin foil. The great flock of birds flew in a massive group that churned and tumbled through the sky, like a rapidly changing cloud of shapes that swooped and spun above the river. The vibrant colors of the sun and sky reflected on their white, blue and green gemlike feathers. Teague and Alastar could hear the intense murmur of the many thousand wings flapping as the birds shifted about to avoid Bress. Their myriad of wing beats reminded Alastar of the rushing sound of wind through tree branches. The great hum of wings sung like a wind's rumbling melody leaping from leaf to leaf.

"What are they?" Alastar wondered. "They fly like the great schools of cold fish in the sea."

"Starlin's," Teague said. "They flock near the river for all the midges, flies 'n such. When the lights 'r set right like now, they look as jewels tumblin' through the sky. Grand at mimicry. We heard one callin' like a hawk earlier, ta warn its flock."

Bress continued to circle the giant cloud of birds and then dove into its outer edge. They watched her come out of the cloud with a starling in its talons. She flew back to them and perched on a nearby branch with her meal - a hand-sized, brown bird with feathers outlined in bright white and shimmered with blue and green. After Bress left the starling flock, the birds settled back down into the trees for the night. Their busy chatter of squeaks and chirps soon died in the low light of the fading sky.

Teague looked out toward the river in front of them. He scanned back and forth carefully for any signs of the enemy in the glowing landscape. "Keep your eyes open for Lorgaire. They'd likely be hidden among the unglowing trees and bushes as we are, but there's chance we'll see one move among the land's glow."

"Right," Alastar acknowledged. "We were blessed in our travels with no signs of the enemy."

"We traveled many miles from any cities," Teague commented. "But a day's march past the river'll bring us close ta Lochtán an Eidhneáin ["Lahkh-tun ahn Eye-nine"], the vine covered city of the Muir Airgid. We'll soon find the road leadin' there, but sure as winter brings ice, there's bound ta be watchmen and scouts near the city. We need ta travel the forests 'n hills in the north if we're ta keep our path due west under cover." He continued to stare intently at the landscape to find signs of the enemy. "I hope there aren't any scouts near us, but we'll set out when the land goes dark and be attentive ta flashes from their eyes as we did that night runnin' out 'a Loch an Scáthán."

Alastar remembered the descent on the mountainside when the Áiteoir party chased them into the plains. The flashing glints from the Lorgaire eyes were like faint sparks that threatened to ignite their calm escape into a deadly fire.

"Be grand ta keep far from any Áiteoir this trip," Alastar noted. "Why is it their scouts have eyes that spark light?"

"The Lorgaire are a clan from the Áiteoir deserts. It's said their ancestral father was a tracker of renown skill. He could spot a single clover on bare rock more than ten stone throws away and find signs 'a game as if the land shouted out ta him. He once tracked a great deer for days through the dune desert ta the Rásúir Mountains. Rain and steamy fog covered the black obsidian cliffs all the days of his hunt, but his arrow found its mark and he carried the stag home. They say the stag was big as the one we found on the valley peak. *That* may be a bit 'a horse's hoof, but seems stories of his eyes glowin' like embers at dusk are true. The whole Lorgaire clan inherited those sparkin' eyes."

"And that uncanny trackin' ability," Alastar added. "The Áiteoir were quick on us that night we ran ta Lacharan."

"They had a fair notion 'a where we'd be," Teague reassured. "They'll be hard pressed ta find us here if we're careful. Quit your worryin', just be mindful 'a surroundin's. Get your rest now. We make the river crossin' after all the land goes dark."

Alastar watched over the gentle slopes of land around them as he leaned against a tree. A slight breeze made the reeds and long grass gently sway along the river bank. The dark and murky river was like an immense winding road of black slate against the bright green and grain yellow of the land around it. Alastar's eyes grew heavy as the land dimmed through the evening and he soon fell asleep.

Hours later, Alastar opened his eyes. He could barely see anything around him, but the peaceful quiet of the river was replaced with a loud cacophony of chirping and buzzing insects. Their noise was deafening. He looked about and rubbed his eyes to help his vision adjust to the low light. Slowly he could see the dark forms of the land and river in front of him. They were barely visible under the starlight.

Then bright blinks of light flashed off to his left. He looked over into the distant trees and saw many dots of light flickering on and off. *Lorgaire!* he worried. He nearly jumped up in alarm but stayed down and put his hand on the grip of his sword. "Teague!" he whispered urgently. "Teague!"

Teague was sitting nearby. "What is it?"

"Glints 'a light ta the left!"

"Ya mean in the trees?" Teague wondered.

"Surely! Don't ya see 'em?!" Alastar said hurriedly.

"Sure, sure, lampróga ["lahm-proh-gah"]," Teague affirmed without a hint of concern.

"Lampróga?" Alastar questioned. "Ya mean Áiteoir foot soldiers?"

Teague chuckled quietly. "Haven't ya ever seen lightnin' bugs? They've been flittin' over there the last hour."

Alastar wasn't familiar with fireflies. "What are those?" he asked.

"Lightnin' bugs - lampróga," Teague said. "Just large flies that light up their bottoms. They come out durin' summer. Scores of 'em 'round the Seascannach."

Alastar eased his sword hand. "I never heard of such a thin'. Have ya seen any sign of the enemy?"

"Not one bit," Teague noted. "Good thin' you're done with that kip. It's time we go. Follow me ta the river. I saw a dry path down. And remember, Lorgaire don't move like lampróga. The flies bob and hover and flash bright. Enemy scouts'll flash faint and not move so erratically, not unless they're dancin' some jig in the dark," he joked.

They got on their horses and quietly slipped down the hill to the river bank. Teague was careful to follow the path he saw through the bog so they wouldn't fall into any deep, muddy hollows. As they neared the river bank, Alastar remembered Neese talking about his scary swim in the river.

"Do ya think Neese saw anythin' in the river?" Alastar asked.

"Ya mean his sea serpent?" Teague remembered. "I'm sure he saw somethin', but it was likely a great pike. They grow bigger than you or me. Menacin' lookin' fish, long, 'n fangs that could hold onta wet ice. Not bad ta eat if ya can get past all the tiny bones stuck all through the flesh."

They stopped at the river bank and scanned the opposite side. The river was less than 100 meters wide, but the water was deep and flowed swift. They got off their horses and waded into the water.

"Time ta swim like a seal," Teague said.

They went deeper and deeper into the water and pulled their horses with them. Their horses didn't like being in deep water and started to slow and pull backwards.

"Swimmin's not your ta your likin', boy, but you can make it," Alastar encouraged Éimhín. They kept pulling on the reins to urge their horses on. Soon they all swam fearlessly and pushed with vigor to the far shore. They reached the far bank without any problems, but they were drenched.

"We'll not dry quick in the night," Teague commented.

"At least the air is warm," Alastar replied. "The river was a fierce chill."

They got back on their horses and started to ride west. Teague led the way at a slow, careful pace. They had barely gone a few meters before a small bird rushed out of a patch of long grass some distance away. Teague watched it fly north and became alarmed when it didn't settle back down. He drew his sword and charged the spot where the bird came out. His sudden movement shocked Alastar. He didn't know what was happening, but he followed Teague with his sword drawn.

Almost as soon as they began their charge, a Lorgaire jumped out of the grass and ran from them. Teague quickly ran him down and struck him with the sword. The scout fell to the ground and Teague dismounted to examine him. Alastar rode up to them as Teague looked through the Lorgaire's clothes and belongings.

"How did ya know he was there?" Alastar queried.

"Birds don't oft startle from distance or fly clear out 'a sight. When it flew straight north without stop, I feared it was an éanshee carryin' a scout's message. Appears it was. Chnámh an Áidh is a short flight north 'a here. We need ta bolt. Whoever lays in Chnámh an Áidh will soon know we're here. The Cairn Cath ["Karrn Kahh"] Road is just west. We can make a full gallop on it, but we can't risk throwin' our horses down in the bog here. Follow me out slow."

They got back on their horses and tried to make their way out of the boggy marshland. Even though they took great care, many deep patches of quick mud were impossible to see in the dark. They were caught in knee-deep mud pits that threatened to swallow their hopes of escaping to the Cairn Cath Road. At times they struggled many minutes just to work themselves free of a single deep pit.

After hours of pulling themselves out of the bog land, they found the road. Alastar and Teague were soiled through with mud and muck, but they were glad to find the packed dirt of the road.

"Was it my idea ta swim through miles 'a bog in the dark?" Teague said in jest. "Remind me ta wait on dawn's break before we do that again!"

Alastar felt all the dirt and debris on his clothes. He could feel his léine was a gritty mess but it was too dark for him to see what it looked like."Right!" he replied. "Ya should've told me ta change before we ran 'cross. Amber'll be right mad seein' what I did ta my fine léine."

"Bah!" Teague scoffed. "It's your war shirt! Made ta soil on your journeys. Besides, she handed ya a spare set 'a clean clothes before we left, did she not?"

"Sure, but they'd not do me good after soakin' in the river," Alastar noted.

"Our run through the night will dry everythin' quick 'nough. We'd best go on. There's no sign 'a pursuit, but the Áiteoir will scour this road soon as they can. We need ta take advantage of it as long as we're able before we break north."

They continued west on the Cairn Cath Road as fast as they could urge their horses. The well packed road made their travel fast and easy. Their horses galloped for nearly twenty miles before they had to stop for rest. The sky began to brighten behind them as dawn approached. They waited on the road and checked their surroundings. No one was behind or ahead of them, but as the land started to take in the sun's light, it revealed a dark mass in the south.

"A huge army marches," Teague noted as he looked south.

Alastar turned to see. "Do ya think it's Laochmarú?"

"From the size of the march, I don't doubt it's the general. They must've come up from Túr an Tairbh. It's time we get off the road. It can't be more than an hour ta Lochtán an Eidhneáin. It'll be slow from here, but the hills 'n forest will give us cover and a diminished pace will help us hold our strength."

"So long as we keep distance from their army," Alastar said.

"Even slowed in the forest we can keep ahead of 'em. They're still far off."

After a few more moments rest, they turned off the road and entered the forest to the north. The area was covered by elm and oak trees everywhere, but the foliage was loose, so traveling through it was unencumbered compared to the dense trees and brush in the River Valley. The sparse forest reminded Alastar of the forests near his home in Netleaf. The last day he traveled in Eritirim came back fresh to his mind.

"Looks just as if we're back home," Alastar said to Éimhín. Éimhín gave a quiet affirming nicker.

"Your homeland is like this?" Teague asked.

"It is. Our forests appear just as this and the plains outside Lacharan are like the green fields around my hometown. I wonder if my mother is lookin' across the fields ta watch for my return."

"I don't know how she could," Teague surmised. "You traveled ages past ta be here. All you've done since comin' ta Rathúnas has long gone ta history for your mam. If ya *could* return, I imagine ya might not have disappeared ta her at all."

"Right, I can smell the brown soda bread and coddle stew she was aimin' ta fix for my return. I miss all the things my mom had on the cooker. If she wasn't tendin' ta the garden, she'd be fixin' somethin' in the kitchen."

They sauntered west through the terrain almost a mile north of the road. The sun rose against their backs and soon the forest took on the bright glow of day. It was quiet compared to the vibrant buzz of animals in the River Valley. Only a few bird calls and the faint skittering of small, puffy red squirrels among the trees accompanied their trek through the woods.

The forest was open and empty as they continued riding through the morning. They thought their plan to bypass the eyes around Lochtán an Eidhneáin would be successful, but as the sun cast shorter shadows across their backs, Teague noticed the prominent chatter of birds ahead of them. He signaled Alastar to stop and listen. The rapid chirping of birds off in the distance gave him concern.

"Ya hear the redpolls makin' alarm calls?" Teague said. "All up front and on our flanks."

Alastar listened intently. "Somethin' makin' them nervous?" he asked.

"*A lot* 'a somethin's 'cross our way," Teague noted. "Could be a pack 'a wolves huntin' fallow deer, but more than not, a group 'a scouts is out huntin' us."

"I don't see anythin'," Alastar said.

"I don't either, but they must be comin' from the city. Let's press farther north," Teague suggested.

They turned right to go northwest deeper into the forest. The fast, sharp calls of the redpolls sounded closer, but the forest continued to appear empty. Teague looked about anxiously. *What are they chattering about? There's nothing in sight,* he thought. They pressed forward cautiously when an arrow came down from ahead and pierced Teague's chest plate. It stuck to his outer armor but did not pierce his chainmail shirt.

"Lorgaire in the trees!" he yelled as he pulled the arrow out and threw it aside. "Swords! Ride fast and weave!"

They drew their swords and charged ahead in zig-zag lines through the trees to avoid the enemy archers. They soon passed the line of Lorgaire, but as soon as the threat of arrows was gone, they heard galloping horses approach from the south. Teague looked and saw a dozen light cavalry riders pursue them.

"The garrison from Lochtán an Eidhneáin is on us!" Teague yelled. "Forward quick!"

They burst forward as fast as they could. Alastar and Éimhín were quick to overtake Teague's lead. It was apparent their many days of racing through the dense forest of the valley with Amber and Muirgel gave them an advantage. Teague never saw anyone gallop so quickly through the trees. However, he wasn't sure of their options. The only thing in their plan was to reach the coast of the Muir Airgid, but what then? Their pursuers would surely follow them there. He decided it best to face them since their numbers were manageable and the cover of the forest could be used to their advantage.

"Lad!" Teague yelled. "Turn and face 'em! Let your trainin' make its mark!"

Alastar looked back to see Teague turn around and charge the riders behind them. He turned Éimhín around. "Time we battle,"

Alastar told him with confidence. He pointed his sword forward and spurred Éimhín toward the fight. A cry of strength rushed out of his mouth as he engaged the enemy.

Teague and Alastar made quick strikes on the enemy and used the trees to prevent themselves from being overrun by their greater numbers. They rode around the trees as easily as the sunlight illuminated every corner of the forest. They struck down most of the riders in minutes. Teague was proud that Alastar was able to fight well in the battle. He had progressed a long way since their first battles together. He remembered how Alastar had to stand away from the fight and needed rescue in the plains outside Lacharan. Now he was certain Alastar could live up to the name of a skillful Eachraighe soldier.

They had nearly finished dispatching the Áiteoir when a loud rumbling shook the forest. They looked about as they fought and saw a long line of dark heavy cavalry rushing through the trees.

"Laochmarú found us!" Teague yelled to Alastar. "*Ride!*"

He moved quick to help Alastar fell the last rider. As soon as they were free, they turned back toward the west and galloped away. They both looked back at the party that pursued them. Laochmarú was leading a charge of hundreds of armored horses. It appeared his entire unit of heavy cavalry chased them through the forest.

Teague and Alastar sped through the trees and kept their distance from Laochmarú, but they wondered what to do once they hit the coast. Could they stand against hundreds of heavily armored riders? Teague remembered how hard the fight was against Laochmarú's men when there were hundreds of fellow Eachraighe to help in the fight. How could they fight back with just the two of them?

They had no time to worry but pressed on toward their goal of reaching the coast. They put all their trust into what the currents told them to do. Many miles flew by and the forest became sunnier as the number of trees diminished. Alastar was a ways ahead of Teague and broke through the edge of forest first. The sky opened up into a bright blue horizon with an immense sea under it. The sight of so much glowing blue and silver shimmering upon the water flooded Alastar's senses. He almost forgot to stop Éimhín from running straight off the cliff in front of them.

"Whoa!" Alastar shouted as he tugged on the reins. He looked backwards and saw Teague burst out of the forest. He, too, was stunned to see the bright, wide open space around them. He rode to Alastar and surveyed the surroundings.

They stood at the end of a high cliff that overlooked the Muir Airgid. The Silver Sea shined of its own light with giant, streaming waves of opalescence that flowed to and fro underneath the water. The flickering white gleams of sunlight on the wave crests at the surface combined with the glowing water below to give a mesmerizing effect. They almost forgot about the army that pursued them.

Teague looked around further and wondered what to do. The cliff extended far south to their left, but on their right, the land sloped downward into grassy hills that blended into a sandy shoreline.

"What now?" Alastar asked.

Just then, Laochmarú's cavalry burst through the forest behind them. As soon as the general saw Teague and Alastar trapped at the end of the cliff, he stopped the charge and trotted forward. He told his men to encircle them so they could not escape.

Alastar looked out to the sea again. He felt a calm peace about him despite seeing Laochmarú and his men come to block their escape. "We've come ta the sea," he said under his breath. "What are we ta do now?"

In that moment, something small burst out of the sea a long distance away. It was so far away he couldn't tell what it was, but when it continued flying up he saw it was a bird.

"Teague! Somethin' flew out of the water!" he told him. Teague was focused on Laochmarú's approach and the hundreds of riders making a circle around them, so he didn't turn to look.

"What is it?" Teague asked.

"*Look!*" Alastar urged. "Ya think it's a gannet?"

Teague turned around annoyed. "Lad! What are ya lookin' at gannets for?!" Then he looked closer and noted the bird didn't have the markings of a gannet. "It's about the right size, but that's no gannet. They have white bodies and black wingtips."

The large bird swooped around and showed the unmistakable markings of the Seabhac Azure.

"It's the Azure!" Alastar yelled.

"Surely is!" Teague acknowledged.

They watched it circle above the water, and only moments later they saw the sea underneath it drain away as if an invisible, great door opened into the depths. The water made a ramp that descended down into the sea and a party of several dozen spearmen marched up to the surface. Teague and Alastar watched in amazement.

"Inta the sea!" Teague said quickly. Alastar acknowledged.

They turned around to face Laochmarú. He had started to gallop toward them when he saw how intently Alastar and Teague stared at the sea. Laochmarú came with a few men by his side, but they were still several meters away. The Áiteoir also had not yet fully encircled them.

"Down ta the hills!" Teague told Alastar.

They burst toward a small opening between the cliff edge and the enemy riders. When they started their gallop, the Áiteoir moved to block and engage them. Their exit was quickly shut by many dark riders. Most of the Áiteoir turned to chase them and make the circle around them tighter.

"Use your speed, lad!" Teague told Alastar, and they turned and weaved separately through any gaps they could see. They ran in tight circles and slashed through several riders to make their way to the north end of the cliff. It was a bold and determined fight through a dense field of solid, moving walls that tried to knock them over at every chance. Teague and Alastar kept their speed up, though, and used their momentum to crash through the blockade. After a tiring push, they found themselves on the far side of the enemy and rushed down toward the hills and beach.

They heard Laochmarú blow his battle horn to regroup his men. The Áiteoir followed quickly, but their heavy horses could not catch up. Teague and Alastar took just a few short minutes to reach the beach in front of the water corridor. They rode into the sea and waded toward the group of guards at the doorway. Teague made a loud whistle call to bring Bress close to them. He didn't want to leave her stranded when they went down into the sea corridor.

The water was up to Teague and Alastar's heads when Laochmarú's men jumped into the sea after them. When Teague and Alastar got to the entrance of the ramp, they slowly emerged out of the sea. The water under them became solid and lifted them onto the floor of the corridor, while the guards at the entrance moved aside for them to pass through.

"Muintir an Éisc ["Mooun-chir ahn Eshk"]," Teague said. "The Merfolk of the Muir Airgid. I've never seen 'em before."

They continued to ride downwards in the large corridor as if they were on a solid floor. Bress flew in ahead of them. The walls of the corridor rose straight up to the sea's surface where the doorway opened to the sky. Farther down the square tunnel, the water roofed in the corridor and made a long passage to the bottom of the sea's depths.

They couldn't see the end of the tunnel, but the water was lit all around them by the vast illuminated forests of seaweed and kelp.

Alastar looked at the Muintir an Éisc as they rode past them. They were all lean muscled and light skinned. Their silver white hair was long, but neatly trimmed. Tight fitting, short-sleeved shirts of thin violet material and tight green pants covered their bodies. They were all barefoot and each of them held up a long spear of gold.

Laochmarú and his men tried to follow, but the guards stood with their spears forward to prevent their passage. Laochmarú tried to press into them but as the guards stepped backwards, the water of the doorway became liquid again so that Laochmarú and his men could not step into the corridor. Instead, the Áiteoir continued to sink into the sea as the Éisc retreated down with Teague and Alastar.

When they had traveled several meters into the corridor, the entrance closed and filled up with seawater. Laochmarú and his men were left splashing in the sea and clamored for the shore.

Murky Passage

*T*eague and Alastar followed Bress as she flew down the long corridor of water. The Éisc guards followed them, and as they walked down, the corridor filled in with water behind them. They descended so far below the surface of the sea, they could no longer see the sun's light from above. The depths were not dark, though, because the water around them was bright with luminescent sea life and foliage. Almost all things with life had a glow and the great forests of seaweed kelp gave off enough silver light to illuminate everything down to the seafloor. Even the water itself had a green glow.

Alastar noted a large school of glowing white fish that swam in a huge, changing mass, like the starling flock they saw along the riverbank. "See," he noted to Teague. "The birds flocked just like that school of fish."

"Right," Teague acknowledged. "Grand sight, but I'm more interested in where Bress is flyin'." He looked ahead and pointed to the end of the corridor. It was going to an immense shining city on the seafloor. Its bright silhouette against the deep green of the seawater was much different than that of a great city on land. Instead of straight edges and spires, the underwater city was made of gigantic rounded trees and tubes everywhere. Its structures were largely glowing white, made of mother of pearl that grew into the shapes of giant coral trees and tubes. The pearl coral buildings were decorated with glowing ornaments and trim of brightly colored, living coral that appeared to have grown into the city's structures. The city had no walls but was surrounded by a hilly seafloor that glowed with red hot lava in the valley trenches. The dim glow of the lava channels spread all around the seafloor like a lattice of red rivers that flowed everywhere.

As they neared the city, they saw its citizens swimming around its massive coral and pearl structures. However, unlike the guards who appeared completely human, the others had lower bodies of different kinds of fish, whales and seals. The Muintir an Éisc swam around, in, and out of the coral buildings like bees living inside elegant hives of branching coral tubes. Some of the branches were so large, Alastar thought a palace could fit inside just one arm. He wondered if they would be able to breathe in the water and go about the city as the Éisc did, but then he realized the corridor ended in a giant air bubble that surrounded the city's square. *Doubt we can travel outside the air bubble,* he thought.

Bress flew into the square's courtyard and rested in a ruby, tree-like coral. It was one of many small tree-like corals that lined the courtyard. They resembled blossoming cherry trees with thick branches, except the trunk and branches were translucent ruby while the leaves and flowers were white spiraling ribbons that lined the outer branches. A contingent of Éisc stood in the center of the square and waited for them.

"I thought ridin' inta Cnoc na Rí was a grand spectacle," Alastar said. "Nothin' could've prepared my eyes for such a sight!"

"Nor mine," Teague agreed. "I know of the Muintir an Éisc through old tales 'a murúch, mermaids and selkies. They can change their legs inta the forms of fins and all sort 'a water beast, but never was there mention 'a their lives under the sea, nor that anyone from above ever saw their kingdom."

Teague and Alastar made their way to the assembly of Éisc in the square. The guards behind them formed lines on both sides and stood still. The group of Éisc in the front wore long robes of thin white fabric. Despite their more elderly faces, they were all fit and lean muscled like the guards. The one at center raised his hand to greet them. He wore a crown of gold wave crests that faced outward from the center. A large round diamond with a starburst pattern in it was set in between the two center wave crests.

"Welcome ta our kingdom, Men of the Soil," the king greeted. "I am Ailbhe ["Æl-veh"], King of the Muintir an Éisc. Please come forward. We have somethin' ta discuss."

Alastar and Teague respectfully bowed to the king and got off their horses. They went forward curiously. Their earthy clothes and ecru skin made them appear dark compared to the bright complexions and clothing of the Éisc. The king's attendants escorted them to a nearby table and chairs that were made of pearl and trimmed with colorful coral that matched the beautiful structures around them.

"Thank you for savin' us from the Áiteoir," Teague said after they settled into chairs.

"We're very grateful," Alastar added.

"The Seabhac Azure called us forth," Ailbhe said. "But in fact we have been waitin' weeks for you, Swan-bearer."

Teague and Alastar were surprised. "You knew I would come?" Alastar wondered.

"I was given a dream that you would," Ailbhe told them. "My young son, Murchadh ["Mer-rah-hoo"], was taken captive two moons ago on the beaches near King Draíodóir's ["Dree-ah-dor's"] mountain fortress. He was warned of the danger, but Draíodóir lured him inta a trap with a gleamin' sword of obsidian. His escorts could not sway his curiosity, and they came away ta tell me after Draíodóir appeared from behind the rocks ta capture my son."

The king shook his head in dismay. "Murchadh, the little warrior, has affinity for uncommon weapons. I sought Draíodóir ta find a way ta free my boy. He bargained ta exchange Murchadh for items of great value - our Bracers of Focus. They give their wearer control over the powers that lay hidden in each of us. Any who wear them can wield awesome power. I dared not give him the pair, but only gave him one ta exchange for my son. But when we withheld the other bracer, Draíodóir went back on his word. He knew our strength comes with the sea upon our bodies, so he kept my son in a stone prison far from our reach ta ensure safe passage for his ships. We were powerless ta save Murchadh so far from the sea's strength. That is why the currents called you ta help us, Swan-bearer."

Murchadh must be the boy I saw in my dream, Alastar thought. *But who is Draíodóir?* "Forgive my ignorance," he asked. "Who is King Draíodóir?"

Ailbhe replied, "He is king of the Áiteoir."

"With all our focus on Laochmarú and his army," Teague said, "we never had occasion ta speak 'a Draíodóir. The general is Draíodóir's top commander, but Draíodóir oversees all the Áiteoir Kingdom."

"Draíodóir is a conjurer of considerable power," Ailbhe added. "His arts of levitation and animation of earthly stone and dust were greatly increased by the bracer he took."

"That must be how the Áiteoir conjured the black stone dragon!" Teague exclaimed. "If one bracer gave him that power, what could he do with the pair?"

"Surely," Alastar thought. "It would be terrible. But how are we ta face such force and free your Murchadh?"

"The dream I had," Ailbhe continued, "showed what I am ta do now." He gestured to one of his counselors. The counselor brought forward a small chest made of clear, green crystal jasper. The bright interior of the chest was vaguely visible through the transparent sides and cover of the chest. It was given to the king and he opened it.

Inside the chest was a white setting of pearl and fabric that had depressions to hold the gold Bracers of Focus. Only one bracer was in the chest, though. Ailbhe picked it up and gave it to Alastar. "Use this bracer ta face Draíodóir and rescue my son, Swan-bearer."

Alastar accepted it and wondered how to use it. It was a solid gold half-tube that clasped onto his forearm. The smooth gold bracer was sparsely decorated with simple trim and filigree. Its main feature was a large engraved symbol of an eye made by the outline of an infinite knot that curled in small loops at the sides of the main circle, like a loop of string twisted to make a small loop on either side of it.

Alastar clasped the bracer onto his right forearm over his leather armor bracer and asked, "How do I use it?"

"Focus," Ailbhe said bluntly. "You will find its method."

"Thank you," Alastar replied. "I will return it when our duty is done."

"No," Ailbhe said. "The bracer is yours, ta keep for your service. I only ask you return my son unharmed."

Alastar looked at Teague with a sense of obligation and then looked back to the king. "We'll do our very best," he said. "And thank you for your gracious gift."

"How are we ta enter Draíodóir's fortress?" Teague asked. "He'll soon know we've come ta ya and suspect we'll go for your son. He will no doubt fortify his position."

"Laochmarú's army marches for Gleann Creagach ["Glæn Krægukh"] as we speak," Ailbhe said. "But you are weary. Rest this day. We will speak of matters early in the mornin'. It will take Laochmarú more than a day's march ta reach Gleann Creagach. We can bring you there in but an hour's time through the sea."

Ailbhe stood up and told an attendant to bring Teague and Alastar to their quarters. "I leave you now ta rest," Ailbhe said. He went toward the edge of the air bubble with his counselors and their legs became fins as they passed through it. They swam away and disappeared into the tallest coral tower.

Teague and Alastar went back to their horses with the attendant. Alastar was not surprised to see Éimhín eating the white leafy ribbons on the ruby coral trees. The ribbons glowed opalescent as Éimhín bit them from the lowest branches. "Ya have a taste for radiants," Alastar told Éimhín.

"Right," Teague noted. "Only horse I knew ta chew more on glowin' blossoms than the fruit 'n leaves around 'em." His horse was eating bushes of green seaweed that made the borders around the trees and walkways. He patted his horse on the neck. "My steed prefers the usual sort 'a roughage."

"Your horses will be safe here," the Éisc attendant said. "Follow me ta your quarters."

They followed the attendant to the rear of the courtyard where the king had gone. When they reached the edge of the air bubble, the attendant raised his hand toward a round tubular tower in the distance and a tunnel of air expanded from their position all the way to a door at the top of the tower. They continued to walk forward in the air tunnel just as they had done in the large corridor that brought them from the sea's surface.

Alastar and Teague marveled at the sights around them as they walked to the tower. It was like being on a high bridge above the great pearl and coral city. Sea life of all kinds swam near and passed through the tunnel of air as if it didn't exist. Alastar wondered if he could pass through the tunnel walls just as easily. He raised his hand to reach into the wall.

"I wouldn't," the attendant warned Alastar. "The water is warm but the depth would crush your hand. We walk under miles 'a sea here."

Alastar quickly lowered his hand.

"Lad, you're always pressin' for trouble," Teague joked. "Save your energy for the mission tomorra'."

They reached the door in the round tower and stepped into a foyer with circular doors on the left and right.

"Enter on the right," the attendant said. "All you need is inside. Stay in your quarters until you are called. The air will not travel for you if you come out. I bid you, sirs, a good rest." He gave them a bow and stepped backwards out of the tower's entrance. The tunnel of air disappeared, but the foyer retained its air. As the attendant floated in the water outside, his legs turned into the rear end of a dolphin and he swam away.

"Right bafflin' place," Teague commented. He looked at the doors and noticed they did not have any handles or doorknobs, but they had lines across them that appeared to be seams. "How do we open the door?" he wondered.

Alastar brought his hand close to the door and it opened suddenly, like a valve or shutter. "A little curiosity isn't a bad thing," he noted with humor.

"Right, lad," Teague said as he stepped into the room. Alastar followed and the door closed behind them. They saw the room was a long, expansive corridor that curved around the outside of the tower's extremity. The floors and walls were smooth mother of pearl and trimmed with blue coral. The interior shone in streams of pearlescent white from light that came through large windows along the walls and ceiling. Furniture of green stone was laid out throughout their quarters, and there were stairs going up towards the center of the tower that went into separate sleeping rooms and a dining area.

Alastar peered through a window and looked down. "Never would I have guessed all this lay under the sea," he said astonished. "I can see the courtyard from here. Éimhín is still eatin' from the coral trees."

"Right large that horse's appetite," Teague said. "I'm surprised he runs so fast always with a full belly! I'd be needin' a chew as well, but I've no strength ta even lift my eyes. I'll leave ya ta your gawkin'." He went up to one of the bedrooms and rested.

Alastar walked around the entire quarters and looked out the windows. The Éisc city stretched for miles around, like a giant lump of white crystal that sat on the dim sea floor. He went to the room at the very center of the tower. It had a full stock of food and drink for them to enjoy - all sorts of edible seafood and plants. The Éisc even had freshwater and fruit juices from the land in stock, but all the food items were from the sea.

He sat down at a table and ate whatever looked appetizing. He even found a favorite from the shores of Netleaf. "Shell-dillisk!" he recognized. He grabbed the plate of steamed red seaweed and mussels. *Wonderful! Tastes just as mom made it,* he noted as he ate hungrily.

Alastar filled himself with the many choices of food set before him. When he finished, he went to a bedroom and sat in a plush chair that looked out a large window. The chair's supple cushions were water-filled sacs, like giant seaweed pods. They were just as comfortable as any plush pillow he'd seen on land.

He sat there contemplating things. Would freeing the boy prince be easy? When would they return home to the valley? How would the Bracer of Focus help him? He gazed at the polished gold bracer on his arm. It looked common enough for a solid gold piece of armor. He didn't feel anything unusual about it since he put it on. He touched the curving eye symbol on its surface.

"Focus," Alastar whispered. Ailbhe said that was what he needed to do to use the bracer. *But focus on what?* His mind was so

cluttered with so many things and concerns. He quickly became tired
and thoughts came to him of riding through the country with Amber,
free from threats of any kind. He soon fell asleep with visions of
vibrant fields and flower covered meadows that passed underneath
him.

Fuar held a new éanshee message in his hands. It read: The boy
was found entering the Muir Airgid with a single companion. They would
enter Gleann Creagach to free the Éisc Prince. I march there to capture
the Swan-Bearer. Send your army to Lochtán an Eidhneáin and block
the boy's escape should he slip through. The land north of Lochtán
an Eidhneáin is the only way back east. They will certainly try to flee
through the passage. – G. Laochmarú

Gilroy was working in the longhouse when quick visions
flashed in his mind. He saw Alastar struggle with masses of enemy
soldiers around him. He was alone and surrounded by soldiers of
both Laochmarú and Fuar. Gilroy paused for a moment to think. *Does
Alastar need help?* he wondered.

Then as soon as he could start pondering what it could mean, a
Greerian report was transmitted to his mind. He saw King Fuar leading
an army out of Rían's Gate. It appeared his entire forces from Cnoc na
Rí marched through. Thousands of soldiers went through Gap Dearg
and turned just outside the gate to go straight west.

*Why would the king lead an army west? Fuar must know
Alastar is at the Muir Airgid,* he thought. The king rarely marched his
whole army and the last time he did was to meet Laochmarú on the
hills of Earraigh where he tried to take Amber captive. *I must speak to
Gearóid and Amber. Alastar will need aid.*

Amber was far from the village. She was used to spending time
riding in the forests with Alastar and resting at the stone arch cliffs, but
since he left she wanted to save those activities for his return. Instead,
she rode up the north side of the valley ridge and went west to find a
high peak to see the land beyond.

The anbobracht continued to dry up the mountain peaks and
expanded farther down into the valley. The thinning foliage made it
easier to find an open cliff that gave a good vantage point, but the
withering worried everyone in Duille Coiréil; Amber especially.
Alastar had told her about the dry desert valley and she worried like he
did whether their efforts to build a new kingdom was doomed to fail.

She felt their kingdom was a small uprooted garden after they
lost Lacharan. Their small community in Duille Coiréil was a new
sprouting plant that sent strong shoots of growth into the ground, but
they needed resources and people outside the River Valley to continue
growing. They couldn't crouch low in the valley forever, but Gearóid
and Conn said there was little short-term hope of bringing Lacharan
back under their control. The king had too many loyal troops holding
Lacharan's walls, but they found most of the citizens were still loyal to
Amber. Gearóid felt Lacharan could be easily won back if they could
depose the king's army from Lacharan.

On top of the mountain ridge, Amber traveled west until she
came to a clearing that faced outside the valley. It was a perfect site,
positioned where the valley curved south towards Loch an Scáthán. It
provided an area of bare cliffs that were free of the obstruction of trees.

She stopped Muirgel there and went to the cliff ledge to look west.

The green hill country and fields beyond stretched as far as the horizon could show. Though she couldn't see the Muir Airgid, she knew it was straight ahead. *Alastar is out there,* she thought. They were only days apart, but the distance stretched out between them, seemingly impassable, like disjoined moments in time that could not be held in one hand. She wanted to call him back and remembered the song her mother sang to bring her father home.

In the years she practiced the song, she never had her Swan-bearer to sing to, but whenever she sung it she always had him in mind. It was only when Alastar appeared to her in Lacharan that she could truly sing it in her heart. She was doing that on the harp the evening he came up from the banquet. She didn't show her emotions then, but she felt a boundless joy when he came into the parlor that night.

She sat there on the mountaintop and admired the beauty of the hill country in front of her. The many hills were like giant wave crests of a rolling, deep green sea that was speckled with vast patches of blue and white flowers. The view inspired her and new words came to her mind as she started to sing the lover's return song, "Ar Ais Chugam ["Ar Ash Hugum"; Return To Me (Woman's Version)]."

"Nuar↘ ahh jimeee↗ toooo↗, ahhh graaa↗ whemmm [When you left, My Love]

Ohh↘ veee↗ maaay boo-arrr↗ kræææ↗-chehhh [I was sadly tormented]

Ba↘ war↗ ah-huug, may↘ graaa↗ dee-iiitch [Yet dearly did I love]

Ah↘ hush-lehh↘ 'saa↗ storrr↗ [My Darling and My Love]

Ah↘ hush-lehhh↘ 'saa↗ storrreeennn↗ [My Heart's Beloved]

Eear-um↗ ort↗, fill-yoo↗ orr-rum [I ask, Return to me]

Mounting Rescue

Nuar ahhh↗ eye-reeeem↘, ahmahk↗ gohh hoooo-igyukkk↘ [When I rise, lonely]

Shood↘ ehh↘ 'noo-airrr↗, ish morrr↗ m'bronnne [At that time, my sorrow's greatest]

Beee-eem↘ eg shmooo-eetoooo, ar meeeer↗-graaa [I think of you, My True Love]

Etaaa whaaaa↗ whem-shehh↘ [Who is far from me]

J'warrr↗ naa↗ krukkk isheeen↗, im-maaay-gennn [Over the hills and far away]

Ah↘ hush-lehh↘ 'saa↗ storrr↗ [My Darling and My Love]

Ah↘ hush-lehhh↘ 'saa↗ storrreeennn↗ [My Heart's Beloved]

Eear-um↗ ort↗, fill-yoo↗ orr-rum [I ask, Return to me]

Nuar↘ ahh dahhh↗ toooo, doooer too [When you left, you said]

Aaahs↗ co ahn↗ teeel [Before the whole world]

Gahhhk↗ orlock↘, j'daaa↗ creee [Every inch of your heart]

Ve-fah ar aaash↗ hugum [Would return to me]

Je-air maay, ort↗ may-ah horch lee-et [I asked, Take me with you]

D'leehin↗ shes↗ fin spairrr [I'd sleep out in the wood]

Ah↘ hush-lehh↘ 'saa↗ storrr↗ [My Darling and My Love]

Ah↘ hush-lehhh↘ 'saa↗ storrreeennn↗ [My Heart's Beloved]

Eear-um↗ ort↗, fill-yoo↗ orr-rum [I ask, Return to me]

Bay↘ roon mo kreee↗-shay↗ [It would be my heart's desire]

Too-ar↗ ash↗ a'reeesh [You return again]

Ah↘ hush-lehh↘ 'saa↗ storrr↗ [My Darling and My Love]

Ah↘ hush-lehhh↘ 'saa↗ storrreeennn↗ [My Heart's Beloved]

Im↘ he arrr↗ vinn↗, aahn↗ jaaay-vehh [I was sitting out on the mountain peak]

Nuar-ah vinnns↗ ahnn↗, greee-ana↗ eyye-reeee [When sunrise always comes]

Ahgus shahs, a'warr↗ aaahn aard [And stood up on the height]

No↘ goeee↗ vek-kin, an joyj ee'geen [In order to see the jewel in the distance]

Ah↘ hush-lehh↘ 'saa↗ storrr↗ [My Darling and My Love]

Ah↘ hush-lehhh↘ 'saa↗ storrreeennn↗ [My Heart's Beloved]

Neel-ahn bronnne↗ aneweh-chehhh [Sorrow is not renewed]

Ha-nig moeee↗ graah↗, aaaah↗ bahnu ahn laaay [My Love's come at break of day]

Too aaar↗ aaash↗ hugummmm" [You have returned to me]"

[Nuair a d'imigh tú, a ghrá uaim]

[Ó bhí mé buartha cráite]

[Ba mhór a thug mé grá duit]

[A chuisle 's a stór]

[A chuisle 's a stóirín]

[Iarraim ort filleadh orm]

[Nuair a éirím, amach go huaigneach]

[Siúd é an uair, is mór mo bhrón]

[Bím ag smaointeamh, ar m'fhíorghrá]

[Atá i bhfad uaimse]

[De bharr na gcnoc is in, imigéin]

[A chuisle 's a stór]

[A chuisle 's a stóirín]

[Iarraim ort filleadh orm]

[Nuair a d'fhág tú, dúirt tú]

[Os comhair an tsaoil]

[Gach orlach, de do chroí]

[Bheifeá ar ais chugam]

[D'iarr mé, ort mé a thabhairt leat]

[Do luífinn síos faoin spéir]

[A chuisle 's a stór]

[A chuisle 's a stóirín]

[Iarraim ort filleadh orm]

[B'é rún mo chroíse]

[Tú ar ais arís]

[A chuisle 's a stór]

[A chuisle 's a stóirín]

[Im' shuí ar bhinn, an tsléibhe]

[Nuair a bhíonns an, ghrian ag éirí]

[Agus seas ar bharr an aird]

[Nó go bhfeicfinn an tseoid i gcéin]

[A chuisle 's a stór]

[A chuisle 's a stóirín]

[Níl an brón athnuaite]

[Tháinig mo ghrá, ag bánú an lae]

[Tú ar ais chugam]

When she finished singing, her hand touched the wood fibulae clasp that hung by her neck. She remembered how Alastar said it was also a soldier's promise to return. His pledge gave her a sense of security that eased her heart. The promise of an honorable man is like a rope of many strands - it is able to support the heaviness of uncertainty and tie the hopes of longing together. She felt his promise brought together those disjoined moments that kept her and Alastar apart. She could grasp his presence in her heart without fear of losing him. *Let separation test your love,* Gilroy had said. Patient resolve filled her so that all fear of being apart from Alastar was gone.

She continued to gaze toward the west when movement was caught in the corner of her eye. She looked right, to the north, and saw many troops in the distant foothills. She recognized the king's red and white banners. *What are they doing?* she wondered. Their march made a straight line to the west.

Amber got up quickly and kept low to the ground to avoid being seen. She mounted Muirgel and rode to the village as quick as they could.

Mounting Rescue

*T*eague and Alastar were back in the city square early the next day. They would have slept much longer if the Éisc attendant didn't gather them in the morning. The passing of time was lost underneath the constant flow and luminescence of the deep Muir Airgid. There was no hint of dawn or dusk at the bottom of the sea. If they didn't have urgent business, they could have lounged in their opulent quarters for days, oblivious to the world above the flowing waters.

Alastar had changed into his old clothes after washing his mud soiled léine. He marveled at how well Amber had mended them. They were spotless and free of their battle tears. He stood at Éimhín and packed the damp léine in a saddlebag. He was groping around in the bag when he jostled his bag of coins inside. They reminded him of something. He grabbed the coins and a small bit of frayed, white folded fabric. He went to King Ailbhe who waited for them at the edge of the courtyard.

"I have a request of you, Sire" Alastar asked him.

"What would the Swan-bearer wish of us?" Ailbhe replied kindly. He already suspected what Alastar was going to ask because he could sense what was on his mind and the hidden content of the folded fabric.

"The bracer is more than enough reward for the errand we go on," Alastar said, "I wish not ta ask favors of you, but seein' how your people are master artisans of precious things. . ."

"Say no more," Ailbhe interrupted. He extended his hand to receive the fabric. "You wish somethin' for Princess Ealaí."

Alastar was surprised Ailbhe knew what he wanted. He put

the fabric and bag of coins in Ailbhe's hand. "The coin is payment for your materials and craftsmanship," Alastar said.

Ailbhe gave a soft laugh seeing that Alastar tried to pay for his request. He gave back the coins. "You've an honest heart, Swan-bearer, but we're glad ta make your request with nothin' more than a grateful heart. We are indebted ta your efforts." Ailbhe unfolded the fabric carefully. Inside was the rough, uncut emerald Alastar bought from the merchant in Lacharan. "I know exactly what you need. It will be ready when you return with my son."

Alastar looked at him with confusion. How could Ailbhe know what he wanted done with the emerald? Ailbhe's comforting smile eased him though, so he didn't question any further. "Thank you," Alastar said.

Ailbhe raised his hand and spoke loud, "It is time! Mount your horses, People of the Soil."

Alastar went back to Éimhín and got in the saddle. Teague and Alastar rode forward and stopped in front of the king. Ailbhe motioned to one of his counselors who came forward to give Teague something.

"Teague," Ailbhe said. "Accept this gift for your brave walk with the Swan-bearer. Your efforts are appreciated as much as his."

The counselor handed Teague a commander's battle horn. It was a semi-U shaped trumpet, like Conall's battle horn. This horn was brilliant polished gold instead of bronze, though, and engraved with swirling designs.

Ailbhe added, "The call of this horn will strengthen your soldiers ta stand like mighty waves of the sea."

Teague nodded in appreciation. "Gracious thanks, Sire," he replied.

Ailbhe turned and nodded to another counselor. The counselor turned to face the wall of the air bubble that surrounded the courtyard.

He waved his arm up and a large tunnel corridor shot out from the bubble towards the surface of the sea. It was just like the square corridor that brought Teague and Alastar down to the Éisc city, except this time it went in a different direction, almost due north toward the shore.

"You will find Draíodóir's keep at the end of this passage," Ailbhe said. "The fortress of Gleann Creagach has a small alcove at its base where its sewers empty inta the sea. You can enter the fortress there. We will wait in the sea for your return with Murchadh." He stepped aside to let Teague and Alastar pass. "Your endeavor have success and winged flight."

Alastar and Teague rode into the corridor. Teague called for Bress to come and they galloped toward shore with Bress flying ahead. As they ascended higher, the bright of sunlight started to appear above them in flickering streams of light. They rode for many miles in the sea's depths through thick forests of towering kelp. At times they had to slow when the seaweed became so dense that they had to push through it like the thick foliage of the River Valley.

It was strange to ride floating in the midst of the tall, glowing kelp forests. Alastar looked down often to see the long strands of silver white seaweed extend far below them. The forests were so high that their luminescent strands faded away into the deep, like a myriad of cloudy streaks that raced away from them.

They couldn't tell how many miles they rode, but it took nearly an hour to reach the end of the corridor at the sea's surface. When they burst out of the corridor it suddenly disappeared as water flooded in to fill it. They found themselves standing in the shallow waters of the beach near Draíodóir's fortress. Teague looked about to gauge their surroundings. The sandy beach's coarse black sand quickly gave way to dark boulders everywhere. Mountains of dark obsidian stone and crumbling black earth stretched into the distance, left and right, while a narrow valley extended directly in front of them where the fortress stood.

The black stone walls of the fortress stood more than three stories over them, while its towers extended another level higher. Though the structure stood high, it was old and crumbling, and its design was simple with stout, blocky towers and no curves at all in the dark cut stone.

"An ugly unassumin' place for a king," Teague noted. "No one in sight, but we'd best move quick." He noticed the alcove Ailbhe told them about. It was on their left where a section of the sea rushed into a small channel toward the cliffs under the fortress. They made a slow trot toward the alcove.

Alastar carefully surveyed the area and noted the mountaintops were not as high as in the River Valley, but they would make for far more treacherous traveling. Most of the terrain was jagged black rock with little vegetation. "Hardly any trees here," he commented.

"This place is grand compared ta the mountains and desert ta the west," Teague said. "The forest here still lives, but in the heart of the Rásúir Mountains, all the forest is but bare spikes 'a charred pitch - burnt and lifeless from the poison heat leechin' from the ground."

They came to the alcove and found it led into a shallow cave where a large sewer pipe came out of the fortress. Teague saw the pipe was covered with an immovable metal grate and there was no door anywhere in the cave wall.

"Grand," Teague said sarcastically. "Ailbhe said this was the way in, but I was hopin' not ta crawl up the sewers."

"Right," Alastar acknowledged. "But how are we ta get in?" He got off Éimhín and examined the sewer pipe. He tugged on the grate, but it was embedded solid in the stone. "It won't move at all," he said.

"There'll be no climbin' inta this pipe."

Teague got off his horse and came to the wall. "There must be some other way in," he said. He looked at the cliff wall just to the right of the pipe. It was a large bare area of rock with no unusual features. They spent some time feeling around the wall to find any hidden crevices, but nothing stood out. Then Teague pondered and he thought of something.

"Step back," he told Alastar. After Alastar stepped away from the wall, Teague picked up handfuls of dark sand from the ground and threw them all over the wall.

"What are ya doin'?" Alastar asked.

"Hold on," Teague said. He kept throwing sand at the wall and it started to collect into some hidden crevices. "Here!" he remarked excitedly and threw more sand around the areas where it settled.

Alastar looked closely. "What is it?"

"A hidden door and lock," Teague noted. He continued to throw sand at the wall and filled in the door's outline and some curving cracks and depressions to the right of the door. When the sand settled, they saw the contours of a round lock mechanism. It had a depression inside its outer circle that was shaped like a razor-backed wolf. A round hole was set near the edge of the circle.

"Do you often break inta hidden passages?" Alastar wondered. "How'd ya know?"

"I just thought Draíodóir was a conjurer, and how they like ta use illusions ta hide thin's," Teague said. "I didn't know it would work! Still, we're banjaxed. Looks like we need a fáelshee shaped key with a turnin' peg."

"I can do that!" Alastar exclaimed. "I just need ta find some wood." He went to his saddlebag and took out his hand axe. Then he ran outside and found a tree with a branch that stuck straight out.

Teague followed him and watched as Alastar carved out a hunk of bark that surrounded the branch. In a few minutes, he had a suitable plate of bark with a sturdy peg sticking out of it.

They went back to the door and Alastar got out his wood working tools. "This'll take some time," he commented. He held up the piece of bark near the lock to gauge the dimensions of the shapes he needed to carve. He formed an image of what the key should look like in his mind and just as soon as he had it pictured, he felt energy rush out of him and the wood transformed in his hands to match exactly what he imagined.

Alastar was so startled from the changing wood that he dropped it and gasped. Teague was tending his horse and feeding him when he heard Alastar.

"What happened?" Teague asked.

Alastar picked up the wood key and showed him. Teague was shocked. It was carved perfectly to match the lock mechanism. "How did ya do that so fast?!"

"I don't know. I was just thinkin' about how ta make the key," Alastar said. Then he realized something. "I was *focusin'* on what it should look like."

"The Bracer of Focus?" Teague speculated. "Is that what it does for ya? Carve wood at the blink of an eye?"

Alastar turned around and cleaned the sand off the lock in the wall. Without the sand to reveal it, it disappeared into the face of the wall. He rubbed his fingers over it and was amazed to find that he could not feel the contours of the lock. But when he placed the key where the lock's depressions were, he found it fit perfectly. He pressed it firmly in and heard a click, but nothing else happened. He wondered for a second when Teague spoke.

"The peg hole, lad," he said. "It's meant ta turn the lock. Turn it!"

Alastar turned the key clockwise and the lock's circle turned with it. When the key was upside-down it stopped and they heard the clicking of metal gears. The door started to open.

"Grand work!" Teague exclaimed. "Who else could've done it but you, Swan-bearer?!"

Alastar peered into the open doorway. It was completely dark inside. "Doesn't look ta be a well used passage. Nothin' but dark."

"Let's hope guards are scarce as the light in there," Teague said.

"We should move the horses before we go in," Alastar suggested. "In case someone comes this way."

"Right," Teague agreed. "We'll tie 'em in another hollow outside. They're all over the beach."

Alastar packed up his tools and the key he made. They led their horses outside and found a secluded area to leave them. Then they hurried back to the door and went into the fortress. Teague led the way as they walked slowly through the dark passage. The light from the doorway soon diminished into thick, dark air that was heavy with a damp musky odor. They had to grope along the walls to continue their way. The damp stone walls were coated with grit that made a scratchy sound as their fingers slid along.

They had gone for a distance when Teague all of a sudden tripped."SCANGER!" he huffed. "Steps up. Feel 'em out."

They climbed the long stairwell until they could see light ahead. Everything remained quiet.

"Be ready," Teague whispered. "Guards could be anywhere."

They stepped slow toward the top of the stairs and listened for any activity. Not a sound penetrated the musty air. When they reached the top, Teague peered out into the connecting hallway. The walls were lined with unlit torches, but the area was lit by many small windows placed high in the outside wall. He saw many doors with barred windows that lined the opposite wall of the hallway.

"Looks like we found the prison easy 'nough," Teague said. "Let's check the cells."

"Murchadh is in a flooded cell," Alastar remembered.

"Right, step quiet 'n stay together," Teague said as he went to the left. They came to the first door and looked through its window. The cell was empty, so they continued to the next door. Someone was huddled in the far corner.

"Hey!" Teague whispered loud. The prisoner lifted his head and squinted at Teague through the bars. He didn't move or say anything. "We look for a boy named Murchadh," Teague said. "Have ya seen 'im?"

"The selkie boy?" the prisoner replied. He got up and went to the door. He was dirty and had tattered clothing that hung from his bony body. He looked out intently at Teague and Alastar and examined their clothes. He recognized the crest on their armor. "Who are ya, Eachraighe? Clearly not Áiteoir jailers."

"You know Murchadh?" Alastar asked.

"Sure," the prisoner said. "He was opposite my wall, but they took 'im the day before. I don't know where or why."

"Draíodóir must've moved him soon as he heard we entered the sea," Teague said.

"Ya came for the boy?" the prisoner asked. "What of me? I been in this room near two years now."

"What was your crime?" Teague asked.

"Just an old servant who displeased the king," the prisoner said. "I failed ta mend a robe as he wished and was thrown in here."

"Tailor, it'd be a grand day for ya then," Teague said. He

checked the door to try and open it, but it was locked. He turned to Alastar. "Get him out, lad," he said.

"Make another key?" Alastar responded. "But I don't know what it needs ta look like."

"Just do somethin' with the door," Teague suggested. "It's solid wood!"

"*Right,*" Alastar said with comprehension. He looked at the lock in the door and imagined a hole around the lock. Just as he thought it, he felt energy leave him again and a hole appeared in the door around the lock. The iron lock fell down to the floor with a loud clanging that rung through the hallway.

The prisoner jumped in alarm. "BANJAX!" he exclaimed startled. "You a conjurer too?"

"I'm not," Alastar said. "Just handy with wood."

"Sure," the prisoner said with unbelief. He pushed open the door and came out. "I've had my fill 'a conjurers. I thank ya for my freedom, but I'll not keep in your presence. My mind's set on goin' as far from Draíodóir as I can. You'd do the same if you know what powers he wields." He quickly ran off and disappeared down the stairs that led to the beach.

"Brief fellow," Teague said.

"He said Murchadh was on the other side of his wall," Alastar remembered.

They continued down the hallway and rounded its corner. They checked every cell for prisoners and freed them all. Most of them fled to the beach as the tailor did, but one man remained to help them find Murchadh. He was an old commander named Gabhann ["Goh-en"]. He was from the Méine Kingdom and was locked up when the Áiteoir took over their lands.

When they reached Murchadh's cell, they looked inside and

found it empty. The room was still flooded with water.

"The boy's not in there," Teague said.

"The tailor said they took him yesterday," Alastar reminded.

"There was much murmurin' when the guards took 'im," Gabhann said. "Talk 'a movin' the whole garrison 'n supplies out."

Alastar worried they moved Murchadh away from the fortress. "What if they left with Murchadh? How are we ta find him?"

Teague thought for a moment. "If Draíodóir knew we were comin' and Laochmarú marches here, why would they empty the fortress? They should be ambushin' us here. Surely they'd not fear us so much as ta run before us."

"Perhaps they *want* us ta follow them out?" Alastar suggested.

"Hardly chance 'a that," Gabhann said. "Murchadh couldn't survive roamin' about land. He's weak as it is sittin' many days in that dank cell. I gather Draíodóir is holdin' 'im here still, where he can get thin's from the sea ta keep the boy alive."

"I agree," Teague said. "Draíodóir would not risk killin' the boy. His use of the sea would be cut off by the Éisc if the prince died. Still, we've no choice but ta search the fortress. We need be certain these walls are empty before venturin' out."

"Ya can be certain they set a trap," Gabhann added.

"We need ta get ya a weapon," Alastar told him. "Do ya know where they keep 'em?"

"'Fraid not," Gabhann replied. "I've not seen any part of this keep but the dungeon. I'll just follow behind ya lads for the time bein'."

They proceeded to the next level through a winding staircase. Halfway up, Teague noticed a small bird standing in an open window. It gazed at them a moment and then flew up and away. Teague jumped to the window to see where the bird went. He saw it fly to another open window in the top level of the fortress.

"Sickle swift! An éanshee sentry," Teague said in alarm. "Whoever's still here knows we're comin'."

They hurried to the next level and looked about with their swords ready. It was the main level of the fortress with a banquet hall and meeting rooms. No one was around everywhere they looked, but they found an ornamental pike axe and tall rectangular shield in the banquet hall for Gabhann to use.

"Sure as clouds coverin' the land, this emptiness doesn't sit right," Teague noted. "Everyone must be on the upper level where the éanshee flew. Back ta the stairs."

They went back to the stairway and proceeded to the top level. The entrance to the third floor was a short corridor that went toward the center of the fortress. There were open windows along both sides of the corridor and a closed wood door at the end. They cautiously stepped to the door and tried to listen for anything.

"Be wide," Teague whispered. "There's sure ta be a fight behind this door. Swords ready."

Alastar and Gabhann braced themselves for action as Teague opened the door. They stood in shock as they saw what lay beyond them - many dark floating panels slid around a large room. The thin panels were black shiny stone and stood in midair. They floated and shifted about just above the floor, like the walls of a changing maze. The room had a high ceiling of wood above the stone walls that was supported by heavy wood beams. There were windows along the left and right walls, but they couldn't see beyond the shifting panels in front of them.

"Banjax!" Teague exclaimed quietly. "Draíodóir's conjurin'."

"Any chance those flyin' walls are illusions?" Alastar asked.

"Sure, as imaginary as that stone dragon!" Teague quipped.

"Let me go first," Gabhann said. He raised his tall shield. "I have cover for a surprise attack."

Teague got an idea and turned to Alastar. "Mind ya make a round shield out 'a the door for me? Gabhann and I will press at front. You keep behind us."

Alastar looked at the thick wood door and carved a sturdy round shield from it. Teague took it and they went forward in slow steps. They watched the movement of the floating panels as they approached. They were dark foggy mirrors that threatened to slice through them, like giant flying blades. When they were close enough, Teague tapped a panel with his sword. It made a clink like metal on stone.

"No illusions," Teague said. "Let's jump through the openin's quick as we can."

Teague and Gabhann jumped through the next opening without a problem, but Alastar came behind slowly and got nicked in the shoulder by the edge of a panel. It punched a deep depression in his leather armor. Alastar grunted and looked at his shoulder.

"Ya alright?" Teague asked.

"Walls have bite ta 'em," he answered. "Nearly sliced through my armor."

They stood in the middle of a hallway made by the traveling panels and watched carefully for the next opening to come close. Teague and Gabhann jumped ahead when the opening slid past them, but Alastar stayed for the next opening. As Teague and Gabhann waited for him, two guards struck at them through another opening toward the front. Their swords caught them by surprise and nicked Gabhann in the shoulder, but Teague's shield and armor protected him well. Before they could strike back, though, the opening slid away.

"Skawly, these walls!" Teague huffed.

"It's too narrow here ta swing my axe," Gabhann added. "We need ta get out 'a here!" He hung his shield over his back so he could use two hands with his long pole axe. Alastar jumped through quickly to join them and bumped into a panel on the opposite side. He hit it solid but it didn't move from its direction of travel.

"Guards in the next passage!" Teague warned Alastar.

They stood ready for the next opening to slide in front of them. When it came, Teague and Gabhann swung their weapons at the guards. Teague only nicked his mark, while Gabhann's axe got caught on the edge of a quickly moving panel. It ripped the axe out of his hands and made it tumble to the ground. Alastar picked it up and gave it back to him.

"We can't fight like this," Teague said. "Jump through with me, Gabhann, and knock 'em over. Lad, you follow behind." Alastar nodded in acknowledgement.

"I'll follow ya," Gabhann agreed, "but I need go through beyond 'em. My spearhead is best from a distance." He went past Alastar in the moving hallway so he could jump through an opening farther away from the guards.

When the next opening came, Teague dashed through. He bowled over one of the guards and made him drop his sword. They crashed into the panels and wrestled with each other. The other guard started to come at Teague from behind and jabbed him in the back with the tip of his sword to try and get through his armor.

When the opening slid a ways down from them, Gabhann burst through with his pike axe held upright. He quickly lowered it and charged the guard behind Teague. He ran the axe's spearhead through him from behind. Teague continued to wrestle with the other guard and pushed him away to get distance so he could swing his sword. He raised it, but the guard quickly charged at his arm and sent the sword backward against the traveling panels. The butt of his sword struck a panel and shattered it. It crumbled to the floor in pieces. Teague hardly had time to express surprise. He continued to wrestle with the guard as they bounced off the panels moving around them.

"Break the walls with your pommel!" Gabhann yelled to Alastar as he jumped through the opening made by the shattered panel. Alastar quickly started to punch the panels around him with the butt of his sword. They all shattered to the floor in dark clouds of shimmering obsidian shards.

Gabhann ran forward to help Teague. He dropped the axe and picked up the dead guard's sword. Together they brought the remaining guard down.

"Grand fight," Teague said.

Before they could catch their breath, they saw dozens of guards run through the large gaps in the floating panels that Alastar made. They ran ahead to engage the guards and shattered panels along the way. Alastar kept smashing panels everywhere and noticed he could see through the large gaps to the other end of the room. Past the running guards stood an old man in a long, dusky red maroon robe. He held a staff in his hand and a boy lay unconscious on the floor near him.

"Murchadh!" Alastar exclaimed. He ran ahead too and charged the approaching guards. He fought with them skillfully, but was not as seasoned as Teague and Gabhann. Bodies piled about Teague and Gabhann while Alastar dispatched the guards much slower. They all continued to shatter panels as they fought and soon there were no more floating about.

Draíodóir stood motionless over Murchadh's body and watched Alastar keenly. He saw the gold bracer on his arm and grinned. He had a chance to get both bracers. His guards were dying quickly, but he remained calm. When his last guard fell, he pointed his staff forward and made all the shattered panel pieces rise up and swirl about the room. They flew around like small, jagged daggers that sliced through everything.

Alastar raised his arm to shield his face from the flying shards, but he noticed none of them touched him. They simply flew right past him harmlessly. Teague and Gabhann, though, screamed as the flying obsidian sliced through their skin. They huddled together, back to back, and crouched behind their shields.

When Draíodóir saw that Alastar was not being harmed, he scowled and waved his arms about. The broken obsidian stopped flying around and lumped together into three large masses in front of him. They quickly coalesced into large stone soldiers who held thick maces.

"Bog bean!" Teague said. "I see now why the tailor ran off!"

Teague and Gabhann stood up while Alastar ran to join them. They braced ready to face the animated stone soldiers. Everyone was still and silent for a moment. Then the soldiers charged with their heavy maces high. Teague and Gabhann held their shields up while Alastar moved quickly to avoid being hit.

The large spiked balls of the soldiers' maces splintered their shields. Gabhann's shield split so badly that he had to throw it away. Teague struck at the soldier in front of him. His sword could only chip off a small chunk from it. Dismayed, he remembered striking at the stone dragon. These things were just as hard.

"Try ta shatter 'em!" Teague yelled to the others. They started to smash them with the butts of their swords and managed to chip off large chunks from the stone soldiers, but they remained fully functional. They continued to fight the soldiers for a time and grew tired.

Alastar was thrown down to the floor when a blow hit him in the chest. He was struck dizzy and regained his vision as the soldier stepped up to him. He saw the ceiling and large beams overhead and got an idea. Alastar quickly rolled away from the soldier and focused on the ceiling above him. He cut it with his mind and made a large chunk of it fall down on the soldier. Then he cut a large beam and it fell on top of the soldier again, shattering it to pieces.

Draíodóir grimaced in surprise. He didn't think Alastar would be able to use the bracer so well.

"Get away from them!" Alastar yelled to Teague and Gabhann. They ran backwards and Alastar cut more ceiling and beams to smash the last stone soldiers.

They stopped to catch their breath, but Draíodóir pointed his staff out and made Teague and Gabhann levitate. He held them in midair and tried to do the same to Alastar but could not. "I see you learned ta use the bracer, Swan-bearer," he said. "Pity my powers are limited while you wear it."

"We only seek ta free Murchadh," Alastar replied. "Leave us and no harm will come ta you."

Draíodóir stepped forward. As he walked, he made Teague and Gabhann hover higher. "Why don't we do somethin' else?" he suggested. "The life of your friends for the bracer you wear. I can throw them outside ta fall ta their deaths in but an instant."

Alastar remembered how Ailbhe said he wouldn't dare give Draíodóir both bracers. He resolved not to let him get it. He approached Draíodóir slowly and noticed his staff was made of wood. Alastar thought quickly and cut the staff into small pieces. Its bits fell before Draíodóir and with them, Teague and Gabhann came crashing to the floor. Draíodóir roared out with rage. He lost his ability to project power onto people with his staff gone.

Teague and Gabhann moaned in pain on the floor, but Teague got up quickly and ran at Draíodóir with his sword. Draíodóir screamed angrily and thrust out his arms. He made the obsidian rubble rise up and swirl in a cloud that protected him. Then the stones coalesced to make a small dragon, hardly bigger than a horse. He quickly jumped on it and flew through the large opening in the ceiling that Alastar had made.

Alastar ran to Murchadh. The prince was still unconscious. Teague and Gabhann joined him at the front of the room.

"Next time we face Draíodóir, we come with the rest of the Eachraighe," Teague said.

"Grand he's gone," Gabhann added. "Hardest match I ever fought." He touched his face and looked at his limbs. His skin stung from many shallow slashes everywhere. He looked at Teague and saw his face cut as well, but most of him was protected by thick armor. "Ya fared well, lad. I must look as if I ran through a bramble 'a thorns.'"

"Just a few more scars ta speak a bit a craic over," Teague said. He went to a window and looked for Draíodóir. He wasn't anywhere in sight. "Time we go. No doubt Draíodóir regroups with Laochmarú. Last we heard, his army marches here."

Alastar sheathed his sword and picked up Murchadh. They went as fast as they could to the lower level and back to the beach. As soon as they exited the alcove, they saw Ailbhe rise out of the sea and walk toward shore with many of his spearmen.

Alastar brought Murchadh to Ailbhe who took him in his arms. He gazed lovingly at the boy. Murchadh's thin, dry body looked as if he had lay in the desert sun, starved and parched for days. "My brave little boy," Ailbhe said. He turned around and gave Murchadh to one of the guards. "My son learnt a hard lesson, but he will be fine. I give my thanks ta you and your friends, Swan-bearer."

Ailbhe gave Alastar a small bow of his head in appreciation. He picked something out of his robe and handed it to Alastar. It was wrapped in a small piece of fine white fabric. "I trust it is exactly what you wished for. Your emerald had ta be cut inta pieces for the fracture it had, but we used all of it. . . and set more thin's of value ta show our gratitude."

Alastar unwrapped the fabric quickly and saw a brilliant gold ring inside. He picked it up and examined it. Teague and Gabhann stepped close to look at it too.

The ring had the largest piece of Alastar's emerald set at center. It was cut and polished as a splendid square gem. Two swans of molded opal were set facing each other on both sides of the center stone. They were the same swans as shown in the Ealaí House crest and the same as the glowing swan symbols at the stone archway. The smaller emeralds were set as the eyes of the swans and at each tip of their wings' feathers.

Alastar was amazed at the detail and quality of the ring. It was exactly what he wanted for Amber. "You have my thanks, Sire," he said. "Would you take back your bracer for such a fine gift?"

"Nonsense! The bracer is yours as I said," Ailbhe reminded. "This will not be the last time you need it. Thank you again for rescuin' my son. We return ta the sea now. You need return ta your people as well. Laochmarú advances on you. We saw them pass the Cliffs of Marmair ["Mar-reh-mer"] just an hour past. Take the coast here as far as you can. They take the inland road so you may round them without their knowledge."

"Won't ya make a way for us through the sea, straight ta the shores near Lochtán an Eidhneáin?" Teague asked. "It would give us the safest passage."

"I'm afraid we cannot help now," Ailbhe said. "The Muintir

an Éisc do not interfere with affairs of the People of the Soil. It is only when one of us is involved, as my son was, that we do so. We take our leave, Valiant Men of the Soil. Fare well."

The Éisc stepped back into the sea and disappeared. Alastar put away the ring as they went to get their horses.

"Quite a bit 'a polish ya have there," Teague teased Alastar about the ring.

"*Very* fine indeed," Gabhann added. "I know the swans on that ring well as anyone on the isle. There's but one lady deservin' of it." He smiled wide. Teague smiled as well and stared at Alastar with amusement.

Alastar knew their friendly prodding was to make him blush, but he wouldn't let them embarrass him about Amber. "Sure," he said. "I can't think of a finer woman ta take it. The Éisc made the most grand ring I ever seen."

"Ya see!" Teague noted, "I knew your grebe huntin' would only lead ya ta the swan. An anxious heart tumbles 'bout many rough stones before it lands soft in its pillow 'a downy feathers."

"Doubtless they're swan feathers the lad'll lay his head on," Gabhann added. "But be easy on the boy. Lads 'n gals alike oft run 'bout in hunt for feathers without a clue what they need look for. Did ya not chase a bird or two?"

"That I did," Teague responded, "and I would've nested with a fine girl if only she waited for me. My years 'a soldierin' unsettled her heart and she married another. Paid no mind ta wishes 'a the heart after that. I will let the pieces lay where they fall, but the lad, Swan-bearer that he is, thought he was a grebe for certain! Would've caught a fine lake grebe if the currents didn't send 'im off ta find his swan. He needed forceful pushes 'a Áiteoir armies chasin' 'im to and fro. He spent a moon with the princess with hardly a feather preened for her, but once he got in his wick, he knew what ta do, swift as a bolt 'a lightnin'! Now they're cooin' as a pair 'a doves deep in spring blossom!"

Alastar started to feel the warmth of blood rush to his cheeks. He tried to change the subject. "Our horses are just round this cliff," he said.

"Doves in spring!" Gabhann continued to muse. "Soon after their cooin', there's a clutch 'a eggs. Many clutches 'a eggs all year round!"

Alastar's cheeks flooded scarlet. There was no getting away from their teasing.

"Right!" Teague added. "Doves and swans make round about the same handfuls 'a young each year. Only swans nest once a year, but doves rear many a small clutch through the seasons. Another year, lad, 'n there'll be swanlin's runnin' 'bout!"

"Ha! For certain!" Gabhann laughed. "The swanlin's always come after the moon 'a nest makin' 'n honey wine!"

They approached the horses. Alastar went to Éimhín and patted his neck. "We're back for another trot through the country," he spoke softly to him. "Let's make a swift ride home and keep the talk of swanlin's muffled in the wind."

"Sure 'nough!" Teague laughed as he continued in their amusement over Alastar's pending engagement. "I forgot 'a the honey-moon! We'll be sure ta stock the best honey wine for you 'n the princess, lad."

Alastar tried not to let his embarrassment show in their teasing. He wanted to remain quiet, but he was curious about the honey-moon. "What's this about a honey-moon?" he asked.

Teague answered, "It's the custom of our isle a newly wed couple leave ta be alone a full month 'n sip honey wine every eve thereof."

"The nest makin' tradition!" Gabhann added. "For a blessed 'n bountiful marriage."

Teague looked around for Bress and found her on a nearby tree. He got out a small piece of paper from a saddlebag and wrote on it. He called Bress to him and put the message in her collar. "Our friends will know we leave for home," he said as he sent Bress flying.

Gabhann got on Éimhín behind Alastar and they proceeded east along the beach of black sand. They often looked up to see if Draíodóir flew overhead, but there were only patches of clouds in the bright sky. Still, they hurried along the coast as fast as they could. The cover of forest would be welcome in their flight to reach home undetected. Some time passed before the black rocky coast broke away into green fields and trees. The shore curved into an inlet where high, grass-covered cliffs began to dominate the shoreline.

"The Cliffs of Marmair are just round the bend," Teague said. He led them inland, up a small path that wound around the hills along the shore. When they got higher, they could see dense forests just beyond the sea. They felt reassured they would reach the safety of the forest, but when they emerged from the hill path they heard the unmistakable deep bellow of Laochmarú's battle horn.

They looked to the west in alarm and saw a vast Áiteoir army in the distance. There were tens of thousands camped on the fields of the cliff plateau. Draíodóir was on a hilltop behind them, still sitting on his small stone dragon. At the sound of the horn, their cavalry rushed forward with thousands of foot soldiers behind them. The quiet ride along the shore suddenly became a howl of thundering hooves and shouting men.

"They were waitin' on us!" Teague yelled. "Brought all their forces near 'n far from the looks of it!" Alastar was astonished by the size of the army. Just a small arm of their troop equaled the entire mass of the soldiers they had in Duille Coiréil. He felt like the Áiteoir would swallow them whole with just a quick glance of their swords.

"They brought the rabid beasts 'a the Rásúir wastelands as well!" Gabhann added when he saw a line of a dozen fáelshee in front of Draíodóir.

"Ride swift along the cliff fields!" Teague commanded. "We'll have more speed than in the forest."

*T*eague burst out in a gallop to the east along the grassy cliff plateau. Alastar and Gabhann followed him closely atop Éimhín. The Áiteoir chased them as a huge, dark mass that descended on them, like a giant arm of darkness. Their light cavalry soon overtook Laochmarú's heavy horses and began to inch closer to the fleeing party.

They surged ahead for many miles with the bright waters of the Muir Airgid on their right and the deep green forest on their left. Alastar looked back at their pursuers often and saw them gaining. Hundreds of light riders were well ahead of Laochmarú's cavalry, but all the Áiteoir pressed on without stop. Their numbers teemed in the distance behind them like a flood of black water that followed them. They would be at their heels soon and their horses were tiring. *We can't keep this pace much longer,* Alastar thought.

He pressed Éimhín to catch up with Teague. "We need ta run through the forest!" Alastar yelled to him. "I have an idea."

Teague acknowledged and they turned to enter the forest. Alastar slowed down to a walking gait and yelled, "Let them catch up!"

"Have ya gone in the head again?!" Teague shouted back.

Alastar looked back and watched the Áiteoir's front edge gallop into the forest. He focused on the trees around them and with a look across the view, he felt energy leave him and cut down many dozens of trees. They fell all around the Áiteoir and made them stumble and fall in a mass of confusion.

"Grand idea!" Gabhann said.

"Right grand altogether!" Teague added.

Alastar smiled, but he felt tired this time after using the power of the bracer. He didn't have time to think about it, though, and they continued forward. They galloped out of sight and focused on going straight east toward Lochtán an Eidhneáin.

When they had gone a while without signs of pursuit, they stopped to rest the horses. They had run for hours since crossing the Cliffs of Marmair and needed respite. Teague anticipated they would need to rush past Lochtán an Eidhneáin when they came near. The Áiteoir would no doubt have a garrison waiting for them outside the city, so he stopped them to rest.

"Gather strength," Teague told them. "We're close ta Lochtán an Eidhneáin."

"Where they came and chased us inta the sea?" Alastar remembered.

"Right," Teague answered. "The forest is settled for the time bein'. Rest in calm."

They got off their horses and relaxed. The bright sounds of the forest soon replaced the constant rhythm of pounding hooves. They listened carefully for any signs of trouble. The air was filled with the peaceful chirping of songbirds and the quiet murmur of wind rustled leaves. There was no threat in the air.

Alastar stared up at the elm and oak trees around them. The sun was overhead. Its light broke through the treetops and he wondered if Draíodóir was flying in the skies over them. "How far behind do ya think they are?" he asked.

"Miles I'd say, after they ran inta your tangle 'a wood," Teague said. "We have time for a rest."

"Minutes anyway," Gabhann noted. "We best keep movin'. There's no space wide 'nough between me and an army that size. Never in all my days 'a warrin' have I seen the land so packed 'a soldiers. When the Áiteoir took down our kingdom, they had half the number! And here we sit in the wood, just three 'a us waitin' for 'em ta come run us down!"

"The lad 'n I have gotten used ta masses 'a Áiteoir chasin' us every which way," Teague said. "Not a bit 'a craic in it. . . not till we've come safe home ta tell of it anyways!"

They laughed. The humor cast off the layer of anxiety fastened around their hearts, but it was no sooner than their laughing drained away that they heard the rapid alarm call of many birds behind them.

"Shhh!" Teague hushed. "The redpolls are shoutin' again."

They paused to listen and looked behind them. Amid the calling birds, they heard loud, deep barks.

"Fáelshee!" Alastar cried.

"Right that!" Teague acknowledged. "Fell the trees here, would ya, lad?"

Alastar cut down the whole line of trees behind them as far as he could see. The effort drained him so much that he became dizzy. He stumbled as they ran to mount their horses.

Gabhann caught him from falling. "Ya alright?" he asked.

"Usin' the bracer's power wears on me," Alastar said. "I'm grand. Let's get out of here!"

They started to gallop east again and heard the barking growls of the fáelshee just behind the mass of fallen trees. The fáelshee climbed and wormed themselves through the tangle of leaves and branches as easily as they would jump through small bushes. They emerged through the trees quickly and leapt after them.

Gabhann looked back. His face stiffened into shocked dismay as he saw the dark, hulking shapes of the leaping fáelshee come near. "Bog bean, lad!" he screamed. "This horse go any faster?!"

Alastar urged Éimhín as fast as he could go. They overtook

Teague and made him press harder as well. Still the fáelshee had no trouble keeping up with them. Alastar's heart beat furiously, but he gathered calm and tried to focus again. He cut the trees just in front of them so they would fall as they passed.

The large trees crashed down on the chasing fáelshee and crushed many of them. Most of them were stopped and yelped in pain, but a few continued to run after them. They were able to keep their distance from the wolves for some miles, but their horses were tiring again from the heated run.

"Flank 'em in the fields!" Teague yelled to Alastar. "We passed the city!"

They burst out of the forest and entered the plains just northeast of Lochtán an Eidhneáin. They saw the Cairn Cath Road to the south of them, but as they charged toward it they were shocked to see another large army directly ahead. Their long lines stretched across the field to block the way east and south.

Teague recognized the army immediately. "Fuar blocks our way!" he yelled. "Mind the fáelshee first! Go round on your left, lad!"

Teague turned his horse right to round back on the three remaining fáelshee while Alastar looped back on the left side. They came at the fáelshee with their swords as the wolves burst out of the forest to follow them. Teague rushed at the nearest fáelshee with the point of his sword held out. When he came close he quickly turned his horse to the side and rammed the sword into the side of the wolf's chest. It slid clean through to the heart, but the fáelshee's hard body caught his sword as if it had sunk deep into a hardwood. He couldn't pull it out and fell off his horse with the tumbling fáelshee.

Alastar charged another fáelshee from the opposite side with his sword held high. He also swerved and struck, but found the wolf's hide was too thick for a swiping blow. His sword bounced off the thick fur harmlessly. The fáelshee turned to face them and Éimhín reared up on his hind legs. Gabhann fell off and gasped for air when he hit the ground on his back, but he continued to hold his sword tightly in his hand.

The third fáelshee came up on Gabhann quickly as he lay dazed on the ground. Teague had worked his sword free from the dead fáelshee and went running to help Gabhann. *The long tip of Gearóid's spear would be grand!* he thought as he sprinted the distance to reach them. The giant wolf was about to pounce on Gabhann so Teague jumped high in the air and threw his sword. It stuck in the fáelshee's side and made it cry in pain. Gabhann quickly got up from under the wolf's shadow and lunged his sword into its underside.

Alastar held on to Éimhín as he continued to rear up at the last fáelshee. It snarled at them as Éimhín kicked his front legs in the air. Alastar couldn't strike at the wolf while Éimhín was on his hind legs, so he swung off the saddle and jumped to the ground. He charged under Éimhín and stuck his sword straight into the fáelshee's neck. It thrashed in pain and swung around to knock Alastar down. He fell backwards to the ground, but his sword remained stuck in the wolf's neck.

Teague and Gabhann rushed to help Alastar fell the beast. They tackled it with their swords as Alastar got back up. It lay dying on the field as they heard a trumpet call come from Fuar's army.

"No time ta celebrate victory," Teague huffed. "The king is not here ta help us."

"*What?!*" Gabhann cried with shock. "Are ya not soldiers 'a Torthúil? They fly your kingdom colors."

"We are," Teague said, "but the kingdom has split. King Fuar has sided with the Áiteoir against Lacharan's House of Ealaí. The Eachraighe stand apart from Cnoc na Rí's House of Lorcán now."

"And where are the rest 'a ya!" Gabhann worried. The thought of facing another army made his courage drain away.

Teague looked at Alastar with a sigh.

"They're home," Alastar said in a quiet, disheartened breath.

"Ya mean the home we're runnin' ta?" Gabhann said. "*Grand.*"

They looked forward at Fuar's army. He had brought his entire troop from Cnoc na Rí - over three thousand men - but many of them remembered the battle at Cnoc Earraigh and how Alastar and their kinsmen fought with surprising vigor and tenacity to rescue Amber. They especially remembered the shocking display the Azure gave and how the Eachraighe simply rode away in the midst of great numbers against them.

The rumors made the king's army wonder what to expect. Many of them still had loyalties divided between Fuar and Amber, but despite his soldier's uncertainties, Fuar ordered them with a calm rigidness. His archers marched forward at the sound of his horn and came within range.

Alastar, Teague and Gabhann got back on their horses and waited.

"Be wide behind us as well," Teague reminded. "Laochmarú's men will arrive shortly."

Hundreds of archers lifted their bows and loosed their arrows, but Alastar was already focused on what to do. As soon as the arrows went flying, he splintered all their shafts and the pieces fell harmlessly to the ground. Fuar's soldiers stood in confusion. They never saw anything like it before. The king, though, grew angry and ordered another volley.

Again the archers raised their bows and loosed their arrows. This time Alastar cut their bows to pieces as well as the arrows. The soldiers had no idea what was going on. They couldn't tell Alastar was splintering the wood, but fear went through their ranks with murmurs of unnatural protection for the Swan-bearer. Their confusion was sending them into disarray, but Fuar commanded his men into order.

"Grand work," Teague told Alastar. "The men don't wish ta fight. There's chance they'll let us pass."

Each side stood facing each other for a time as Fuar rode about and rallied his men. Alastar, Teague and Gabhann were hopeful the army would stand down, but the king showed no signs of giving up. He called everyone to raise their weapons and wait. Thousands of men stood with spears, axes, and swords held ready, but their eyes did not match the tough metal of their weapons. Most of them second guessed their loyalty to Fuar.

"What are they waitin' for?" Gabhann asked.

"Reinforcements," Teague said.

Gabhann burst out in delighted amazement, "Amaideach, lads! This old dog has seen it all now - an army hesitates ta attack three men in open field! This'll be the grandest craic of all time!"

Just as Gabhann finished speaking, they heard another battle horn from behind. It was the low bellow of Laochmarú's call to charge. They looked back and saw scores of Áiteoir cavalry gallop out of the forest as far as it stretched, north and south.

"The reinforcements," Alastar said calmly.

Teague assessed their options and decided to run to their left, toward the only opening without troops in their way. "North!" he shouted.

They shot forward toward a large, distant hill of grass and massive boulders. They could go through the gap there if the Áiteoir and Fuar's men didn't close it off. They pushed their horses as fast as they could go. Streams of enemy soldiers followed them to close the gap. They almost reached it when a large shadow flew over them. They looked up and saw Draíodóir on his stone dragon.

"BANJAX!" Teague yelled. They would need cover from attacks overhead too. He looked forward through the gap and trained his eyes on the forest beyond. "Bolt ta the trees!"

They pressed their horses even harder and swiftly narrowed the distance to the gap, but Draíodóir circled above and made a scooping motion with his hand. The ground in front of them all of a sudden shot up to make a high wall. Their escape through the gap was completely cut off. Their horses gave loud neighs in alarm and quickly stopped just before hitting the wall of grass and dirt. The men struggled to stay on their horses after the sudden jolt of stopping.

"Bog bean!" Teague exclaimed. He looked back and saw both armies still approaching fast. They came from all directions to pen them in. Then Draíodóir flew over Fuar's men far to the southeast. They didn't have time to wonder where he was going.

"Turn 'round and battle Fuar's men!" Teague ordered. "Try ta break through 'n run east. Keep swift on open ground, do not let 'em slow ya!"

They turned their horses back toward Fuar's men and charged. They had nearly reached them when another battle horn sounded. Its loud, mid-tone timbre came from behind Fuar's army. The sound was familiar to Teague. He slowed his horse and stood up in the stirrups to see over Fuar's men. Alastar slowed as well to stay with him.

Teague saw another army behind Fuar's make a charge toward them with a thousand spears bristling at the forefront. Draíodóir circled over them just out of reach of their lances and arrows.

"Our kinsmen!" Teague yelled joyfully. "Press on, lad, 'n meet them center!"

Alastar charged ahead again with a yell of valor. Gabhann shouted as well. They held their swords ready and chopped at many soldiers as they rode through Fuar's ranks, but Teague remained in the open field with enemy cavalry bearing down on him. He picked up the gold horn that the Éisc gave him and blew a long note to affirm their presence to their friends.

Its bright, powerful sound rushed through the field so thick that its waves could be seen in the air, like a golden, dewy mist that blew out to cover everyone. Wisps of it settled on Alastar and Gabhann and it continued onward to settle on all the Eachraighe rushing to join them.

Everyone that the gold mist settled upon immediately felt resolve and strength lift them. All fear quickly left and they could even move faster. The effects surprised Alastar and he remembered Ailbhe said the horn would make them stand like mighty waves of the sea. He felt his focus sharpen as well. It made him remember to use the bracer and in the midst of attacking with his sword, he also turned every wood shaft, shield and weapon into splinters. The only arms he couldn't disassemble were swords completely made of metal.

Gabhann felt so invigorated that he jumped off Éimhín and fought on foot. The tattered rags on his thin, old frame waved about his body, like a worn banner of battle held high. Despite his lack of clothing and armor, he fought as if he had the full assurance of a knight's heavy armor surrounding him.

Teague charged ahead again to join Gabhann and Alastar. The Áiteoir were just behind him, though, and pressed into Fuar's men to get to them. At the same time, Gearóid and the Eachraighe crashed into the other side of Fuar's army with their spears plowing through the field. Fuar's men quickly split into such confusion and panic that they started to attack the Áiteoir as well as the Eachraighe.

Fuar was in the south end of the battlefield, far from Alastar and Teague, but he saw how quickly his men were falling. His army would not survive this battle, so he ordered a retreat. His trumpeters called it out and he left the battlefield to flee south.

"Fuar retreats!" Gearóid yelled when he heard the trumpet call. "Let his men leave! Engage the Áiteoir!"

Fuar's men quickly retreated and followed the king south, but many of them shifted allegiance to the Eachraighe and remained to fight with them. The battlefield was still a huge mass of soldiers everywhere. The vast Áiteoir army continued to stream out of the forest in the east. They greatly outnumbered the Eachraighe, but when Laochmarú saw Fuar leave the battle he became furious. He resolved to make Fuar pay for it, but he had to focus on getting Alastar first. It would be an easy task to separate him from the others since the Eachraighe were spread thin to engage his huge numbers of soldiers.

Fuar looked back at the battlefield as he rode away and saw Amber in the outskirts with Gilroy and many guards and archers around her. They were keeping Draíodóir at a distance as he continued to fly over them. Fuar grimaced in anger at Amber and ordered his royal guard to take her. If he couldn't win the battle, he could still steal her away and reunite his kingdom by marrying her.

Fuar continued to retreat south as he let his guard go after Amber. Nearly a hundred of them charged toward her. Gilroy had a horn blown to alert Gearóid of the threat, but he and his men were too busy fighting the swarm of Áiteoir.

"Archers!" Gilroy ordered.

Their archers shifted their attention from Draíodóir and aimed for Fuar's charging guard. Draíodóir saw an opportunity and swooped down at them. He plunged through the line of archers with the edge of his dragon's stone wing and sent them tumbling.

Gilroy ordered their guards to charge. They went forward to stop Fuar's guard from advancing, but they only had half the number.

Many of Fuar's men continued to charge toward Amber.

"Stand firm," Gilroy urged her.

Amber watched the riders charge and looked around her. All her men were injured on the ground or too far away to help. Then she looked toward the battlefield and saw the massive movement of flailing men and horses. Her Eachraighe were fighting valiantly with the great vigor Teague's horn gave them. They were holding well against a force more than ten times their number. She thought quickly and made Muirgel gallop toward the battlefield.

"Princess!" Gilroy yelled after her. *What is she thinking?*

Fuar's men followed Amber toward the battlefield as Draíodóir watched them from above in disbelief. He smirked thinking that neither she nor the Swan-bearer would come out of the battle alive. He set his dragon down on the rocky hill in the north to watch over the battle.

Amber charged straight into the battle and looked for Alastar. Her men didn't notice her enter the field, but the Áiteoir who saw her were confused. They simply let her pass by since they had no orders to take the princess. Fuar's guards, however, watched Amber go through the great crowd of fighting. They dared not to enter for fear the Áiteoir would turn on them. They retreated and returned to the king to make a report.

Gilroy watched Amber in disbelief. "Right grand ailpín!" he exclaimed. "A fair dose 'a stout-headedness from her Swan-bearer has rubbed off on the girl. They'll be the death 'a me!" He rode forward and ordered all his men to enter the battle and protect the princess.

Every Eachraighe except Gilroy was now in the battle. He was the only unarmed man in the field, so he stayed on the outside and watched. His kinsmen slowly chopped away at the Áiteoir ranks, like a grinding stone methodically crushing grain. It was obvious the Áiteoir were falling in far greater numbers.

Fuar's guards told the king how Amber got away, but he resolved to not give up. He ordered two guards to go back to the battle and infiltrate the Eachraighe. They would easily fit in since many of Amber's men came from Cnoc na Rí and still wore their old uniforms. Fuar told them to stay with the Eachraighe discretely until they knew where Amber's base camp was. They went back to the battlefield and joined the ranks of Conn's men who fought in the south of the field.

Amber went through the middle of the large field for many minutes trying to find Alastar. She finally saw him near the north end with just Teague and a few Eachraighe nearby. Laochmarú was pressing toward Alastar, but Gearóid and Conn were trying to intercept him. They knew if Laochmarú fell, the Áiteoir would give up easily and Draíodóir would have to retreat.

Gearóid was getting closer to Laochmarú, so he looked around for a spear. He was most expert with them, but he lost his spear in the first moments of battle. When he saw one on the ground, he sheathed his sword and jumped down to get it. Conn was just behind him and covered him as he grabbed the spear and remounted his horse.

Gearóid took off in a charge toward Laochmarú with the spear held high. He aimed for a joint in Laochmarú's plate armor at the left shoulder. Gearóid threw the heavy spear with a shout and its point hit the exact mark. The spearhead slipped right between the links in Laochmarú's armor. It had such force that it snapped the chainmail rings underneath and pierced him. Gearóid and Conn shouted with zeal and rushed forward with their swords to finish him off.

Laochmarú grunted in disbelief. He stuck his long sword into the ground and yanked out the spear. He charged at Gearóid and Conn in anger and threw the spear back at Gearóid. They were galloping so fast that the momentum sent the spear clear through the center of

Gearóid's chest plate and mail shirt. He fell off his horse and tumbled to the ground. Amber screamed in alarm when she saw Gearóid fall. She galloped forward to get to Alastar as fast as she could. She had to get him off the battlefield before Laochmarú got to him.

Conn continued to charge at Laochmarú. He struck at him with his sword many times but could not get past his thick armor. Laochmarú was unarmed and blocked Conn's blows with his armored forearm. He quickly grew irritated of Conn's quick strikes and used his strength to push Conn off his horse.

Laochmarú rode back to get his sword and saw Amber rush past on Muirgel. He retrieved his sword and followed her to Alastar. She yelled at Alastar to look and go with her, but he couldn't hear her above the battle. The clanging of metal was a droning roar everywhere around them, but as Amber got closer Alastar heard her voice.

He looked at her with surprise and shock. He couldn't understand what she was saying, but he saw Laochmarú chasing her and the distress on her face ran his blood hot. He screamed at Laochmarú and charged. To Amber's dismay, Alastar galloped right past her and engaged Laochmarú.

She brought Muirgel to a halt and looked for help. The battlefield was scattered there. Few Eachraighe were nearby. She had seen Teague before. Where was he?

She spun Muirgel about looking for him. She found him many meters away fighting on foot with an old man in rags. She galloped to them and screamed, "Alastar needs your help!"

"Princess?!" Teague acknowledged wondering what she was doing on the battlefield. "What are ya?" he asked pausing, but then continued to fight as more Áiteoir attacked him.

After he and Gabhann dispatched the Áiteoir around them, Amber yelled again, "Go help Alastar! Laochmarú's on him!"

They ran forward to help Alastar. He was striking at Laochmarú with his sword but doing little damage. Amber watched them from the distance when her guard caught up with her.

"We need brin' ya ta safety, Princess," one of them said.

"Pay no mind ta me!" she said quickly. "Go help Alastar!"

They acknowledged and most of them rode to Alastar, while some of them stood guard around Amber. When the guards reached him, Teague and Gabhann were pulling Laochmarú off his horse. They stood around him and pinned him to the ground.

Draíodóir saw his general subdued and took off flying on his dragon in a rage. He circled the hill he was on and focused his power on it. The ground rumbled and shook as the giant boulders and earth of the hill rose up and formed a colossus hunchback troll.

Everyone stopped as they saw the earth troll take form. It stood many stories high and had a head and back of granite boulders. The rest of it was dark earth and green grass. Clumps of dirt fell from its body as it stepped forward.

Most of the Áiteoir knew to get out of its way and scattered, but the Eachraighe rushed to regroup and protect Amber and Alastar in the north end. Most of them had to cross the huge field, though, and the earth troll was right in front of Amber. Despite many dozens of guards protecting her, it ran through them and swiped a giant arm at her.

Muirgel rose onto her hind legs wildly and threw Amber off. She tumbled to the ground as Muirgel ran away. The giant continued to swing its heavy arms at everyone and made them run about. They didn't know how to bring down the troll.

Alastar charged toward Amber as the others attacked the troll. Laochmarú took advantage of the distraction and freed himself. He gathered his few remaining soldiers nearby and told them to get

Alastar and Amber. They rushed toward them on foot with swords and spears as Alastar helped Amber onto Éimhín. He didn't get on, though, and slapped Éimhín to make him run. "Take her safe away!" he yelled and raised his sword to face the Áiteoir.

Éimhín jumped forward. Most of the Áiteoir moved out of the way, but Laochmarú held a spear ready. He waited for Éimhín to come near and plunged the spear into his underside. Éimhín rose up and screamed in pain. He fell over and Amber rolled off him.

"Éimhín!" Alastar screamed in horror. He raced forward to get to Amber but the Áiteoir intercepted him.

Laochmarú looked down at Amber with a sneer as she went to comfort Éimhín. He walked past her to fight Alastar. Amber looked about for help, but the men around her were trying to fight the giant troll, and the Eachraighe who ran to join them from the south were still a ways off.

Draíodóir saw it was time to get the bracer from Alastar. He landed near them as Laochmarú overpowered Alastar. The general threw him down with Amber and the Áiteoir stood guard as Draíodóir walked up.

"Are ya hurt?" Alastar asked Amber.

"I'm not," she replied with tears in her eyes, "but Éimhín is dead." She brought her hand to his arm to comfort Alastar and touched the bracer. She immediately felt energy leave her and go out to Éimhín. But before she could say anything, Draíodóir reached them. His men took Alastar and held his arms firmly.

Amber got up and tried to go to Alastar, but they restrained her. Laochmarú grabbed the bracer on Alastar's arm and tried to get it off. He struggled violently when he remembered that Draíodóir should not get both bracers, but they were too strong for him. Laochmarú took the bracer off and gave it to Draíodóir. He received it with a grin and looked downfield at the Eachraighe coming closer.

"A valiant fight, Swan-bearer, but this battle is lost for you," Draíodóir said as he put on the other bracer. "Finish them," he ordered. He got back on his dragon and took off.

Laochmarú raised his sword and pressed its tip to Alastar's throat. Amber screamed and struggled, but Alastar stood still, ready to face death.

"Your courage has been a surprise, Swan-bearer," Laochmarú said. "You meet death with honor." He gripped his sword firmly with both hands and prepared to lunge it forward.

At that instant, bright light came from Éimhín. It blinded everyone. Alastar couldn't see, but he quickly lunged backwards and broke free from the Áiteoir. When their eyes adjusted to the bright light, they could see something happening to Éimhín. He got up, still glowing bright, and large wings of feathers grew out of his shoulders. He whinnied loud and reared up to kick at the Áiteoir who held Amber. They let go of her and she rushed to Alastar.

Laochmarú was still mostly blinded, but Alastar was quick to regain his vision. He stared at Éimhín in shock. Everyone did. Even the giant troll stood motionless now and looked at Éimhín's brilliant, shining hide. He was the same ruddy, powerful horse, but bright light shown from him like the radiant, glowing blossoms he was fond of eating. His new wings gave him the strength and majesty of a glowing golden eagle.

Éimhín reared up again and whinnied loud. He ran over to Alastar and shoved over the Áiteoir along the way. Alastar regained his wits and quickly grabbed his sword on the ground. He jumped into the saddle with Amber and they took off flying as the Eachraighe reached the north end of the field.

Laochmarú couldn't believe what happened. Alastar had

slipped away again and was now flying on a winged horse. He saw the Eachraighe led by Captain Conn in the south. They were dragging Fuar's three ballistae that he left on the battlefield. He needed to regroup his men, so he brought his battle horn to his lips and called for a retreat to Lochtán an Eidhneáin.

Draíodóir was already flying there when he saw the area flood with light from Éimhín's transformation. He didn't know what happened or what to do about Alastar and Amber now. They flew over the battlefield and tried to distract the troll while men attacked from below. Soon they had the ballistae aimed at it and fired.

Giant arrow bolts shot from the ballistae. One bolt stuck through the troll's chest of dirt, but the other two dismembered its head and an arm. They quickly reloaded the ballistae and shot again. The bolts sent the troll spinning out of balance and it went crashing down to break into pieces.

Draíodóir grumbled and flew toward the city in a rage. Most of his army was in retreat near the city. He needed to secure his army there, so he thought to see how much power both Bracers of Focus gave him. He focused his effort in a giant circle miles around the great port city. A huge amount of energy drained out of him as the earth broke away and lifted the city of cliffs and vines into the sky. The soil on the city's docks and beaches was too loose to hold together, so immense chunks of earth and seawater fell away as the city rose up.

Draíodóir became visibly aged and weak as he made the great effort, but he continued until Lochtán an Eidhneáin floated as high as the clouds. Most of his army was now on the floating island and the bay that the city sat in doubled in size. Water from the Muir Airgid rushed into the massive crater left by the rising island. The disturbance created such huge waves that the Éisc could feel the water's thrust in their city many miles away underneath the sea. The waves snapped some of their tall structures and sent debris from the sea floor everywhere. The bright waters of the Muir Airgid became a murky pool of churning mud and dirt.

*T*he Eachraighe had cheered in victory after reducing the giant earth troll back into a pile of dirt and stone, but their jubilation was short-lived when they felt the great rumbling come from Lochtán an Eidhneáin. The battlefield on Cairn Cath Road was a mix of emotions for them. They couldn't believe Éimhín sprouted wings like an eagle and carried Alastar and Amber to safety. It was another miraculous triumph for them, but it was overshadowed by the rising of the Áiteoir's new fortress into the sky. Lochtán an Eidhneáin blotted out the sun and cast a heavy shadow on the battlefield. All their shouts of joy were silenced when they saw the massive city rise into the sky.

Then the aftershock of death set in under the shadow of the enemy's floating city. Gearóid's death was a sharp hammer blow that cracked the anvil spirit of Lacharan's men, like Conall's death shook that of Loch an Scátháin's. The sight of their dead kinsmen sent their hearts into a lament.

Alastar landed Éimhín near Conn and Gilroy. They hovered over Gearóid's body in mourning. Amber went to Gearóid and knelt down by his side. Alastar followed and gave her comfort. She wept with the dismay of sorrow and uncertainty. The enemy just raised a powerful stronghold, while they had to huddle hidden away in the River Valley. The anbobracht withering put doubt in her heart about whether their efforts for their kingdom would survive. And now the strong and watchful protector of her house, who she remembered had always stood firm, lay lifeless in the green field. The spear was still stuck through his chest.

Teague came up to them and pulled the spear out. "Our mightiest have fallen in these days 'a blood soiled earth," he said.

"Gearóid 'n Conall fight t'gether in the endless heavens. May they laugh and sing while they wait on our joinin' 'em." A murmur of recognition for the dead went through the crowd, and someone began to sing a lament for them.

Gilroy put his hand on Amber's shoulder and said, "We mustn't linger under the shadow of the enemy. Let us gather up and return home."

Amber nodded in silence and everyone prepared to march to Cnoc na Raithní near Loch an Scátháin where they could bury their dead. Hundreds of their kinsmen had fallen and they would take them all back to rest the ages with their ancestors.

Gilroy took off Gearóid's gold penannular ring and fibulae clasps. He stashed them in his robe and stood up. He gazed up at the island that hovered high over their heads. "How could Draíodóir raise such a mass?" he wondered confused.

Alastar stood up. "I'm afraid it's my fault," he said sorrowfully. "He took my Bracer of Focus."

"Banjax!" Teague exclaimed. "If he can raise a mountain inta the sky now, what could he do ta our homes?"

"Bracer?" Gilroy asked with confusion. "What do you speak of?"

"It was a gift from the Muintir an Éisc," Alastar said. "For the rescue of their prince and ta match the bracer Draíodóir stole from them."

"It was the bracer that healed Éimhín," Amber added. "When I touched it, I felt its power go inta him. Then he lived again and became. . . as he is."

"Is that what happened?" Conn said amazed. "And now the Áiteoir have this power?"

"Not exactly," Alastar replied. "It wasn't just the bracer that brought Éimhín back. Amber, it was your gift of healin' the bracer brought forward. Éimhín could not have lived if not for you. The bracer let me wield my skill ta carve wood with just a thought. For Draíodóir it strengthens his powers over earth and levitation. The pair of bracers together must've given him enough power ta raise the city."

"All the more reason ta march quick away," Gilroy warned. "No tellin' what Draíodóir will conjure next."

"I think Draíodóir will not conjure any more today," Alastar said. "Usin' the bracers drain you. He will need much rest after raisin' the city."

They gathered everyone up and marched back to the east. Amber rode on Muirgel while Alastar got used to Éimhín's wings. Éimhín wanted to take off flying at every other step, but Alastar held him to the ground as they went along the Cairn Cath Road. It would take them just north of Loch Chnámh an Áidh where they could cross the River Seascannach on a bridge.

Normally they wouldn't take a major bridge controlled by the enemy, but since the bulk of the Áiteoir army was lifted away on Lochtán an Eidhneáin and Fuar's army fled south, they had no fear of enemy troops along the way. Amber's Eachraighe still numbered more than 2000 men, so any garrisons along the way would be of little threat.

The sun dwindled into the horizon and the land's glow overtook the light of day. They were glad to be far from Lochtán an Eidhneáin, but they could still see its huge bulk hanging in the sky behind them. It was like a black mark in the midst of the landscape's beauty. It stood out like a patch of dry, shriveled dirt in a field of vibrant green and blue. The two men Fuar had inserted into their ranks, though, were well concealed. Everyone was oblivious to them as they kept to themselves and followed the army in the rear where the dead were hauled on carts and horses.

They made camp for the night before reaching the River Seascannach. The next day, they crossed the river and passed Chnámh an Áidh without incident. The watchmen in the bridge and city towers were alerted but no troops were sent to intercept them. Later in the day, they swung toward the southeast to head for the mountain ridges of Loch an Scátháin. Just hours away, they saw a small group of people far ahead going in the same direction.

"I would send a scout ta inspect 'em," Teague said to Alastar, "but since ya have wings, I think you should have a look. Éimhín's been set ta bolt inta the sky all day. Try not ta scare 'em flappin' 'bout."

Alastar acknowledged and flew toward the group. He quickly came upon them and stayed behind their path so his shadow would not alarm them. He looked down and counted about two dozen men and women but only a handful of horses. They did not display any colors or crests, so he came down closer to see who they were. As he swooped lower he recognized Flann and Ula in the group. They could hear Éimhín's wings in the still air and looked up. Many people let out screams when they saw Alastar on a flying horse.

"Dragon!" someone yelled.

Cathal, Rónán and Bearach drew their swords, and Neese quickly turned around to aim at Alastar with his bow. Éimhín flapped his wings intensely at the threat and whinnied. When Neese saw it was no dragon behind them, he held his bow taut and waited.

"Lower your bow, Neese," Bearach said. "It's Alastar!"

"The Swan-bearer lad?" Neese mused. "Emmm. . . he's got wings."

Alastar landed in front of them and dismounted. Flann and Ula ran to him first while everyone else gathered close. They examined

Éimhín and wondered what happened to him.

Flann filled with joyful tears as she hugged Alastar. "Fáilte ["fahl-chay"; welcome], Alastar!" she said. "We hoped ta see your face on our return, but never did I think ta see ya comin' from the sky!"

"There's much ta tell of," Alastar said with calm. He was thinking mainly about Conall's death, but they looked at him with such enthusiasm he didn't have the heart to tell them. He turned to point at their approaching army. "We march home from a battle near Lochtán an Eidhneáin. Wait here while we join you." He got on Éimhín and flew back to the front of the march.

"It's the group rescued from the north," Alastar told them.

"Grand altogether!" Teague exclaimed. "We've a spot 'a bright t'day."

"I couldn't tell Flann and Ula about Conall," Alastar replied. "They were so glad ta see us."

Teague sighed mournfully. "We'll tell 'em t'gether, soon as we reach them." He ordered a group of men to ride fast ahead and tell everyone in Duille Coiréil to meet at Cnoc na Raithní and prepare for burial ceremonies. They would reach the ferta burial grounds before the sun set.

When the army came closer, Flann and Ula scanned the soldiers at the front for Conall. They thought he would be at the head of the march, but they began to worry when he was nowhere in sight. The bright gleam of Conall's polished bronze would always bring warmth to their hearts when he returned from battle, but as they watched the army approach somberly without him, their spirits sunk into despair. They were already thin and ragged from working the mine and walking many days from Cloch Lom. Conall's absence only made their faces even more downtrodden. They ran up to Teague when they found no sign of Conall.

"Where is Conall?" Flann asked urgently.

"I'm sorry, Flann," Teague replied. "Conall fell the day you were taken from Loch an Scátháin. Many have fallen that day and since."

Ula cried and held onto Flann while her mother let out a wail of sorrow. Amber came and comforted them. For a time they wept on the open fields. They found their return home to be honey spilled on coarse sand. Hopes of returning to life and family as they knew it seeped hopelessly away from them.

Amber let Muirgel carry them home while she rode with Alastar. They came to the high hills of Cnoc na Raithní with the sun casting its last rays along its back. Fionn, Mab, Nola and the others from Duille Coiréil were waiting for them.

They quickly buried the dead at the ferta under cairn piles of stone and gave their last wishes for the dead. Mab had brought Conall's gold ring clasp and gave it to Flann. Flann held it tight as she stood at Conall's grave. She remembered his steady resolve and fearlessness as he left them to fight the enemy. She looked at his penannular clasp and stroked its gold shield. It symbolized his leadership.

Flann went to Amber and gave her Conall's ring clasp. "This belongs ta the next leader of Loch an Scátháin," Flann said.

Amber accepted it and gave her a reassuring smile. "Don't lose hope. You lost your husband, but you're surrounded by kin. We're you're family, as strong in support as Conall's love was for you and our kingdom."

After the sun disappeared and the land was letting out its last breaths of light, everyone returned to the River Valley. They passed the burnt shell of Loch an Scátháin. Many longed for their lost homes and wept for a return to peaceful times, but there were speckles of hope that glowed bright in the abandoned fields. Sprouts from the crops they had planted many weeks ago came out of the dark earth. The dry weather held back the crop, but despite the poor conditions, new life was returning.

King Fuar led his army southeast from Lochtán an Eidhneáin to find refuge in Lacharan. They fled away even faster when they saw the fields and cliffs of Lochtán an Eidhneáin rise up behind them, like a giant uprooted plant. Fuar lost nearly half his men in the battle and wanted to regroup with the soldiers he left in Lacharan. He took most of them out and left a garrison of many hundreds to defend Lacharan. Then he marched back to Cnoc na Rí and waited for his spies to reveal where Amber hid. They came back to Fuar a few days after the battle.

"They hide in a village near the center of the valley, Sire," one of the guards told Fuar.

"Hid right well deep in the forest," the other guard added. "Set against the north mountainside."

"And what of foul beasts there?" Fuar asked. "The scouts reported nothin' but enormous fanged bats."

"We dared not venture out at night. But we hardly saw anythin' 'a harm in daylight. Right grand place the valley, really."

Fuar scowled realizing Amber was hiding just miles away. "How do they enter the valley?" he asked.

"There's a narrow pass outside the hill country 'a Loch an Scátháin, Sire. The forest is thick everywhere 'round 'em. An army can do nothin' but enter scattered or in thin lines."

Fuar dismissed the guards and thought about what to do. He

sent messages to the Áiteoir about where Alastar and Amber were, but
he got no response. He wondered if his retreat in the battle cost him
the alliance with them. He wanted desperately to capture Amber and
get rid of Alastar, but he worried the Áiteoir would act on their threat
to siege him, so instead of sending his army into the valley, he planned
to fortify Cnoc na Rí and Lacharan. It would do little good for him to
unite the kingdom with Amber if the Áiteoir captured it.

Draíodóir was so weak after raising Lochtán an Eidhneáin
he could hardly walk for days. The great effort he made in raising
the city made him look fifty years older. His hair thinned into patchy
sections and his skin turned to dry, cracked leather. He spent the time
recovering inside the palace of pale green and gray marble stone. The
vine covered palace was the seat of the Méine Kingdom before the
Áiteoir conquered them a few years before. Draíodóir had just finished
moving his throne from Gleann Creagach to Lochtán an Eidhneáin
and now rested in the lush palace. It was a bright and elegant contrast
to the dark, crumbling fortress he abandoned. Lochtán an Eidhneáin
was so full of polished stone and green life that it gleamed like an
oasis in the drab desert and rock of the Áiteoir homelands. Draíodóir's
withered complexion was like a dry corpse in the midst of a vibrant
garden.

While he hid in the palace, everyone else in the city was
restless and flocked to the outer edges of the floating island. Mobs
of people went to see the views of Rathúnas from the height of the
sky. The panoramas were spectacular. The north and east were never
ending pictures of deep green forests, fields and hills. From the great

height, the mountains of Torthúil could be seen as tiny bumps on the horizon. To the west, the Muir Airgid stretched out, but its opposite shore was still hidden over the horizon. And in the south, the great mouth of the River Seascannach could be seen like an arm of the Muir Airgid trying to expand into the land. The river's transition from the clear blue water of the sea to its muddy hue in the northeast appeared like a lively root of the sea had withered dry as it crept inland.

Many residents of the city worried their isolation in the middle of the sky would permanently separate them from the rest of the isle and cut off their supply, but all the farm and pasture land around Lochtán an Eidhneáin was raised up with the urban center. They could easily survive in separation, however, Draíodóir never meant to cut off the city from the rest of the isle. He wanted the high expanse of air around them to be an impenetrable moat and wall to protect his new kingdom seat. No one could attack them now.

As Draíodóir gathered strength, he made plans to move his army back to the ground and bring an end to Torthúil and its hopes in the House of Ealaí. Fuar told him where Amber and Alastar hid in the valley, but he knew his army's size would have little advantage in the dense forest of the River Valley. The strength of his army was on open ground where Laochmarú's cavalry had its greatest strength and where his great number of soldiers could surround and overwhelm their foes. He had to get Alastar and Amber out of the valley or find a different way to fight them.

The Eachraighe settled back into Duille Coiréil after the exhausting battle and the long march home from the Cairn Cath Road. They mourned for days afterwards and kept watch for any signs of enemy movement. However, neither the Áiteoir nor Fuar took any visible actions against them.

It was early summer and the anbobracht withering continued to dry out and crumble the River Valley. Not a drop of rain had fallen in the valley for weeks, though some areas just outside had minimal rain. The water levels on Loch an Scátháin and the River Bradán crept lower each day.

"The fishin's scarce here now that the water's gone low," Niall told Alastar and Gabhann. They had fished for over an hour without a nibble. "We'll have ta go downstream for the catch 'a grilse today."

"Right," Alastar agreed. "Let's go up another mile." He was wearing his léine while Gabhann wore Alastar's white shirt and leather pants. Alastar had given his clothes to Gabhann so he had something respectable to wear. There was a shortage of fabric in Duille Coiréil, so they couldn't make him a new set of clothes. Any extra fabric they had was used to mend the soldiers' clothing damaged in the battle. Amber and the other women spent much of their time repairing clothes and armor as much as wounds of the flesh.

Gabhann started to wrap up his newly made fishing pole. "It'd be nice ta feel the yank of a gill or two. Your stories 'a bright grilse jumpin' every minute have me restless ta catch some silver."

"The summer run just began," Niall said. "Plenty a silver ta grab yet."

They wrapped their poles and began to walk downstream under

the cover of the forest. They traveled along the river with their senses alert. They wanted to keep vigilant from being seen in the open, but no one knew their village's location was already given out to their enemies.

"Do ya know what the fuss is about t'night?" Niall asked Alastar. "Gilroy called everyone ta gather at the longhouse."

"I haven't a clue," Alastar said. "No one's told me anythin'."

"Royal chancellors are always fussin' over somethin'," Gabhann noted. "Must be talk 'a King Fuar. Gilroy said he returned ta Cnoc na Rí."

"Can't be that," Alastar said. "They don't call ta gather unless there's a formal."

"A *formal?* And the princess didn't speak of it ta ya?" Niall asked Alastar.

"Your bird must've found that ring ya had made for her," Gabhann joked. "The gatherin's a ruse ta announce your betrothal! Royals love a public proposal!"

Alastar blushed. "Quit your slaggin'! I'm not goin' ta propose in front of everyone!"

"A ring?!" Niall said curiously. "Ya have it here? Let me see it!"

"Sure he's got it," Gabhann said. "The lad carries it everywhere just waitin' for the chance ta brin' that bit 'a sparkle ta her eyes!"

Alastar flushed with embarrassment. He had the ring in a sleeve pocket of his léine. He was going to retort when a loud splash came from the river ahead. They stopped and listened. Something large was splashing around in the river.

"A long boat paddlin' this way!" Niall said.

They quickly ducked farther into the forest and crept behind the trees to get a closer look. Just a little upstream, they saw something swimming with just its head above the water. It had a large salmon in its jaws.

"A brown bear," Gabhann recognized. "It's got the same ideas a fishin' as we do."

"Hadn't seen one in the valley before," Alastar said.

"They roam high on the mountains most 'a the year," Niall noted, "but always come down for the run 'a salmon. They usually gather upstream where the water's shallow. Hunger must've brought this one inta deeper water."

"Keep wide 'a this one," Gabhann suggested. "Never heard a bear with a meal ta be kind for sharin'. I don't believe we'll get any fishin' done here."

The bear swam to the shore toward them. It had appeared to be a normal bear underwater, but when it came out of the river they could see its enormous size.

"Be wide!" Niall exclaimed quietly as he drew his sword. "Never seen one that big!"

Alastar and Gabhann drew their swords as well.

"Big as those rabid fáelshee dogs!" Gabhann said.

"Let's go back," Alastar said. "We don't need ta fight a bear for fish today."

They turned backwards and started to slip back to the village. They had only made a few steps when they saw another large bear come toward the river. It saw them and stood up just a few meters away. Its massive body stood over ten feet high. They stared stunned at the bear for a moment and dropped their fishing rods in case they had to fight with their swords.

"Do not run, lads," Gabhann whispered. "He's sure ta run us down. Hold your ground."

The huge brown bear let out a roar and it dropped back down

on all fours. It moved its stout muscled body toward them and made a low growling noise.

"Use trees for cover if it charges," Gabhann said.

Niall slowly stepped back from the bear and went toward a large alder tree, while Alastar and Gabhann stood still. The bear charged at them and they ran behind the closest tree. They prepared to face the bear with their swords as it rounded the tree to get at them. Its heavy, clawed paws swiped at them and knocked Alastar down. The others poked their sword tips at the bear to try and make it turn away, but it continued to attack them and roared loudly. During the commotion, the bear from the river came and approached slowly behind them.

"The other bear behind ya!" Alastar yelled as he got up. He faced the other bear and pointed his sword at it. Niall and Gabhann continued to poke their bear and got it to run away, but the bear from the river charged at them just as Niall and Gabhann turned around.

Alastar jumped out of the way just in time and slashed at the bear's side. He was only able to make a shallow cut through the thick fur. The bear continued forward and bowled over Niall and Gabhann with a wide swipe of its paw. Gabhann's shoulder was slashed by its claws and they both fell to the ground in a daze. The bear pounced on them, but Alastar jumped at it from behind and plunged his sword through its thick neck. The great bear roared in pain and slumped down dead with its heavy head square on Niall's chest.

Niall pushed the bear off him and scurried onto his feet. Alastar stepped up to them and helped Gabhann up.

"Thank ya, lad," Gabhann said. "Caught more than we bargained for t'day."

"Banjax!" Niall huffed as he picked up his fishing pole. It was broken. The tapered half hung loose like a broken, limp arm. "Still want ta fish yet?" he joked.

Gabhann picked up his pole from the ground. "Sure thin'," he said with a moan. His shoulder hurt from the gashes. "I doubt the bear will come back for a time. I can still swing my rod about."

"Ya can't be in your wicks!" Alastar said stunned. "I've no stomach for fishin' after that. Who knows how many bears want ta come down for grilse today." He gave his pole to Niall. "Here, you can fish. I'll keep watch."

Niall and Gabhann fished while Alastar watched for any danger. They enjoyed hours of catching good sized salmon while Alastar relaxed after the first hour of silence in the forest. He got to skinning the bear for its thick hide and then dumped the rest of it into the river so its carcass would not attract scavengers, especially more huge bears.

They returned to the village carrying long strings of hanging salmon. Some women and children ran up to them in the courtyard. They took the fish and went to prepare them. Alastar saw Amber brushing Muirgel nearby and went to her. She was trying to soothe her as she brushed Muirgel's golden hair.

"I skinned a bear today," Alastar said as he showed her the bear skin. "This ought ta come handy in the winter."

Amber smiled at him but was distracted. Muirgel was not standing still and tried to bite Amber as she brushed. "Grand," she said. "Muirgel's antsy. . . There's somethin' I want ta ask you."

"Anythin'. What do you need?"

"Muirgel and some of the other mares are in estrus," Amber noted. "Many of the riders want me ta ask for your permission ta mate Éimhín."

Alastar hesitated. "Emmm. . . but he's. . . I'm not sure he's a horse anymore. He'd rather fly off inta the sky than gallop the fields."

"Of course he's still a horse!" Amber retorted. "Besides his new wings, he's still the same - ready ta run and jump as ever he did."

"That is sure," Alastar agreed. "Alright then. We can pen Éimhín with the mares. Would ya like anythin' else of me?"

"Just clean yourself for the gatherin'. You smell of bear and fish!"

Alastar took the bear skin to the cliffs and laid it out in the sun to dry. He looked around at the mountains and then back toward the village. He felt a peaceful sense of belonging and couldn't believe he helped build their community, much less that he was an Eachraighe cavalry soldier. He felt he could call his friends kinsmen now, instead of feeling like an outsider - the babe lost in the woods during his first days on Rathúnas. All thoughts of returning to his life in Eritirim were gone, but he did still wish to see his mother again. She was the only reason he felt the desire to return to Netleaf.

The fires were set around the longhouse and everyone gathered around. A band played music on the stage with Gilroy, Amber, Alastar, Teague and Conn at a table next to them. People were tending to roasting meat and bread on the fires while everyone else sat in a low murmur waiting to see the purpose for the gathering.

When the band finished the song, Gilroy got up and went to center stage. He addressed the village, "We've had many upheavals in our journey ta this place; victories and defeats. Our last battle outside Lochtán an Eidhneáin cut both ways - for us and for our enemies. We came ta aid Alastar and Teague. In that we succeeded!"

The crowd cheered boisterously and Gilroy continued, "But

the Áiteoir gained advantage in the raising of their city, and we lost our greatest commander and many friends. May Gearóid's spear and sword be at his side in the afterlife and all our lost clansmen be forever at peace."

A roar of recognition for their dead friends and family went through the people. Many grieved with tears and utters of short laments. When the crowd quieted, Gilroy spoke again. "Our grievin' may be fresh, but our spirit of hope has not foundered. Look forward, Brothers and Sisters. Tonight we appoint new leaders ta replace those who sleep for the 'morrow." He looked at Teague and Amber, signaling them to come forward.

Amber held gold ring clasps and a royal blue fabric in her hands. Gilroy extended his hand to Teague and asked, "Son, your commander's clasps and mantle, please."

Teague unfastened the clasps that held on his red mantle and gave them all to Gilroy. Then Amber unfurled the blue fabric. It was a royal blue mantle similar to the one Gearóid had worn. She fastened the left side of the mantle to Teague's shoulder with a new gold fibulae clasp that had four slanted bars engraved in it. It used to be Gearóid's clasp and showed his rank. Then Amber secured the other side of the mantle with Conall's old ring clasp. Its gold shield signified that he was a lead commanding officer and district governor.

"We appoint you Governor of Loch an Scátháin and Commander General over the swords and spears of the Eachraighe," Gilroy said as Amber finished securing the ring clasp to Teague's mantle. Teague nodded in acknowledgement and everyone cheered. Then Gilroy looked at Conn and said, "Captain, come forward."

Conn went up as Teague sat back down.

"Your clasp, son," Gilroy requested, referring to his captain's fibulae.

Conn looked down toward his left shoulder and noted his clasp was still replaced with a bent pin. "My betrothed wears it, Sir," he said calmly.

Gilroy smiled at him and looked out to the crowd at Nola. "And may she continue to wear it proudly." He turned to Amber and gave her Teague's old clasp. As she replaced Conn's makeshift clasp with the fibulae, Gilroy stated, "We appoint you Lead Commander Captain under General Teague."

Conn nodded in acknowledgement and everyone gave a cheer.

Then Gilroy looked to Alastar. "Come up, son."

Conn went to the rear of the stage to get something while Teague gave Alastar a reassuring grin. "Go on up," he told him, but Alastar went up to Amber and Gilroy with hesitation and a perplexed look on his face. "What am I doin' here?" he whispered to them. Gilroy and Amber just smiled at him.

Conn came back to the front of the stage with a polished bronze breastplate and chainmail shirt.

"Take off your armor vest, son," Gilroy commanded.

Alastar took off his leather armor and Amber took it from him. She set it down as Conn put the chainmail shirt over Alastar's head. He then secured the bronze breastplate on him. Alastar stood still and composed, though his spirit raced with the joy and pride of receiving the armor. His heart beat with an intensity that could hardly be contained.

When Conn finished with the breastplate, Flann came up to them carrying another bundle of blue fabric with gold clasps set on top. Alastar knew what they were and felt a nervousness about what they meant. *Am I expected to lead soldiers too?* he wondered.

Flann approached them and gave the things to Amber. Flann gave a loving smile of appreciation to Alastar and went back down to sit near the front of the stage. Amber proceeded to unfurl the fabric as she did for Teague. This time, though, she unfolded a mantle of blue-gray instead of the royal blue and placed it around his shoulders.

"Accept this fallaing ["fah-ling"; mantle, cloak, robe], son," Gilroy said. "Its color stands for the foundin' of Lacharan and the Eachraighe Clan when Grandfather Ealaí said the skies were blue-gray each day he built his new home in the land of Lacharan."

Amber proceeded to clasp the mantle on Alastar as she did with Teague. She fastened the left side with a gold fibulae that had three slanted bars on it. Then she fastened Gearóid's gold ring clasp to the right side.

"We appoint you Captain Protector of the House of Ealaí and Regent of Lacharan under Princess Ealaí," Gilroy stated.

Amber stepped away from Alastar with a smile of endearment and the entire village cheered loudly. Alastar nodded in acknowledgement as Teague and Conn did and returned Gilroy and Amber's smiles with one of gratitude and belonging.

They went back to the table and sat down in great elation. The band started to play music again and food was brought out. The village celebrated in renewed strength and hope with the appointments. Teague and Conn's appointments did not surprise them since they were the next in rank under Gearóid, but for Alastar the appointment as a commander was a shock. He was thrust so swiftly into the life of Rathúnas and his role as Swan-bearer that he still hadn't fully adjusted to being a soldier and champion. He still felt like a simple woodcarver, but he took his duties to serve and protect Amber's kingdom very seriously.

The many weeks of training and fighting had etched a soldier's fortitude into him. He hardly knew it as he sat trying to eat clumsily in his new, rigid breastplate, but the noble Swan-bearer knight that Amber dreamt about had finally materialized. He sat next to her enjoying what felt like a simple celebration to him, but for Amber it was a turning in the currents of destiny that helped her continue to reach for the great promises of the future with him.

When Alastar and Amber had their fill, he asked her, "Let's come away from here and find a bit 'a quiet."

She followed Alastar to the stables where they found Éimhín in a pen with Muirgel. Éimhín was tied with a long rope to the pen wall so he couldn't fly off.

"Grand evenin' for a ride," Alastar told Éimhín as he put a saddle on him. He mounted and helped Amber get on Éimhín in front of him. Then they took off flying toward the mountain peaks just over their heads.

Alastar had Éimhín go east to fly over the griffin roost and stone arch. One of the griffins lay relaxed in the nest, but the other saw them coming and flapped its giant wings. It leapt into the sky to intercept them and let out a loud screech that blew through them like a gale wind.

Amber got nervous seeing the huge griffin fly toward them, but Alastar held Éimhín steady. "Are ya mad!" Amber cried. "Did ya not learn they do not want ta be touched?!"

Then they heard another griffin call out from a distant peak. The third griffin took off and came toward them as well. Éimhín held a straight course forward as the closer griffin approached. It swooped up over them and passed by with a huge rush of air. The turbulence from its great mass nearly blew them over. It quickly turned about and followed them just off their left flank.

Amber couldn't believe how close it was flying to them. Its wingtip was just behind Éimhín's waving tail. Then the other griffin came to them and swooped low and around to join them on their right side. They continued to fly down the valley together fixed in formation. The glowing foliage of the valley was alight underneath them, like an immense river of sunlight bordered by the dark mountain peaks.

"The valley's like a burst of stars gathered inta a streamin' river!" Alastar commented.

Soon the city lights of Cnoc na Rí came into sight and the dimly shimmering waves on the dark waters of Bá Rí ended the valley's glowing stream of life.

"We need turn back," Amber said. "We can't be seen in Cnoc na Rí."

Alastar made Éimhín fly upwards and the griffins followed.

"Hold tight!" he told her. "Show her what we've been practicin'," he said to Éimhín.

Éimhín made some vigorous flaps of his wings and then brought them tight to his body and swung quick around and spiraled.

Amber screamed and closed her eyes tight. "LAY OFF IT!!!"

Éimhín straightened out and they were flying back toward the east again.

"Hardly a tumble," Alastar said reassuringly. He looked back to see where the griffins were. They hardly missed a beat and still followed closely behind.

Amber punched him in the leg. "Mind the spinin' 'bout! I'd rather you fall off than the both of us!"

Éimhín gave an affirming nicker.

"Right then," Alastar said. "Forgive me. We'll be straight and level from here."

"I want ta show you a place," Amber said. "Go west along the ridge."

They continued flying east along the northern mountain ridge for a time. The griffins left them when they came to the roosting site.

"There's a clearin' on the summit just as the valley bends south," Amber said. "We can land there."

They flew past the village. It was still well concealed. They couldn't tell it was underneath the glowing forest canopy, but the distant sounds of music and celebration faintly drifted to them from below. Soon they reached the clearing and landed. Alastar got off and helped Amber dismount.

She led him to the cliff where she spent time looking out to the west. They sat down and she said, "This is where I looked for you when you had gone ta the Muir Airgid. It's straight west from here."

At night, the plains and hill country glowed dimmer than the dense life in the valley. The horizon stretched out into a faint green glow and Alastar remembered the battlefield outside Lochtán an Eidhneáin. The great floating city was a dark speck in the sky during the day, but at night it couldn't be seen at all.

The loss of the Bracer of Focus weighed on him and he wondered if he could get it back. How could he face Draíodóir when he could wield so much power? He gave a soft sigh, but tried to hide his concern. There was something else he had his mind set on.

"The stars are full out tonight," he said. He looked at her with a loving resolve. "I couldn't have imagined bein' surrounded by such beauty of things when I came ta Rathúnas. . . I need ask ya of somethin'."

Amber returned his gaze with a reassuring smile.

"Amber, I came here with a few bundles of sticks and none but that willful Éimhín ta keep me company. Almost didn't go through the gateway, but I felt I needed ta reach through and see all the life showin' its abundance in this green valley. Now look at where I am and what I have. . . a clan of my own, a future of promise here. . . and you. I wish ta make it permanent." He reached into his pocket and grabbed the small bundle of white fabric that protected the engagement ring. He hid it in his closed hand and brought her hand to cover his. "Would ya like ta hang your wash with mine?" he asked and opened his palm to place the fabric in her hand.

Amber saw it and smiled wider. She knew what he was asking. "You hardly have a wash ta hang anythin' with," she teased. She paused a moment and feigned contemplation. "Of course I would," she answered.

Dictionary of Names, Irish Slang, English-Irish, and Gaeilge
["Goo-el-gah"] (Irish Gaelic ["Gayl-lik"])

About pronunciations: There are many Irish dialects that sound vastly different. This book generally prefers a North Irish "Ulster/Donegal" accent when pronunciations are given.

Words labeled Gaeilge are Irish Gaelic in origin.
Words labeled English-Irish are Anglicized words. Much modern Irish is Anglicized Irish Gaelic.
Words without a label are English or are not completely Irish Gaelic or Anglicized Irish Gaelic.

Pronunciation Key:

Consonants that repeat, such as in "karrn" for cairn should be pronounced with a longer, more emphasized sound of the consonant.

'æ' is an 'a' sound as in ash, cat and hat, not 'ah' or 'ay' as in ago, pa, or hay.

'ah' is an 'a' sound as in pa or fah, lah, lah.

'ay' is the long 'ā' sound as in hay or neigh.

'ee' is the long 'ē' sound as in seen and knee.

'eh' is an 'e' sound as in peck or heck.

'ih' is an 'i' sound as in pick or sick.

'kh' is a hard, long 'k' + 'h' sound.

'g' is always a hard 'g', "guh" sound, not a 'j' as in jay or gee-whiz.

'ny' is an 'n' + 'y' sound, like the Spanish 'ñ' in niño, pronounced "neenyo".

'oh' is a long 'ō' sound as in woe and low.

'oo' is the ooh 'o' sound as in flu or shoe.

'oww' is the "ow" sound as in cow and plow.

'uh' is a "u" sound as in muck or slug.

a chara ["ah kahr-rah"](Gaeilge) – Used when addressing a friend; means "my friend or dear friend"

ádh mór ["ah more"](Gaeilge) – "good luck"

Ailbhe ["Æl-veh"](Gaeilge Name) - King of the Muintir an Éisc; means "white"

ailpín ["æl-peen"](Gaeilge) - a stout-headed stick

aindeiseoir ["æn-jeh-shor"](Gaeilge Slang) - an unfortunate person or thing

Áine ["Æn-yeh"](Gaeilge Name) - a nurse servant from Cnoc na Rí; means "radiance"

áirneál ["ahrr- nya-ul"](Gaeilge) - a friendly night visit

Áiteoir ["Æ-chor"](Gaeilge Slang/Name) - Kingdom controlling most of Rathúnas; means "argumentative man"

Alastar Duer ["Ah-lah-stahr Doo-er"](English-Irish Name) - woodcarver from Netleaf of Eritirim; Alastar means "Swan-bearer", Duer means "heroic"

amaideach ["ahma-jawkh"](Gaeilge) - silly, absurd, idiotic, foolish, daft, or crazy

Amber Lyn Ealaí ["Ahm-ber Lin Ah-lee"](English and Gaeilge Name) - Princess of Lacharan and the House of Ealaí; Amber (English) from the precious gemstone; Lyn (Gaeilge) means "lake, waterfall and lightning"; Ealaí (Gaeilge) means "swans"

anbobracht ["ahn-boh-brahkt"](Gaeilge) - a withering wasting sickness

Azure ["Ah-zure"] - see Seabhac Azure

babby ["bah-bee"](English-Irish Slang) - baby; a term used to call someone a baby or child

baile ["bwhy-leh"](Gaeilge) - town or home

banjax ["bahn-jæks"](English-Irish Slang) - broken, ruined or tired

banndaire ["bahn-dehreh"](Gaeilge) - a disappointed person

Bá Rí ["Bah Ree"](Gaeilge Name) - the bay at the mouth of the River Bradán and River Valley; means "King's Bay" báthlach ["bahh-lokhk"](Gaeilge) - an awkward clown

bean ["bæn"](Gaeilge) - a wife or woman

Bearach ["Bæ-rahkh"](Gaeilge Name) - a royal guard of Lacharan; means "sharp/ intelligent"

bird (English-Irish Slang) - a girlfriend (lover)

bodhrán ["buh-ron"](Gaeilge) - a traditional Irish handheld drum

bouzzie ["bow-zee"](English-Irish Slang) - a young good-for-nothing person, trouble-maker

Braede ["Bray-dah"](Gaeilge Name) - the mill keeper of Loch an Scátháin and an envoy for the Torthúil Kingdom; originally a mine owner from Cloch Lom in the Méine Kingdom; means "from the dark valley"

fallaing ["fah-ling"](Gaeilge) - a mantle, cloak or robe

Bress ["Bres"](English-Irish Name) - Teague's primary messenger hawk; means "exhalted one"

Brónach ["Broh-nahkh"](Gaeilge Name) - the wife of Braede and sister of Mab from Loch an Scátháin; means "sorrow"

burster ["bur-ster"](English-Irish Slang) - someone powerfully built or intimidating looking

cairn ["karrn"](English-Irish) - a burial mound of piled rocks

Cairn Cath Road ["Karrn Kahh Rohd"](English and Gaeilge Name) - a road leading from Lochtán an Eidhneáin to Loch Chnámh an Áidh; means "Burial Mound Battle Road"

Canal Valley - also called the Desert Valley; it is the River Valley of Eritirim in Alastar's time

Carraig Mhór ["Kar-rig Wor"](Gaeilge Name) - the site on the north shore of Rathúnas where the first harp is made; means "Great Rock"

Cathal ["Kah-hul"](Gaeilge Name) - an Eachraighe soldier of Lacharan; means "battle rule"

céad míle mar aon ["kayd meel mar een"](Gaeilge) - "a hundred thousand as one"; it means a multitude of people moving with unified mind and purpose of spirit

céilí ["kay-lee"](Gaeilge) - a social dancing party or get-together

chancer ["chan-ser"](English-Irish Slang) - a dodgy, risky character

Cliffs of Marmair ["Cliffs of Mar-reh-mer"](English and Gaeilge Name) - cliffs along the northeast shore of the Muir Airgid; marmair means "marble"

Cloch Lom ["Klukh Lum"](Gaeilge Name) - a city in the north mountains of Rathúnas controlled by the Áiteoir Kingdom; means "bare stone"

Clochán na Láimhe ["Kluhkun nah Læveh"](Gaeilge Name) - a city in the southeast of Rathúnas controlled by the Áiteoir Kingdom; means "Stepping Stones of the Hand"

Chnámh an Áidh ["Krahv-aw"](Gaeilge Name) - see Loch Chnámh an Áidh; means "lucky bone"

cnoc ["kruk"](Gaeilge) - hill

Cnoc Earraigh ["Kruk Ah-ree"](Gaeilge Name) - site of an old castle in the east of Rathúnas; means "Spring Hill"

Cnoc na Rí ["Kruk nah Ree"](Gaeilge Name) - capitol city of the Torthúil Kingdom; means "Hill of the King"

Cnoc Seamair ["Kruk Shæ-mer"](Gaeilge Name) - the market district of Cnoc na Rí; means "Clover Hill"

Conall ["Kon-nul"](Gaeilge Name) - Governor and Commander of Loch an Scátháin; husband of Flann and father of Ula; means "strong wolf"

Conn ["Kon"](Gaeilge Name) - Commander Captain of the Eachraighe in Lacharan; means "war hound"

Coral Leaf - English for Duille Coiréil; see Duille Coiréil

craic ["cræk"](Gaeilge) - to have fun or a good time; also to have casual conversation

cré-umha ["kray-oo"](Gaeilge) - bronze metal or ore

Cré-umha Draíochta ["Kray-oo Dree-ehkkta"](Gaeilge Name) - the trademark bronze metal alloy of the Torthúil Kingdom; means "enchanted bronze"

Cnoc na Raithní ["Kruk nah Ræh-nee"](Gaeilge Name) - the ancestral burial grounds of the Torthúil Kingdom near Loch an Scátháin; means "Fern Mountain"

cupán tae ["kupahn tay"](Gaeilge) - "cup of tea"; an expression used to offer social tea

dadaí ["dah-dee"](Gaeilge) - daddy or dad

Desert Valley - also called the Canal Valley; it is the "River Valley" of Eritirim in Alastar's time

Donavan Ealaí ["Donah-vin Ah-lee"](Gaeilge Name) - Amber's great, great, great grandfather; founder of Lacharan and the Eachraighe Clan; Donavan means "strong fighter" and "brown-haired chieftain leader"

doss ["daws"](English-Irish Slang) - used in "on the doss" to mean "playing truant"

dradairín ["drah-dah-reen"](Gaeilge) - a small, useless potato

dray (English-Irish Slang) - a horsedrawn cart, sled or sledge, low and strong, usually used for heavy loads

Draíodóir ["Dree-ah-dor"](Gaeilge Name) - King of the Áiteoir Kingdom; means "magician"

Duille Coiréil ["Dul-yeh Kor-rel"](Gaeilge Name) - a town in the River Valley founded by Alastar and Amber; means "Coral Leaf"

dún ["doon"](Gaeilge) - a fort or to close/shut

Dún Liath ["Doon Lee-ah"](Gaeilge Name) - a castle fortress on the east coast of Rathúnas; means "Fort Gray"

Dún Tearmann ["Doon Tear-mun"](Gaeilge and English Name) - a fort village west of Loch an Scátháin belonging to the Torthúil Kingdom; means "Fort Tearmann"

Eachraighe ["Ahkh-ree"](Gaeilge Name) - the clan of Lacharan and a clan of the Torthúil Kingdom; means "People or Kingdom of the Horse"

Éanshee ["ayn-shee"](English-Irish) - a bird mimic (animated bird of stone) used by the Áiteoir to carry messages

Earraigh ["Ah-ree"](Gaeilge Name) - see Cnoc Earraigh; means "spring"

Éimhín ["Ay-veen"](Gaeilge Name) - Alastar's horse; means "swift or prompt"

Éisc ["Eshk"](Gaeilge Name) – short for Muintir an Éisc; see Muintir an Éisc

Eritirim ["Air-rih-cheer-rim"](English-Irish Name) - the isle of Rathúnas in Alastar's time; means "dry land"

fáelshee ["fahl-shee"](English-Irish) - the giant black lion wolves from the Rásúir Mountains

fáilte ["fahl-chay"](Gaeilge) - welcome

fallaing ["fah-ling"](Gaeilge) - mantle, cloak, or robe

fallsáin ["fæl-sine"](Gaeilge) - a very lazy person or sluggard

Féile Plandála ["Fay-lah Plahn-dah-lah"](Gaeilge) – Planting Festival

fella (English-Irish Slang) - boyfriend (lover) or man

ferta (English-Irish) - ancestral burial grounds

Fionn ["Fin"](Gaeilge Name) - a farmer from Loch an Scátháin; the husband of Mab and father of Nola; means "fair-haired" or "fair/white"

Flann ["Flahhn"](Gaeilge Name) - wife of Conall and mother of Ula from Loch an Scátháin; means "red"

Fuar ["Foor"](Gaeilge Name) - King of Torthúil with his seat in Cnoc na Rí; means "cold"

Gabhann ["Goh-en "](Gaeilge Name) - an old commander from the Méine Kingdom; Gabhann means "smith" and "audacity"

Gap Dearg ["Gap Jair-reg"](English and Gaeilge Name) - the gap through the Torthúil Mountains near Cnoc na Rí from the River Valley to the north; dearg means "red"

geata ["gæt-tah"](Gaeilge) - gate or gateway

Gearóid ["Ger-rudge"](Gaeilge Name) - Duke of Lacharan and leader of the Eachraighe; means "spear carrier" or "brave with a spear"

Gleann Creagach ["Glæn Krægukh"](Gaeilge Name) - the capitol city of the Áiteoir Kingdom on the north shore of the Muir Airgid; means "Rocky Valley"

Giant's Hammer - a huge, sheer cliff face in the south mountains at the mouth of the River Valley

Gilroy ["Gil-roy"](Gaeilge Name) - royal chancellor of the Torthúil Kingdom from Cnoc na Rí; he addresses himself as Gilroy Mac Dáithí, Giolla Rí ["Gil-roy Mahk Dah-hee, Gil-la Ree"] means "Gilroy, Son of Dáithí - the King's Servant"

Glasa ["glah-sah"](Gaeilge Name) - refers to the Prophecies Glasa or Green Emerald Prophecies; "glasa" is the plural form of the color green

Greerian ["Greer-ree-in"](English-Irish Name) - golden guardian sentry eagles of the Torthúil Kingdom grilse ["gril-sheh"](English-Irish) - refers to salmon that come up rivers to spawn, typically during early summer and through fall

hardchaw (English-Irish Slang) - a rough, tough person or someone overeager for a fight

honey-moon (English-Irish Slang) - an old Irish tradition where a newly married couple takes a month (a moon) to be away from others; it is often accompanied by the drinking of honeywine during that time, which is what the "honey" part of the term refers to; the modern word "honeymoon" came from this Irish tradition

horse's hoof (English-Irish Slang) - an exaggerated, embellished story

jig (English-Irish Slang) - an Irish dance or tune set to a beat of six

kip (English-Irish Slang) - a nap or rest

Lacharan ["Lah-kahr-run"](English-Irish Name) - port city on the east coast of Rathúnas belonging to the Torthúil Kingdom; seat of the Eachraighe Clan; founded by Donavan Ealaí

ladhb ["lyyb"](Gaeilge) - an awkward looking young man or boy

lagharitshee ["lye-irtch-shee"](English-Irish) - a swamp bog lizard the size of a wolf that breaths sleeping fumes

lampróga ["lahm-proh-gah"](Gaeilge) - fireflies

Laochmarú ["Lee-ukhk-mahr-roo"](Gaeilge Name) - Commander General of the Áiteoir Kingdom; means "killing warrior"

lashing (English-Irish Slang) - a heavy rainfall or a lot of something

léine ["lay-nyah"](Gaeilge) - refers to the ancient, traditional Irish "war shirt" tunic that predate kilts; typically hangs just above the knees or down to the ankles and has long hanging, flared sleeves; modern skirt-like kilts come from Scottish influence

local (English-Irish Slang) - pub or bar

loch ["lahkh"](Gaeilge) - lake

Lochtán an Eidhneáin ["Lahkh-tun ahn Eye-nine"](Gaeilge Name) - port city on the east of the Muir Airgid; means "Ivy Terrace"

Lorcán ["Lorkh-kun"](Gaeilge Name) - son of Rían and was King of Torthúil after him; Father of the House of Lorcán and great, great, great grandfather of King Fuar; means "little fierce one"

Lorgaire ["Lore-geh-reh"](Gaeilge Name) - a clan of the Áiteoir Kingdom famous for scouts; also refers to the Áiteoir scouts; means "tracker, pursuer, detective, seeker, searcher"

Loch Chnámh an Áidh ["Lahkh Kroww an Eye"](Gaeilge Name) - city in the northeast of Rathúnas; means "Lucky Bone Lake"

Loch an Scátháin ["Lahkh-in Sky-hine"](Gaeilge Name) - town in the west of the Torthúil Mountains; feeds the River Bradán of the River Valley; also called the Mirror of the Mountains; means "Mirror Lake"

Mab ["Mahhb"](Gaeilge Name) - wife of Fionn and mother of Nola from Loch an Scátháin; Mab means "happy"

mainidh ["mah-nee"](Gaeilge) - lunatic or crazy person

Mairéad ["Mah-raid"](Gaeilge Name) - Amber's attendant servant; means "pearl"

mam ["mahm"](English-Irish Slang) - mom

Marmair ["Mar-reh-mer"](Gaeilge Name) - see Cliffs of Marmair; means "marble"

Méine ["Meen-yeh"](Gaeilge Name) - Kingdom that had controlled the northeast of Rathúnas before it was conquered by the Áiteoir Kingdom; means "ore"

midge (English-Irish Slang) - a small fly or gnat

millie up (English-Irish Slang) - term to get ready or fight

Muintir an Éisc ["Mooun-chir ahn Eshk"](Gaeilge Name) - the mermen/mermaids of the Muir Airgid; means "Fish People or People of the Fish"

Muir Airgid ["Mooer Ar-gedge"](Gaeilge Name) - an inland sea at the center of Rathúnas; means "Silver Sea"

Muirgel ["Mer-gel"](Gaeilge Name) - Amber's horse; means "bright sea"

Murchadh ["Mer-rah-hoo"](Gaeilge Name) - Prince of the Muintir an Éisc; means "sea warrior"

Murtagh ["Mer-tah"](Gaeilge Name) - a merchant in Cnoc na Rí; means "skilled in the ways of the sea"

murúch ["mur-roohkh"](Gaeilge) - merman or mermaid

nawful (English-Irish Slang) - terrible, awful

Neese ["Nees"](English-Irish Name) - an archer from Lacharan; means "choice"

Niall ["Neel"](Gaeilge Name) - a royal guard from Lacharan; means "champion" or "cloud"; Anglicized as Neil or Neal

Netleaf - a coastal town on the east shore of Eritirim; Alastar's hometown

Nola ["Noh-lah"](English-Irish) - daughter of Fionn and Mab from Loch an Scátháin; means "famous" or "fair-shouldered"

Nuala ["New-ah-lah"](Gaeilge Name) - Alastar's childhood friend from Netleaf; means "famous" or "fair-shouldered"

peckish (English-Irish Slang) - to feel hungry

Potaire ["Pot-teh-reh"](Gaeilge Name) - a coastal town on the east shore of Rathúnas; means "potter"

pram ["prahm"](English-Irish Slang) - a baby's carriage or stroller

Prophecies Glasa ["glah-sah"](English and Gaeilge Name) - prophecies written in walls of emerald; "glasa" is the plural form of the color green

rashers (English-Irish Slang) - pieces of bacon

Rásúir Mountains ["Ræ-soor"](English and Gaeilge Name) - a mountain range in the north central of Rathúnas; Rásúir means "razor"

Rathúnas ["Ræ-hoon-us"](Gaeilge Name) - the name of the isle; it is called Eritirim in Alastar's time; means "Prosperity"

Rathúnas Tnúthánach ["Ræ-hoon-us Troo-ah-hun-ahkh"](Gaeilge Name) - this book's title; means "Aching/Yearning Prosperity"

Réalta Mountains ["Ree-ahl-tah"](English and Gaeilge Name) - a mountain range outside of Rathúnas; Réalta means "star"

Rían ["Ree-en"](Gaeilge Name) - Amber's great, great, great, great grandfather; first king of Rathúnas and founder of the Torthúil Kingdom; father of Donavan Ealaí and Lorcán; founded Cnoc na Rí; means "kingly"

Rían's Gate ["Ree-en's"](English and Gaeilge Name) - the large gateway at the north end of Gap Dearg; built by King Rían

River Bradán ["Brah-don"](English and Gaeilge Name) - the river of the River Valley and Torthúil Mountains; Bradán means "salmon"

River Seascannach ["Shæs-kon-nahkh"](English and Gaeilge Name) - the river flowing northeast from the Muir Airgid to the North Sea; Seascannach means "boggy"

River Valley - the valley formed by the Torthúil Mountains

Rónán ["Roh-nahn"](Gaeilge Name) - an Eachraighe soldier of Lacharan; means "little seal"

scanger (English-Irish Slang) - a rough, poor person

sciathánshee ["skee-hahn-shee"](English-Irish) - a large bat creature seabhac ["shawwk"](Gaeilge) – a hawk or falcon; used to carry messages in the Torthúil Kingdom

Seabhac Azure ["Shawwk"](English and Gaeilge Name) - the special, supernatural white hawk with blue beak and markings who guides people

selkie (English-Irish) - the seal-human equivalent of a mermaid

siosóg ["shish-og"](Gaeilge) - a puckered, sucking kiss

skint (English Irish Slang) - to be broke or have no money

sláinte ["slan-cheh"](Gaeilge) - an expression for making a toast; means "health"

slán ["slahn"](Gaeilge) - bye or literally safe as in have a safe journey

Teague ["Teeg"](English-Irish Name) - scribe, bird keeper and commander under Conall from Loch an Scátháin; means "poet storyteller"

tine ["chin-neh"](Gaeilge) - fire

Torthúil ["Tar-hool"](Gaeilge Name) - Kingdom controlling the southeast of Rathúnas, mainly the Torthúil Mountains and Lacharan; founded by Rían, father of Donavan Ealaí and Lorcán; means "fruitful"

Torthúil Mountains ["Tahr-hool"](English and Gaeilge Name) - the main mountain range of the Torthúil Kingdom in the southeast of Rathúnas; means "Fruitful Mountains"

Túr an Tairbh ["Toor ahn Tahr-rev"](Gaeilge Name) - a city in the east of Rathúnas controlled by the Áiteoir Kingdom; means "Tower of the Bull"

Turnmor (English-Irish Name) - a watch post on the east shore of Rathúnas belonging to the Torthúil Kingdom and Lacharan

Ula ["Oo-lah"](Gaeilge Name) - daughter of Fionn and Flann from Loch an Scátháin; means "jewel of the sea"

Rathúnas

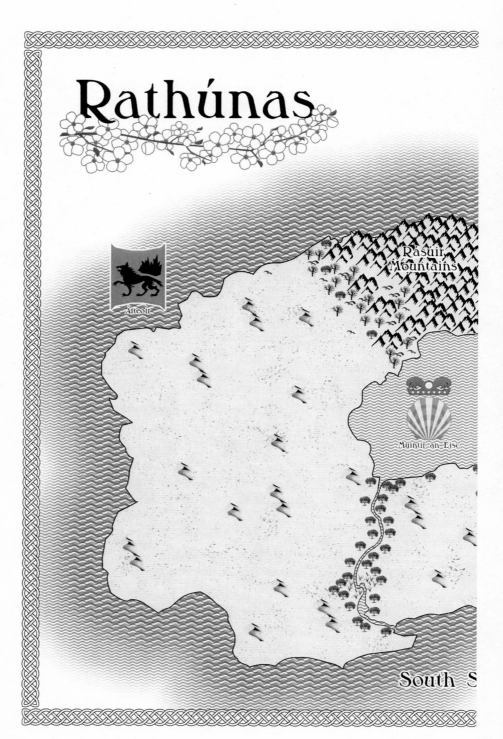

Rásúir Mountains

Áiteóir

Muintir an Éisc

South S

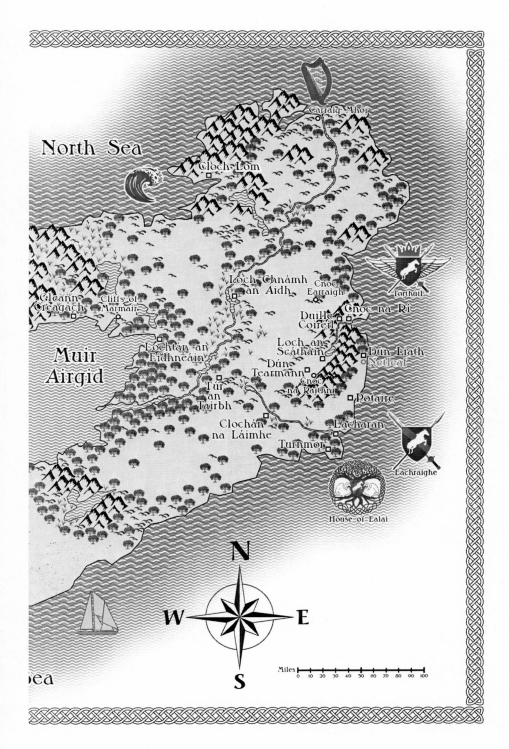

North Sea

Carraig Mhór

Cloch Lom

Gleann
Creagach

Cliffs of
Marmair

Loch Chnámh
an Aidh

Cnoc
Earraigh

Torthúil

Cnoc na Rí

Duille
Coireil

Muir
Airgid

Lochán an
Eidhneáin

Loch an
Scáthain

Dún Liath
Netleaf

Dún
Tearmann

Cnoc
na Raithní

Túr
an
Tairbh

Potaire

Lacharan

Clochán
na Láimhe

Turnmor

Eachraighe

House of Ealai

N

W   E

S

Miles
0 10 20 30 40 50 60 70 80 90 100

Sea

Edwards Brothers Malloy
Thorofare, NJ USA
February 25, 2016